Praise fo

Alan Warner is one of Scotland's best loved literary figures. His debut, *Morven Callar* is a contemporary classic; both it and *The Sopranos* have been made into famous films. He has been nominated for the Booker Prize and many other awards. He teaches at the University of Aberdeen.

KITCHENLY 434

Alan Warner

Illustrations by Mark Edward Geyer

WHITE
RABBIT

First published in Great Britain in 2021 by White Rabbit
This paperback edition published in 2022 by White Rabbit
an imprint of The Orion Publishing Group Ltd
Carmelite House, 50 Victoria Embankment
London EC4Y ODZ

An Hachette UK Company

1 3 5 7 9 10 8 6 4 2

ISBN (Mass Market Paperback) 978 1 4746 1954 7
ISBN (eBook) 978 1 4746 1955 4

Typeset by Born Group
Printed and bound in Great Britain by Clays Ltd, Elcograf S.p.A.

www.whiterabbitbooks.co.uk
www.orionbooks.co.uk

For a true star: Irmin Schmidt.
For Hollie.
For Simon Bain & Catherine Ryan.

Give an account of thy stewardship.
Luke 16:2

1

As I did two or three times a month during those summer afternoons of the late 1970s . . . Crofton approaches Kitchenly Mill Race – Dan Mullan chief gardener – a previous owner Lord Halmer – a window situation – curtains and the questions of pulling them – a night arrival – an intruder.

As I did two or three times a month during those summer afternoons of the late 1970s, I found myself returning from the shops in town, driving the hatchback Volvo through ancient Sussex hamlets mentioned in the Domesday Book – back towards Marko's main residence of that time: Kitchenly Mill Race.

The slipstream from the wound-down driver's window was satisfyingly tapping at the sleeve of my T-shirt. I was much earlier than usual, so at least I wasn't stuck behind the damned school bus. Or had schools broken up for summer?

Yet more phenomenal weather. Vast, slow tarpaulins of shadow were moved across the fields by pure white cumulus perpetuated above; yet beyond the blackthorn silhouettes on Ablemyre Hill, these vertical clouds seemed unmoving. Muddy puddles were now just dust along the uneven roadsides; you'd come across the scowling county-council squad, smoking roll-ups while hacking away at the verges with hand scythes.

Kitchenly village is really just one single street of houses: a steep-gabled thatched cottage, the doctor's surgery, a post office annexe penetrating out from a semi-detached, the ancient dovecot, the garage with two- and four-star petrol pumps. There's the Babbacombe Lee pub, the disused schoolhouse, the village green, where a wire litter bin traps a few recognisable Cornish Strawberry Mivvi wrappers and crushed Lilt cans. A little estate of council houses is thrown out into the edges of the fenced fields somewhere beyond the roofs of the high street; I've never had cause to drive around back there as you can always find parking on the main thoroughfare – such as it is.

When we first moved down here in 1973, Kitchenly village lay in darkness at night – an old Elizabethan darkness – a darkness which it had cowered in each night since Merrie England; since the German bombers bulked northwards above. But a few years ago they fitted street lighting on ugly unpainted lamp posts – a giddy, whisky-coloured light, which drops down onto the widened, tarred black pavements, until the wide open fields recommence once again.

With the reversed, grammatically odd, *Welcome Kitchenly* road sign in the rear-view mirror, I always keep to thirty alongside the new bungalow development of Brockleberry Rents, with the crazy-paved chimneys on their ends; the chalky-soiled gardens are hardly grassed over but there are kiddies' swings in some of them.

Four hundred yards east, I glanced adoringly as usual across the greenliness of Foul Mile – that vast empty meadow which actually belongs to Kitchenly Mill Race but which has been rented out to a farm as rough grazing since the previous ownership. I always repeatedly sneak helpless glimpses over the empty passenger seat, across the meadow towards our ochre-coloured eighteenth-century perimeter walls on the far side of that same field; dark carpets of ivy are thrown across the wall and they mantle along the top of the bricks. The garden trees beyond are in full leaf. Ash and horse chestnut are there, plane trees with their scabby bark; deeper in are ancient beech, lime, elm, walnut, holm oak and cedars of Lebanon from the forest of the Cedars of God in Bsharri, all fully shielding the historic residence. I wondered again at the age of the widest trunks – growing since long before Waterloo – at the negligible movements of their leaves held against such skies. The green trees of Keats's England – their emerald rugs of moss so patched upon them in those numberless and shadowed arboretums.

Even when some of these trees are seasonally undressed by winter, the maturity of the grounds means that it's only around Christmas time when the auburn and bluish weathered brick of the northerly Tudor chimney may be quickly glimpsed from the public bus route. Or say a January gust parts evergreen branches – then perhaps you might spy the H of the television aerial on the scalloped roof tiles of the larger mill house; possibly you could just spot the verdigris on the stilled, ornate clock tower above the converted saddlery. It is recorded in *Patterson's Sussex* that the diligence, the four-in-hand mail coach up to London departed in the 1820s from the stable courtyard of *Kitchanly Mills* (sic) which is why the clock tower was added.

Surprisingly, from the vantage afforded down on the main road, the tallest architectural feature of Kitchenly Mill Race – the chimney stacks of Adam Elvetson's celebrated 1933 addition – could almost never be spotted; perhaps because the huge, crenellated chimney tower is more or less sideways on to where the public road passes a quarter of a mile away? What the public can distinguish is only the upper portion of the naked white flagpole on the roof, which needed a new lick of paint. Two years before, Marko had us run up the Union Jack for the Silver Jubilee. That flag had slopped, languid in the hot air for weeks, till he had it taken back down.

No one behind, so I slowed the Volvo hatchback even more to gaze across, a single hand on the steering wheel. I was one of the few inhabitants of the vicinity who knew the concealed topographies beyond that calculated assemblage of trees; a frieze of multicoloured leaves – just like those dark Chinese Coromandel screens with their decorative lacquer in the master bedroom, behind which Marko's unbearable lady – Auralie – changes into and out of her latest international fashions, two or sometimes three times daily.

Within those perimeter walls, I knew the tristesse of every weeping willow along those crawling waters' edges. Overlooked by the precipitous manor house, I knew the laburnum slope with its stepped rill in ornamental brick, its rivulets channelled down from the moat to the twin culverts at the riverbank, cascading the acoustic steps. I knew the double mill buildings now connected by their two modern, triple-glazed air bridges.

Every time I approached Kitchenly Mill Race, I began to anticipate the paradisal compound of dolorous laburnum and lavender banks which scent the decorated interiors when the summer manor windows are fixed open on their ornate securing arms. All of these enchantments which were hidden from common view.

Without fail, when advancing on Kitchenly from east or west, or down the farm track to the north, I would feel the same occult conviction, the same magic of its acreage. I fully believed in the abstract energies of its frequently absent young owner. His aura which, to my mind, reached from the soil of his extensive grounds to beyond the very tips of his trees.

Even the lands around the house: solitary elms midfield, encircled by cultivator markings, or the semi-transparent beech hedgerows split by unpainted tubular metal gates; the roadside walls, the ditches, the pasture corners trodden bare by jostling livestock gathering at their troughs; surely these hinterlands must be alive to the aura of that dwelling close by? Could meandering Sunday motorists not sense world fame on their approach? I was crazily convinced that every part of this landscape around Kitchenly Mill Race vibrated with an overpowering presence. Like a leaking nuclear power station, the radiation of Marko's vast talent, his mystique, settled and shimmered like dust on the tops of telephone wires, on the flowers and leaves, nettles and bitter dock, lanes, fields and sunken tracks for at least several thousand yards about. I was dumbly certain everything was infected by his main residence and its glamorous pollution.

For six years in the smaller mill house – with its clamped but still-functional water wheel – I had held my staff flat of two small rooms and a kitchenette beneath. Sometimes, stepping through the gravelled car park from some chore in the big house, moving towards the white, fretworked wood of the footbridge across the headrace, I would spot a wood pigeon launching itself with a slap from one of the far pine trees on the other side of the boundary wall. That grey bird would slide across the public road, clear the orange brick and ivy, cross the driveway lawns and make upward ascent onto the corner guttering of the larger mill house. There it would resume its coo-cooing loop of song and I would feel a sense of outraged sacrilege. The feathered ones alone did not acknowledge the demarcated boundaries of this private Shangri-La. The impunity of the birds' trespassing from public land into Marko's haven was still somehow astonishing to me. Birds may fly free, but the very airspace above the renovated manor, the mills, the river gardens and outhouses was, as far as I was concerned, privileged and private too.

Down on the main road is that mundane, tar-daubed wooden GPO telegraph pole with its small blue identifying disc, standing on a lifted verge just at the access road junction. A clad cable droops blackly off the pole, crossing Kitchenly's walls and away it goes through the leaves. I indicated for a left turn here and swung the hatchback onto the single-track supplementary public road. After the hundred yards of wall echoing to my right come the two original 1933 Elvetson columns of the main gateway to Kitchenly's drive – each topped with a finial ball of stone and tonsured lichen. Both brick pillars are chipped and blemished here and there by the historical entrance and egress of many large and clumsy loads on carts, tractors and lorries, down long decades. I would need to get the gardener's nephew – Johnny – with barrow and spade, to scrape the public tarmac clear of horse droppings for Marko's return from the United States. (That lad Johnny was always just lossocking about.) Marko had taken Auralie and their six-year-old, Molly, over to America to scout East Coast recording studios. There was some concerning debate over where the next Fear Taker album was going be recorded.

I nosed the Volvo up to the closed gates with their weathered, lathe-turned wooden roundels. I put the automatic gearstick into P and stepped from the car, leaving the driver's door open and the engine idling. It is at this point I always vainly wish for a vehicle coming from – or towards – the two upper farms to pass by, or better still, two jodphured ladies: a mother and daughter, riding high, side by side on tall brown horseback, boots and stirrups almost touching, witnessing my scruffy but authoritative figure. I casually tapped in the four-digit security code – which I can still remember to this day – to begin the near-silent drive mechanism of the now electrically powered gates.

No one came and no car passed under the leaves of the lane, so I peered into the wooden postbox fixed to the left pillar – its slit specifically fourteen inches wide to accommodate packaged LP albums. Nothing. Above the mailbox was the live, steady buzz of the imported American intercom system connected not to the main house, but to the kitchenette beneath my rooms. The owner of this home invites only those he wants to and has no stated interest in any random callers – they are my responsibility. We stapled those intercom wires and painted them ochre, so they blended with the original brick; round the pillar they run, then down into that verge along with the automatic gate wires, then they travel up a buried duct adjacent to the driveway tarmac. Above the intercom is the KITCHENLY MILL RACE brass plaque – slightly blemished from not being rubbed with Brasso often enough. On the right-gate column, in gloss white and red paint a **PRIVATE. STRICTLY NO TRESPASSING** wooden sign is rudely bolted.

I drove the estate hatchback through the opened gates, halted, then climbed back out of the car. The gates are on a three-minute timer until they close but I always feel pedantically protective about leaving them wide open behind me. I crossed to the small winding motor in at the base of the wall. I stretched out my leg and, much like the way that Marko engages or disengages his preamp Echoplex guitar pedal onstage with one smart tap of his foot, I clicked the polished stud downwards with a plod of my worn Kicker. The front gates immediately swung shut.

It gives me a vague and unjustifiable satisfaction to observe those gates lock flush back into place; partly a throwback to the early years when four mentally unstable peacocks roamed the grounds. Rather inconsiderately, the remote control keyring for the gates is kept locked in Marko's car. I lost the other one.

The curvature of the driveway veers past topiary bushes and the cedars of Lebanon which drop their dark, uneven puddles of total shade and crisp sheddings onto the mowed lawn – as if they were rusting in leisure; this curve of tarmac kills any possible view through the main gates down to the actual dwelling houses themselves. That hundred yards of driveway to the gravelled turnaround and car park is lined on both sides with nine-foot-tall decorative park lamps – sixteen of them in total – forever blowing their damned bulbs. They are operated by a wall switch just inside the front door of the main air bridge.

The Volvo tyres crushed on the gravel as I swung into the wide car park then rounded the glass booth. Mrs Hilary is our housekeeper and her old rusty banger – a Triumph Dolomite – was parked as usual a little too closely to the two pillars and stairway up to the main house entrance on the air bridge. Why noisy gravel instead of tarmacadam on this wide parking space? Well, when Marko began renovations to Kitchenly – including the tarring of the driveway – he was advised by the tree surgeon that the many mature oaks and elms on the fringes of the lawns needed the rainwater seepage for their far-spread roots; if we tarred over the car park gravel then they might well have turned brown.

The sun still fell wide over this gravelled space and directly onto the faces of patterned brick, the quoining, the flint and mortared concrete of the upright manor house; its enormous

9

singular shadow, including that of the huge porch and the twin-arched moat bridge, was thrown onto the eastward gardens in a black seepage, down the rearward laburnum slopes towards the river's edge, where the elongated silhouettes of the topmost chimney pots and the distorted strip of flagpole lay across that curve of slack brown East Sussex stream water.

Every single day I would reacquaint myself, stare across the water of the narrow moat and up at that house, still baffled to be connected to a millionaire's dwelling like this one. I would lay siege to the fortified building with my eyes.

I always gaze at the four Tudor window sets and then I follow the line across to the blended stitching where the brick of the collapse meets the flint and concrete of Elvetson's grafted addition. I gape at the vertical tube of windows on the Turkish staircase and at the purple-stained glass of the minaret window, with the moustache of its ogee arch at the stairhead. I often study the horizontal parades of miniature Arts and Crafts windows along each of the three floors on the 1930s wing. Let me tell you, legging it up a ladder with only the narrow moat bank beneath you, those second- and third-floor windows are damned pesky to chamois from the outside. Believe me, that Elvetson was no bloody window cleaner.

The high lattice glass walls on the porch of the 1930s entrance are like a conservatory; what I relish is that you see right through the west window and clear out the other side towards the distant eastern skyline. And if you find yourself, in summer, down in the lavender banks and laburnum slopes looking the other way, a furnace of clementine sunset is trapped within that burning porch.

Inside the porch, the large brass chandelier floats on its thin chain as if suspended atop an invisible fountain. That chandelier is illuminated every night for effect, though we hardly use this locked, 1930s front doorway across the moat bridge any more.

On summer nights, moths tap against each rippled, antique lozenge of glass in a forlorn seeking of the chandelier bulbs.

Each year as Christmas approaches it's me, Dan Mullan the gardener, daft Johnny and a few borrowed Fear Taker road crew who wind that chandelier up on its chain and secure it hard against the ceiling, in order to erect a twenty-foot Christmas tree in that vaulted porch. It looks like part of an ersatz Norway has been glassed in for scientific study. There we cut free its tethers and decorate the tree in tinsel, fairy lights and baubles from Harrods boxes, while Mullan's nephew scrubs all the tree resin off the floor tiles and double front doors where we rammed it through. Then we would stand outside looking in at the fairy-lit tree on those winter nights of the 1970s and sometimes even here down south it was nippy; Jack Frost had strode across the counties so the lawn was iced, tree angles and shapes of the pre-floodlit garden showed pitch black against the whitened grass-blade tips and the little letters of my Timex digital watch glowed red at me under the pampered heavens.

Extending north of the manor house is the first of the two air bridges. At the manor house end, this larger air bridge now encloses the once exterior – and now interior – Elizabethan doorway with the clear 1602 date on its grey stone lintel. Despite their tall, triple-glazed windows and the jardinieres of indoor rubber plants all the way along them, these two modern extensions remind me of a modern railway carriage, or the rectangular fuselage of some queer aircraft which has been winched down from a height and into position. The first air bridge spans the moat and connects the main manor dwelling into the first and larger mill house, then a further suspended air bridge extends over the mill race water itself into the smaller secondary mill house where I dwell.

Thus – on average – in one minute and fifty seconds, I can march with steady pace right through the entire main-floor living spaces of Kitchenly Mill Race: from the 1930s porch, through the manor house with its Tudor panelling and Arts and Crafts restoration, over the first enclosed, centrally heated air bridge above the moat, across the open-plan drawing room with its colour television set in the large Georgian mill house, beneath the pale classical archway, on to the carpeted floor of the second shorter air bridge which spans the mill race waters beneath – again, panoramic windows on either side – then into the first floor of the secondary mill house on the further riverbank, along its corridor with the original plaster ceiling until finally I step outside the exterior doorway on the stables' side. Overhead is a late eighteenth-century oil lamp suspended on two elongated wrought-iron stanchions. Like the one outside 10 Downing Street. You could, if required, ascend the pathway from here to the stable-wall side door and continue into the courtyard with its own Georgian clock tower.

One minute and fifty seconds. Back in old Stafford town it takes me three seconds to cross the ground floor of my elderly mam's front room. I have counted, making the direct comparison.

Up in my rooms at Kitchenly, among all my albums, books and music mags, I had Pevsner's classic, *Buildings of England*. Old Nikolaus would have been horrified by those 1970s air bridges, but I read and reread our entry from the 1950s in his book so often that I can recite much of it by heart:

> . . . *thus, moated Kitchenly Mill Race and its magical water gardens is an edifying, extraordinary sanctuary; uneven in eccentricity but finally satisfying in its defiant melding of Elizabethan, Tudor, original Queen Anne, Georgian additions and modern. A summation of England's history in solid form . . . Adam Elvetson's bold, perpendicular additions soar . . . the entire southern side of the Tudor construction collapsed into the moat during extensive renovation work and the 1579/1602 dwelling appeared lost, until the current owner undertook the bold reconstructions of 1933 . . . Elvetson*

grafts an entire new section and a glass porch with decorative moat bridge onto the surviving edifice, placing it flush to the original moat bastion wall . . . the strange clerestory of the roof atrium . . . horizontal parades of lattice window screens flood the interiors with a generous light. The ceiling heights in the two sections are at complete variance. The original staircase was lost in the collapse . . . adding a flamboyant and monumental, 'Turkish Staircase' to harmonically fuse these interiors together . . .

But that day, turning off the car engine I noted something was amiss. I got out and stood beside the Volvo, resting both hands on the top of the open driver's door. I frowned up at the third-floor windows of the master bedroom in the salvaged Tudor section. The daily, or Mrs H, or most likely, nosey Dan Mullan (who is always trying to gain entry to the interior of the house) had sealed two windows closed after wrapping both frames in black plastic gardening sacks! Strips of electrical duct tape had been used to clumsily affix the plastic to the noble exterior brick.

My initial summation was that a whole window frame must have become unfixed on its securing arm and, though the hinges are stiff, had somehow swung outwards in a breeze and broke some glass against the walls; some of those lattice panes were original early-nineteenth, possibly late-eighteenth century. I hoped Dan Mullan had at least shed his dirty work boots at the bottom of the Turkish staircase carpet. Yet, if a glass pane was broken, why was it that the second window was also lashed and clad with black plastic? Could both windows really have broken a pane on a near windless day? A patch of that ugly black plastic breathed and oozed out an inch.

I slammed the car door then walked across the crunching gravel to observe the northerly façade, staring up and across the flat roof of the air bridge which links the earlier and later stages of the dwelling. The two bedroom windows *there* were similarly

13

bound in black plastic, sealing out all natural light from entering into the en-suite master bedroom and bathroom.

The secondary doorway into the mill house kitchen was embowered with cream-white roses; I huffed aloud and pushed it then began making my way through the ground floor, across the sunflower tiles of the wide, modernised kitchen, then out again at the split Dutch doorway above the riverbank, giving me a vantage across those private inner gardens.

I stood in cool shadow, listening, and I could hear the sweet monotony of water from the rill cascades; that pleasing, ambient certainty, that clepsydra of the afternoons which you become so inured to around Kitchenly Mill. I also noted the pump in its small wooden hutch down by the river bend was running silently once again. It forced water uphill from the riverbank, directly into the evaporating moat – keeping the surface constant and teasing a steady spill through the sluice pond then back down the brick rills with their acoustic steps, producing that playful sound of constant and industrious waters. The pump did good work but it needed frequent maintenance to stop it running rough – which Marko's musical ear would detect day or night in the first ten minutes.

I wished we could get round to laying an off/on switch wire from my kitchenette; one which journeyed across the secondary footbridge over to the pump. In winter, when on occasion it rained hard, I had to monitor the rill flow and if necessary, manually shut the pump off, sometimes dashing in the dark across the bridge, wearing my wellies with no socks, my parka hooked by its hood on the crown of my head, pyjamas underneath. Frankly it was a fiddle-faddle, but it kept the moat fresh.

I yelled, 'Dan?'

I sniffed, detecting the slightly acidic fresh-mown grass on the banking. I could see the cut extent where the Flymo had been prematurely halted. Telling to note that while I was in town, the mower had been ushered away over the footbridge to the storeroom up in the immured stable yard, as if it were obvious that there would be no further mowing on this day. Late in the morning, Dan Mullan's idiot nephew had swung the Flymo across the only extension cable and cut clean through it – and they claimed the bank was too steep there for the big petrol mower.

I listened and I squinted along the dozy river to beyond the second footbridge where the willows showed the waters' slow curve round and out of sight, down among the ash trees on our eastern boundaries. Across the frutescence of the shrubbery, I could just hear the steady intensity of bumble- and honeybees in the Illawarra flame tree. A momentary movement caught my eye on the far side and I squinted beyond the bright white-painted wood of the crossing. It was Mingles the friendly cat, stooping in an obscure and cautious stalk, perhaps after a butterfly? Unless his rival ginger, Corbisher-the-Swiper was about – rabbit stalking?

Then I saw a manifestation of the man before I physically located him. The sun had driven in among the willow trees, forming panels of silver; bright green with cracked segments of black shadow; yet from behind one of the willow curtains escaped a cloud of pale cigarette smoke, upwards. The smoke was almost silver in colour that day.

There lurked Mullan, our gardener. Dan Mullan. No. Dan Mullan doesn't communicate how we said his name back then. It was more: Danmullan – one quick word.

Two summers before, Dan Mullan noted with some distress that Marko had fetched one of his antique brass telescopes down from the roof atrium to the window of the master bedroom; the lens turned away from heaven's crowded stars to instead direct its magnifications towards the far reaches of our gardens. Marko could now observe anything displeasing which came to his eye's

15

attention: the pump hutch needed repainting, or there was a flotsam of twigs, leaves and scum jammed up against the base of the secondary footbridge. Such garden matters were indeed reported to us, but it was the potential for furtive surveillance which kept Dan Mullan so furious during his frequent fly smokes and sudden disappearances in under the vaults of the willow tents.

His nephew didn't display any such caution and rather than barrow it to the midden, I still caught Johnny each summer, tipping grass cuttings from the large sit-on mower hopper straight into the mill race. Even when the flow was sluggish. Or his reluctant form could be observed sitting on the earth, back fully rested against an ash tree – surveying the work he had yet to do rather than that which he had already accomplished. He didn't even bother to hide under a willow umbrella.

But the real reason for the telescope was little Molly Morrell. When Molly first got bold as a walker around the manor house, Mullan had to spend a full week sledgehammering in the temporary fence of wooden stalks bound with a securing top wire, around the eastern moat and sluice pond, then right along the lip of the ha-ha wall and the far riverbank's curve. All in case the infuriating nipper somehow got down onto this more obscure far side of the moat and fell into the water unnoticed. Through his telescope, Marko believed he could witness his daughter's attempted escapes, or the condition of the riverside fences – if he was sober enough.

Frankly, I found Marko and Auralie's thoughtlessness and their stoned, deeply relaxed attitude to child-rearing, flipping alarming. They had not fenced the car park moat edge – the presumption being that the child was always going to be supervised in this area. In truth, Kitchenly Mill Race was a death trap for a six-going-on-seven-year-old who couldn't swim.

Sometimes Molly was suddenly located alone, roaming the grounds at will, without any of us having been warned she had been let out of the main house. I have had to waste many hours following her around the grounds, looking for fairies and toadstools, leading her this way and then that way, but away from water. Until my patience ran out and I rapidly lifted and carried her – wailing – back through the flower beds and across the footbridges to the manor house, to be plonked into Mrs Hilary's waiting arms. Mrs H bearing that sorrowful look on her face as wordlessly the situation was understood.

I really adored the gorgeous kid – she was inquisitive, gentle and a mix of her mum and dad's very good looks – but she was getting heavy to lift and I wasn't paid to be a childminder as well as everything else. What was I paid for? I was The Help. But what exactly is The Help?

Molly can be a little pest, falling forwards with her hands held out onto the gravel of the parking area. Out come the sticking plasters which I keep especially in my kitchenette drawer for her. I was starting to fear Molly fell deliberately and came to me with her grazed hands held out for cleaning and plasters, just because she sought affection. Which she often wouldn't get from her parents. On the sixth or seventh US Fear Taker tour – that one in the winter time – when he took Auralie and Molly along with them, before the child began attending the Waldorf school place (which I don't see eye-to eye about), Marko must have trekked through thirty-five American hotels, many with their own heated indoor swimming pools. Still Molly couldn't yet swim a stroke.

Since they couldn't obtain a small enough life jacket back in those days, for a period, Molly waddled through our gardens with a variety of non-matching, inflatable, brightly coloured armbands forced up under her oxters. On several occasions I had found these inflated swimming bands painfully lashed with Sellotape to her skin, round her biceps and even bandoliered over a shoulder. But at the first opportunity, the kid peeled the armbands off and deposited them behind bushes. Or she even made play of dropping the flotations from the footbridge down into the alluring, deadly water of the mill race below.

When a breeze got up around Kitchenly's gardens, a single, sun-faded, partially inflated armband would always suddenly materialise, rolling in from some other sector of the grounds, jamming beneath the parked cars or against a raked pile of leaves; or lodging deep into a flower bed – usually the spiky roses. I've also had to use the extending window brush to coax many an armband in off the moat surface. Who knows how many have headed off downstream towards Maxtelham, the next village, there to worry the gathered swans?

'Dan!' I stepped along the limestone-slabbed garden path towards the willow tree where he hid. Dan Mullan was just an old pain. Baraclough, Marko's housekeeper up at his London place on The Vale in Chelsea, had stated it to me years before. 'I'll tell you about country life, Crofton. Don't employ locals, not even the gardener's boy. Get them from a good few villages away or they'll only form a web of gossip. Employ immediate locals and there will be an inventory of Marko's tapestries, guitars, telescopes, Auralie's jewellery, and a map of the house with its doors, circulating around the village pub. It encourages break-ins.'

Baraclough is a stuck-up old fairy and paranoid. Immediate locals! But he probably knew what he was talking about. He'd briefly worked for George Harrison before Harrison shifted to that Friar Park pile, to all kip in sleeping bags, I'd heard.

Anyway, Dan Mullan did come in from the village beyond Maxtelham – but I was always unable to look at our gardener without thinking about tied cottages and bestiality. We inherited the gardener with the house. Dan Mullan had been at Kitchenly under the previous owner, Lord Halmer, or the 'Colonel' as he preferred to be called.

18

Colonel Halmer inherited Kitchenly from his own father and personally escorted me and Marko round on that first day when we drove down from London, actually holding the current copy of *Country Life*. It's funny – these years I meet kids who genuinely believe nobody in Britain got rich before Maggie Thatcher. But in the late sixties, the money had suddenly shifted in Great Britain. The blue bloods were clobbered with the rise in wages and inheritance tax – no cash – and the sixties brought a whole generation of working-class film- and music-business nabobs, crashing down into the Home Counties with ready bread, hot to buy into historic countryside property. Marko wore even longer hair in '73, and I saw the glances of incomprehension from beneath the tweed cap at Marko's Renaissance barnet, at his South London accent, at his unlikely youth – yet here was a cash buyer with a Coutts cheque book.

You had to feel a bit of sympathy for the old blue bloods. I had heard the stories. Despite their new bread, guys like Marko, or film-star blokes, house-hunting, being escorted from the grounds of stately houses to the gate lodges by sellers or even butlers, on account of their long hair and common accents. People who refused to sell their house to someone else who was five times richer but without the correct accent. They really had standards, and best of respect to them. You can't accuse the old set of worrying what the neighbours would think either, as these florid monarchists didn't have any neighbours. Yet old Tory, Colonel Halmer, who'd stopped a coin of *Wehrmacht* shrapnel at El Alamein, seemed surprisingly casual. Wanted a quick sale to get himself and the old lady into a nice thatched cottage with low maintenance costs. Auralie had ensured her eminence by getting in the family way very quickly, as most of these girls did. Marko wanted to provide a family home and he fell in love with Kitchenly on that very first day, though I cautioned him that it was only the second property outside

19

London we had driven down to view. We had earlier called at this corking pad, The Mill House in Byfleet, which was then owned by the actress Sarah Miles and her husband, Robert Bolt – after hearing a rumour the house and its river grounds might be up for sale. It was not and we were bluntly told so. Lucky escape, really, as the M25 ended up going through the bottom of the garden.

Kitchenly Mill Race was a right funny old place back then; seen much better days: no central heating, piled ash in forgotten bedroom fireplaces – even some of the bathrooms had fireplaces in them – linoleum and gruesome metallic wallpaper of hunting scenes. Lady Halmer had some neurotic obsession with pure drinking water, so every single sink had these strange, enamelled filters bolted onto the splashboards, producing a chalky dribble of drinking water through thin, horizontally positioned aluminium tubes. It was a bit like a sanatorium. Old fashioned electric geysers trembled and burped above many sinks. The range fitted in the inglenook of the Tudor kitchen was an old anthracite burner, so Marko had the Scholtès hob and the Thermador ovens put in with an oil-burning triple Aga which did the central heating as well. A pantry *and* a larder – whatever the difference between a pantry and a larder is?

The problem with historical Grade-1 listed properties is always the same. Rewiring the electric and the plug sockets without shutting the whole house down for months, ripping out the skirting and getting the bloody council inspectors nosing back round with their clipboards. So half the house had been done in modern 13-amp rectangular peg BS1363 plugs and the rest in pre-war round peg, and you got Marko in the middle of all this, lurching around trying to plug in practice amps, tape reels, Putney synths, FM stereos and colour television sets going at full commotion; my jacket pockets always hung heavy with adaptors.

It's embarrassing to admit it now, but we were a bit stuck without Dan Mullan in those first years. Marko purchased Kitchenly Mill Race in the February of 1973 and all the old staff were immediately paid off. I didn't even know on which day the ash-bucket lorry came from out beyond the village chain to collect our domestic rubbish. Marko had been on the road for three years solid, touring with the band, and he was already somewhat out of touch with conventional daily life – What *is* a bin day? he'd queried. Honest. He had never thought about where the rubbish goes. And sure enough there *were* no bloody neighbours to ask. I had to walk a mile up to the top farm, knocking on doors and try to ask what day to put the ash buckets out on, but they were all away in the fields, or wherever farmers go to. We were quite isolated longhairs. I put a bin by the public road with some junk in it and checked each evening when it had been emptied. Thursday mornings, for historical interest.

By the second summer the garden had gone au naturel and we realised we didn't know how to keep a moat. I mean who does? They didn't teach you that one in school. Marko's fairly hopeless suggestion was that I telephone Percy Thrower at the Chelsea Flower Show – ask him. I urged that Marko give Old Wykehamist Colonel Halmer a tinkle, tell him the moat had turned emerald. I was stood right next to Marko when he called on the ancient Bakelite black telephone – one of those ones with the hairy cord, which the Colonel had made a point of generously leaving behind – though he had taken every single electric light bulb from all three buildings with him. Even the bulbs out of the hoisted porch chandelier. That old telephone was not in the main house back then; rather it remained placed on a single freestanding table by a window in the larger mill house, since its modern ringing – perhaps once a month in those days – bothered neurotic Lady Halmer. Back then, when dinosaurs roamed the earth, phoning between Sussex villages was only three flipping digits on a rotary dial. Even to this day I remember our number: Kitchenly 434.

'Hey, eh, Colonel Halmer? Eh, it's Mark. Morrell. The guitar-player geezer. You sold me the Mill Race down at Kitchenly, two years or so back. Yeah?'

'Mr Morrell, why good day. How on earth are you?'

'I'm good, man, I'm good.'

'Did you get the Wolseley Ten out the stables, Morrell? Isn't she a beaut? Had her since the war. The seats do need re-upholstered. She's in there beside that old thresher; all yours.'

'I'll get to her someday, Colonel. I got my own wheels for now. Ferrari Dino, the 246 GT.'

There was a sharp pause of suspicion at this Italian name.

'Drive the Wolseley round the grounds, my boy. Round the grounds, I say! House all right? Still in the pop music game? Enjoying life there? No second thoughts? It was never the same for me after my good lady wife insisted on those beastly modern joiny-up bits. I was quite content to stretch my legs over to the mill houses but I dare say it suits you with your . . . dear little one. Who will be growing. A boy came, I believe?'

'A yeah sort of a, eh, girl really, but yeah. Most beautiful house in England, Colonel. Just like you said. But look, I have a bit of prob down here. Something that's come up, hasn't it? The moat has gone bright green on us, hasn't it?'

'I beg your pardon? The moat's gone green, Morrell? Well it is a warm summer but it shouldn't have overgrown in one year.'

'In one year?'

'Since last year. You had it cleaned last spring. Yes?'

'Cleaned?'

'Yes, Morrell. You did have Dan Mullan clean it out, did you not?'

'Oh man, look, Colonel. I had to let that old geezer go. Just watching him potter on the lawn spitting and kicking at things

22

the day we moved in. He's so slow.'

A longer silence came on the other end of the phone.

'Mr Morrell. That was a grave mistake. Dan Mullan was chief gardener at the Mill Race since 1961. He knows your gardens there better than anybody. A gardener is like part of the house, Morrell. Get a new one and they will kill off half your blooms in a season. Mullan can coax colours out of any corner; he knows where to lime, where to manure and how much. Precisely. A wizard with a dung load, that man, and knew when the horses needed their alfalfa. So nobody cleaned the moat at all last year?'

'Eh. Nah.'

'That's your problem, Morrell. You have to shuck it clean every spring.'

'Oww. What, like a swimming pool, chuck in a box of powder or something?'

'No. No. No. Mr Morrell. You must have the gardeners and seven or eight hired hands climb in, form a line together and move ahead in an orderly manner, tearing out all the weed growth and reeds from the bottom. Otherwise it takes the air from the water and the bloom is quite phenomenal. Then every decade you take a damned good dredge at it with a mechanical digger.'

'Crikey, Colonel. Who would have known?'

So that was Dan Mullan back on the job at Kitchenly, stood in the moat with a big set of chest waders on, the hired hands yelling and laughing as they swung gluts of slimy weed out of the moat with their fists and deliberately tossed them up towards the manor windows.

'Dan. Dan!' I stepped further down the table-top-sized blocks of limestone on the pathway, calling out more assertively.

The grizzled head nodded free once from the willow fronds and there was a reluctant step ahead to brush the hanging

23

leaves clear of his shoulders; he even raised a hand, but without looking at me, as if we were just passing acquaintances in some Thomas Hardy market town, with a forgotten transaction on a cow one decade behind us. He was facing upriver, towards the three large buildings and their connecting air bridges behind me.

'What's with their bedroom windows?'

'Busy in town, Crofton?'

'The windows?'

'Get that flex? Not really seeing flex strung 'bout you there.'

'A forty-footer up in the car. About the windows.'

'In the car. That'll do for tomorrow.'

I tried a new approach and paused. Stretched my arms out to the sky and faked yawning. I looked up the slope of the zig-zagging water rill. 'Lovely mowing weather. Today.'

'Ah, the windows. Yar. There was a call. On the telephone. From overseas.'

'Overseas. Marko?' I frowned.

'Well now I dursn't say if it was the one or other. The other I would reckon.'

'What one's that then?'

'The fast piece. Fancy lady.'

'Dan. She's little Molly's mum and you know her name fine. Mrs H took the call?'

'Hilary wasn't in that brisk. The daily took the call — fair jiggered her with the fast piece queering on, and the word is they'll be wheeling back during your small hours. The fancy lady hasn't been sleeping, I hear; worried over beauty sleep; that her curtains are like cheap hankies and dunt keep light out is what the daily told me was the very words spoken. Didn't she want the glass painted jet black with a pot of paint? Would have spoilt those old windows forever. I told Mrs Hilary: use bloody plastic and that wapple won't know the difference.'

24

'Those curtains are the thickest she could get.'

He began rolling another cigarette, chuckled mysteriously. 'Do with a shovel's dunt on the head that one if she's so sleepy.'

'So they're coming in at five in the morning or something, are they? Why don't they just stay with Baraclough up in London tonight?'

His stumpy fingers made business with paper and Golden Virginia. 'Up in that bedroom I never saw so many smalls and undies in a lifetime and I had three daughters. Good God. Smalls and undies.'

'Mmm.'

'God sake, man. Carpets of smalls and undies thrown round the bedroom floor like she was spreading grass seed. Wouldn't see such in the Colonel's time. I tell you, lad, could have bent down and scooped up armfuls; Johnny would've made a fair interesting trade in the Babbacombe Lee tonight. I'd to walk on top the things to work the windows. In my bare stocking feet!'

'Good to hear you took off your boots.'

'I'll wash between my toes tonight, Croffie.' He grumbled a laugh. 'First in a while.'

'The flex's in the car so you better get Johnny to mow down this bit to the edge.' I swept an arm across the banking for emphasis. 'Tell him to take care with the flex. He can pay if he runs over this one.'

'The mower's up in the stable. Scraped it clean myself.'

I turned and started back up the path. 'Best get it done all the same,' I called. 'And the horse shit needs scraped off the public lane too.'

'Don't put a flaw on yourself, it's not tottle grass. Tottle grass always best done with scythe if it was, not this electric razor. They won't be seeing nothing in the dark, horse dung or whatnot. Keep till tomorrow. Or next day. They won't see nothing out those windows come morn, Crofton. I trussed 'em

25

up good and proper. Two layers of the plastic. Then you'll find 'em beseeching us for peeling the plastic back off again. Undies and smalls, colourful forms, things you wouldn't have fathomed up in your nightmares. Good mind to throw my new socks away and go back to the darned ones, dip my feet in the water right now.'

'Not a bad idea, Dan.'

His words were behind me and I heard the cigarette lighter click desperately as he aggressively attempted – four or five times – to ignite it.

Back at the Volvo I lifted the coil of new Flymo extension flex and carried it through the kitchen to chuck it onto the limestone path, just outside the Dutch doors, where Dan Mullan could fall over it. I glanced down the river. By Jove. He was unlacing his boots at the river edge.

I closed the back hatch of the Volvo. No need for locking down this way. I came off the gravel and went past the other two round stone finials at the bottom of the stairway. I jogged gently up then through the front double door into the larger air bridge where I hung the car keys on the hooks next to the others.

Here I stood in the dense atmosphere behind the triple glazing, listening to my left – towards the mill houses, and listening to my right, through the 1602 doorway into the manor house. I was listening for the sounds of a hoover or a pot chinking. Mrs H's location. Olivia, the daily, would have headed home by now – she just came in the mornings to take cleaning instructions from Mrs Hilary. Mostly, Olive arrived and departed by the bus, walking from the main road up the wall-side lane. Or her bachelor brother dropped her off and picked her up at the gates; occasionally, in bad wintertime weather, I would give her a lift home to her council house on the outskirts of town, or on the odd Sundays that she was called in. Olive often returned home with freshly sliced ham or chicken from the fridge, wrapped up in her lap as she sat primly in the Volvo, telling me how it was a sin for good food to go to waste. Pilfering and pinching, pure and simple, but I hadn't raised the matter yet with Marko.

Below my feet, under the corridor of the air bridge, was the moat. The entire bridge was secured by vertical metal supports sunk directly into the smooth water; or angled tube struts which were clamped to concrete panels in the grass embanking with wisteria run up them from a circle of glazed pots. You could argue that these double-glazed corridors of glass, plastic and pine panelling communicated an intent to turn Kitchenly into the country-based headquarters of some mid-sized business conglomerate, full of electric typewriters and Xerox machines; but they were a really successful feature. As I stood there I looked out through the corridor's panorama windows back down the gardens and the river; beyond the footbridge Dan Mullan had his canvas trouser legs rolled up his calves and was sitting on the banking, his feet in the tail race of the millstream.

I shook my head. Still no sound. Usually in summertime there were a few flies, bluebottles or a wasp, tapping against the long glass sheets of glazing all down this air bridge; at night daddy-long-legs, awkward for swatting behind the flat leaves of the mature potted plants. Fly spray meant cleaning the interior of the windows all the sooner. Unless it was a honey- or bumblebee of course, which had to be caught with a glass and paper, then taken out. You can never harm a bee.

With the new kitchen and modern Aga relocated in the mill house, any prepared food had to be sent up the dumb waiter and wheeled on trolleys or carried on trays through this corridor to the main manor house's dining room; but for a couple who appeared to subsist on Rice Krispies and Corn Flakes, this wasn't too much of an ergonomic detour. The Tudor dining room with its fake Tudor table for twelve was never used. Tea, coffee and

Auralie's distressingly weird herbal infusions were all brewed with an electric kettle or the percolator in the morning room of the Elvetson section. A silver biscuit tray with Marko's Blue Ribands and Gypsy Creams also rested there.

Once, a bit before Molly was born, when I was briefly away up in Stafford visiting my mam, Marko and Auralie arrived back in Kitchenly Mill Race and it was found that the fridge was completely empty. There wasn't even a single bottle of fresh milk. Marko and Auralie had no idea how to go shopping for a pint of milk in the area. So they simply went off again on a holiday to Bali rather than go to the village shop or the supermarket in town for themselves.

Walking all the way through, it was in the morning room where I found Mrs Hilary, standing with her back to me next to the vitrine which held Marko's rare LPs – including a signed Elvis. Using the polished silver gravy boat which was also seen on Christmas Day, Mrs H was watering the flowers, freshly snipped from the garden, which Dan leaves obediently but anonymously on the stairway to the front door every few mornings.

Without turning around, Mrs H said, 'They're back awful late tonight.'

'Dan Mullan said.'

'Oh, Crofton, it's another strange one. Auralie wants the bedroom windows blacked out but I don't think Mr Morrell knows, so I'll carry the brunt.'

'Don't worry.'

'She wanted them all done over in black paint.' Mrs H turned to look at me with a distressed expression. 'Paint.'

'Daft.'

'Honest to goodness. She told Olive she needed to sleep for two days. Dan said to just wrap them up in that plastic. You know we're not allowed in the master bedroom, but to turn down or change, yet she was screaming on the telephone from somewhere over in *America* that we had to do it. Mr Morrell won't like it. What on earth are we to make of it?'

'Never mind. I'll handle it tomorrow.'

'Oh, Crofton, you're an angel. Imagine to goodness. How much does a telephone call from America cost?'

Mrs H was a great fusser. Which is what you want in a housekeeper.

I glanced out the multi-panes of the window. 'Dan Mullan better finish cutting that grass on the riverbank. Give the devil his due. They cut that cable on the Flymo deliberately, 'cause they knew I wasn't going into town. Meant to be my day off.'

She coughed, for some reason. 'Would you like me to make you a nice cheese and pickle sandwich then? There's fresh cheddar. If Olive hasn't carted it off.'

'No thanks. I'm going for a nap if they're coming back late. Is there anything we haven't thought of?'

'I was just chewing over that but I don't really think so. Plenty fresh milk in the fridge too for Rice Krispies.' She paused. 'Wonder how little Molly liked her holiday?'

'You get home when you're done. I'll do the curtains myself tonight.'

'Are you sure? Well, have a pleasant nap. I'll put out Corbisher and Mister Mingles's food. Don't forget now and lock the top of the Dutch door or robbers could just reach in and undo the bottom half.'

'Quid's in I won't be woken up by a lawn mower, that's for sure. I hear Dan Mullan took his boots off to go upstairs?'

'He did. And the whiff was atrocious, but I squirted Glade all the way down after he was done.'

'Must be why there's no flies on the corridor windows; died when he unlaced his size elevens. See you tomorrow.'

*

29

I walked out from the morning room and past the bottom of the Turkish staircase with its minaret-shaped balusters ascending like a complex Escher into the heights to the smaller chandelier and zodiac-painted ceiling above. Corridors went from landings to the Tudor wing, the Elvetson rooms and to the third-floor atrium. I went on through the Tudor corridor with its dimpled, worn flagstones and original wooden screens. That screen panelling was incredible and I would often pause to study it. Lower down by the flagstones the wood was a crumbly cheese of wear and damage, the beading resculpted by four hundred years of clumsy human contact; centuries of kicking boots, moved furniture, rough children, dropped water bowls, woodworm-conquering varnishes and modern revarnishing. Three panels up and five along was a mysterious graffito artfully edged out by a sharpened knife and inlaid by these many dark varnishings, which spelled: *L.M. Redue 1797.*

By the ancient doorway through to the new air bridge is a deacon's bench and a genuine Elizabethan chest, shamefully used to deposit bark-shedding chopped firewood in winter. Beside this chest was always a scattering of Auralie's discarded footwear: distressingly yellow platform shoes toppled over onto their sides with loosed buckle straps, high boots of soft cordovan leather, their uprightness keeled in their middle by gravity. I often noted some shoes were odd, with one of the pair missing.

Auralie was so tall that the first of her many complaints on taking up residence within the historic English spaces of Kitchenly, was that her hair snagged on the roof timbers and beams of the low ceilings where stunted Tudors once shuffled. She could not wear her high heels with her feathered Gainsborough hats and mad, bejewelled Stetsons without knocking them straight off. On bright days, Mrs H or the daily could often be found, standing on a dining room chair covered with a cloth, extracting coloured feathers and individual snarled strands of the shameless groupie's blonde hair from the dry wood beams above.

On finally conceding that the ancient ceilings could not be raised for her convenience, nor the scalloped stone floors lowered, the sole solution – to Auralie's fury – was the removal of her heeled shoes on entering into the Tudor wing and the putting on of plimsolls instead. And conversely, the reshoeing of herself on exiting the older sections of the house as she moved into the modern corridor and higher ceilings of the mill houses – or the 1930s Elvetson wing. Thus she would wear numerous different pairs of footwear, or the same ones reused, throughout an average day, depending upon the frequency or infrequency of her domestic ventures. Sometimes I had witnessed her in non-matching boots. A friggin' pair of comfy slippers was unknown to this woman and, inevitably, single shoes and boots were dropped and scattered throughout the home, or dragged away by Molly. They became difficult to suddenly locate as Auralie screamed down descriptions of them from the high staircase in her Norse accent, directed at Marko or, far more frequently, at us.

In the mill house I went to the downstairs utility-room closet to wash my hands after handling that lawn mower cable. Mrs H had the toilet brush suspended horizontally over the bowl, the handle trapped under the lowered seat; a distinctive technique of hers to drip-dry all toilet brushes. I returned it to its holder on the tiles and used the sink.

Upstairs in my staff flat I pulled the curtains, took off my Kickers and lay flat on my back upon the unmade single bed. I always place my house keys in the Drake Hotel Park Avenue New York ashtray. I reached out for the pile of books to the side – I was rereading Mauriac's *The Son of Man* – but then I withdrew my hand and sighed.

31

With my frequent insomnia I had discovered the joys of afternoon napping. I awoke from my snoozes in a transformed state, with a well-being that shrouded me for one hour or more, something womblike and transformational; intimations of the next world. Afternoon snoozes had a far more noticeable and beatific effect upon my life than had my readings of the *I Ching*, the Upanishads or *The Late, Great Planet Earth*.

A bearded old man with sage-like demeanour was in a small cabin; a blue military uniform of the American Civil War era hung on the dark wall behind him, the buttons well-polished in silver – or were they brass? This gentleman stepped from a small doorway to reveal a peach dusk above the deck of a large vessel made from old iron and huge rivets, slowly moving up a wide river with verdant banks. Who was this figure he looked towards? Why it was myself! Sitting reading an ancient, heavy book in my lap, out upon this rusted, ferrous deck, as two identical shores slowly moved backwards behind us. The leather covers of the book were as thick, red and brown as the rusted metal. It was as if the book had grown from the iron ship. I was wearing an open, sea-blue tunic from which my slight beer belly shiningly protruded. The man told me that as night approached, I must gently close my Holy Bible, or the gilt lettering from the illuminated pages could glint in the torch flames or lanterns, giving away my exact position to Confederate snipers.

I awoke, blinked; my waking brain initiated responses. I had indeed been reading the Bible – as was usual – and also a history of the American Civil War. I wished there were somebody to relate my dream to, but of course I had nobody in this world but my old mam. Slightly tubby, long-haired, unshaven and unloved I was. But curiously, I lived in the glorious house of a world-famous man – or such as fame consisted of then.

32

Outside it was still light, yet I could tell by the cautious, testing silence of the birdlife in the gardens that it was now the last rallying efforts of daytime which surged a dusted illumination through the trees. I yawned and swung my legs off the bed to sit up. I nodded.

I occupy the annoyingly vague position of The Help at Kitchenly Mill Race, for a very modest monthly stipend. I am *not* part of the housekeeping staff of this substantial home; but one of the unresolved problems for housekeeping staff in an enormous and sprawling residence – as dusk approaches – is which curtains to pull across its many windows. Do you draw all of them? Even in those rooms which remain unoccupied? There were rooms in Kitchenly Mill Race which were only ever entered once a fortnight and even then just by the daily, to dust or to hoover. It is possible, in fact probable, that neither Marko or Auralie had entered many of these rooms in the two mill houses for several years; excepting those very rare games of hide-and-go-seek with Molly, who was good at hiding, and always became rapidly undetectable. Playing but intoxicated, Auralie and Marko would soon become frustrated with the demands of the game and together, arm in arm, amble back through the corridors to the main manor house, Auralie kicking off her higher shoes, calling out the child's name half-heartedly back over her shoulder.

Later, myself, or Olive or Mrs H would detect Molly, crying alone in a disused room's fitted wardrobes. Several of these chambers contained Auralie's many cast-off costumes, roughly folded into cardboard boxes which the various colour television sets or studio-recording equipment had been delivered in.

Is there not even a strange likelihood that there could have been a room within Kitchenly Mill Race – let us say the very far corner room of the secondary mill house, with its singular small window, facing the downstream mill race, but yet from

33

which you can still see the edge of the stable building – could there not be a very robust certainty that the purchaser, owner and sometime resident of this house, its trees, gardens and water features, had in fact never ever set foot in – or even never physically *seen* this room?

Yet does one draw the curtains on such a habitation nightly? Or do you leave the cool black glass exposed to the blank eye of night? Are we trying to shut out the rarefied and curious gaze of the Lord himself, who might peer in to witness us watching a repeat of *Cathy Come Home* on the colour televisions of our forty-two-roomed abode?

If curtains are drawn at dusk, the inevitable corollary exists, that one is obliged to open all the curtains come the morning daylight, after we have survived through the hazards of the moon's transference.

If you do not include the porch of latticed high windows with its rarely drawn drapes, and the air bridge extensions which are fitted with electric blinds, then there are fifty-four windows – very large, large, and small, all fitted with curtains or blinds throughout all of Kitchenly Mill Race. I have excluded the windows in the saddlery (partly a recording studio) over in the stables.

Of course, as well as light bulbs, canny Lord Halmer had departed Kitchenly leaving not a shred of cloth to draw across a single piece of glass. Marko had the whole house curtained by Liberty and the van had arrived each morning from Great Marlborough Street for a full week and two days – they worked the Sunday too!

Marko had admittedly economised by not having every set of curtains fitted with valance boxes or pelmets. Many of the window curtains merely drew across on wood loops and rustic-style fitted bars. Need it be confirmed that Auralie herself was placed in charge of choosing the materials, fabrics and designs

34

for the many curtains? She leaned towards a taste for thickest, back-lined silks with delicate motifs. I calculated that the final bill for the fitted blinds and house curtains of Kitchenly Mill Race could have bought a small terraced house up in Stafford. My part of the country.

As they will do, the housekeeping staff (though let me reiterate that I am *not* a member of the housekeeping staff) fell to bad habits. Most markedly when Marko and Auralie were absent from Kitchenly. Which was a great deal of the time. There were US, European and Japanese tours with Fear Taker; there was business in London, the pad in Chelsea where time was spent, and then there's Marko's gaff somewhere up in bonny Scotland which, admittedly, he never goes to. Then there was the full year of tax exile in 1976. Marko spends only about half his existence lodged at Kitchenly. I often noticed how, at dusk when he suddenly stood up, Marko would forget the locations of light switches in different rooms. Much as he would in hotel rooms. Rather than instinctively step towards a light switch, he had to look around the walls of his own house before moving towards one. The helpless itinerancy of his life was revealed in relation to his surroundings.

We had a tendency, at dusk – in case of an unscheduled return by our masters – only to draw the curtains on the ground floor of the manor house. Which in itself feels unnecessary because the moat creates such a distance from the water's edge to the lattice windows that for any outside observer there would be almost nothing to be glimpsed within the dwelling, apart from interior roof beams and tall vases, or perhaps the last gleam of eastern twilight through a far window, similarly uncovered, on the opposite side of a wide room.

If they had all been pulled, then in the mornings they had to be opened. That much is certain and is beyond debate. Mrs H scooted round the ground floor of the manor, opening the curtains, then she herself withdrew. Later in the day, she quietly accessed the curtains of the guest rooms, library and atrium on the upper floors; and the cute mini-flaps of cloth across the little portals which light each floor of the Turkish staircase a different colour from their stained glass.

It was the going-to-bed hours which presented problems because of Marko's irregular habits. With the two of them sequestered through in the manor and rarely venturing along the air bridge corridor to the main mill house, it was a sensitive question as to when – as dusk fell – to go through and begin the drawing of the curtains there. Often on summer nights Mrs H would have left for her home by fall of darkness and the responsibility of timely curtain drawing would fall to me.

Sometimes yet another raucous drinks party could be heard in progress – involving Auralie and Marko alone. Or at other times there could be guests – some of them, like Marko, world-famous figures. Goodness knows that on a few very rare occasions, Marko and, even I am forced to admit, Auralie herself had actually stepped up to draw a curtain themselves! Hardly credible but it had happened.

Then there was also the issue of displaying the moat and river floodlighting during the hours of darkness. Marko had areas of the moat, the laburnum slopes and river footbridges gently floodlit; he even had placed submerged swimming-pool lights into the moat and mill race water itself, fitted just beneath the surface, revealing a swirling, sub-aquatic night world of weaving reseda-coloured ferns and millpond tendrils. At midnight as you departed the manor house and passed through the elevated, connecting air bridges – to your immediate right – the lit garden presented a splendid vista; a sort of magic, nocturnal playground of general mystery and specific detail was revealed; floodlights creating delicate perspective as they picked out the river edges, highlighted intricate individual water sprinkles shooting from

36

the busy brick rills. Then the artificial lighting receded down-stream, showing the willow trees' fragile canopies, their leaves trailing in the defined water surface like lazy fingers, until the pure darkness in the firmament fell to the ground at last, around the far river bend.

We tended to lower the electric blinds for privacy only on the car turnaround side of the air bridges, but maintained the garden-side electric blinds open and the interior corridor lights off, to display that spectacular dark parkland of night gardens, shadows and bleaches of clawing, upright floodlight. Why conceal such splendour behind remote-operated electric blinds?

So in my *Magic Roundabout* Dougal slippers, I pad-footed through the deep pile carpets, over the parquet, the tiles, the 400-year-old flagstones and across the corridor rugs of Kitchenly Mill Race, drawing curtains onto the outside dusk. I pulled them all. On the ground, first and second floors of both mill houses, even in those bedrooms of north-easterly aspect whose windows can never be seen from the manor. I tugged across curtains in all the rooms which Mrs H, Olive and I utilise nicknames for; names which Marko often frowns at, as he would not know to which room we referred.

I pulled the curtains in the pink bedroom, the blue bedroom, the attic nursery (which despite being decorated, Molly had never used), the maid's room, the hatch room, the two-sink room, the electrician's room (so-called as once, during the power cuts, an electrician had to stay with us overnight to fix an ongoing problem), my kitchenette window, the venetian blinds in the mill-wheel parlour, the studio room (Marko actually only stored recording equipment here, which was being shifted across to the new studio he was assembling in the stables). There's the river room, and the balcony room, where the tall shutters for a millstream winch once lowered filled sacks down to small barges, in the days of Constable and *The Mill on the Floss*.

37

This outer wall opening has been converted into tall, double-glazed French windows and a narrow balcony of white wrought-iron railings. I pulled all the curtains with their sunflower pattern around the main kitchen.

I pressed the switch and brought down the upstream-view side shutters in the smaller air bridge across the millstream. Then I initiated the heavy hum of the shutter-drive motors in the main linking air bridge – standing with a certain pathetic self-importance next to the operating switch which only has two positions.

I entered the three-storey Tudor section of the complex, pulling as I went, tugging at the heft of the heaviest curtains – for instance, the beautiful eastern oriel window with its gold-cushioned love seat, where the drapes across are like the entrance flaps to some huge marquee. I switched on the porch chandelier for the night, jerking open the inner door and glancing fleetingly upwards to ensure it was illuminated. Tenderly, I used the brass-beaded strings to descend the double-layered blinds in the Elvetson morning room, where the window strips are far too long and narrow to accommodate conventional pulled curtains. Auralie and Marko could never be bothered to use the original fitted, bracketed wooden shutters designed by Elvetson, which recess into the walls and concertina out perfectly along those windows. Ditto for the enormous third-storey atrium – once a 1930s dance floor – with its roof solarium where Marko stored his antique telescopes, dumbly pointed upwards on their stands towards the Tiffany-style skylights. On the floor of the atrium was his eighty-plus-strong guitar collection, electrics and acoustics, all uncased and ranged upright on their stands in precise but obscure platoons and phalanxes, with walking aisles between them for access. Marko ensured they were all maintained perfectly in tune by having his guitar tech visit the house each month to adjust them. The daily had orders to gently feather-duster them all every week, which evoked a strange orchestra of open tuning which I had often overheard at the stair bottom.

I closed the curtains in the three upstairs en-suite guest rooms and their bathrooms (some of these rooms are named after nineteenth-century British prime ministers). I could not resist opening the door to Marko and Auralie's master bedroom. My hand reached inwards, sliding onto the original Tudor wood panelling of the bedroom walls until I found the 1930s brass light switch with its little end ball which moves down so softly. Each window was like a dead eye and, as on the exterior, Dan Mullan had sealed all light out with the multi-layerings of black rubbish bags and tape. I hesitated, but crossed the large room and pulled all the curtains across the ugly plastic bags so they did not show. I moved beyond the telescope and those Chinese screens, to Auralie's deep walk-in closet, where there is a tiny exterior porthole with a flap of curtain. Then to the bathroom, with its shower cubicle, outlandish bidets and imported pine steam sauna, constructed by a Danish friend of Auralie's – at great expense. All curtains drawn, I tried to be mature and not glance downwards at her scattered undergarments littering the floor like crushed tropical birds.

Putting out the lights and closing the master bedroom door, I finally moved down the corridor to the 'Ghost's Room'. Sir Lawson Starley. As usual, I executed a fake yawn of feigned indifference as I crossed over beside the four-poster bed, snapped the curtains closed, turned around then smartly departed, pulling the door behind me, listening tensely for any sounds; but I made it to the top of the staircase and descended rapidly in silence. I do not believe in ghosts.

Downstairs I hesitated at the house's main entrance. Despite having housekeepers and watchmen like me, Marko still carried a Yale key away with him on his tours, so I didn't turn the house key in its hole, I just released and let the single Yale click locked.

I left the burglar alarm off at the box – we hardly ever engage it. It was then I illuminated the courtyard and driveway standard lamps and also the garden floodlights, in anticipation of our masters' later arrival.

Conventionally at night, when Marko was in residence, I would close the 1602 door of the manor house at the top end of the enclosing air bridge to allow them to lock it from the inside – if they so wished. They never did, since locking that door implied a total responsibility on their part for whatever went on within that section of the house. Opening the curtains in the morning for instance. I left ajar the aged, heavy wooden door with its rusted caged peephole.

I made my way back through, checking all the other doors were also locked: both of the kitchen doors, including the Dutch door, (but the cat flap definitely released for Mister Mingles and Corbisher-the-Swiper).

Up in my room I changed into my pajamas for bed. I was looking forward to sleep, hoping for a continuation of my dreams.

I was awoken by the white telephone of the extension, ringing on the other side of my bedroom. I could hear also the slightly differing timbre of the second wall-mounted telephone downstairs in the kitchenette, like a teasing dream-phone in some alternative part of my mind. I blinked my eyes clear and was crossing the room in unsteady steps, tugging up my pyjama bottoms. I put myself on the padded stool and lifted the receiver, slightly helpless in the darkness. I whispered, 'Kitchenly 4-3-4,' expecting Marko's laconic south London voice to reply.

'Crofton and your Christian army of one.'

It was Baraclough up there in London. A right dinger. I cleared my throat, crushed up my face in distaste, looking towards my glow-in-the-dark Mickey Mouse alarm clock, trying to discern the hour.

40

Baraclough continued. 'How is your relationship with Jesus this evening?'

'Benign. I hear Marko's back.'

'You know? Thought I would do you an enormous favour and put you wise to it, darling. Came into Heathrow from Kennedy on some late Pan Am thing, then round here. Now they've gone. To see someone. Should be down yours late. With Lawless Limos. To keep your cute little arse warm in your scratcher, darling, I even gave the driver the gate code so you don't have to get up and ring him in. She's on something; says she isn't sleeping. He was on Courvoisier and cans of that American 7 Up stuff.'

'Okey-doke. Appreciated. How's little Molly? She's my lady.'

'Crying. You owe me. What's the scandal down in deep country? How do you endure it?'

'Life is life.'

'Well, hard lines. Yours isn't much fun.'

'Do you want to hear my dream?'

'Certainly not.' Baraclough put on an awful, cod-American Baptist voice, 'Remember, Craftan. Maybe life ain't no album at all; maybe it's just a double A-side single.' Strangely, he sounded like the old man in my dream. He rang off.

All the airs regarding our importance and the greatness of our respective houses, yet between both of us we didn't own so much as a chipped cup in either of the lavish homes we so faithfully served. We were but myrmidons. I imagined him up there in London, lodged in its colossal networks of potential error – his massive dissatisfaction fuelled by frizzy Chelsea cocaine. Marko's house on The Vale once belonged to Alex Korda's brother. A French vintage brass hall light engineers gentle shadows due to a trendy new dimmer switch I had noted on a rare visit. The strip of carpeting on the white stone stairway leads upstairs like a water rill in reverse.

41

And around 4 a.m. I was awoken once again from my dreamless state by the lush, oceanic sound of a vehicle curving in upon the raked gravel of the wide-open turnaround space. From my bed I crossed to the window and knelt upon the small couch which is placed there. I took the stance of a boarding school boy praying for his missed home. I timorously moved aside the curtain to peer outwards and across. Fiddlesticks! First thing I noted was that a bulb had blown on the most necessary park lamp, the one just along from the main entrance of the air bridge. This now conferred an added gloom onto the spectral scene around a long dark limousine which was halted there, its boot sprung open. Daft, but why did I then imagine Henry VIII alighting at night-time Hampton Court from one of his royal barges, in the oily shadow of some vicious diplomacy, after having been secretly oared down the Thames? I tried to spy out my own slim king.

Marko was featured in so many magazines and music papers of those days that it always amused me to see if I could actually recognise his jacket or flamboyant blouse from one of the numberless press photographs which exist of him. Hidden beneath my bed was my own private archive of Marko Morrell's frequent profiles and front pages in *Creem*, *Crawdaddy*, *ZigZag*, *Disc*, *Rolling Stone*, *New Musical Express*, *Melody Maker* and the *Encyclopedia of Rock*.

Across that distance I spied another slim figure which moved rapidly sideways then turned around confusedly beside the limo: the flailing, needy limbs of Auralie and indeed, long pale hands shot up immediately to adjust her broad hat. Then she leaned in and stepped backwards more slowly, cradling a dark weight in both arms. Little Molly in her slumber.

Stooped forwards, I recognised the slightly unsteady marionette slouch of Marko – and it seemed to be a shirt and jacket unfamiliar to me which he wore. Shopping in New York. But what were they doing hesitating around the estate Volvo where I'd parked it earlier? They were opening up the back! Then I understood. Rather than carry them up the short stairway and into the air bridge themselves, the limo driver was placing their considerably outsized suitcases, and even many small shopping and duty-free bags, into the back of the Volvo for the night, so I myself could hoist them up the steps come morning.

Did something creak in my heart at that moment, directed with caution towards myself? Just for a calamitous second, did I feel suddenly helpless, as if I had nothing to do with that absurd landscape around me, the floodlit night park and this extravaganza of living space? Did I doubt, and feel as if my purpose was close to questionable? Answers on a postcard to the *Blue Peter* studio.

Marko moved warily on up the front steps above the two stone finial balls, a long tube under one arm. Another Civil War-era telescope for his collection in the atrium? I saw his elbow draw backwards to unlock the door, the same elbow whose thrust had driven so many electric guitars to frenzy down these many years, as the instruments careened into a symphony of meaning, which lesser or less-lucky musicians could not achieve; a mighty noise of consequence and of economic empowerment, the results of which I lived in.

The slim figures of that nativity scene entered into their lavish home – there was room at this inn, through the main doors together – babe-in-arms – they were gone; the door closed and hid them behind the electric shutters. I might as well have been just a mere fan, lingering by a stage door in the gloomy alley at the side of some famed theatre, desperate for a glimpse, a quick commission to mysterious fame.

The limousine noisily circled the glass booth in the middle of the parking area and there was a distinct cut into silence as it mounted onto the tarred surface and the tail lights of hellish

43

red began to silently curve in among the creepers of the cedars of Lebanon and back up the driveway. It occurred to me that Auralie and Marko would not have instructed the driver how to reopen the front gates. I should have gone downstairs and pushed the 'Front Gate Open' button, but doubtless he was resourceful in negotiating the private gateways of the privileged. To hell with him.

Then I frowned and tutted. They hadn't switched off the driveway lights and conscience would dictate that I had to go downstairs, walk through the corridors and do this myself. Just as suddenly the car park and courtyard turning area fell into a complete and cleansing darkness.

I felt a surge of affection. Marko had remembered where this particular light switch was.

2

And kneeling by my small staff room's window in the secondary mill house . . . foreign night clouds – a dream – Fear Taker – a light bulb change – Maude – an unauthorised arrival – a second unauthorised arrival – a barrier.

And kneeling by my small staff room's window in the secondary mill house that same night, I had continued to stare over to the turnaround area in its mysterious theatre of darkness, which it seemed Marko himself had initiated by his guitarist's fingers upon that light switch. I gave him credit for everything – even the darkness.

Beyond the corner guttering of the main manor house where he now slept off his jet lag within that shrouded chamber, I observed how gently luminescent clouds still moved across the night-time sky which had delivered our master down. Low, fast and silent clouds – within gantries of blue-packed stars showing their busy rotations: one grouping revealed then another respectfully shrouded – the curtains of heaven themselves, being opened and then closed to their own cryptic schedule.

Clouds of differing sizes. You could calculate that if you drew some of those clouds down and in among we earthbound things, their vapours and foggy dimensions were modest enough to only perfectly enclose Kitchenly Mill and its immediate acreage.

Yet if choosing others from these airborne floes, some clouds could just as well extend their vastnesses right across all the pastures and jurisdictions to the next village, beyond Ablemyre Hill – which it would also envelop.

And some clouds which passed above were so comprehensively mammoth, that you could take a fair guess that their extent would stretch from Kitchenly village all the way to the brown silken horizon, indicating those new orange sodium streetlights on the very outskirts of town itself.

The local villages were incapable of projecting enough upward streetlight to bruise the bases of these low clouds, so I imagined

49

those shifting bulks moving onwards across the dark fields, over the lowered necks of cattle, above the milestones of the still sheep, a fox sneaking, a badger lumbering, and the bare-backed horses too, who waited uneasily for dawn.

The slim crescent moon was a tipped white umbrella upon the manor roof, placing almost invisible shadows onto this earth. This great and uncontrolled migration of clouds above silent, perfidious Albion, seemed scarcely credible but was somehow unsettling to me; I sensed the hours these clouds must have hung over foreign lands and also above the English Channel; all in their vague, north-easterly urging; to who knows where, to what other lonely places, as they voyaged hereby? Yet the unanchored wanderings of this skyfleet were nothing compared to the indefinable pulsing of the stars, pinned in senseless configurations between.

Then something deeply unsettling occurred. I can now trace the convulsions that came upon my life back to that very instant. Let me say, the moon slice was sheathed by a large cloud, but still my eye caught some minimal change in the fizz of darkness close by the main door of the air bridge. It was at the bottom of the stairway by the two round finial stones. Of course, the court-yard lights were still extinguished, so what I thought I saw was really no more than a phantasmical charge within many degrees of blackness. I dipped my chin as I frowned at this dark thing outside.

In the absence of light I was absolutely convinced, just there, stock still, a sitting human figure paused, seated casually on one of the bottom stairs of the exterior staircase. I immediately concluded that something vital – or at least something significant to Auralie – had been remembered within the car. Marko had been ordered back down to retrieve it. I believed the figure might have tipped their head backwards to take some kind of drink – a whole

50

bottle? I waited for Marko's telltale cigarette end to erupt, or a match flame to dash. But as I watched, I detected no movement in or around the more reflective metal, from where I knew the Volvo to be parked. Why the furtiveness of such a figure? And then. And then I was certain I saw this intruder stand up, pass on foot along the silent grass verge beside the gravel; coming towards me, it crossed knowingly onto the tarred driveway where a foot falls silently. My own head moved this way and that way at the window pane, twisting like Corbisher the cat as he tried to pinpoint a fly circling the room, his straight whiskers splayed out like dry white fishbones. A believer in Christ must surely countenance spirits; had I seen the fabled ghost of Sir Lawson Starley himself, from the haunted top bedroom?

Glaring towards the cedars by the driveway I saw nothing. Was it my imagination which made me see a humanoid form, a dark advancer, turn away from the driveway towards the foot-bridge and on down and away by the riverside? I watched this stillness for long minutes.

All sorts of bizarre and threatening unlikelihoods paraded through my considerations: one being that Dan Mullan's nephew was somehow sleeping high up in the linen cupboard, exiting and entering the house at obscure hours, doing unspeakable things while tangled among the ironed cotton sheets.

I pulled on my parka and slippers then descended from my staff flat to the kitchenette beneath. I keep an electric torch here, useful for any night manoeuvres throughout the linked compound of houses – one of the waterproofed, black Eveready torches with the on and off switch permanently sealed under rubbery hoods marked: + for on, and – for off. Torched up, I didn't have to bother crossing the large rooms to light switches on the walls, or reaching under the shades of standard lamps.

When I came to the main outer door across the larger air bridge, of course it was locked with the mortice key still positioned in the black metal box of the inside lock where Marko had turned it a short while before. So the only possibility was that Marko had left the house through the old lattice glass porchway, crossed the ornate moat bridge there and then skirted around to the car park from that direction. Why on earth would he take such a weird and unnecessary route? I didn't want to enter the Tudor section of the house to check if the porch door was or was not unbolted and neither did I relish going out into the open air. If I was detected there I would be asked why I had not brought in all the New York shopping yet. So I stood amid my spooky, aimless torchlight in the long shadowed corridor, listening for something I didn't know; the chlorophyll light of the gloomy hanging gardens out there behind me in the night, through the triple glazing.

Should I have kept vigil until break of dawn? Something halted me and birthed an indifference. Was it to do with that presumption of them leaving their luggage in the Volvo for me? Maybe Marko couldn't sleep as well as her and had gone for a stroll – though odd he didn't put any lights on. Lights would disturb nobody. Perhaps he had just taken a long route round the stables to his recording studio. Burdened by a sudden inspiration?

Then it was daylight and I awoke to the loud alarm clock: the white gloves of Micky Mouse vibrated, each pointed finger pedantically indicating a specific numeral or some oppressive zone in between. During the night I had dreamed of a conveyor belt which moved through all houses and all dwelling places, irrespective of technical problems; a conveyor belt which hugged the wallpaper, climbed and descended like a funicular railway, carrying along a constant stream of black or blue or red-covered hardback books, passing into my room, and then out of it, through a neatly shaped tunnel mouth, plunging down into the ground and moving onwards through a complex of tunnels and channels like a subterranean pneumatic post system to the next habitation, where this countless abundance of books re-emerged once again, and we could each reach out and lift free one of these tomes whichever way our reading pleasures tended.

Birds were abroad and chirping while a solitary light aircraft could be heard aloft in that ecstatic sky above, clawing eastwards, or perhaps towards the coast? A whole bright sunny day in southern England was in promise. Then I remembered the luggage and parcels which had made their transatlantic journey, slung low in a cold aircraft hold, to Kitchenly. To find themselves lodged in the rear of the staff Volvo with its wispy shreds of dried lawn grass – and even a sniff of the hedge-cutter oil. I felt a weary, hostile necessity to attend to that luggage straight away.

I removed my pyjamas and put yesterday's clothes back on; of course I casually tugged open all curtains as I made my way downstairs – for that whole opening and closing rigmarole now recommenced because our masters had returned to roost. Since it can be cool in the outdoor shade of the summer mornings, as I left my bedroom I had grumpily shrugged on my green parka.

Passing through the smaller air bridge connecting the two mill houses, I poked the button to re-elevate the electric shutters while I continued onwards, not pausing to witness the upstream and downstream views on both glass sides, as the interstices between each blade of venetian blind rose, parted, tautened, leaking a convoy of thin light striations across the carpets.

I then traversed the open-plan television floor which was slightly cool with earliness. The vertical oak supports of the old mill warehouse sprouted straight up out of the mustard deep-pile broadloom and into the whitewashed ceiling with its metallic spotlights, which could be aligned and angled this way, or directed that way. Their unpainted alloy recalled the airliners of American Airlines, their silver livery which I witnessed at airports over in the United States.

As a point of hysterical . . . sorry . . . historical interest, in various permutations, Auralie, Marko and Molly sometimes came through from the Tudor wing, walking down the air bridge to watch the colour television set. Sometimes Marko brought one of his three Wechter acoustics with him, and more than once I had delighted in hearing him picking out guitar lines from a famous Fear Taker song.

Marko did not believe a television set should be placed in the Tudor section of his house as it, 'Wasn't fitting to the eh, atmosphere.' So he would traipse in from the connecting corridor with Molly or Auralie, or sometimes just alone, throw himself on the huge porridge-coloured L-shaped couch and watch favourites. Just before the evening news on weekday evenings he would often rush through with Molly to watch the five-minute cartoons. And sometimes he would come through by himself for *Ivor the Engine*, *Roobarb*, or *Charlie Brown*.

Let it be known at Kitchenly Mill we have always taken our periodicals, the *New Musical Express*, the *Melody Maker*, the *Financial Times* and the *Radio Times*. Marko would check his stocks and shares listings carefully in the *FT* but rarely looked at anything else in the salmon-pink newspaper.

It was another of my duties to scrutinise the pages of the *Radio Times* and circle possibly appropriate television programmes, to alert Marko when his favourites were being broadcast. He'd get shirty if he missed anything, yet he had unpredictable tastes: black-and-white cowboy films, *The Good Old Days* variety show, a new show on Southern TV: *Worzel Gummidge*, which that last Dr Who did. He also liked *Mr Benn*, *Multi-Coloured Swap Shop*, *The Banana Splits*, *Casey Jones*, *Whacky Races*, *Marine Boy* and *Bagpuss*. Or sometimes current affairs broadcasts like *Panorama* or *Nationwide*. Christ, looking back on it I suppose he did not have unpredictable tastes, he liked everything. *The Liver Birds, The Likely Lads, On the Buses,*

Steptoe and Son, *Some Mother's Do 'Ave 'Em*, *It Ain't Half Hot Mum*, *Dad's Army*, *Python* . . .

For a spell, when he had come back home off the road from the eighth, or maybe it was the ninth American tour, Marko told me how much he had missed English telly and produced an old bicycle air-horn hooter with a squeezable rubber end. Maybe it was cannibalised from the Colonel's wartime Wolesley, still hooded under its waterproof canvas up in the stables? Marko told me to sound this horn off a couple of times before any potential viewing – even though I had already clearly circled programmes for him and placed the *Radio Times*, with that day's pages appropriately open, on the table of the Elvetson morning room.

As I pointed the hooter and honked the bike horn a couple of times down the air bridge corridor, he'd be off listening to some album in the morning room. He wouldn't hear me. Somehow the placing of a quadraphonic music system in the morning room *was* in keeping with the, eh, atmosphere of the Tudor wing. Perhaps he justified it because for a long period he only played Rick Wakeman's *The Six Wives of Henry VIII*, and after he went to see the performances up in Wembley, *The Myths and Legends of King Arthur and the Knights of the Round Table*. Often I had to walk through to tell him *Roobarb* was on. 'Can't be bothered,' he might shout, listening to the music of an ersatz England and gazing out eastwards through the severe grids of the window frames in the morning room.

In the main air bridge corridor I punched the 'Up' button, rehoisting the shutters on the turnaround courtyard side; to my left, the garden and the willow procession on the bankside were already sunlit in matutinal green splendour.

I switched off the garden night-lighting. I turned the brass house key twice – one good turn deserves another – to open the main door which I had checked was locked the night before.

On the cool air, lavender scent from outside wafted back in at me from the shadowy side of the house. New fresh light seemed to move absolutely horizontally across the lawns, slashing out shadows from any tussock, while blackbirds busied and signalled in the cedars.

To reduce noise, I tried to keep my Kickers off the gravel and wended my way along the grass strip towards the old Volvo. I looked down for canted and compressed grass blades. Footprints of the imagined intruder from the night before – but there was nothing I could detect. Some dew in the soaked grass had already marked dark serrations onto the sides of my shoes. I tip-toed around on the gravel and lifted the car's rear door open, moving my feet softly, glancing up at the plastic-lagged bedroom windows above, where our master and lady still slumbered.

From the car, I heaved out two large suitcases – made by Goyard of Paris, a present from Marko to Auralie – which had the feel of pieces of furniture; then seven shopping or duty-free bags. The duty-free bags could be distinguished by the *VAT 69* logo. At least the cases were not too laden – truth be told, they were light.

I carried all the luggage items up this exterior stairway between the two stone balls on the low pillars. Several of the shopping bags read, *Saks Fifth Avenue* or *I Miller Shoes*, and one, incomprehensibly *I. Magnin*. Their cord handles were sealed with ribbons which mainly obscured their contents – some seemed to be folded garments in tissue; others, bottles, lotions? Heaven knows what else the packages concealed – sexy underwear for Auralie, no doubt, slinky camisoles or short nightdresses which would lay like coloured jellyfish on the faultlessness of her reclining upper thighs. She could have been on a Roxy Music album cover for sure.

Breathing heavily, I had placed the suitcases and the shopping bags just in past the 1602 doorway then I remembered: I had to change that damned blown bulb on the park light at the bottom of the stairs. And the extending stepladders were away over in the stables, because Dan Mullan had been out pruning with them at the bottom of the mill race stream the week before.

I did not move through the house interior but left by the main door, trudged beyond the car park area and over the top end footbridge across the mill race, up past the old tennis courts then towards the stables and converted saddlery quadrangle where the archway doors were always open.

At that early hour, the ornate clock tower cast a shadow across the cobbled stable yard. Several months before, listening back to demos in his new studio there, Marko had been hearing an odd, very faint beat through his 24-track recording desk – a sound which was exasperating him. He came and talked to me about it. He couldn't detect where this slight phantom beat was emerging from until, during a quiet passage of basic guitar track, he suddenly honed in on the unmistakable sound of the tinkling quarterly bell of the coaching clock tower on the roof above. He had explained to me how, despite the soundproofing, his live Neumann microphones were so sensitive they were picking up not just bell tolls, but the mechanism's actual ticking above the rafters, inaudible to a human ear. This clock had ticked since 1824, timing out the London horse-drawns until the railways came. Yet the clocksmith was summoned from town within the hour to disconnect the mechanism and there the gilt clock hands were, unified and still at six minutes past three on all four faces.

On the corner of the stable block, I noted a fat trespassing pigeon on that thick black cable which comes in over the perimeter wall and droops through and among the tree leaves. I clapped my hands and reluctantly the bird crashed forwards, down into a birch where it grappled for lodgement. I clucked my tongue and I looked up at the black cable which shipped the juice into that

57

makeshift home recording studio where Marko would sketch out ideas, tracking down palimpsest guitar textures for subsequent albums. I remembered the headline once, from a music press article, 'Master of Modern Electricity: The Fear Taker's fearless guitarist, Mark Morrell'.

Rather than just from the national grid, Kitchenly Mill had refracted back a much rarer variation of electricity, conducted down through Marko's remarkably ordinary fingers, out of his guitar lead socket and then it was projected from his Hiwatt and Marshall amps to the 50,000-watt PA – each amp casing and road case stencilled in white spray paint: *Fear Taker London*. Disseminated further outwards, through 24-track recording studios, into vinyl grooves; on the electrically spun turntables of young men – sometimes even young women – within innumerable bedrooms throughout the Western hemisphere and Japan; onto cassette magnetics, 8-track and live broadcast sessions of national radio. The 'Sounds of the Seventies'. Sound made into long-playing plastic, sound sheathed in paper roundels and the gummed cardboard of gatefold sleeves. Expensive materials when not distributed and sold, but vastly profitable when shipped in huge numbers. Like a radio echo, this alchemical force had travelled back to this corner of England for many years. From the stages of the Oakland Hippodrome, the Cow Palace, Fillmores East and West, from the echoing concrete walkways above and behind the stage of New Madison Square Gardens, from the Ontario Motor Speedway, the Sunshine Festival at the Diamond Head Crater, Hawaii, or just from the Rainbow, Earl's Court, Hammersmith Odeon or Empire Pool, up in the smoke to the north.

Of course this monumental force, as well as the profound, mysterious energy of world fame, was also that of absurd wealth, and it came in among the birdsong of quiet Sussex from those deafening concert stages which I never saw or even missed any more. Those stages with the ruby amplifier 'On' buttons glowing scarlet pre-show, like patient demons' eyes. Stages that are no longer the beer-sticky, club platforms of the early days, but are now sealed in super-grip plastic sheeting. Maracas and tambourines, twin-necked acoustics, mandolins – lined up just behind the stage-left amp stack, Marko's Fender Strat' guitars, each stencilled number 1 and 2, (the '68 Strats) through to 7. Everything is as precisely arranged as the sharpened instruments upon a readied cancer surgeon's tray; the still penumbra of the unoccupied stage only given animation by the strident and moody dynamics of the light-show rig suspended above.

White folded towels for wiping away toxin sweat are stabled lengthwise along the tops of his black amplifiers with their protected metal corners – preferably, the towels are pilfered from New York's Drake Hotel on Park Avenue. We had a few of these hotel towels at Kitchenly, in the huge, high linen cupboard with its rolling Edwardian access ladders. These dark towels are starched hard as card, since Marko despises new, soft, white towels provided by the venue. Their fluff tends to catch in his dark stubble and the cotton fibres stick there, blemishing the contact sheets of many Kodak in-concert photos.

Microphone flexes are taped down by electrical duct tape, hysterically flush to the stage floor, and guitar leads are laid out like powder trails; one enormous museum-quality Afghan carpet reaches from frontman Alvin's microphone stand, all the stage distance backwards to the drum riser. On the corners of the riser will rest Marko and Alvin's two Jack Daniel's and Coke cups, each precisely mixed to their own exact specification at showtime. The horror on those occasional nights they had mistakenly sipped from the paper cup of the other! Rick Thomas on bass, stands stage right. Larry 'Sticks' Stephens, aka Styxie, is up on the drum riser behind his hyperbolic kit, a taped-down, sawn-off umbrella stand of spare drumsticks round by his dinner gong. Glen 'Gasser' Garrett on keyboards and synths is stage left, with the chintz shade of his trademark household lamp which he maintained lit up beside his keyboards throughout the show, and the rotary telephone he kept on top of his Fender Rhodes so he could call the sound-desk bloke and shout at him any time.

Alvin and Marko flick their extra-length Marlboro butts well clear of the carpet: Alvin's landing marginally closer to the carpet edges. Marko bid for that carpet at Sotheby's and he wants it back scorch-free to hoist and suspend beside the chandelier on the back porch wall at Kitchenly – which he had me measure for its fit – though right now that carpet is rolled up in some high-security New Jersey warehouse, awaiting the next US tour.

I had fetched a new light bulb and the extending ladder down from the stables, carrying it across the footbridge – the ladders hoisted up above my head so I looked like the pivot on a see-saw. On the gravel beneath the bedrooms I placed the ladder quietly against the cast-iron post, then I soon had the glass side hood of the park lamp open on its satisfyingly rust-free hinges.

Up that ladder, somehow I didn't hear its approach, but suddenly Mrs H sped her Triumph Dolomite in off the tarmac driveway onto the crunching gravel of the courtyard and swung it into a wide, loud, swishing left turn, heading back round the glass booth for her ever-questionable parking place right in front of the main doorway, by the two pillars with the round stone tops, beneath the master-bedroom windows. I tried to signal: reduce your speed, reduce your speed, by repeatedly moving my flat hand in a downwards manner, but I could not gesture upwards to my lips with my finger – indicating the need for silence – because I held the bulb in my fingers; then when I finally did, the new bulb bumped my nose and fell from my fingers to the ground beneath. Sod's law, it missed the grass verge and broke with a smart pop on the gravel.

Mrs H leaned straight out her car window and yelped, 'You've gone and bust your bulb when Maude is coming down this very morning. Dash it all!'

'Stow it. A bit of hush.'

She looked up, remembered they were asleep above and formed a zero shape with her olden lips, then she gingerly turned the ignition off and just sat there looking at the dashboard.

I dribbled down the ladder in sharp, childish steps, tiptoed up the grass verge to the side of Mrs H's car then leaned over; I whispered, 'Maude's coming? Strewth. That's gone and torn it.' I turned my face to also gaze up at the façade of the manor house above us, with the plastic sacking stuck over the windows. I dropped my voice further, into a hiss. 'Just what we need. We can't wake up sleeping beauty for Maude.'

'I know, I know, Crofton. And I better get in there and open the downstairs curtains.'

'All right. Watch you don't fall over their luggage and shopping from America; I piled it all up by the door for now.'

'Where will we put Maude tonight? That Benjamin Disraeli?'

'Course.'

As well as my and Mrs H's nicknames for bedrooms, when Marko bought Kitchenly Mill Race, bedrooms in the surviving chunk of the Tudor section bore names already: almost all of them belonging to one-time British Tory prime ministers, who for some reason or another had allegedly spent a night or two as house guests at Kitchenly. It seemed a bit historically sniffy to me, like the place was just a sleeping annexe to Downing Street. But we were left with the Robert Peel room, the Smith-Stanley, the non-en-suite Gascoyne-Cecil, the Bonar Law with its dripping toilet cistern, and Arthur Balfour, the very bed of which he was meant to have kipped in beneath our roof. There was also the Eden Czarogan guest room on the second floor – some 1930s Turkish landowner who Colonel Halmer's father had cut a pretty rewarding land deal with 'outside Constantinople', back in the days of Atatürk. Enough to elevate Mr Czarogan immediately up among all these British prime ministers. I often thought the glaring absentee, Art Wellesley, might once have featured, but perhaps his name was scratched out shortly after that Turkish land deal? I raised this with Marko once and he didn't half get shirty and snorted at me defensively – 'Don't you know nothing, Crofton? The Duke of Wellington's was one of them rooms that fell down.'

Bollocks.

I told Marko back in '73 that this named-rooms malarkey was all a bit 'country house hotel' for my tastes, but he liked the small, hand-painted, gilt name plates screwed onto each bedroom door; so they remained there, and the names have stuck. More or less. We usually placed Maude in the Disraeli room with its old wardrobes and dresser, which, like much of the furniture, had been assembled inside the bedrooms as the wardrobe could not have been fitted through the door space.

Maude always pitched up at Kitchenly with very little warning: suddenly to be found outside the main gates at the top of the driveway, standing, tall and upright in her twinset with matching skirt and jacket, between the two separated round stones of the main gate posts.

She would appear on weekdays from her journey, sometime after rush hour, having taken the many-doored commuter train down from the large and modern bungalow Marko had bought for her in south London, in his old manor: Sutton. Maude would alight at Kitchenly's nearest station: British Rail Maxtelham, to which I would often return her in the Volvo. British Rail Maxtelham is the station beyond the summit of Ablemyre Hill, out there among open meadows. Strangely for the station's rural positioning in a landscape of rape fields, sloe-blossom-dotted hedges, farms and cultivation sheds – as well as Strabney's Country Garden Centre – it is served by both up- and down-line double tracks. The railway station has a main stone building only on one of the two platforms, a footbridge, and a shelter on the northbound platform – though ironically that is the most heavily used direction for waiting passengers who drip in the rain and indulge in the ever-so-British mental health activity of slagging off BR.

The station ticket master would, as usual, telephone a local taxi for Maude. There is only one taxi round there and it is driven by a farmer's bachelor son – a man of fifty – who opens the rear car door for this lady, yet conducts his vehicle shod in wellington boots.

However, before this taxi would reach British Rail Maxtelham to collect her, Maude would have carefully walked out from the station to the red telephone box by the car park. Here the tufts of verging and bright ragwort around the phone box were actually just a continuation of the open field directly behind that old tensile wire fence. While you talk inside the box, blades of grass lean or jerk in the silent breeze outside. From this GPO box, Maude would routinely telephone our housekeeper, whether Mrs H was working in the spread-out dimensions of Kitchenly Mill Race, or whether – as on this morning – she was in fact, busy within the confines of her own neat and tidy semi-detached in the town. Mrs H would then have to warn us of Maude's imminent approach. It was through some strange formality that Marko's mum only ever communicated her visits to our housekeeper.

Mind you, this said, Marko was notoriously slippery to reach on the end of a telephone line. Down the years even his mum might have got a bit cheesed off trying to call him – maybe that is why that conversation with old Colonel Halmer concerning the moat still stands out so much for me? Even the Fear Taker's manager, Roger Schillings (inevitably, behind his back, he was called: 'Pounds, Schillings and Pence'), even Schillings had to struggle for a confab with Marko on the plastic-horned devil.

63

Each of Marko's two personal accountants considered a phone communication with him deeply special. You can't just phone up someone like world famous Marko Morrell – though believe me, people have tried.

Onto the back seat of that taxi, by her tweed-skirted thigh, Maude would place the soft, gift-wrapped package of her own knitwear – knitwear even in summer. And often something from a local bakery. When *Pascal's Moon* was at number one in the American album charts, Maude once knitted an alarming tank top for Marko with the album logo emblazoned upon it, which he then felt obliged to wear onstage – one night only – on a winter UK tour of university dates. These knitwear packages were almost always for Molly – Maude was never deluded enough to even try and furnish her daughter-in-law with garments knitted in her own front room in Sutton; or if she ever did give anything to Auralie, it was never to be seen again. Burned in the wide Tudor hearth, no doubt.

One summer, Maude brought down a crocheted hot-water-bottle cover in lime and orange wool, which I coveted.

So without detaining her further, that taxi – a Ford Cortina, with those extended wing mirrors of sometime-caravan-towing – would head south over the level crossing at British Rail Maxtelham. Often lashed by weeds sprouting in the live green summer verges, or during the season of autumn, spinning brown leaves in its wake, shaking the raindrops on the road-side cobwebs, that Cortina motored on downwards through the shire lands; roadsides sunk in grass, by the ducking lanes and glades it came, alongside the wide open fields, by the reeds, by the millponds, by the water meadows, dells and coombes of East Sussex, the car made its progress.

The taxi would pass the headwaters of our very own mill race as it came in from the eastern side of Ablemyre Hill then joined the main road for a further two miles of motoring towards the telegraph pole where it would suddenly take a right onto the single track alongside our boundary walls of Kitchenly Mill.

As far as I know, Maude never once permitted the taxi to enter through the main gates of her son's property. Parked with the engine running, the driver would wait while she buzzed me once on the intercom, but she would never talk into it.

She would be standing there in her high heels by the main gate pillar. The north pillar, I suppose you could term it. Maude had a stance – how can I describe its impression? Her head tilted over with its slightly greying bun, her high cheekbones; she was still a handsome, slim woman, pushing fifty but made older by her respectable clothes. She would be positioned slightly to the left of the humming intercom console – it was as if she was not associated and would never associate with the intercom and its functions; as if the modern device had played no part in her arrival and my interception of her, and that her arrival was simply, somehow, a prophetic one.

Mrs H in her high-mileage Triumph Dolomite or myself in the Volvo, would drive up the curvature and around the cedars of Lebanon to the front gates. As if dismissing a coachman, Maude would nod to the taxi driver politely as the gates were swung open and it would be us who would shuttle her back down the driveway to the main doors of the manor air bridge where her son might await – often with his arms folded in that manner which I recognised from press photos.

On one occasion, Marko himself had spurted his Ferrari Dino around the cedars with no more than a touch to its accelerator, to fetch his mum back down. Maude would have none of it. 'Markus, now really, how do you expect your poor mother to climb down elegantly into that blooming thing; let alone get back up out of it, my dear?'

'Come on, Mam, I'll give you a good tug back up.'

65

'Not at all, off you go now, back down with your silly car and wipe Molly's face clean and proper before I get to see her; careful now. Ooo, why it's as small as that old pedal car your dad brought you back from Woolworths.'

And that was it. Mums. What can you do with them? Marko with his long, rich hair canted round, looking over his shoulder, arm chucked out across the top of the passenger seat, reversing that temperamental Italian oil-leaker back along the driveway; retreating, with Maude primly following along the tarmac on foot, her green croc handbag bouncing on her horizontal forearm.

That was in the good old early days down at Kitchenly, before the brown came in, when Marko like all the others still threw a few parties every year. The aquatic lights had not yet been fitted into the moat or the river, so for those rare party nights, braziers of anthracite and upright burning torches were set all along the riverside paths. Chinese paper lanterns hung from trees, windows in the manor and mill houses were thrown open to the lavender nights, slashing bars of butter light down the lawn flanks.

I know what you're all thinking: young girls screaming for rescue from the upper-floor windows before being dragged back inwards by members of both sexes, to undergo unspeakable sensual awakening; but nah, man. It isn't like that – rock-star parties were very demure, even cautious events. After all, it was about ego and pecking orders by the seventies. Who had come out of the sixties with the most? Everyone's checking each other out and there is no room for error in that.

Musos, world famous or getting there, they would all come down to Kitchenly with their old ladies in tow, and the chicks were checking each other out as well, making sure they knew what each other had or had not – and making sure they soon got it too, if they found out Kim, Ginger or Auralie had it. None of them hung around long about getting pregnant under their fur coats either, I'll tell you that. It was as if wealthy young male musicians were unusually fertile. Groupies, ultimately, the lot of them, no matter how you bake the feminist cake. It's all: oh, so my new swimming pool's bigger than yours – and Brian Jones's was big enough for sure. Then, next time everyone would go to someone else's place for their party. Back then they were called: the jet set.

Their houses were crammed with useless antiques, so you couldn't be falling around smashing things; no one needs the opportunity to make a fool of oneself in the eyes of your peers. All that looning about; that happened on tour and usually just in the early years, before the serious bread and drudgery started, and everyone woke up, realised that rock music could be a crushingly serious and profitable financial business. People forget that when we started out in the sixties we didn't really think there would be much bread in rock music. Same way we didn't think growing our hair was about image – we just did it. Then all the silver poured down from those clouds of coloured dry ice above the stages. Hell, even in 1966, The Beatles were still living in modest enough stockbroker houses up St George's Hill way. By 1973 all the members of Fear Taker were registered company directors. The counterculture had become the counting of pounds and dollars culture.

If you were smart, you saw America was where the honey was – it was a big country, being opened up by slick radio stations sweeping their airwaves across all those cities of the plain. You saw it all coming – at last teenagers had a bit of money in their pockets – and everyone saw what happened to The Cream in America. Look. The Cream were playing in Hoveton village hall outside Norwich in 1966. It really was a village hall, with reluctant short-haired blokes in suits standing moodily up the back looking appalled at what was going on. The fuse box kept tripping from the amps. I know because I was there with Nobby Charles. Nobby was later to be Marko's guitar tech (1971–78) on my recommendation. Just a swift eighteen months later, The Cream were sold out at the Royal Albert Hall and the Winterland. That's how quickly really big audiences opened up for rock bands. We thought The Beatles had topped it, but they just pioneered it. And once we all saw Woodstock, well. What would you think if audiences were your livelihood and a half-million people turned up at your gig? Everyone wanted a bit of that. It was always about the money then the ego – the beautiful music just happened to fit in, and don't let any cultural historian try to tell you otherwise.

America was like stepping onto another planet back then. Americans dressed differently, baseball caps and sports shirts that didn't button up the front. They had good teeth compared to our horrors, and their cars really did seem enormous. There wasn't just spaghetti, over there was this stuff called pasta! There were liberated girls who looked like nothing we had seen. Not like careful doxies from Tamworth with a bit of eyeshadow on. Concorde didn't even exist. Nobody had tasted a Dr Pepper or a Hershey bar before. And sometimes, back in England, Marko and Auralie left Molly with Mrs H, Maude or a nanny, and they went to the parties of other musicians who had also brought back a whole lot of Yankee gold – and I got to drive them over there to where the other rich lived, always down small cul-de-sac lanes off main roads, always called Mill Lane, or Rectory Close, Church Lane or Partridge Lane.

Keith Emerson. Now there was a nice bloke who could hammer the Joanna. I remember him backing P.P. Arnold at Windsor, and I won't hear a harsh word spoken against that first album by The Nice. He never bettered that album really; based his whole future career on it, plus the onstage looning. I play that album every bloody year, especially round about Christmas time – there is something of the old English Yuletide contained in it.

68

Now it was Keith who had one of the most beautiful houses in all England back then, in his ELP Manticore years; a timber-framed Wealden place in Chiddingly, not far from Kitchenly Mill Race: used to belong to the Scotch fellow who wrote *Peter Pan*. Strangely, that handsome house on Gloucester Road once belonged to J.M. Barrie as well – the house Marko tried to buy in '75, when he was looking for a London pad. Odd also that Marko and I used to live on Gloucester *Terrace* in Westbourne Green, hard by the railway lines into Paddington. The J. M. Barrie house that Marko fancied was on Gloucester Road, Kensington. *Peter Pan* man had good taste in property – a red-brick Christmas cake frontage peppered with little balconies.

Marko almost made a down payment on that Gloucester Road semi. Nice looking gaff, nine-foot walled, long back garden. I checked it out for him; toffee-nosed estate agent giving me dirty looks as he followed me across the parquet, from room to room; but on my reckoning it was just too accessible to the general public for my 'client', plonked as it was right on Gloucester Road. There was only a six-foot gap front garden, and the traffic was going to get worse. This was before unleaded petrol; the M25 wasn't near done and juggernauts would still come straight through central London. There was a pub right next door, across the side lane, as well. That meant noisy drinkers outside on a Saturday night and blokes pissing against your garden wall; security-wise, the rear of the pub with a few tables and faded sun umbrellas overlooked the back-garden wall. From the roof of a car it was all too easy just to vault into the back garden with the help of a lovely old cherry tree, too gorgeous to cut down.

This was way before John Lennon got shot, but Charles Manson seemed very recent and there was always the memory of The Beatles being mobbed by fans, but Fear Taker were not household faces and it really was Les Paul and Strat guitars getting nicked that you feared most back then – not assassins.

Mind you, a crazed loon had shoved Frank Zappa off the stage at the Rainbow in 1971 and put him in a wheelchair, so I was always on my guard for Marko's welfare.

I'll never forget the party in that Hansel-and-Gretel dream home of Keith's though. You walked in through an original arched front door marked 1564 – the year Shakespeare was born – and it was timber-beamed Tudor all inside, then you went straight through the guts of the dwelling and out onto this terraced garden and lakeside; and when you turned around to look back onto the house, it had been transformed into an Arts and Crafts beauty on that side – with swooping roof lines, russet tiles and tall crenellated chimney stacks, all reflected in the blackberry water of a small lake now before you – a divine place.

I plucked up the mettle to talk to Emerson when I found myself standing next to the guy that night. I simply said what a lovely place he had here. It seemed an honest thing to say, yet I braced myself for an icy reply; but he instantly said, 'Yeah and on a sunny day I jump in the car to Eastbourne, get an ice cream cone down by the sea side.' Those exact words. Happier days for everyone.

Keith had a huge practice room off to the side – actually part of the house, with his complete set-up in there: concert grand, his full synth racks and a tortured Hammond organ. There was a great jam that night. I was meant to be out front in the little parking area, waiting with some other drivers, but fuck that. I snuck in to listen. Alan White on drums, a roadie called Dobson on bass. Marko was on a low-slung Gibson with too high an action – not one of his own. Keith had had to go find a guitar for him. Keith had quipped, 'That's the great thing about ELP. No bleedin' guitarist,' winking at Marko strapping it on before they cantered away: a version of 'Peter Gunn' that turned into Bernstein's 'America'. That turned into the fanfare section on

70

'Rule of the Evil Ones'. If you asked me, they should have segued into 'Karn Evil 9 First Impression', but they didn't. That was some line-up, I tell you – with Emerson on keyboards and Marko on lead.

Then Marko got obsessed with – and tried to buy – The Pines, this London house for sale up on Putney Hill, in which that nutso poet Swinburne had lived. Marko thought he had to have the house – like it was a feather in his cap; especially after he read a copy of Swinburne's *Lesbia Brandon*, which I got for him off Martin Stone. The edition illustrated by Simeon Solomon, from whom Marko owned a series of five framed oil sketches.

Marko sent me in to case that joint too. I told him I had my doubts about The Pines. The car-parking issue to start with; a 1970s world-famous rock star doesn't need to park his car outside on the street, getting pestered by the occasional punter on the pavement, trying to get their copies of Fear Taker albums signed when he came back from Prestos with the cat food. That's no good. It had also been converted into individual flats on each floor, so it needed a lot of work. Besides, it was a semi-detached. There is a sure rule in life which wisdom has tested. Neighbours are always trouble. Don't have any near neighbours when you can afford not to have any neighbours at all. But after I cooled his heels on The Pines, Marko sort of took me off the job as property scout and bought that place on The Vale in Chelsea, before I even had a chance to see it, with all its light and big studio windows. I suppose I felt hurt by that. It was all a long way from the late sixties when we both lived in Gloucester Terrace.

Ah yes, Kitchenly parties. Marko had an idea at Kitchenly so all the expensive cars and limos would not get into a confusing mess over parking on party nights, like they did out front of Keith Emerson's place in Chiddingly that time. Keith's lovely house only had a small turning place out front, so you had these Volvo roadsters, E-Types, Mini Coopers, Rollers, Mercedes and a Jensen Interceptor parked one hundred and fifty yards all down the narrow public road.

So, at Kitchenly, Marko had a wood-and-glass car park attendant's booth constructed right in the middle of the gravelled turnaround courtyard, for me to sit in and direct the delicate parking operations all night. All arrivals and all departures. It was a bit like National Car Parks out there and for a while – as a gas – Marko had an NCP sign stuck on the side of the booth with a 50p-per-hour tag.

The rule of thumb with the parking on those party nights was – any one of them must be able to get their limo or motor out as easily and quickly as they can. It was a bit like chess and I was Bobby Fischer: *My 60 Memorable Games*. No one can block in anyone else. If the party was going well, no problem, but there was always a battle of egos as to who was going to leave first, or last – it depended on the mood and the politics. Was it cool to leave parties early – or late? And whose parties? It might be cool to leave this musician's place early, but it was cooler to leave this other one late. It might depend what position their latest album occupied on the current chart. Marko's albums in those days were always high on the US and UK charts, and his parties were always pleasant, so folk would stay late and he had so much room in the big courtyard area that I never had any problem getting everyone parked, or with them leaving. It was a cinch. Unless, perhaps, if Keith Moon had rolled up with his driver, and there had been a sudden rush for the cars. But Moony never did, God bless him. Townshend did once. Pete was there with his wife, who was surely the prettiest girl in all England. Karen Astley – a real nice, artistic person who would talk to you. Her dad was a composer. There was a lot of culture in that house.

I miss those parties a bit – eventually that booth got woodlice in it, and we had to tack a double-folded bit of tar paper up there on the roof to stop the damp from the rain. 'Get a good dollop of Araldite on up there,' I recall Dan Mullan growling.

That was all back in those good old early days when Molly was still confined in her pram. It was round then Marko shipped in those barmy bloody peacocks to the grounds of Kitchenly Mill Race. Marko thought the world of those feathered blighters, he really did. They played ruddy havoc with Mullan and me round the gardens. Vicious buggers that went straight for your arse, or the crown jewels themselves. Lifted up Auralie's gypsy skirts with their beaks. The Ferrari Dino had just got delivered down from Berkeley Square. Been parked out front about a week and one morning Marko descended the interior Turkish staircase and out he went onto the top steps of the air bridge entrance above the parking area. Casting a proud eye over his grounds and his Italian motor. And his car park booth. Folded his arms in that way; yawned then frowned. Since dawn broke, in first light, hadn't the peacock thugs surrounded the newly-buffed Ferrari, taken offence to their own damned reflections jutting about there in the red, glossy, wax-polished, deep paintwork, and pecked their way right along the driver's side, then around the passenger side for good measure? Looked like someone had got down on their knees, then hammer and chiselled a horizontal line right round that car. That was the last we ever saw or heard of those bloody peacocks and good riddance to them too; they were shipped out to a sanctuary somewhere near Tunbridge Wells long before the Ferrari came back from the paint shop.

So I said to Mrs H, didn't I, that day after I saw the dark shadow in the garden: the intruder, the figure, moving in the night-time grounds, I said, 'Yes. Put Marko's mum in Disraeli.' I nodded, looking upwards at the open hood of the park light. I had to abandon that chore. It could wait.

When the intercom buzzer sounded in my kitchenette it was Mrs H in her Triumph bone shaker who went up the driveway to collect Maude from the taxi at the main gates. I was still in the main kitchen where I'd casually flicked on the kettle while crossing the bright floor tiles. Then there was Mrs Maude Morrell herself, standing alone at the open exterior kitchen door.

'Crofton. Love. Now is that the kettle on I hear?'

'Hello, Mrs Morrell. Yes it is. Always a pleasure to see you.'

'You look tired out, my dear; it's all this country air. Bad for you in the long run. Nuts to that; look what I've brought you down.' She thrust out a paper bag with a transparent grease stain on it. 'It's a lovely custard finger. From Mr Gromley's Bakery. A custard finger. Just for you, Crofton. I hope it hasn't turned a little tough on the outside, or got any bad air in them railway tunnels.'

Before stepping into the ginormous kitchen, with its bright yellow sunflower floor tiles, Marko's mum turned around; she looked out across the lawn and sighed, 'Fancy that. You got the chrysanths looking ever so gorgeous, Crofton, and them azaleas are to be proud of. Ever so.' She took off her pair of gloves with little pearls fixed onto their inner cuffs and she put them away in her ever-snapping handbag. Then she leaned over to the flowers outside the kitchen door and said, 'And I am pleased to see you have been tending to your window boxes.' She reached across and went momentarily out of sight from the doorway. I knew exactly what she was doing. With her fingers she was severing off a flower's dead head in the window box. She came back into the kitchen and her voice hammered on, 'Would have been here sharper but that British Rail is defective. Know what Morecambe and Wise say? British Rail coffee. It's terrible. I hear it's gone up ten pence a slice.'

74

She cackled slowly, her eye on me.

I laughed back.

'Here. I'll warm the pot,' she stepped in past me. Then she declared, 'I'm going to get in among the linen cupboard today. Me and Mrs H are going to give it a right good sort out, we are; note down everything that's in there in correct order. What's it called, Crofton? An invitationary?'

'An inventory.'

'That's the number.'

When I eventually explained the situation about the blacked-out bedroom windows, she frowned across her tea cup and some ridges of disturbance showed momentarily on the cuppa's reflective tan surface. 'Well fancy that. Well just fancy that! I knew he was back today. Phoned me from America to keep me abreast of it, so to speak. So little Molly is all shut up in there with them both, is she? Fancy that. See! That's what I object to. She'll get bad air. Now they might not smoke in bed, but they breathe it out all night long, don't they? Especially her. On account of those long legs of hers. And that little pet should be in her own bedroom.' Maude used her eyes to gesture around us both, to the dimensions and possibilities beyond that modernised kitchen. 'God knows her mother has enough rooms to choose from. There was upstairs too that was even made up as a lovely little nursery, wasn't there?'

Pleadingly, she looked at me and I felt obliged to agree. 'Yes, yes,' I claimed, nodding smartly.

'And there was us all in a one-bedroom in the years after the war, Markus crying all night in a cot, and Jeffrey off onto the buses at dawn. Here we are, seems like just the blink of an eye with this ruddy great pile and he has Molly all shut up in the same room as him, just like us, back of old Sutton High Street in the fifties. Fancy that.' She sighed and looked into the middle distance. 'Doesn't bare reflecting on it all really, does it? Make you fed up to the back teeth if you did so. Not going to try your custard finger then?'

I nodded, 'Well one of them will wake up sooner or later.'

'Yes. Molly. The poor little peach. Fed up with those slumber-pussies.'

'Would you be okay in Benjamin Disraeli tonight?'

'Beg your pardon?'

'The first bedroom off the stairs.'

'Oh yes. Well I am having none of it. Going to fix myself up in a nice comfy chair with a pot of tea and some biccies, right there on the stairs outside my room and wait for little Molly to come downstairs to play with her gran. That's what I'm going to do. I've got all the time in the world. Mrs H and I can go through the linen cupboard any other day now, can't we?' She nodded once.

About an hour later, looking downcast, Mrs H came over to tell me, in her worried voice, that Maude was sitting halfway up the Turkish staircase.

By then I had cleaned up the broken bulb glass, picking individual slivers of it from in among the gravel. I had to resort to a pair of tweezers from my bathroom which I utilise for my nostril hairs. That very day I had pulled a longer hair out my nose with the same tweezers, and I tell you – there was a touch of ginger to the blighter! Genetics. Finally, I changed the bulb on that park lamp – tested that it worked – then to spite him, I hid the shorter set of ladders along the side of the mill-wheel house by my kitchenette door, just to annoy Dan Mullan.

Later, I was sitting at the long kitchen table, adding to the left-hand expenses column: the price of that length of Flymo wiring I had bought the day before in the town branch of Strabney's Country Garden Centre. This figure was placed in the 'expenses' school notebook, which I keep in that drawer under the gate buzzer switch and intercom speaker. Without noticing, I had started the accounts book in a jotter the rear pages of which I had used to monitor Corbisher the cat when he had that bad bout of diarrhoea. The vet had given us special cat biscuits and advised me to shut Corbisher-the-Swiper in and keep a cat tray so we could maintain an accurate record of his stools and their specific appearance. This I did religiously, and it was with great pleasure I saw Corbisher's stools return to a healthy appearance. I looked at my comments and descriptions:

Tuesday 17th afternoon. A linked series of poems. What a contribution. Evening 17th a chocolate-themed sculpture octet. 18th late afternoon. A shit to aspire to. A grand performance. During night of the 18th a bulletin of prime importance is delivered. Afternoon of 19th a royal message from this fine cat. The 20th: dawn, the dainty prancer produces a major evacuation of his main movement. As firm as rosary beads. 21st morning. What an outstanding addition. 22nd, lunchtime. What a display: the force that through the tight arse drives the pong, that blasts the roots . . .

And so forth.

That enormous kitchen table at which I sat had been brought up to Kitchenly by the Fear Taker road crew in a tour truck in 1974, from a former monastery in Devon. The talk round that table had got more interesting than in its former days, I am sure. Or had it? It's a bit like that time I met Chappo and told him that 'The Weaver's Answer' . . . no . . . it isn't. It isn't really like that at all.

Mrs H returned to timidly update me that Maude had now nodded off upon her armchair on the stairway landing, and she had dropped her tea cup onto the carpet but no tea had been spilled as the cup had been empty at the time; as we all knew, she was a real 'tea jenny', and the cup hadn't broken but, Mrs H added, her snoring was echoing up the stairwell and might awaken Marko and Auralie.

'Good.' I said. 'That would solve everything if they all woke up.'

I was just making myself a nice cheese sarnie, dropping the sliced cheddar onto the thickly smeared butter, when the gate buzzer went. I trotted to the intercom, ready to hear Mullan with his van telling me how he had made it as far as the gates but now was being forced to turn back, beaten by some unstoppable dark resistance which was testing him harder than I could ever believe.

'Crofton? That you? James Burton of Burton and Anders.'

I was already standing but I jumped bolt upright and erect. One of Marko's personal accountants! Not the ones that handled the band finances, a personal accountant.

'Jim. Hello. Was Marko expecting you?'

'He should be. He asked me to come down.'

'Asked you to?' I added, 'To arrive today?'

'Oh. Yes. Told me he was back from being overseas; we needed to go through some figures together.'

'Definitely today? It's just, Marko's not expecting anyone today. He's sleeping off his journey, to be quite frank; asked not to be disturbed. Auralie too.'

'Oh. Really?'

'Perhaps you could rejig another appointment.'

'But, I've just driven down from Guildford; cancelled the lot at the office. Tomorrow morning too. Marko mentioned I might stay overnight. Thought that would be nice. And useful. Yes. Useful in going over these figures.'

'Stay the night? Marko's mother is here and even she can't get to see him right at this moment, Jim.'

'Marko's mother? Well. I'd love to make her acquaintance; I don't think I've had the pleasure.'

I interrupted and blurted out, 'Actually, I've heard she's sleeping as well.'

'Really? Have you an outbreak of tsetse fly in there?' James Burton laughed that chuntering and rich coil which was his.

I resigned myself and poked the switch. 'Open Gate', which was written in my own handwriting, on a rectangle of white adhesive sticker beneath. 'Come in then,' I said.

James Burton (yes, like the guitarist!) is a lightly breathless and short man who has tended towards real stoutness; he never touches alcohol and has a habit of putting his arm around you – which initially I thought unusual, if not suspect, behaviour from an accountant. There's nothing in it all; he doesn't drink or smoke as he only has one lung from a childhood illness. He flings his arm around the back of any unoccupied chair which happens to be next to him, or he fires his arm out and supports himself when he pauses in a doorway, looking at you and talking. It is as if he is, unconsciously, standing on a slightly undulating ship deck; perhaps his missing lung, as well as making him fussy about draughts in winter, somehow unbalances his weight distribution? I don't know if it doesn't make me feel slightly seasick as I look at James Burton gently supporting himself. James also had a habit of talking only about accounting matters – or rather, a habit of managing to reduce all earthly phenomena so that accounting is in some way relevant to it. He doesn't half go on; for my tastes, he isn't quite breathless enough. Marko liked him though because, as he once put it – Jim Burton is so damned straight he doesn't even know what a curve is.

James Burton probably had a much better handle on reality than me, and he drove regularly renewed Austin Allegros; his latest, in chrome and banana yellow, crunched out widely across the gravel of the turnaround in a generous arc, casting a side spray of noisy stones. I grimaced through the row of cute, small kitchen windows along the wall in front of the twin kitchen sinks. I clicked the kettle on again. James Burton positioned his car right in next to Mrs H's Triumph. He racked on the handbrake then I heard every one of his enthusiastic steps across that gravel towards the main kitchen door. I hoped this latest arrival might rouse the hibernators into some form of rise and shine.

'We have to keep it all moving, Crofton, and that is the way of it. As accountants that's all we can ever do. Keep it all moving.'

James told me this across the huge kitchen table. He was having a cup of tea I'd made him, his hairy left hand slid clear of his jacket's tweed cuff and the mustard jersey sleeve, resting along the curved wooden back of the pine chair next to him. He grinned at me as if we had settled some deal.

'Uh-huh,' I said.

'You see, Crofton,' James told me, with that serious, digging, enquiring tone people use to other people who have no interest at all in seeing anything. 'You see, it's evasion versus avoidance. Might not be much difference in those words on a Saturday football pitch. I'll assure you of that.'

I nodded.

'Senseless Ambition Holdings. There are so many expenses on a pop music tour, it gives ground for real creativity in arriving at a net figure. Can I put it like that? Or a tour of Europe, or of Japan. Now look. Crofton. Crofton?'

'Yes?' I said softly. Perhaps even with fear.

'Crofton, I am only an accountant. Not a tax advisor, but I can point out to you the likelihoods of any given series of acts. If you had earnings of that type, you would be taxed on those net amounts that you remitted back into the British Isles. You understand?'

I pulled myself together. 'Progressive, Jim. They're a progressive rock band, not pop.'

'Yes, well. I'm not one for the lively arts.' He chuckled that way again. 'Pop or . . . Progressive.' He coughed. 'That's no matter of distinction for Her Majesty's Inland Revenue. Let me tell you. Mantovani man myself. Pure and simple. Mantovani and Mozart. You can't beat that for some relaxing strings of an evening with my wife in the kitchen. Anyway.'

'Fancy a custard finger, Jim?'

'Oh. Well. Don't mind if I do.' After taking a bite he frowned, licked his finger, 'So you pay all foreign earnings into a company account in one or more of those three sterling areas which keeps the Exchange Control Act happy, then, carefully, you remit the money back into England to the company directors, when for instance, domestic income is lower. So we declare. Or when it was nil. Such as it was, say, when a certain individual was non-resident. Like when Marko spent that year out of Britain and left you and Mrs H here running things.'

That was a very good year. The year of the open curtains.

'You understand? And of course you ensure you have lots of expenses. Tax write-offs. A home recording studio. A set of offices in central London, have a documentary film produced, where you can imply huge expenses, issue invoices and keep a second set of books. Finance part of a motion picture. The outbreak of fellows in Marko's line of work having home recording studios is nothing to do with their love of music, Crofton. It's a fabulous way of writing off hundreds of thousands in expenses that might well not have been spent. If you get my meaning. We can then insinuate that remitted money was if fact spent on item a, b or indeed c. Get me?'

He talked on for quite a considerable duration of time; well into the second cup of tea, I heard Mullan arriving in his van. Instead of listening on to James, I focused mercifully on the sounds of the approaching vehicle. Mullan had let himself in through the main gate – always a sign he wasn't going to make an excuse and flee for the day. I heard the van, going too fast, taking its usual tradesman's left at the driveway junction, off the tarmac and onto the track, the uniform drumming on the thick boards as the vehicle crossed the little Victorian coach bridge across the top mill race stream, up the short incline then by the disused double tennis courts with their cracked asphalt, the green weeds pushing out. Obviously, I couldn't hear the van by then, but he'd have parked it up in the stables quad.

Fifteen or so minutes later, behind me, I heard the distant, hysterical whine of the electric lawn mower bleeding into the tranquil day, up on the terraced banks above the willows, where the dried-out stalks of April's daffodils lay flat, looking like caramelised drinking straws; the Flymo's whirr catapulted against the manor's north façade. I couldn't take any more of Jim's accountancy – it was like an afternoon with the Moonies.

'Just nipping out. Check on the gardeners, Jim.' I stood up and backed off, still facing him as I went, reaching behind but familiarly, to unhook the upper and lower sections of the Dutch door onto the riverbank side – all to escape the full extent of Jim's continuing and infinite lecture. He kept talking as I went, speeding up his delivery slightly as I reached the door.

Outside: birdsong as well as the lawn mower. Sweet liberty. I didn't hang around. I cast my eyes up the terracing and there was Mullan's nephew, Johnny: jeans and checked shirt, one arm casually stretched out, knees bent in support as he leaned backwards, one garden-gloved hand on the handlebars, the lawn mower swinging below him on the slope of banking. The lad used gravity to sweep the machine widely from one side to the other like a pendulum.

At the decorative brick stepping stones I crossed the water rill then walked over the lower footbridge. I could see the nephew had his insolent look upon me, his molars working away at the usual gum. I raised a hand in acknowledgement without really facing him, while I strolled on round to the rear door of the secondary mill house, below the stable pathway. I passed under the wrought-iron lamp and walked in the glossy black doors, through the house and across the first air bridge. I was blatantly avoiding Jim in the kitchen below by circling and moving over like a bird. I traversed the television floor in the big mill house then entered the larger air bridge. I was listening out for Mrs H as I came onwards into the manor house, under the 1602 lintel. Blow me if those suitcases weren't still there. Suspiciously, all the shopping bags had been removed. Glancing cautiously upwards at the base of the stairs I turned my head to establish if Maude could be seen. I moved quietly through the corridor of ancient wooden panelling and turned into the Elvetson morning room, then stopped dead.

'Oh. Crowftun. *There* you are.'

It was the tall figure of Auralie, taller than I, standing in the morning room wearing pyjamas with a loose blanket thrown across her shoulders. She had thick wool socks on, the patterns of which did not match.

'Auralie. Hi. How was "La, la, la, la America"?'

She frowned and looked towards me with the solipsism of an animal. 'Oh Crowftun. Didn't you have problems sleeping? And now me too, and Marko. Poor Marko.'

'His mum's here.'

She leaned towards me, both hands rising to hold the blanket on her shoulders and she lowered her voice. 'I know. She is asleeping in a chair on the stairways. I sneak past on toe tips. Is she drunken? What is she *doing* there?'

'Well she came down from London this morning. Is Marko awake then?'

She tutted, 'No-no, of course not.'

'But I thought he was having problems sleeping?'

'He is asleep. That's why I am down here; not to wake him. I must take a draught of something. I can't sleep. It's terrible.

83

It started in Manhattan.' She looked around herself and frowned, not as if the room with its oak wainscoting and ornate cornices was unfamiliar, but as if she was looking for something to pick fault with; she strode to the table, by the coffee percolator and the biscuits, and there she tested the kettle for water; I could tell the way the kettle only half rose in response to her long and thin fingers upon its black handle, that it was filled. She switched it on. 'I mean what is she *doing* here?'

'You mean on the stairs?'

'Yes. Here. And there? I mean we are just back. Returning.'

'She said she was waiting for Molly to wake up. How is Molly?'

'She is fast asleep.'

She had spoken curtly and as if I had no right to enquire after her little girl, though many was the time Auralie would hype up a false, affectionate relationship between Molly and me, then fob her daughter off on me for hours while Auralie attended to some triviality – speaking to fashion-modelling friends on long-distance telephone calls without being interrupted. Often conducted in Danish.

I said, 'You must all be very tired. It's just . . . what will I tell Maude?'

'Don't waken her, for God's sake. Tell her nothing.'

'What will I tell Maude when she does wake up?'

Auralie grunted and shrugged so the plain wool blanket across them slid a bit up then down on her slim shoulders. 'Tell her Marko is dreaming of her.' She sniggered and sniffed, lifting a finger quickly to touch her very small ear.

I dared to say, 'Maybe Molly will want to see her gran?'

But she just ignored me, swiftly lifting and looking at the dark tins of Twinings teas, one after the other, frowning monstrously at their names then dismissing them. She spoke between gritted teeth, 'Molly has two grandmothers.'

Meaning her own mother, over in wherever land, who we never saw – or only on a singular occasion at Kitchenly. Auralie and her mother did not get along. You could tell the mother was jealous of her daughter and all the spoils of her world-wide foraging. Kitchenly, a reminder of her daughter's success at advancement was not where Auralie's mother wished to spend any time. She had visited the London house much more frequently.

A familiar silence then began between us. The sound was disappointingly subtle but I could still just hear the steady tone of the lawn mower, round on the other face of the building. Auralie seemed not to have noticed it.

I quietly spoke. 'I see the bedroom windows are covered over in plastic.'

'It is because of the jet lag. You arrive in a country, Crowfton, and you don't know what time it's going to be, and to sleep correctly we must have night – wherever I go the sun is always damned-bloody shining when I arrive, just outside a set of curtains, like someone wanting in. No matter where I go to. It was the same on tour with the band or even when I was model-ling. You would arrive, halfway round the world, go to your hotel and tell me what? Tell me no matter what time where it is, a strong, strong sun is just outside your curtains. It is never night.'

'It was night when you arrived here.'

'When we got here, yes, but it was light in London when we truly arrived, and I tried to sleep in Chelsea but it was day. I don't have time to wait for night. I am sick of it. But no, you painted the bedroom good. Or you put plastic not paint. Not a little bit of light is getting in.'

'It wasn't me who did that. It was the gardener.'

'Who?'

'The gardener.'

'Oh yes. That man. Corbisher.'

'No, Auralie. Corbisher is the cat. Dan Mullan is the gardener.'

'Oh yeah. Dan Mullan. I guess you're right.' She paused. 'This man was in our bedroom?' There was a split second of contemplation, but oblivious as ever, she suddenly snapped, 'He took down my hanging crystal by the window that was spreading good crystal energies. Instead he should be getting all that bloody damned fucking cow shit off our road.'

'I did tell him that. Well it's a public road, but yes. I will ask him again to clear the mess. It's horse shit actually, not cow shit.'

She sniggered. 'Cow, horse. Shit is shit, Crowfton. Why are you always so right? Right all the time. Cat. Gardener. Shit. You are like my high-school teacher, Mr Poulsen. Always have to be right. Mr Right Man?'

'I'm not. Mr Right Man. It's just. It's horse shit. Cows are fenced in the fields and don't get herded past this way.'

'Whoopee, Crowfton. You know all about shit. Look. I know the difference between a horse and a cow. Even English ones. And you are wrong.' She suddenly whispered to me, 'Halfway up the stairs here is for sure a cow.' She turned and laughed – her face opening up through her tiredness and looking younger; beneath the raised chevrons of streamlined, golden eyebrows, the pupils sparkled. She was so annoyingly beautiful. I smiled. 'Have you seen Mrs H?'

'I saw her. Before we went to America.' She opened the lid and peered into a tea caddy. 'She must be over in your building.'

My building. That's what she called the second mill house along, through the air bridges, where I lived. As if I owned it. Poor Auralie. As far as she was concerned it might as well be Trumpton Town I dwelt in. It all belonged to her as much as to Marko, but she hardly ever went into the second mill house. Kitchenly Mill Race was like a linked spaceship to her, moving relentlessly through some unknown void, oblivious to passing planets of no consequence. The air bridges were the umbilical corridors connecting the three linked sister ships and their humming life-support system.

It crossed my mind Mrs H might have somehow slipped through by now to encounter James Burton in the kitchen, and that she might say something compromising to him. I was about to move away to the morning-room door when Auralie, smiling, turned to look at me; she changed the tone of her odd voice, 'Crowftun?'

'Yes?'

'Our suitcases.'

'Oh yeah. I'll take them up then. Leave them outside your door.'

'Noo, noo, noo, you might wake her or Marko. It's mainly all dirty washing, my little undies and so forth, so just take to Mrs H. Or leave them by washing machines.'

I nodded. 'Look, there's a situation.'

'A what? A situation?'

'One of Marko's accountants, James Burton, is here.'

'Who? Accountant?'

'Yeah; that James Burton guy. Jim?'

'The boring fat one who talks always? He is here now as well? Ah min Gud.'

'Yeah, he says Marko asked him down today to go over some figures?'

She frowned. 'That seems weird. Marko only decided to come back yesterday at the very last moment.'

'Yeah, I thought it was unusual, but James is not the type to make stuff up. I sort of wondered if Marko had invited him down after he'd had a couple of beers and perhaps overlooked it?' I gave a quizzical look.

'Oh, fuck knows.' She shrugged and showed no further interest. 'Here. See. Val-a-reean. That helps, look.' She lifted a foul-looking little tea bag of herbs – a rangy string was attached

87

with some handwriting on a small label. It had come from a head shop somewhere.

'Valerian. That's been there a long time. Did you try a pill?'

'We took all pills and there are none left, but you feel horrid in the waken times. We need to see the doctor. That band doctor, not a shitty real doctor in your villages.'

'All right; if Marko wakes will you tell him his mum and Jim are here?'

'He is not to be woken. He is exhausted. Okay? Nobody on the top floor.'

'Okay,' I shrugged, walked away from her, back past the ancient panelled walls, beyond the base of the staircase and its monumental balusters. By the 1602 door I grunted and stooped to pick up the suitcases, one in each hand, then walked onwards through the air bridge as if I were in Heathrow Terminal 3. At least the cases didn't weigh much. I swung up one case then the other into the dumb waiter in the alcove at the end of the corridor. I pulled across the sliding door and pushed the button to send them below.

Bracing myself for more of Jim, I walked through the television room and went down the half-twist of spiral stairs which places you in behind the kitchen where the pantries – or larders – or whatever they are called, are positioned. Mrs H was in the kitchen with her pink pinny on, but there was no trace of Jim Burton.

'Hey, I just had the pleasure of meeting Auralie. Where's Jim?'

'He's gone to stretch his legs in the garden.' She coughed. 'Is Maude still up in that armchair? She'll finish with a crick in her neck.'

I ducked my head slightly to look out of the kitchen windows behind the sinks, to scan around. 'Gone for a walk, has he?' I said, suspiciously.

Mrs H nodded. She seemed a little dazed and I could only assume she had received a broadside of Jim's accounting wisdom.

She must have recognised my sympathetic expression. 'I've been told to keep on stamping my books,' she said. She continued looking at me, somewhat put down.

'I bet you have. He goes on a bit. Think of his poor wife. Marko's still asleep but Her Ladyshit is up and about. It's like she's keeping him and Molly prisoner up there. She brought us both back a lovely present, from New York,' I said.

Mrs H turned round, briefly hopeful.

I slid up the dumb-waiter door. 'Ten days of their dirty washing.'

'Gracious.' She sighed. 'Plonk them down by the Bendix then, and I'll see to them.'

I left the garments within the suitcases in the large utility room by the two washing machines, then I nipped on across to the next mill house. I was heading through my kitchenette, towards my room to see if I could have a little lie-down. The front gate buzzer sounded. I stood still and looked at the receiver box on the wall as if I had never seen it before. I crossed over and depressed the button, putting on my tough, stranger-repelling voice: 'Yeah?'

'Marko?'

'Who is this?'

'Oh, Crofton? It's Martin Dimelon up here at the gate.'

I widened my eyes and my voice fell into its normal timbre. 'Martin. Ah. You don't have an arrangement to see Marko, do you?'

'I do, I do.'

'Gosh. It's just, you see, Marko had a hard journey back from America and he is actually asleep right now.'

'That's no bother. I can understand if he's having a nap.'

'He's sedated. I don't see him having a head for figures.'

'Sedated? I'll just wait. I have all day. I closed the office and came down here as he asked.'

89

'Right, right. Okay. It's just . . . I think he's changed his mind.'

'Changed his mind?'

'Yes. Auralie made it quite clear he is not to be disturbed and nobody is permitted onto the top floor of the house, so I'm afraid he's had a bit of a change of heart, Martin. I am really, really sorry.'

'But he needs to sign off on this land deal. I had looked it over. I mean we know it was all done and dusted, but there's been such a delay to it. Brockleberry Rents. And how it will fit in to the year's income. He wanted to put it to bed.' He paused, 'And now he's gone to bed.'

I felt he was looking around himself ever so cautiously, up by the gates, with fields behind and around him. Cows with their heads down in the grass, ripping up the grass with a sideways tear of their mouth. Rippling, leathery leaves dimpled the light above him. He wasn't in the city any more. He half whispered, half rasped, 'Well, I can't discuss it out here.'

'Brockleberry Rents by the village?'

'Yes. The building land. All squared off now and the money in, so Marko wanted to go over it.'

I was dumbfounded. I said, 'Martin. Just hang on there and I will come up to let you in.'

'Oh. Right-oh.'

I walked with an odd, stiff-legged, swinging motion back to the kitchen. Mrs H was over the sinks, wiping around them with a cloth. 'You won't believe this. It's Martin. Martin! Marko's *other* fucking accountant.'

'Crofton. Language, please.'

I dropped my voice, peering out the windows, looking anxiously towards the Dutch door. 'Sorry. One accountant doesn't know that the other exists; to make sure both come to exactly the same conclusions on what tax Marko pays. They always do but. I mean. It's like having two wives. If one accountant finds out about the other, it doesn't look good. Jesus. They might start conferring. He must have been in a bloody state to manage to invite both of them down here on the same bleedin' day. What is it Marko says?: "I live in a stately home so I get in a state in it."'

'Can't the gentleman just come back some other day?'

'These accountants don't take no for an answer, Mrs Hilary. They are like the police. We can't stand up to them. But we can't let them meet for a single second either, or the game's up. If you're talking to them, don't let one know what the other does. Are you listening, Mrs H? Make something up. Say one's from the Land Commission or something. Or an astrologer, come to give Auralie a reading. The Musicians' Union, anything.' Mrs H gave me a curious look. 'Put Jim over in one of the rooms on the stairs, Bonar Law perhaps, but not the top floor. Her Ladyshit doesn't want us up there. We'll put Martin over on my side in – say – in the electrician's room. Closer to me. Keep them apart! I'm off.'

I dashed straight up the driveway, swaying in double time with that slight limp I unconsciously cultivate whenever I am very nervous, perhaps to try and generate sympathy for this potential victim. But sympathy from whom? I knew I wanted to see Martin in person before opening the gates. It was as if I wished his existence, his genuine presence confirmed.

My lurching passage was scattering birds which were hopping on the lawns. My head was swivelling around though, trying to spot Jim Burton's heavy figure and where he might be located, rolling steadily through our gardens, reaching out to lean against walls and tree trunks, or grabbing on to the drooped net up on the dry dust of the uneven tennis courts, holding on to it as he moodily swayed. I tried to walk normally.

Martin Dimelon was quite unlike Jim. Younger, with a handsome and proportioned forehead which he held low and slightly protruding, studious, yet as if the determined brow were always prepared to butt aside commuters on a crammed underground train. His personality was more restrained, curt, always seeming as if he was dealing with something slightly more important than you, just somewhere out of your sight. I suppose he always was? I liked him though: a family man with a couple of young kids up in London: little boy and a girl. He kept photos of them not only in his wallet, but behind the sun visor above the steering wheel of his brown Volkswagen Scirocco. He had that car right there, pointed at the main gates, when I walked up to him.

'Hi Crofton, been a while,' Martin called out between the wooden roundels of the ornate gate. He had a gritted-teeth expression, as if he were caged behind those bars and I was bringing him prison food on a battered metallic tray.

To open the gates I crossed to the foot stud and depressed it – once again imagining Marko clicking off his Echoplex pedal onstage – then I rode down the driveway in the passenger seat of Martin's car. I asked him a little hurriedly how his kids were and I had a crisp report by way of reply. Simultaneously of course I was casting my eyes through the windscreen, which, seen from outside, would be reflecting back oily gyrations of the strobing racks of tree branches above. I looked to my left, this way and that way, between the trunks, and in among the pointillist ground shade from the leaves, in anticipation of seeing Jim – the second accountant – wandering somewhere, perhaps leaning against something as if holding it up, his shirt recklessly untucked. Martin might have been studying my behaviour; he was looking at me oddly.

I had to keep glancing at Martin as he talked. I noted the crisp collar of his shirt, wondered if he had them laundered or if his wife herself carried his damp white shirts out into an area of their back garden where a clothesline was tethered. Did she occasionally place a clothes peg in her mouth while squinting upwards at the London sky? And where was that washing line in relation to his house? We had similar considerations to address with regards to the placement of the clothesline at Kitchenly. I felt like asking him about the laundering of his neat shirts, but following the doubtless more judicious route, I said nothing.

I directed Martin not to the gravelled turning place before the manor but to the left, off the main driveway, over the Victorian coach bridge and instead of up the incline towards the tennis courts and finally the stables – the route Mullan had recently followed in his work van – I gestured Martin to halt his car in front of the Regency building of the secondary mill house. He tutted and blew some air out his lips, announced, 'I can never get over what a huge, huge place he has here.' Quite right I suppose that he used 'he' and not 'you'. Despite my pivotal role in the running of Kitchenly Mill Race, it had to be accepted that someone like Dimelon knew the financial power behind our settlement here was Marko's – despite Marko's dependency on me.

We were talking, but my mind was not fully on the subject as I wanted to ask another question. I was carrying a large plastic carrier bag containing some files into the mill house, while Martin bore a leather travel bag which doubtless held his presumptuous overnight accoutrements. As we went beneath the wrought-iron bars which supported the oil lamp, and through the gloss-black door, I said, with a false air of familiarity about the subject, 'So that's Brockleberry Rents all done and dusted?'

He glanced at me, hesitated momentarily and said, 'The paperwork finally is, yes. And about ruddy time. I mean the houses are long built down there, are they not? I drove in from the other direction.'

I turned to look Dimelon fully in the face. 'Oh yes. Yes they are. Childrens' swings are up in the gardens.'

'The paperwork should have been completed long before, but no harm. That's what happens the minute you get county council planning and developers involved.'

I nodded. 'I must say I was a bit surprised Marko agreed to that. Selling off a strip of land from the estate. You know? Why would he bother?'

'Well, housing is short for young families down here. In the sticks. The council and the developer approached us – I mean the estate – asking if it would be considered, since it was the outskirts of the village. In retrospect I wish Marko hadn't gone ahead, but the developers had to pay a very high price and the council cleared it for residential,`so everyone ends up happy. It makes Marko look less . . . You know? Less stand-offish. Not that he is; but that's the impression people get, isn't it? And have. From the outside.'

'Yes. Yes,' I said. 'From the outside.' I repeated that yes with such relish that it surprised me.

I led Martin up the corridor to the Regency staircase and we turned hard right on their elegant curve to ascend the carpeted stairs to the top floor where I took him directly into the electrician's bedroom – so called.

He seemed more than satisfied with this habitation, of course. The use of central heating throughout the linked houses in winter – with scant regard for the final oil bill, combined with that year's splendid summer – meant not a trace of damp lingered in any of these rarely used bedrooms. The electrician's room had small French windows opening out onto a tiny white, wrought-iron balcony suspended above the slow millstream beneath. Of course, this room had not the full-sized balcony and double doors of the neighbouring room: the 'balcony room'; but Martin was just an accountant, not a visiting world-famous rock star. I had a gentle hierarchy always established in my mind. Now conceive if Dave Mason of The Traffic, or say Peter Frampton (mocked, but no slouch on a guitar) turned up by wild chance at Kitchenly as house guests, and Marko ordered me to put them into 'the balcony room', above the dense mats of wild watercress upon the gentle millstream race below. Imagine I had to report to my superior that the biggest guest room in my wing was presently occupied by his accountant. *One* of his accountants. Unthinkable!

Closing the door, I left Martin Dimelon alone in the electrician's room, going over his papers and documents, telling him I would return when there was news about Marko's possible awakening — or otherwise.

I hurried directly back up to the stables.

Several years before, a county council squad had dug up then tarred over a section of the single-track road by the boundary wall, to repair a collapsed culvert; they then left a roadside barrier to shield the small, freshly tarred area. But it remained in place week after week, although the cement and road tar had fully dried and set. I became so fed up squeezing past it in the car — it was also obstructing occasional limos, often belonging to world-famous figures — that one winter evening I simply loaded the barrier thing into the back of the Volvo hatchback and I took it all away. I threw in the flashing warning light on its metal tripod stand as well. I knew somewhere there, among the empty horse stalls, we still kept that length of yellow and red plastic road barrier which had been pinched straight from the verge, along with the slow-flashing, orange/yellow warning light.

I located this stolen barrier in the northmost corner horse stall, dusty and slightly cobwebbed but otherwise as I recalled it. The flashing light was still there too. The plastic barriers were not at all heavy — they were much lighter than the stepladders — so I carried them down from the stables and in through the Regency door, making as little noise as I could.

I then began the task of blocking up the smaller air bridge over the millstream at its carpeted opening place into the secondary mill house. Using the plastic road barrier and its base pods, which were hollow with screw caps, enabling them to be filled up with water to weigh down and secure them — presumably against wind and vehicle slipstreams, I blockaded the way through the air bridge. I worked swiftly and as quietly as possible. I had to add a few empty cardboard boxes and some chicken wire rectangles. After filling the base tanks with water, which took many trips to the closest bathroom with a watering can, I incorporated a detached door which I had also spotted up in the stables. Incongruous in the main thoroughfare of a millionaire's dwelling, the road barrier and its wall resembled some hastily assembled street barricade in a time of Parisian student riots. It would be impossible to pass through this barricade without causing quite a commotion.

Much like I did as a child on paper, meticulously drawing out plans of complex roadworks and round-verged airport runways with networks of connecting taxiways, up in my bedroom I used a sheet of blank foolscap to sketch and fill in with red pen a clear sign in large lettering:

FLOOR UNSAFE
NO ENTRY AT ANY TIME

I sellotaped this paper signage onto the barrier then stood back to admire my fine handiwork. Why, even a dog could not get through a blockade such as this, though I admit that Corbisher and Mister Mingles, could probably have wiled their feline way through the structure in that slithery manner. For added effect, I used a matchstick to press in the little recessed operating button on the flashing roadside lamp, which still worked. I hung it onto the barrier so the slow semaphore would be more dramatically delineated with the closing of curtains and fall of dark night.

As instructed, Mrs H had placed Jim Burton over in the Bonar Law bedroom and by late afternoon Jim had retreated there on a permanent basis. Maude too had made Jim's acquaintance, and for a while she had tolerated him – or so I later learned from Mrs H. Maude and fat Jim had sat together for a time in the Elvetson morning room taking tea. Of course as the afternoon wore on, Marko's mum made her understandable retreat to the sanctuary of Benjamin Disraeli – her allocated room – to escape Jim's favoured method of communication: the accountancy monologue, where the monologue was always being delivered by him alone.

It was my own bedroom in the secondary mill house which I made my refuge as usual, standing before my hi-fi, changing record albums: The Heep, Wishbone Ash, Mogul Thrash, The Tull, then slowly circling the small room, lifting books or old *Melody Maker*s down off the bookcase and flipping through them while I listened to the music. At relatively/extremely high volume, I played the first and the third album and side 2 of *Pascal's Moon*. I then put on the Steve Miller Band's *Sailor*, but I eventually took it off the turntable and once again put on the classic second Fear Taker album. Surely Marko's guitar solo on 'Hysteric Atmospherics', remains among the most beautiful in rock? When it had finished, I noted the sounds outside. The lawn mower had long fallen silent. Afternoon had stretched into early evening, but still – though we all awaited his descent and passage among us – it seemed Marko had not emerged from his blacked-out bedroom suite at the top of the stairwell. Nor Auralie, or Molly.

The melancholy of another day having uselessly passed was sounded by the numerous birds, each like individual listening posts, positioned at varying depths within the ornamental gardens which surrounded me.

Once again it was that time: to commence the drawing of the curtains throughout Kitchenly Mill Race. Obviously, I could not use the smaller – now blocked – air bridge, and I wandered quietly over to the manor building by way of the gardens. The low sun was slicing its way through the cedars of Lebanon in

97

vertical copper sheets, as if the trees were torn black curtains with high-powered stage lights placed directly behind them.

Mrs H had already gone home, and beside James Burton's parked yellow car at the front door, the chevron shape of her car tyres remained imprinted in the gravel where she had reversed, paused, and then come forwards, but curving over to the left.

Within the manor house, dear Mrs H had pulled the curtains and all was silence. All was spick and span, as she herself would term it. I wondered if she had dared to close the curtains on the top floor? There was no sound.

I tiptoed up the Turkish staircase lit by the citrusy stained-glass slits which illuminate each landing in a pleasing and different colour and which Mrs H had left uncovered. I passed Maude's now-vacated armchair on the first landing. Out of my pocket I took the key to Bonar Law which I had removed from the huge board of keys on the wall by the utility room. As quietly as I could, I inserted the key into the lock from the outside. I had not been quiet enough though: from within the large bedroom I heard Jim's hollow voice gently say, 'Hello? Is there somebody there?' Fearing he could spontaneously begin a swift monologue about accounting – despite the thick wooden door between us – I turned the key, left it in the lock and stepped away, carefully descending the stairs. I heard the handle of the bedroom door turning behind me. It rattled once again with a higher degree of irritability. But then there was silence. Put an accountancy spin on that, I thought. He really was so boring he deserved to be locked in for the good of everybody.

Jim would be deliberating the outcome of his actions. If he made too much of a fuss and began screaming and knocking for release from the bedroom – complete with its own luxury bath-room, which was just as well considering the pots of tea he had devoured – it might reflect badly upon him. Jim's shouting and drawing attention to himself might very well wake up Marko and cast Jim down, into a state of persona non grata. On the other hand, if he quietly endured his unexplained sequestration, he might, by obscure means, emerge as something of a heroic figure who Marko had to apologise to.

Leaving Jim with this dilemma, I made sure the main entrance door was locked on the Yale. I lowered the electric blinds on the car park side of the main air bridge and I switched on all the floodlights and river illuminations in the gardens. I exited the house through the kitchen, after ensuring all curtains were pulled and that the doors were locked and cat flap un-snibbed, since Mrs H had put out their food and saucers of milk. I locked the kitchen door from the outside, posting the key in through the old letter box which remained there. Obviously I couldn't come all the way back around the interior and cross the blockade in the smaller air bridge, in a blatant contradiction of the rules.

I had collected the key to the electrician's bedroom and once over the footbridge, and by way of my kitchenette, I was planning to approach Martin Dimelon's bedroom on the first floor of the secondary mill house with the same intention of locking him in, for an as-yet unspecified period. Then I would draw the curtains in the other, empty bedrooms.

Once I had reached the interior, pulling all curtains as I went, it was with some horror, as I approached the bottom of the Regency staircase, that I saw, through the shape of the archway and beside the entrance to the smaller air bridge, the unmistakable jet-black silhouette of Martin Dimelon's trim figure. He was halted, his suit jacket was off, but with his inquisitive forehead clearly thrust ahead, contemplating the barricade which I had constructed to block his possible escape from this area of the house. In a slow rhythm the flashing orange (or was it more yellow?) traffic beacon bloomed up then sunk back into darkness, rendering Martin Dimelon almost invisible, then visible in stark profile.

In a cheery voice I greeted him, 'Hi Martin.'

He visibly jumped.

'I have just been over to the main house and Marko is still asleep. The whole family are. So we are locking up for the night.' I reported this with some delight.

'What's this?' he nodded down the smaller air bridge at the barricade facing him there, with the oddest frown on his forehead.

'Oh. We had a spot of bother. With the air bridge floor there. The floor isn't safe. You could fall straight through it into the mill race underneath.'

'Why is the barrier just on this side then? Facing this way? If the floor's a danger behind it? Why isn't there another barrier on the other side?'

I looked down to the far end of the air bridge. It was a fair question. 'Everyone down that way' — I pointed along the air bridge, towards the darkness of the far end, to the unilluminated colour television room in the main mill house building — 'Everyone down that end is well aware of the danger here and has been briefed. We tend to put up any visitors to us here in Kitchenly, in this building. So those likely not to be aware of the danger are always going to be on this side of the barrier, you see. Your side.'

'But, if the house insurance is all up to date, I don't see the need for delay. Is the floor really that unstable it might fall down at any moment? You really need to get that seen to if Marko's daughter is here. That's really dangerous for her.'

'Dangerous for everyone, Martin. We will have tradesmen out very soon to see to it. Better safe than sorry. Now you aren't in your room, I see; is there something I can help you with?'

I stepped up to the switch for the shutters and pushed the down button; they began their work on both sides, darkening our surroundings even more as the last light of the day was cut off.

'Well, to be honest, I was wondering if I could grab a bite to eat?'

'Aww. Did Mrs H not come to see to you? I'm sorry, Jim. I mean Martin. We're not a hotel though. This is a working household. Truth be told, not a lot of square meals get dished up round here these days. Marko is very keen on Rice Krispies or sometimes three fish fingers between two slices of Nimble. I am a bit of a veggie myself. I seem to get by with cheese sarnies on Nimble with a good smear of Branston Pickle. Bring out the Branston, I say. I could make you one up if you wish? You go back to your room now, and I'll bring you it there, and a good mug of hot char. Okay? But first we have to pull all the curtains. You go thataway, back upstairs, and if you'd be so good as to pull the curtains in the empty rooms around you that would be very helpful to me. In fact, pull every curtain you see. I'll go thisaway. I'll make you a sandwich and bring it back from the kitchens. I am afraid the kitchens are out of bounds to you now. All the staff have gone home.'

'You're here, aren't you?'

I narrowed my eyes. 'Yeah. You go that way and pull the curtains. I'll go this way and I'll be back with something for you to eat shortly. See you in your room. Best you stay in it. The ghost of Sir Lawson Starley comes out after dark.'

I walked angrily towards my kitchenette, closing curtains here and there, and locking all the outside doors from that end. I wasn't making bloody sandwiches for surprise visitors whom I hadn't been correctly informed about. I had an important job to do round there; I had an estate under my control to think about. He could wait till his damned breakfast, or jump in his fancy car and drive to the Mumbleton Arms out towards Maxtelham. They might still serve him dinner in their roomy dining salon. You've got to take the rough with the smooth in this life. I made my way up to my rooms and immediately went to bed to try and sleep. Staff, indeed.

101

3

I slept with much more purpose than with which I embrace my waking hours . . . a lie-in – a dream – Crofton & Marko – guitar players – a family departure – a housekeeper.

I slept with much more purpose than with which I embrace my waking hours.

In my dreams I was at that place of constant fascination for me as a child, after a formative school visit: the Science Museum in Kensington, London. Yet in my nocturnal mind at dark night, it seemed mixed up with a geological museum – if such a place exists. In this dream, the museum floor I stood on vibrated beneath my thick-soled shoes; the floor was made of a fibreglass-like material of variable opacity which could be seen through only vaguely. The whole floor was uneven, in fact in some areas it presented full-sized hillocks which you could clamber up and over, though I stood quite rooted to the spot. Underfoot it was lumpy and blistered in texture, and it was landscaped, like the accurate-scale model of some smaller territory. What I stood upon was obviously thick, semi-transparent plastic. The areas of light showing beneath clearly had as their primary sources the banks of orange-coloured electrical lights, fitted and arranged beneath this false floor with the intention of dramatic effect. The entire diorama beneath me seemed to simulate glowing magma under the earth, in places flowing in molten rivulets. My terror in this dream was of falling through this thin crust; I could feel the heat beneath. Like Hell, awaiting my just punishments.

When I awoke, my two bare feet were sticking out of the bottom of the bed, clear of the sheet, and benign sunlight was shining upon them both. I chuckled aloud. All those curtains which I had pulled – I had finally rebelled and not closed the curtains across from my single bed.

I lay there stretching my jaw open and flexing my arms and legs as I am wont to do upon waking. I even wiggled my warm toes.

105

The dream had been stimulated by a combination of the night-time garden lighting at Kitchenly Mill Race, Fear Taker's on-tour show, the coal-effect electric fire in the front room of my mam's house in Stafford where I grew up, but also by the steadily flashing light of the roadworks beacon which I had attached to the barricade the night before. I turned my head to look at the Mickey Mouse clock and I thrust forwards to find myself sitting upright.

It was ten minutes past two in the bloody afternoon! I was aghast I had slept so long. I had done my best to keep Marko's two accountants separated the day before, but surely in all the hours of morning which I had granted them, they would now have conspired to finally unite and foil my intent? And what of all the other vital issues which I had to apply myself to on this day? But what duties did I have to fulfil that day? None. And even if the accountants had discovered each other, was I not certain that all my crimes could be disguised?

I dressed slowly. As well as the change of socks and underwear, I needed a clean T-shirt. Years before, a harsh remark from Marko had stopped me from wearing my collection (it is complete) of Fear Taker tour T-shirts around Kitchenly Mill, but he never objected if I wore any other band T-shirts. I chose a relatively new one: the Alan Parsons Project in black with the album cover of *Pyramid* on it.

Patting that T-shirt flat onto the bump of my tummy in lieu of ironing it, I tiptoed through to the stairway landing and down to the exterior door facing the stables. Outside, the coolness in the building's shade could be felt up the sleeves of my T-shirt and in under my arms, but you could tell it was warmer over in the direct afternoon sun. I saw then that Martin Dimelon's car was no longer parked where I had told him to berth it the previous afternoon; I felt myself bristle at the idea he had moved his car over to the main-house parking zone without being accompanied by me. How dare he?

I walked quickly through the gardens after crossing the mill race on the footbridge. I was squinting in the sun, but when I had a clearer view across to the gravelled car park and the booth, neither Martin's car nor in fact Jim Burton's yellow Allegra were anywhere to be seen – just Mrs H's Triumph Dolomite, parked as usual at the bottom of the stairs.

And another astonishing change – when I glanced up at Marko and Auralie's master bedroom, two of the plastic sheets across the north-facing windows had been torn free. The action appeared to have been perpetrated from the interior of the room and in a somewhat hasty manner; the black plastic had been ripped away from the top and at the sides but then left to flop loosely out and downwards where it hung vertically from its remaining attachments, bumping gently against the brick in the lightest of updraughts; its tattered ends almost reached the window frames of the second floor. I found myself speeding up my walking pace.

I realised I was looking forward to having a good old natter with Marko about New York, the changes since I had last visited, and the recording studios of the East Coast: Electric Ladyland and the Record Plant on West 44th, versus Sigma Sound on 56th, or even Criteria down in Miami and the ocean-side pleasures of the old Doral Hotel where I was in residence once when the band were on tour; and if – as was intended – the prestige of having Fear Taker record their next album in one of these studios would allow Roger Schillings to negotiate a substantial discount for the hourly rate which these studios demand. Also, my mind turned to the Brockleberry Rents issue and if I could possibly use this opportunity to plumb Marko for further information on his deeper thinking there about selling the land to the development.

I suppose – I know – some people question our relationship. No. Our friendship. It's very simple. Marko and I go way back, we were once flatmates, for God's sake, and he feels sure he can trust me – he is a man surrounded by sycophants, as most men are in his position, and with me he can count on honesty and clarity.

Sycophants are a common sight in my line of business. Whatever that is. Like Fear Taker's singer – natural frontman Alvin – he always has two or three young blokes surrounding him. Literally, that's how I see Al in my mind's eye: one bloke on either side, another standing behind him, jabbering over his shoulder, into his ear. It took me a while to understand what the disciples' purpose was: it was to appreciate Alvin's jokes, to hang on every word of his stories and laugh in the correct places; it was to act as symbols of an unimaginably huge army behind these men, an army who similarly adored Alvin to the limitless extent that they did.

These sycophants always have their own little quirks and their own stories, but don't for one minute believe they are anything other than supporting characters to the starring role. If they stole a single scene from Al, if attention was lavished on any one of them for a moment too long they would be retired – they would mysteriously vanish overnight to be replaced by another replica; another whispering cocaine friendship in motion, until the friendship dissolved up some orifice as well.

I first met Marko in '68 just after I came down from up north and started to roadie. The position of 'roadie' didn't even really have a name back then. I was seventeen years old. Marko was like Steve Howe at that point, a great guitar player but without a steady group; he was jumping from band to band. Neither the classic Yes line-up nor Fear Taker's had fully come together. Marko was peeling off bristling Telecaster solos with an outfit called The Sorochinsky Assessor, and I'll tell you something remarkable. The Sorochinsky Assessor are *still* playing at the time of writing! In Spalding of all places, I saw a rubbishy poster for them pinned up at some pub venue. Couldn't believe they were still on the road: *The Sororchintsy* [sic] *Assessor, Here Wednesday Night*.

It would be my guess it was lead singer, Paul Hartford, who had kept the whole thing ticking over. He always was a persistent gasbag. Good band though, in their time.

Marko and me first bonded in some back lane behind a village hall, standing beside a Ford Anglia (the 123E model I believe) – he was guitarist for The Assessor, lighting up a cigarette. I was heaving amps. We bonded then and often re-bond over the unlikely subject of Christmas Day, 1966. Among other gifts on that day we had both asked for and received the exact same two presents. Isn't that remarkable? Even miraculous. Admittedly, he had received his presents from his beautiful, posh young girlfriend of that time who had just left some public school (or sometimes, I got the feeling she was still at it, due to her extended suspicious absences during school term times). Caroline Proudfoot, like in the Tolkien books. And she did have very nice feet.

What a Christmas 1966 was for a young guitar fan who was, like me, intent upon building up a comprehensive record collection. Mam got me an album and my sister got me a 45-rpm single. You got your Christmas Day presents in a pillowcase pinned to the mantelpiece back in them days, and you got an orange in the pillowcase too. Honest. I really mean it – in Stone Road, Stafford in '66, an orange was really exotic. As well as my Jaffa, the long-player was *Fresh Cream,* on Reaction Records, and the single was 'Hey Joe' on Track. How about that for Christmas presents and a lifetime of listening? I already had that Electra compilation, *What's Shakin'* with the Powerhouse; had both Blues Project albums and Butterfield's *East-West* with Bloomfield's unearthly playing on 'Work Song' and the title cut. Owned the Bluesbreakers' *Beano* album too, with that flooring solo on 'Have You Heard'. Had *Revolver* too. But nothing quite prepared you for *Fresh Cream* and that fourth cut on side one, 'Sweet Wine'. Three entwined guitars – one feeding back, one

109

comping, one which explodes into the top of his solo. That was the moment when I realised what electric guitars and overdubbing could really do; that and Hendrix. 'Hey Joe' was out just before Christmas '66, but it wasn't really 'Hey Joe' that mattered, it was the flip side: 'Stone Free' – with its solo. Another molten explosion. When 'Stone Free' meets 'Sweet Wine' (and a bit of Dave Davies's 'You Really Got Me' riff), then you got hard rock born right there at the end of 1966. I saw, by the look in his eye, Marko knew exactly what I was pontificating about when I said the whole future was contained in those records. He asked me if I played, and I admitted that I did not. I could also see the disappointment. I was always tone deaf and could only pick out a few chords on a guitar though I still try. I could never aspire to being his guitar tech like Nobby Charles did (1971–78).

When Marko and Schillings were putting together a road crew for The Fear Taker's first British tour in '69, they raised the topic of me tour managing. I turned it down on the spot. Even though that tour raised the Fear Taker to headliner status the road wasn't for me; I was sure there would be something better for me, something which kept me intimate with Marko. I believed in his talent so strongly then. Still do. I already had a little room in Marko's flat in Gloucester Terrace, right beside that bloody locomotive depot for Paddington station. It was down there below our back rooms (and my bedroom); changing over from steam engines to restless diesels in them days, but they were both just as noisy. Shunting nightly. There was no point building any recording studio there. Unless you were recording music for *Thomas the Tank Engine* with Johnny Morris.

After the first album went flying up the charts and the tours kicked off, I was a flat-sitter for Marko in Gloucester Terrace, guarding the couple of telescopes and the early guitars which weren't on tour; feeding bloody Corbisher and Mister Mingles

– those same immortal cats, while he was up north, on the Continent, or even overseas – which was most of the time.

Caroline Proudfoot would still come round to play with the cats since she had wanted the kittens in the first place. She looked wan and so young, but she quickly fell by the wayside with Marko out on the road and mostly in the States. There were tearful scenes and I got the unfortunate job of pushing her away which made her dislike me. As if we were in competition for Marko. She was quite bitter towards me.

But I'll tell you another thing Marko and I bonded over, to demonstrate there was nothing but sincerity in our connection. We bonded over Ray Fenwick. We were both huge fans of Ray. Not a lot of you will remember Ray Fenwick now but he was in the Syndicats. Steve Howe was in the Syndicats too before he went over to the Tomorrow and then to Yes. Ray filled that little guitar vacancy in the Syndicats nicely, thank you very much. Ray was just a wild player in those days. Check out his slide solo at the end of 'Crawdaddy Simone', a 45-rpm on Columbia. Was it Syd Barrett – who we saw downstairs on the Tottenham Court Road supported by The Tomorrow – or was it Ray Fenwick, who got that non-blues, atonal slide-guitar sound first? Ray found himself in a jazzed-up rock-fusion unit that Ian Gillan from Purple (Mark IIa) toured; that was in '76/77 when it might still have seemed to the suits that young people would go on buying jazz-rock-fusion records – before punk and new wave swiped it dead. Death Threat Dave soundboarded some stuff with Gillan, and when the Taker were off the road, Dave once took me round to Gillan's house. Up past Goring way, but not Thames-side. When I got inside there I didn't know if I was inside a house or inside a hotel and subsequently it turned out indeed to be a hotel – with a guitar-shaped swimming pool. Small world, the south of England and Home Counties, as a few years later Purple's keyboard man, Jon Lord, had his place just down the Reading Road from there.

111

Ray Fenwick was one hell of a nice bloke, not pushy or cleaved by ambition. Clem. Clem Clempson from Colisseum, Humble Pie and Rough Diamond – there was another lovely fellow, a brilliant player once considered for Purple (Mark IV). Then there was Ollie Halsall from Patto, the Tempest and Kevin Ayers's band – another cracking guitarist. Maybe one of the best British guitarists I ever heard. Bloody good players those blokes, and they could have ended up with mansions in the country, like Marko and Steve Howe did. Well, in Steve's case, a lovely seventeenth-century farm in north Devon which he rehearsed in and liked so much, he bought it. However, the dice just did not fall for those other chappies. That's the way in the music biz. There really is no in-between in the rock world. You either reach up for the big coin in the sky and it comes down so you wind up in a mansion, or else you end up disappointed and broke (which is always the same thing). Or dead. There really is no middle ground in the music dream. You make it big or you do not, and a very few of the big – like the Fear Taker – make it bloody huge.

People don't understand the seventies and how the music industry functioned. They will tell you it was a great time for excitement and innovation, but basically it was that the suits didn't have a clue what would sell to long-haired kids and hippies. All kinds of albums came out because the suits were shooting in the dark – they didn't have a notion what would go hot and what would not and when something did go hot and sell, they all rushed out to try and grab some more of it. Jazz-rock fusion or disco – it didn't matter to them as long as it shifted plastic. In the eighties, taste got stratified. As Marko once said, stratified was a good pun on the Fender Stratocaster, and he wanted to call his first solo album (if he ever got round to doing one) – *Stratified*.

It would be great to see Marko again and catch up, so I nipped in through the kitchen side door, crossed the sunflower tiles and trotted up the spiral stairs to the main air bridge. Nice to note that

112

Mrs H had raised the electric blinds on the car turnaround side. Bless her heart. Mrs H was usually a little cautious about those intimidating Up/Down buttons, as if they might bite her or the blinds would surely jam and she would end up getting the blame.

I went through the 1602 door, passed the stairwell and the wooden panelling – heading straight for the morning room. I was surprised not to hear conversation going on. I approached, hurrying slightly, and when I turned the door corner there was only Mrs H in her pinafore, checking on the fresh flowers in the vases.

'Goodness me, Mr Sleepy Head. Didn't you have a long lie-in?' She looked at me. It immediately felt like a reprimanding expression.

'Sorry. Where is everybody?'

'Everybody is gone, Crofton.' She glanced down at the vase she was holding and then she pulled some slightly wilting flowers out of it and lay them in an old sheet of newspaper. 'The two accountants left; Mr Morrell, Auralie and Molly all headed back to London in a car to try to sleep there and they took Maude with them to babysit. Just as well you were sleeping, there was a bit of a fankle.'

'Marko's gone back to London?' I actually sat down on the chesterfield sofa. 'But I didn't even get a natter with him.'

'Wait till you hear. I came in this morning to find one of your accountants in the kitchen eating scraps for the cats out the fridge, claiming he's been starved steadily since yesterday. Tea and toast with no butter was adequate enough fare for him and he was out the door directly.'

'That one is Martin.'

'Yes. Out the door and into his car saying this house was a crazy place. Asking if there was something wrong with you. That you had cluttered up a corridor with a load of old junk to stop him passing through it. I didn't believe him so I went and

113

took a look-see. Oh, Crofton. What a messy prospect. It's like something from that awful Steptoe and Son pair.'

'Well I didn't want them two meeting up, did I? Where's Jim?'

'Wait just a little tick now. Martin took a wander in the night. Said he couldn't sleep with hunger and was trying to find you. Climbed over your . . . contraption.'

'Did he now?'

'Said he came to an upstairs door, heard a man inside, whispering that he was locked in his room and to please, please unlock him. That he was hungry too. Another one.'

'Maybe I went a bit far.'

'Crofton. Really. How could you lock him up?'

'Did he let Jim out?'

'No.'

'Oh. No harm done then.'

'Turned tail, since you had told him about our old ghost, Sir Lawson Starley, who I once had the pleasure of encountering. Then when Mr Dimelon was coming back over to your side, in the glass corridor, he told me he was sure he saw someone sat out in the garden down by the main stairs. Scared the living daylights out of him. Was that you trying to scare him? I wouldn't put it past you to put a white sheet over your head and dance in the gladioli. I really wouldn't.'

I sat forwards in my seat. 'Someone. Who? It wasn't me.'

'Oh now, Crofton, don't be silly; who else could it possibly have been? It certainly wasn't Dan Mullan, doing the nasturtiums at three o' clock in the morning. Anyway, Molly eventually got the blame for locking up chatterbox Jim in his room, though it was a toss-up between her and Maude, who of course denied everything. When Auralie and little Molly finally appeared, it had been the usual. Her Ladyship against Maude, them both fighting it out for poor little Molly's attentions. Now suddenly around noon, there's this almighty yell from the top of the stairs.

Me, Auralie and Maude all jump up and dash to the bottom of the stairs. I thought it was Sir Lawson Starley himself, with his icy fingers, setting about Mr Morrell, but there's Mr Morrell up on the top landing, hair shooting outwards in all directions, a good while since he's shaved. Down the stairs he comes too with not a stitch of clothing upon him, shouting at the top of his voice, I won't say the word, but shouting, "It's f—ing daylight out here. I thought it was the middle of the night. What f—ing bleedin' day is this?"'

I burst out laughing.

'It isn't amusing, Crofton. Not in the least. Mr Morrell was shouting about why it was dark in his bedroom but light outside. He was taking quite a turn.'

'Because his common-law wife is stark raving bonkers,' I suggested.

'He was yelling for his accountants. Like the king in his counting house. I had to explain to him that they arrived early yesterday and had already given up and gone home this morning to allow him to sleep. "And what bleedin' day is this then; is yesterday today or is today yesterday?" That's what he asked me and let me tell you, I was somewhat stumped for an answer. Mr Morrell was furious. He'd missed a whole day because of Auralie blacking out the bedroom for herself. She never even told him she had it all trussed up like that. He was in there days, waking up, thinking it was still night-time and going back to sleep. So they both started on each other; Molly was frightened and the poor little soul had another howling fit. Oh, there was quite a commotion all right. Mr Morrell had finally wanted to introduce these two accountant gentlemen to one another after all these years, and to congratulate them both on their work which had always balanced out. When he said that, Maude had drawn his attention to the fact that if he wanted to introduce anyone to anyone he would be better putting some clothes on first. By this

115

point he was standing covering his shame with the lifted end of a curtain.'

I said, 'Oh. Which curtain? And what happened to Jim the fat geezer?'

'I'd had another sermon or two from him across the breakfast table. He had accepted a fried egg without too much encouragement and after the second tea pot was emptied it was all I could do to get him out of this house. I actually walked him to the bottom of the front steps, to his car. He was still sermonising his socks off as I went back up and he put out his arm onto the pillar there at the bottom, leaning on it as if he owned the place, jabbering away, his hand against the big stone ball on top and heaven's above doesn't that stone ball just go and fall right off the top of the pillar. He must have had his whole weight on it. And the big fool he is, he bends over and tries to move the stone, him in his suit too small for him. I was waiting for the seat of his trousers to rip right open so I would have to fetch the sewing kit next but somehow they didn't tear. He soon climbed into his car after that. He was full of apologies through his window even as he was reversing off. I must say, I felt a bit sorry for him. You could see he didn't want to face Mr Morrell after the night and now after breaking the stone ball. I was put a bit out of sorts, Crofton, so I shouted to him that the stone ball falls off all the time. Just to lift his spirits, so to speak. Nice colour of car he had there.'

Later that afternoon, as usual, I cursed Dan Mullan for not turning up to work in the garden but around five I heard sounds of metal scraping against stone and, when I walked up to the main gates in order to investigate further, I found that, although Marko had already departed, Mullan and his mouching nephew had finally shovelled the road by the boundary wall entirely clear of all the horse droppings – into a wheel barrow for the roses. Better late than never, I suppose.

116

4

At least this latest and sudden flight of our masters . . .
concerning clothesline placement – laundry – a barricade
clearance – rolling (a) stone – a front gate buzzer sounds!

At least this latest and sudden flight of our masters from their East Sussex estate meant we could all once again proceed with our respective duties around that great property. You could almost go so far as to say that Marko and Auralie's arrival – and their very brief stay, along with young Molly – and all the other unexpected callers they dragged along with them, had been something of an interruption or even an inconvenience to our routine, to the disciplined running of our dwelling and the proper maintenance of its grounds – but of course that would be absurd. Wouldn't it?

For sure we were left with chores to be getting along with. For instance, I suppose I had to roll away that stone ball plonked on the grass verge, ridiculously toppled there from its normal lodgement by that natural Bill Withers fan, Jim Burton and his inveterate bad habit of leaning on everything around him. Or perhaps I could find some way of reattaching the blasted stone ball?

I also had to clear that barricade out of the smaller air bridge. While Maude's ambitious task of collating an inventory of the linen cupboard had been postponed by her sudden departure until her next visit.

Mrs H still had the ironing of the New York laundry to complete. And she also had the bed linen from four used bedrooms to get into the washing machines, as well as making up the four beds in clean sheets in case of more sudden arrivals.

In the fair-weather hours of the previous day, Mrs H had hung the New York laundry out on the clotheslines and had gathered it back in again before she left for her home. Mrs H ironed everything: underwear, socks, cloth napkins, tea towels and handkerchiefs too. My mam had never bothered with any of those.

I have previously alluded to clotheslines – I believe when I was observing Martin Dimelon's ironed shirt after his surprise arrival the day before. (I would still define it, an *unauthorised* arrival.)

It might be useful, or at least of note – no, perhaps of some historical value – to consider and acknowledge the delicate nature as to the correct positioning of a clothes-drying line around an illustrious property like Kitchenly Mill Race. In other words, to make the conundrum vulgar: where did a world-famous rock star hang up his washing to dry?

For many years, shyness and modesty has led me to wash my own underwear in my sink and allow it to dry in the privacy of my own small rooms – which initially spread a sour rumour that I wasn't washing my underwear at all. I was teased about this by Mrs H and even once – insolently to my mind – by the daily. I had to take Mrs H up to my bedroom (after tidying a bit), and display to her my own little improvised drying line of string between the window handle and the sofa corner. She chuckled. I think the malicious personal-cleanliness gossip may even have reached Marko's ears. Perhaps I felt my own underwear was not worthy to fly in the wind next to that of my guitar idol?

Three Victorian ceiling pulleys remained in the utility areas of Kitchenly Mill Race – useful for smalls of course, as well as for sheets, towels and also for general winter drying when inclement weather plays havoc with any laundering schedule. Mrs H would have had to tell you all about that.

Everyone agrees, I am sure, that in a countryside free from any sniff of silage upon the prevailing breeze, outdoor drying of clothes is far superior, to air them and to freshen them up. Many is the time, in from the washing line, I have held my Purple (Mark IIa) *Stormbringer* T-shirt – no, my rare road crew ELP Manticore T-shirt – held it to my whole face and inhaled

122

deeply. What is it I smell there? England, of course! In all its oak and dell glory before the South Downs descant to the south coast. The same England I love; the England you sense when you listen to *Liege & Lief*, an older, better England we all discover in that album, manifested through those ancient, remarkable songs – taken there by wonderful young people of my own generation, and a voice of astonishing technique and expression, thus rendered new and alive yet timeless.

Though it has come to my attention over the years of serving in a big rural property how much of and how often our green English countryside honks of animal shit.

It is obvious that in a great house such as Kitchenly Mill Race the clothesline cannot be positioned in a location where it is visible to the residents. Likewise, it should not be visible to passers-by, visitors or tradesmen callers – even of the most casual type. Yet at the same time the clothesline cannot be positioned in a location too far away from the dwelling house and washing machines for reasons that are obvious, but which I will doubtless state anyway. There is the ease of access for the staff getting to the washing line with often-weighty garments, towels and sheets which are to undergo drying, and likewise when these items are dry, they must again be available for convenient and swift collection.

There was no absolutely perfect solution to these complex criteria at Kitchenly. The linked sequence of dwelling houses had so many windows – as you know by my earlier and very useful explanation of the many curtains which are to be drawn and opened with cosmic regularity – giving views through the windows in all directions of our grounds.

The exception to this open view from the manor – apart from the most far-flung quadrants of the garden around the river bend and at the far end of the older moat-bridge approach way – is clearly the hidden area immediately behind the secondary mill house on the far side of the millstream, which is unseen from the manor house. Here is the much smaller car-parking area up against the black door and the two storeys of Georgian windows where I had forced Martin Dimelon to park his Volkswagen Scirocco. A slight grass slope commences in this place, upwards to the stable-yard wall with the arched door in it; a broad, paved and climbing pathway – the gradient far too gentle for steps – which continues from the gravel in a dead-straight line in direct lateral relation to the big, gloss-black door. And the suspended coaching lamp. This slope is planted in snowdrops and narcissi on either side of the pathway, which flourish seasonally.

Somewhere in this area would have been the ideal location for a clothesline, from a purely practical viewpoint. Especially in 1976, during Marko's year of tax exile when he could not return to the United Kingdom – and when, despite his total absence, Mrs H would still strip and wash bed linen quite regularly as we awaited the return of our exiled king. This location would really have sped up her process of putting out articles and garments to dry and – again, the necessary opposite, collecting the dried laundry back in. But even a – shall we say – 'officially sanctioned' clothesline in this area would have meant that technically, if any of the rarely used bedrooms which face the 'front' (north) of the secondary mill house were occupied – however briefly – the occupants would gain a direct view onto any clothesline and its hanging load.

Another possible candidate as a washing-line zone lies on the far side of the main car turnaround area, where the screen of trees reaches right up to the far boundary wall. But this would be an inconvenient location for any clothesline because it would have to be positioned in among the mature copse and here it would be unduly sheltered from the required breeze and direct sunlight. The staff would be seen transporting the laundry back and forth from this location as they must by necessity cross the

124

gravelled car park and well-tended lawn. Unthinkable. New pathways might have to be laid. It was wholly impractical.

The only sensible location for the clothesline was up by the disused tennis courts, but far enough back so that even a casual visitor to the stables could never glimpse the tethered line with its dancing fabrics. No tennis was ever played on the courts, or was contemplated – even later on when Marko always seemed to be conveniently on tour during Mrs H's and my temporary enthusiasms for the Ashe, Connors, Borg, Nastase, Billie Jean King, Evert, Goolagong, Wade, Wimbledon finals – on the colour television set.

The simple solution was to use the grassed, sunken garden area next to the courts which had been converted out of an old 'paddling pool' or 'fish pond' in the 1930s. (Contemporary maps of the garden confusingly named it as both.) The area had later been a kitchen herb garden but neglect of this charming feature had led it to return to grass at some point prior to Marko's purchase of the property. It was here, by the planting of some fast-growing privet and the construction of a new set of stone steps down into the declivity, that we finally placed our clotheslines. A generous five-cord network was hoisted up and strung between black cast-iron poles planted by Dan Mullan which stood rooted in this crater-like grassy zone. Only the most vigorous of winds might tease a large item – like a dazzling white sheet – to flick a linen corner upwards, showing above the rim of ground to the right (or south) of the tennis court surface.

A disadvantage of this location was the distance Mrs H or the daily had to walk from the side door of the kitchen, across the footbridge and then uphill on the track to the coaching doors of the stables' arch in order to reach the clotheslines. It often meant several relays of the blue plastic wash baskets if Mrs H was working on her own. Thus – though I felt the task beneath my station – I frequently accompanied the older woman with damp washing up to the lines. Blinking in the light, slightly bent forwards to the gradient, one often felt one was partaking of a country stroll, but this was a notion made incongruous by the large blue plastic laundry basket held in both arms which could often be quite heavy with damp fabric.

I may as well admit I felt less guilty about allowing Mrs H to carry the lighter dried laundry loads back from the drying zone by herself, with the down gradient now in her favour. Often I would peek a look at her from the edge of my bedroom window while I was busy – listening to records for instance.

Many times through the years of my service, in a completely unexpected rain shower, Mrs H has shouted to me along the communicating corridors of our large dwelling and I have understood immediately, detecting the first spattering of excited raindrops outside. Like a lifeboat crew we have both scrambled to her rusty Triumph Dolomite and she has sped us halfway up the driveway, hard right turn over the Victorian coach bridge with the beams clattering beneath the tyres, ascending the small incline then hard left into the area behind the tennis courts. Here Mrs H and I have speedily whipped down the laundry, allowing the mix of old wood pincers and coloured plastic clothes pegs to fall indiscriminately onto the grass. We have gathered the garments into huge armfuls then rushed to cram them onto the cramped rear seats of her car, or even into the boot out of the rain. Then we have driven back down to the house with the windscreen wipers on to try and rehang the quantity on the interior pulleys of the kitchens.

It was still full sunshine as I carried the differing parts of that road barrier back up to the stable-wall door. Compared to coming the other way the night before, I made quite a noise getting all them bits back through the door; just shows you what adrenaline can do. Marko often talks about adrenaline floods when he's gigging. I know it's not the same but . . . in some ways it is.

126

Firstly I had to drag the water-filled pontoon bases into the bath of the left-hand ground-floor bedroom, invert them and open the caps to drain the water out. They were one hell of a weight. I won't say I was not concerned about marking or damaging the creamy beige carpet where I had to drag the pontoons behind me with both hands as if I were a soldier heroically pulling a wounded comrade to safety and out of the line of fire.

I had not thought through the unfortunate consequences of filling the bases so full of water the night before. Why had I bothered when there was no wind or passing vehicles to blow over the barriers indoors? I suppose I felt it would make the barrier 'stronger', should the accountant, Dimelon, have chosen to charge and to breach it. Which he did! Always a possibility when dealing with accountants. I saw then that road barriers are not intended for use inside a house with expensive carpets. Duly noted for future reference.

As I worked, my mind was very distracted by this latest report of an intruder prowling at dark night in our grounds yet again. Perhaps this was why, while I was up at the stables transporting sections of the barricade back to storage, I checked the recording-studio door was locked and also peered in the tiny gap between the triple doors to ensure that the Ferrari and Auralie's Mercedes 350 SL were still secured in that segment of the building converted to a five-vehicle garage.

Sometimes I get to drive the fire-engine-red Ferrari Dino myself. Marko might be heading off somewhere. Occasionally he just likes to drive through the countryside with no set destination; sometimes even after dark. So to save him trekking up to the stables' garage, I myself will valet the car down for him, leaving it outside the front door stairway with the two round stone— correction, *one* round stone finial at the bottom. This is why I have often insisted Mrs H parks her banger further away from the formal front entrance.

Many times I have returned the Ferrari back up to the garage when Marko is going away or not planning to use the vehicle for several days. Alas, Marko has regrettably but understandably not insured the car for me to drive on the open road. I am confined to carefully manoeuvring it only on private property within the confines of Kitchenly Mill's grounds. Frankly it's difficult in such a powerful car to get up into third gear on the curved driveways, never mind fourth. How I would love to get into fourth with the Ferrari Dino.

After I had completed stowing the road barrier and the detached door, the sheets of cardboard and even the chicken wire back up in the stables, I turned my dedications to the round stone ball sitting on the grass verge by the front door.

Here I was back again only a few feet from that damned park lamp whose bulb I had changed with some difficulty and interruption the day before. I looked around me then bent over to test the weight of the dislodged stone. By Jove. Forget it. I could barely rock the blighter to and fro. So it was back up to the bloody stables, this time to visit the 'tool shed' – which incidentally had been stripped clear of all contents apart from some rust-encrusted trowels, when Colonel Halmer vacated the premises. I came back with: the older metal wheelbarrow, a five-foot crowbar and a couple of uneven sections of four-inch by two-inch planking/lumber. It was only when I had reached the main car-turning area once again, that I realised I was going to need a saw to even out these lengths of wood, so it was ho-hum. I dropped the wheelbarrow handles and trudged back up to the blasted stables. Hot work this. In fact on my return I stopped off in the kitchen to check the fridge. There was a can of Tizer, so I stood on the sunflower tiles gulping it back, listening to the moat water trilling down on the steps across from the silent mill race.

I placed the planks together to find the matching length and nicked a scrape with one of the gravel chips to indicate where to cut, then I sawed this end piece off by securing the plank under my knee across the wheelbarrow. I burped a bit with the exertion. So far so good. I dropped the sawn-off wood scrap into the barrow. I jammed the two planks against the barrow but the angle was very steep for one man to attempt rolling that stone up them. There was a lot of sawdust on the grass verge though, so I would need to somehow clear that up. I tried kicking the white dust in towards the moat but this made matters worse.

I took the crowbar in both hands and, to test it, eased it in beneath the large sandstone sphere which sat on the grass, then using both hands I shoved the crowbar forwards with real force . . . The stone rolled forwards with surprising ease, covering a few inches immediately, reaching the start of the slight banking to the moat. 'No!' I yelled and I let go of the crowbar to lunge ahead. The crowbar fell, its top glancing my collarbone with a painful strike as I twisted, trying to dodge in front of the rolling ball, but the orb's weight responded to the developing slope with an amazing acceleration and even though I got my hands briefly onto its rough surface, it scraped at my palms and fingers – pushing them away like a racing whetsone. One more revolution and the enormous finial, like a medieval cannonball, crashed into the still edges of the dark moat water and sank in an ascent of grey bubbles. It sent forth an enormous wake which spread outwards on the smooth, lily-scattered moat water, wavelets clucked and slapped all up and down the moat banking as far round at the ornamental bridge emerging from the porch doorway.

I bent over and struggled back up the banking, rubbing at my collarbone which felt intact. I studied all the blank windows above, fearful of any witness. Mrs H, I suppose. Though perhaps the intruder was peeping from some stinky dell. I glanced around and maybe for the intruder's benefit I said aloud, rather half-heartedly, 'Well. At least it's out of sight. We'll get a new one,' and I nodded once, sharply. I stood for some moments contemplating whether harmony could be better restored by simply knocking off the other stone ball as well and rolling it into the moat. Or trying to break it off directly into the waiting wheelbarrow below – which it would most likely destroy?

Then I heard a familiar sound which now filled me with trepidation rather than with my usual feelings of power, responsibility and authority. It was the damned front-gate buzzer far over in my kitchenette. I ignored it and commenced loading everything back onto the wheelbarrow but after a few moments the intercom insistently started up again: irritating long buzzes then shorter ones then long ones then some kind of da-da da-da da dah dah annoying pattern of buzzes. I walked resignedly back across the gravel towards my kitchenette in the secondary mill house.

5

'Yeah?' I drawled at the intercom receiver with the button
held down . . . two visitors – a 24-track home recording
facility with synthesisers – a courteous conveyance – talked
to harshly.

'Yeah?' I drawled at the intercom receiver with the button held down – using my threatening voice. When I released the button, I heard the active buzz of an open but functioning line; there was someone out there listening on the other end, standing by the main gates, but they were not responding. I pondered: could the accursed night intruder be showing their face in broad daylight at last?

Then a voice spoke – surprisingly, a female one, but it was not Maude. Fresh and slightly high-pitched in excitement, the unmistakable and wavering tones of youth or even of late childhood in the accent of Sussex. It was an attractive, bright voice. 'Hello there? Hello-oh-hoh,' it repeated.

I frowned and pushed in the button again. 'What is it I can help you with?' I said – as if I were a doctor – then added, 'This is a private property and a private intercom system.'

The girl-voice spoke again. 'Wow. Hi-yah. Is that you that plays guitars?'

'What does this concern?'

'What?'

'What is it?'

'Is it you that's the big guitar guy?'

'What is your business, please?'

'You what?'

'What do you want?'

'Are you the guitar man?'

I was about to respond, but a rustling sound came and the voice slightly lowered in volume – a result of the speaker taking her head away from the grille. 'He doesn't make any sense,' it said. It went on, stating, 'He's speaking in all these clever words.'

135

I frowned, then suddenly a similarly youthful voice, but much more faint and in a different accent − much more well-spoken − announced, 'Give it up, Rose. I've got an itchy tit and I need to poo.'

There was a loud guffaw.

'Natandra wants to know if you're the guitar man?'

'I don't, I don't, it's all her,' the other voice shouted.

I pushed the button. 'Are you referring to Mr Morrell?'

There was a silence then the girl-voice yelped, 'Yeah! Is that you? Are you Marka thingamy? It is so smashing to talk to you. I've seen your picture in the magazine. We tried to phone but you're not in the directory-thingy up the phone box.'

The more distant voice shouted, 'Rose is in love with you,' and laughed.

'Shush, you cow. No I'm not.'

I sighed. I enjoyed saying the lines and had often said them, so I delivered: 'Mr Morrell is not in residence at this time. You can try to reach him through his management at their offices in London.' My tone of voice was like my mam when she answers the phone out in the hallway.

'But we're not in London. We've come up from the village; took hours and I tell you what, it was right jittery along that roadside, mister. Hold on. What? Nat? *What?* She wants to know what it is you play then, mister?'

'State your business, please?'

'Well we've got some of your records here and Nat wants you to write your name onto them.'

'No I don't. She does.' The distant second voice had come much closer to the intercom.

'Well I do then.'

Fans. Female. I was surprised. 'You have Fear Taker albums in your possession, do you?' I sounded like the Old Bill.

'Yes. Yes. Fear Taking. Taker then.'

136

'They're her big brotheeeeeeeeeeer's.'

'Well if you leave the albums in the box there, please, I will pass them on and see if that can be arranged. Or not. For them to be autographed. By Mr Morrell. I can't get the other band members to do so. But we would require a stamped, addressed package so we can return them to you.'

'You what?'

'You will need to have the albums in a stamped, addressed envelope and leave them in our mailbox there so we can return them to you.'

'But we want to meet you.'

'It's not him, Rose; it's not *him*.'

'So? Can we just come in there for a little moment, if you please? Nat needs to use your toilet.' She emitted a raspy bubbling noise, trying to hold in a laugh.

'This is a private property,' I repeated, threateningly, but I had suddenly stopped believing it.

'C'mon, Mister Envelopes. We're all puffed out now with the walk and Nat needs to do a poo.' She broke down in laughter, huge shrieks and gulps of air; utterly immature stuff.

Even separated by the intercom system I felt my face colouring. I have a sort of fear of teenage girlies. They can really tease you about the smallest thing and they wield some ridiculous power over you. It's nothing to do with sex, it's to do with them possessing a youth you squandered before you fully appreciated it. I thought about walking away from the intercom, re-establishing the powerful barrier of silence and unreachability which must be in place to protect Marko at all times. A cordon. Like the barrier last night. Which oddly shelters me also from the outer world.

It was almost always blokes who came calling round at Kitchenly to try and meet Marko: awestruck young fellows in leather jackets. Maybe seven or eight groups a year would call unannounced, sometimes in cars, once even in a taxi from town, *à la* Maude. Though in recent years, it had to be accepted, fewer people were calling at our main gates. This punk and new wave music was starting to hit home. Though also, in those days, folk just didn't really know where famous people actually lived. It was very difficult to find out and folk weren't so obsessed with the rich. There was Buckingham Palace and that was that.

Yet I only ever remembered one previous female caller at the gates of Kitchenly Mill Race who wanted albums signed as a surprise gift for her husband's fortieth birthday. I had strolled up to the main gates to encounter a very stout woman in leathers with her large motorbike parked by her side. Marko had been in residence at the house at that time so I took the albums down from the gates to him in the home studio. The husband had owned all seven albums including the live one. The record covers were quite worn with use. A real fan. Marko had asked what she was like – if he thought he should go up the driveway and do a bit of punter-pleasing. I replied that I believed she was a Hells Angel's wife, and it was her husband's fortieth birthday. He hummed thoughtfully and handed each album back to me as he autographed them with his swirling signature. On the final album he signed – which was *Radiance of the Kings* – he added the words: *Happy Birthday. Rock On!*

The lady did not seem in the least disappointed not to have met Marko in person and I felt a sense of insult about this as with both hands she enthusiastically reached in, grabbed the wad of albums back through the wooden roundels of the gates, turned her back on me after saying, 'Ta very much, son,' and swung her sturdy thigh over the saddle, bending around to shove the albums into a leather pannier at the rear while she sat. If you asked my advice I would have said some clear PVC sleeves to properly protect those albums would have been well in order and I almost stated this to her – but she suddenly kicked her deafening bike into life and drove off down the side lane, neatly swerving around the latest scattering of horse droppings.

It amuses me that Fear Taker autograph hunters always transport the vinyl inside the album covers as well, though of course it is only the album sleeves which Marko finally signs; yet invariably punters bring the album in its complete form. Why risk mislaying your actual vinyl as you traipse around, trying to get the album cover art signed by Alvin or Marko or Styxie, or Gasser? Or even Rick, our silent bassist. Perhaps they feel some totemic power is gained as the vinyl album itself — the source of those cherished and familiar sounds — has been held for a few sacred moments in Marko's very fingers? Maybe I used to feel such a similar emotion myself, but time has dulled that sense of wonder along with many others.

I depressed the intercom button. 'I am afraid you would need to deliver the album with the required postage,' I rather pompously repeated.

'Oh but that's a bit silly, mister. We just live in the new houses by the village. What would be the point in posting them and all postage stamps and stuff for the distance we are now?'

I paused. 'You live in the new Brockleberry Rents bungalows?'

'You know where we live! He knows where we live, Nat. Yes, yes we do. I promise. We just moved in, both of us.'

'Stay there a moment,' I said. I left the kitchenette, pausing to pull my long hair back behind my ears and check my beard growth in the reflection of the door glass. I realised something. I stood awkwardly pensive then I dashed up the stairs. In my bedroom I had my other underwear drying on my little line and I snatched the damp garment, shoved it into the tallboy and yanked down the string line.

On my way up the driveway through the signalling and chirruping of garden birds, I disciplined myself not to adopt that odd limp of mine. I knocked some sawdust off the front of my jeans as I quickly walked.

The curves of the driveway even out just before the front gates, so as I rounded the cedars of Lebanon I saw the two figures before I reached them. They stared towards me with sullen intensity through the roundels of the gates but they accompanied this alert stance with continual uneven giggles and visible smirks.

They were shockingly young-looking – but I myself was of that age when a man becomes unsure if the soft face of a young woman is twenty-one years old or fifteen. They both initially seemed tiny beings to me, but this was oddly misleading for as I came close to the gate itself I noted they both stood almost as tall as me in their awkward girlhood – but thin and svelte with it which made them seem slighter. One girl – despite the warmth of the August day – wore a bright-blue stuffed anorak above her jeans. She had blonde and high curly hair which made her seem taller; as she chewed gum her curls reacted in staticky jerks. A real doll. The other one, a delicate, petite person despite her height, wore a tucked-in black shirt with several metal badges pinned on it, the sleeves fully down, and dark jeans – Wranglers, I suspected. Her kind face was as white as a round dinner plate, her brown eyes were moody with liner. She didn't seem like a rocker chick. There was no way of avoiding the fact that they were both extremely attractive which for some reason discon-certed me even more. Especially the dark one with her neat facial profile as she turned aside. A perfect-featured young girl, so pretty she resembled a Jane Austen silhouette on a miniature.

The giggles continued until the blonde blurted out, almost into my face, 'Are you gonna let us into this place then?'

In her left hand the dark, prettier girl carried a supermarket bag with a name on it: 'Keelers', the telltale shape of long-player albums inside, and she shook it – as if I were a dog of some description.

'Hello,' I said.

'What do you play in the band then?'

'He's not in the actual band, Rose.'

I stood before them both, the gates between us, and I didn't quite know what to say but found myself asking, 'Are you sisters?'

They both burst out laughing, turning to look delightedly into each other's face.

'Not likely,' the blonde said. 'She's at number 2 and we're at number 4.'

The pale-faced girl laughed a sort of throaty escape, then as an aside, 'And it's a number 2 that I need right now.'

They both became physically unstable with laughter, holding on to the roundels with their curved fingers, the nails bitten low on those three hands – but with scrappy black nail varnish on the brunette's right one. I desperately tried to stop my face colouring at the laughter, but found the only way to cover this up was to walk immediately to the left where the wall curved gracefully upwards in height to fully shield me.

'Oops-a-daisy. He's gone away,' the blonde's voice announced.

The other one chuckled and again sighed deeply inwards to take breath after the exertions of mirth. A beautiful sound.

I paused a moment out of their sight and took a gulp of air for myself, controlling any blush which might have been developing; hopelessly committed by my position there, I stood on the stud to open the gates, not even knowing if I had wanted to do so or not.

'Oh, clever man. Look, they open with a . . . With an electric way.'

Though the gates were opening inwards as I moved back towards them, neither crossed the holy threshold to enter the grounds. This charmed me. I said, 'You've just missed Marko, I'm afraid. He actually left this very morning.'

I noted it was the blonde who turned directly to the dark girl and asked 'Mark-oh. Is that the thingamy, guitar player?'

'Yes,' the girl in the black clothes said curtly.

I told them the frank truth, 'So I can't get your records auto-graphed by him today. What have you got here then?'

The girls looked at each other and the pale girl handed the albums in their carrier bag, out flat towards me like the roofed bird table on the laburnum slope where, in winter, Mrs H places a lard block. Dan Mullan had fitted it on an especially heightened support, so the cats couldn't leap up there, though they both linger beneath, sitting stock still in truce, their heads bent upwards with frustration. I took the records off her but I didn't look at them.

'Will you really get him to put his name on them then?' the curly girl suddenly queried, seeming more impressed.

The skinny girl in black asked brusquely, 'Do you sort of work here then or something?'

'Yeah,' I nodded. 'Yup. I'm the retainer. I am in charge of the place when he's not here.'

'Do you get loads of records for no money then? Do you get to sort of go free to their big concerts and all of that stuff?'

I shrugged my shoulders at the blonde. 'If I wanted to, yes.'

'You could get us tickets for the Brighton Dome then, could you?'

I smiled. 'The band isn't on tour just now.' Though I felt the girls were not genuinely interested, I added the informa-tion, 'They are getting ready to go back into the studio and do a new album.'

'What, do you not really like his concerts then?' the brunette chuckled, testing.

Sewing seeds of disunity in our ranks already. 'Course I do. They're brilliant. I've been with the band since they started out. I used to go on tours, but now I am sort of a manager really. There's a manager who looks after the band, and a road manager and I'm manager of looking after this place. Personally for Marko.'

142

'A manager like Harry Marley is at the Mumbelton Arms Hotel?' She turned to the dark girl and nodded affirmatively.

'Perhaps a bit like that, yes.'

'So you are sort of in charge round here? You're not just the janitor, like at school, you're more like . . . the headmaster?'

'I suppose I am, yes. The headmaster. Perhaps the deputy headmaster.'

'So you're here on your own then? But not him, you say?'

'That's right. He left this morning.' I added for some reason, 'With his wife and daughter.'

The curly one turned to her pal and spoke as if I were not there, or as if I was still on the intercom. 'Just missed him, that's bloody bad luck. And he's gone and married somebody, like Paul McCartney and that . . . Linda.' She tutted scornfully.

I turned and looked down the driveway then I heard myself say, 'Come along then for a minute and you can leave your records with me. I'll get them signed for you and we'll find a way of returning them.'

'Will you? Will you? Oh, that's brilliant.'

They began to follow me somewhat cautiously down the driveway of Kitchenly Mill Race, looking from side to side, but then the blonde one called out towards my shoulders, 'You will give us them records back, won't you, mister? They are my big brother's.'

'Of course I'll give them back. I can't say when though. Marko's gone away for at least a few days I would expect.'

They continued to follow me down the driveway, giggling, chuckling, looking around constantly.

'See, it's got streetlight things like on a whole street. That's fab.'

'Yeah,' the pale-faced one said.

The blonde skipped and jumped, turned round and looked back the way we had come, snorted and constantly glanced at her friend. 'But this is too brilliant,' the blonde told us.

143

It was then it occurred to me I had forgotten to hit the stud to close the main gates behind us. I gritted my teeth at this. A real bit of neglect, especially with this prowler in our grounds at dark night. Very lax of me. Women. A distraction already. I would just have to accept that any moment now the autotimer would shut the gates anyway; but it couldn't be denied I was disgruntled at my performance.

As we came around the curve in the driveway beyond the shield created by the cedars of Lebanon and across the top of that deep triangle of vanilla, red and yellow rose heads, the two teenage girls had a clear view of Kitchenly Mill Race manor house with its three large, interconnected buildings.

'Heaven's above, Nat, would you look at this? It's bigger than the Mumbleton Arms. It's almost as big as our whole flipping high school. And hoi, do you live here by yourself?'

'Yes, well I live in that bit over there.'

'Oh, look at all the dainty little bridge thing and big wheel stuff and that. Natandra, look. Oh, look at the . . . that thing. Oh, this is smashing.'

Blankly the dark girl squinted across at the manor house and went, 'That's a bit spooky that place is.'

'It's big. I mean *big* isn't it?'

I was unsure if she was addressing the dark girl, myself or making a general statement. I replied, 'Yes, I suppose. Bigger than your houses at Brockleberry Rents, is it?'

They both looked at me with those charming bright eyes of young kids.

'You know it is. Miles bigger,' curly locks laughed.

'Do you live here all the time then?' the gruff, darker girl deadpanned.

'Yes, I do and have for a good few years now.'

'Look at all this, Nat. Look at all that. Imagine actually living here.'

144

'It's totally ginormous. What a party you could throw; could be brilliant as anything,' the one called Nat or Natandra finally admitted.

Then the blonde one – Rose – suddenly pointed. 'Hoi. But you're missing one of them round ball things on your stairs over there.'

Christ. The blonde one had an eye for flaws.

I could sense their disappointment as I turned away from the larger house and made my way towards the footbridge, connecting to the far mill house. On the footbridge itself they both instantly paused, folded their arms onto the gloss white tops of the handrails then stared down into the barely moving mill race beneath.

'Nat. We shoulda took our cozzies and gone right in swimming.'

They both screamed with laughter.

'You could play Poohsticks all day on this. I would if I lived here.'

The one called Natandra smiled, 'Oh, you say such angel things.'

I glanced carefully towards the manor house, worrying if Mrs H had overheard all their unfamiliar and combined racket yet.

Then Natandra actually dropped her voice and suddenly asked, 'Excuse me please but may I make use of your lavatory?'

Rose laughed and countered. 'She talks so posh and all that sometimes.'

I nodded, 'Of course. I'd gathered you might need that.' I led them in the side door to my kitchenette.

'Oh this is a nice little place you have, isn't it?'

After checking the surface was clean, I removed the albums from the plastic bag and placed them down on the kitchenette table then I pointed to the stairway. 'The loo is at the top on the right.'

'Thank you very much.' The dark girl slouched up the stairs, herself sort of swinging wearily from side to side, slightly

145

limping, as if bored with the whole endeavour of movement. I noted how she was so skinny that her black jeans hung around her legs but I still saw the garment was smartly tight over the taut little bum and yes, Wranglers.

Without waiting to be asked Rose sat down on the chair at the table.

I looked through the albums. Three. It was the eponymous first album as well as *Pascal's Moon*, and *Rule of the Evil Ones*, in the 1973 gatefold sleeve.

Rose turned her head continuously from side to side observing everything in my kitchenette; when she saw me looking at the albums she told me, 'I'm not that much into music really, I suppose. I mean it's okay and all that but there are better things.'

I smiled at her, 'Oh yeah. Like what?

She frowned at me and said, as if it were self-evident, 'Ponies. And pets.'

'We have two old cats here. A right couple of rascals.'

'Oh nice. Where are they then?' She looked around again.

'Who knows? They roam the grounds at will.' Like that bloody intruder, I thought.

She started swivelling her head once again. 'Mister, would you have anything to drink? If you please?'

'Yes. Milk.'

'Oh right, thanks. It's true I'm not into music that much. Don't even have a record player but Nat does. Nat's bonkers for music, she is.'

'Is she?' I said, got two glasses with the floral pattern on them down out of the cupboard above the cooker.

'Can't you tell? With her Tubeway Army badges and stuff. She's a Numanette.'

I had opened the fridge door and I was filling two glasses with milk by the sink. I turned to look at her. 'What's a Numanette? A school or something?'

146

She laughed. 'Naw. Don't you not know what a Numanette is? She's one. She is mad about Gary Numan. She's in love with him.'

'Oh yeah. Gary Numan. I've seen that guy on *Top of the Pops*.'

'Do you still watch that even at your age?'

I grimaced and placed one glass of milk in front of her. Without saying thank you, she took the vivid pink gum out of her mouth with two fingers, lifted the glass straight to her lips, drank half and wiped the back of her hand across her mouth before popping the pink blob back in beyond her cute, goofy front teeth.

'Well, we're in the music business here, aren't we?'

'I suppose you are. A Numanette is a girl thing that's just starting up all over the place; she's in the fan club and she's gonna try starting one round here. Huh. Fat chance. I mean I'll join but who else will round here? Maybe a few weirdos at school. Yes. A Numanette is a girl who is just mad about Gary Numan and his Tubeway Army. And wants to be like Gary. Like a machine.'

She made a brief robotic movement, holding her arms out horizontally and turning mechanically.

I chuckled.

'She has loads and loads of posters up in her bedroom. Just of Gary and the Tubeway Army. Knows the words to every single song. And she's got the tickets bought for going up to London to see his new concerts. She'll be going to a real Wimpy Bar and everything. Her mum's going too. Imagine going with your mum.' She laughed scornfully but then thoughtfully added, 'Her mum likes Gary too though. Probably fancies him too, 'cause Nat has no dad. Her mum's awful nice.'

'Is she?'

I knew Marko wouldn't countenance Gary Numan music. For starters there were few bloody guitars to speak of. I had seen this Gareth Numan only a month or so before. I was sitting alone in the big salon of the main mill house, watching *Top of* *the Pop*s on the colour television set while Marko was away. Mr Numan was in the BBC studio, pinioned to his microphone stand, turning his young, hurt-looking face from this side to that side like Yul Brynner in *Westworld*, with a wonky fuse. 'Our Friend was Electric', or something it was called, and if I am correct it was bloody number one in the UK singles chart. Typical.

However, I was still rather impressed by the synthetic sweep of Numan's damned song, the vulnerable-sounding spoken-vocal part and android machine aesthetic. The problem was, Numan was part of this dreaded new wave fashion which had transformed rock in the wake of punk music. The same new wave which heartily condemned bands like Fear Taker as bloated capitalists, out of touch not just with the kids in the street but with reality itself. They thought we – I mean Fear Taker and really successful bands like us from the seventies – they thought we were a pathetic joke. Dinosaurs. We felt really shocked when these kids started coming out with all this venom directed towards our generation of bands, but maybe we should have seen it coming?

Truth be told, I always had to be cautious mentioning any new wave acts around Marko and the whole Fear Taker family structure. It felt like a betrayal, and worse, I was guilty of actually liking a lot of the new bands which I heard. I bought their albums on the sly when I was in town or up in London. Played them through headphones. I would listen to John Peel's Radio 1 show alone on many a weekday night but with the sound turned down as if I were in occupied France listening to a wartime broadcast on the BBC. Peel had just stopped playing music from the earlier seventies altogether which he had been playing enthusiastically just months before and it was nothing but new wave, punk and reggae. I was really shocked.

We had to start thinking: maybe our day was gone? Everyone's record sales had really dropped, including major seventies acts like Fear Taker. America was still okay – so far – but not good old Blighty, and that hurt. It was home after all. The younger brothers of Fear Taker fans were now buying The Stranglers' latest albums not the Taker's. And The Stranglers were damned good. Even if the composition 'Down in the Sewer (a) Falling (b) Down in the Sewer (c) Trying to Get Out Again (d) Rats Rally' was clearly progressive rock, just roughed up a bit.

Punk was a sudden and exciting revolution but like all revolutions it had replaced one tyranny – the popularity of bands of the seventies – with another: the tyranny of fashion and an ahistorical hatred of any music created before 1977. Or at least it sometimes seemed that way.

Being able to play an instrument very well was suddenly frowned upon. In a way it created such a surge of creativity that I loved the illicit thrill. I mean look at Island Records releasing MX-80 Sound's *Hard Attack*. Brilliant. From 1977 on, I looked forward to every edition of the *New Musical Express* and the latest on all these new bands; but in another way, many things got overlooked. Really great bands I dug, like Upp, National Health, U.K., Fairport, and the Jack Bruce Band, were coldly dropped by their record companies and could hardly get a gig. Careers of really talented musicians were stalled or even ruined.

The music business changed overnight; the suit clones just went for new wave, handing out record deals left right and centre to anyone who pretended they couldn't play very well. In some respects it was like the sixties and early seventies all over again; the suits suddenly didn't know what these short-haired younger people would buy. So many bands could suddenly get a record deal on a major, and of course some great stuff came out of that liberty. Smart guys like Peter Hammill and Bill Nelson – who is a superlative guitar player – made the transition into new wave very intelligently. Ultravox! were a great new band too. But the scorning of musicianship, that was the fallacy. These new wave guys didn't come from the blues and this was fair enough. But you knew fine all these new guitarists had been practising Fear Taker, Free, Zep, McLaughlin, Be-Bop Deluxe and prog rock guitar riffs in their bedrooms just six months before. They'd cut off all their long hair or stuffed some of this weird 'gel' in it, then pretended they only knew four barre chords on a Telecaster so their band could get a gig. It was all about the bleedin' look.

On Stiff Records, The Damned had made this album, *Music for Pleasure*, up at the Floyd's studio on Britannia Row with Floyd's drummer producing – so the 'We hate hippies' principle was discarded on the first day of the new regime. It was a cracker of an album too. Got slagged off, but it has sax, free jazzing – killer metal riffs all over it. Great Moon-style drummer; star quality frontman vocalist dressed as a vampire. The Damned were ace: real English music hall with Gibson guitars; show business as art. Bit like the only good Stooges album, *Fun House,* which it was permitted for punks to like, I believe.

Here is another very important and valid point about new wave music to which I would like to draw your attention. The—

The toilet flush went upstairs, and of course Rose found this an occasion for great, bawdy laughter.

I said, partly to cover up the intimate noise, 'So she's a Numanette, is she?' I heard the upstairs sink tap running.

'Course. That's what's with the black gear and the white make-up. Didn't you know? Haven't you heard Gary's new one, "Cars"?'

'No. I haven't.'

'But it's so brilliant. Even I like that. We were just playing the single again and again in her bedroom this morning. Really loud. And laughing all the way along the main road walking up here, 'cause car after car almost run us over.'

'There's no pavement once you're outside the village; you should be more careful,' I told her.

'Tell me about it.' She looked thoughtful. 'Gary's a bit of a weirdo, though, but Nat would strip right off and let him do it to her anytime. She would too. She think's Gary is God. She lies in her bed looking across at Gary's poster every night.'

I suddenly felt disgruntled that I hadn't heard this new song. I fancied crossing straight to the wireless and turning it on to Radio 1, just in case the song was playing, but I never listened to the radio much any more. Since Marko had been away I wasn't really following *Top of the Pops* or John Peel either. I always like it when mad old Jimmy Savile presents *TOTP*; he seems a great bloke. You go in and out of moods with music, don't you? Well I do. In the Volvo I usually played my loose cassettes. The old stuff. All my faves: okay, I admit there was a cassette of *Pascal's Moon*, but also Crimson's *In the Court of the Crimson King: An Observation*, the Tull, Purple (Mark IIa), Fairport, Sabbath, Floyd, the Moodies, Zep, the Dead, Slowhand, El Becko, CSN&Y, BOC, ELP, RTF, KGB, UK, APP, CCR . . .'

'Here she is, back from poopland; and we were just talking about you,' Rose lied, as she heard Nat coming down the stairs.

I had noted the distinctive creak of my floorboards and knew fine she had taken a gander in at my bedroom, so just as well I had got my drying underwear down.

'Would you like a glass of cold milk?' I motioned towards the other full glass with my hand.

Nat stood across the table from us. Neither of us could sit down after all, since Rose had commandeered the only chair.

'Oh no thank you. I don't much like milk. Unless it's got Creamola Foam in it.'

I grimaced again. 'Can you put that in milk?'

'I do. You stir and stir.'

'Oh. Well, I'll have this then.' I felt a bit damned foolish but lifted up the other glass of milk and drank from it. Then I gulped a swallow and stopped so quickly that it's lucky I didn't

151

commence with a coughing fit — much to their amusement. I asked, 'Would you like some water instead?'

'No thanks. You're all right.'

There was a silence and the two girls just looked across at me. A silence was unusual from them. Frankly, I felt a bit on the uncomfy side that so pretty a young girl had just had her trousers down in my vicinity. I lifted my hand and touched where the crowbar had hit me on the collarbone. It was sore.

I said, 'What's it like in your new houses then? Are you happy to have moved in? I know them 'cause I've seen them getting built every time I drive into town.'

The two girls looked at each other and Rose shrugged. 'It's great I suppose, 'cause the council estate was a bit grotso, but she's not from round here, they've just moved down.' She nodded to her pal. 'Haven't you?'

I looked at Natandra. 'Have you? Where did you come from then?'

She looked glumly at me and said, 'Scotland.'

'Scotland. You don't sound Scottish.'

'Well I'm not.' She suddenly seemed a bit reluctant but added, 'I went to a boarding school there for a long spell and all the other girls seemed to be English so I just ended up talking like this.'

Suddenly Rose spoke to me. 'Listen to you though. You've got . . . an accent and stuff.'

I smiled, 'You've got an accent too.'

'No, I don't.'

'Course you do.'

'Get lost. You're like from . . . what's it? From *oop* norffff.'

Both the girls giggled and wrinkled their noses at each other.

'I'm from Stafford.'

'Whereabout's that then?'

'Kind of close to Birmingham. Hey, do you two know that your houses there at Brockleberry Rents were actually built on land that belonged to Marko? To this place?'

152

Rose looked at me and then at Nat. 'No way? We own it now. It's my dad and mum's, not like in the council estate.'

'No, no. I know you own it, but the land your house was built on originally belonged to this place. It's true. Marko sold it just so folks from the village could get better houses. How about that? That big field there beside you is called Foul Mile. That's not a very nice name for some houses.'

Rose snorted out a cruel laugh.

'So they called your houses Brockleberry Rents 'cause way back, we're talking during the last war, there were some growing allotments there and they were rented out from the estate for villagers in Kitchenly to grow veg and stuff.'

'But that's a bit away from here.'

'Maybe so, but the big field is part of this estate.'

'Huh. I didn't know that,' Rose said rather testily. 'My dad was saying it's like . . . like funny that the first house we ever have owned is bloody called Brockleberry Rents. We've only just got *out* of renting.' She laughed.

'Did you grow up in Kitchenly, Rose?' I asked.

'Yes. Did. Worst luck. I tell Nat everything, like who is who and all that. All the stories. Don't I?'

I nodded. 'I see.'

'My dad's always lived in the village, but he works in the town now at Keelers.'

'What's Keelers?'

'It's sort of electric things. Fridges and that.' She nodded her curls towards my fridge.

'Oh yeah, I know where you mean. Up past the Belisha beacons on the roundabouts.'

'And Mum is from Maxtelham. My big brother, who those records belong to, he's off at the agricultural college. He's into bloody plants, flipping tractors and all that. Stupid rally bikes. Know what he is? He's a right yokel. A bloody country bumpkin.

153

That's what my dad even says. Nat doesn't even fancy him. Do you?'

'No.'

'Do you like the new houses then?'

Rose raised one shoulder. 'Yeah,' she pursed her lip, 'They're great, I suppose. I've a big bedroom to myself now.'

Nat seemed to feel she should contribute so she just mumbled, 'It's all new to me. And my mum.'

'You're settling in though? Do you like it down here? Better than being in a big smoky city, is it?' I said this encouragingly.

'It's all right. We lived in the countryside in Scotland too.'

I pushed on as I was curious as to their real ages. 'So will you have to go to school here after summer, Nat?'

'I caught the tail end of term there, worst luck. I will, yeah, in the town. I don't think I'm going away to a school any more.'

'Don't Nat, oh don't go away to some daft school. Stay here with me and it will be brilliant. All the boys on the school bus are gonna fancy her, right? She's beautiful, isn't she?' Rose smiled at Natandra, seemingly quite genuine and proud. 'They'll all be asking, the ones who get on in the middle of nowhere − bumpkins − they'll all be asking me, "Who is she, who is she?" And I'll say that's Natandra Losey − my best friend ever.'

I looked at Natandra and she just smiled at Rose then shrugged. 'I ain't beautiful, Rose. Bet you Gary wouldn't think so.'

'You are too. He would.'

I said, 'Fifth form, will it be? More exams.' To disguise my leading question I added, 'I hated school. Left as soon as I could and came down to London to work with bands.'

I saw Rose turn to look at Nat and she let a smile touch out from the sides of her lips, nodded just a bit too quickly. 'Yeah, we'll be going into fifth form, won't we, Nat?'

Natandra said nothing but nodded quickly at Rose.

Lying imps. So they were going into the fourth form – they were fifteen years old, maybe just turned sixteen. 'You can . . .' I was looking at Nat, right at her secretive chestnut eyes. I thought of that sad, beautiful song, 'Your Eyes' by The Damned, but my train of thought had drifted away. 'What's your mum going to get up to round here then?' I suddenly said.

'I beg your pardon?'

'I mean your mum. What's she going to do round these parts?' I admit it was a bit poorly expressed. 'I mean for work? Is your mum working round here?'

'Why?' Rose butted in and I looked at her rather sharply. She asked, 'Why? Are there jobs going here as bloody cleaners or something?'

'No. No, I was just asking.'

Nat looked down at her feet – she had on black, slightly pointed little boots, now crusted with country mud. I felt a bit guilty for pushing her. 'So, I hear you're really into Gary Numan?'

Her face brightened up at this new prospect. 'Yeah. Too right. Do you like him? Can't wait for the new album to come out. I've tickets for his London concerts next month. Hope I don't die before them. He's so fantastic. It's brilliant he's at number one again.'

'Is his new one at number one as well?' I couldn't help an edge of annoyance creeping into my voice. Fuck it, Fear Taker were always a classic *albums* band. Singles were for kids like them. People forget that old distinction about singles artistes and albums artistes. Many at Motown for example, were singles artistes. It's like my sensible and perfectly sound, carefully expressed argument, which everyone objects to: Springsteen is essentially a brilliant singles, not an albums artiste; history will show this, and—

'Yeah. Didn't you know?'

155

In a dead voice of final condemnation Rose declared, 'He hasn't even heard "Cars".' She tutted, raised her eyes and sighed at the tragic boredom of this fact.

In a tiny voice Nat said, 'Have you ever met Gary Numan or known anyone like, from here' – she nudged her head over towards the compound of buildings – 'that met Gary?'

'I haven't. I've met lots of musicians. World-famous ones, not just Marko, but I haven't met Gary Numan and I don't know anyone who has. Bands tend to sort of . . . keep to themselves in a way. Especially all these new ones. They can be a bit competitive. Like football teams.'

'Do you think you could ever get to meet him?'

I pondered on his. 'Well, if he's touring I might know blokes up in London who have met him? Sound guys and lighting guys and the like. Or some folk from his record company. Look, I'll ask around for you.'

'Oh wow. I'm going to start up a fan club in this area and maybe make up a sort of . . . a sort of newsletter thing for this bit of Sussex. Use all my drawings of him. Imagine I could get to interview Gary!'

She did this dizzying lift of her brown eyes then they settled again.

'That would be great,' I lied. I said, 'I know this bloke Andy Fallon and he runs the Fear Taker fan club. Up in Didcot of all places, but he has thousands and thousands of folk who buy his mail-order fan magazine. Twice a year he puts one out. It's even in colour now. He knows more about Fear Taker than anyone. I mean probably more than me. Or even Marko. If you ask Andy, this guy can recite the tour dates of any American tour. He can tell you what songs they played each night: the set list. *Taken*, his fanzine is called. I can show you a copy if you wish? I have every copy upstairs in my room.' I glanced encouragingly at Nat. 'He does it all himself, pays for it to be printed. He's visited here twice to interview Marko and he's

156

always very welcome. He even stayed the night once. He really hero-worships Marko, he . . .' I broke off.

The girls were both staring at me, bored shitless, no doubt.

Nat asked, 'Do you have any synthesisers here?'

I smiled. 'We do actually, yes.'

'Oh, wow.' Charmingly, they both looked around as if one might be propped up in a far corner, which they had overlooked.

'Marko has a few up in his studio. Do you want to see them?'

Natandra really brightened up at this. 'Oh, yeah. That would be amazing.'

'Finish your milk then, Rose, and I'll quickly show you.'

Rose looked and me and frowned. 'Okay, headmaster.'

I ignored her as she gulped the rest of the milk, somehow directing it around the chewing gum still in her mouth. 'The guy you really want to talk to about synths though, is Gasser. The keyboard player in Fear Taker.' I lunged forwards and Rose blinked but I grabbed *Rule of the Evil Ones*' gatefold cover, opened it and indicated with my finger the inner-sleeve photograph of Gasser onstage. A photo taken by – correct me if I am wrong – Jim Marshall. In semi-darkness, Gasser was sitting down behind all the many rows of black and white keys on his equipment; a pink stage light was clamped high above him, angled so it shone across and through some of his hair, his face turned aside in concentration as he executed trills on the high notes at some forgotten show.

I found myself standing there indicating the photo as if I really were a teacher, demonstrating some point in a high-school textbook. I forgot what point I was making – if any – and I closed the album cover.

Rose frowned, 'Does he live here, too? Like hippies that live all in one place and all that sort of thing.'

I laughed. 'No. This isn't a commune – far from it – just Marko's place.'

'All this just to himself, eh? How brilliant.' She nodded adamantly in support of this.

'Gasser lives out towards Newbury now,' I found myself confessing. 'Actually I've never been to his house.'

'Can we see that studio thing?' Nat reminded me.

'Yeah, sure.' I put the album back down and went over to my hanging board of door keys. For the purposes of security – especially in an era where we had a night crawler in our grounds – the use of each set of keys was not indicated on the hanging board, but I knew them all by heart: the garage keys, the main stable door keys, the tool shed key, the old rusty stable-wall door key, the new bunch of studio keys. I snicked the bunch off the board and rattled them in my hand, taking the old stable door key with me as well. Sometimes, with the only other copy of the two old keys which he has in his possession, Dan Mullan will lock the stable courtyard wall door on random days, just to catch me out. The thought of Mullan cast a momentary gloom upon me. How long till he found out I had lost the stone finial into the moat waters? He'd get a month of laughs out of that if he knew. And how was I ever going to extract it out of the moat? If the stone remained in there even after I had surreptitiously replaced it with an identical one, the team would find it next year when the moat was due its clean out.

Rattling the bunch of keys in my hand aggressively at these turbulent thoughts, I led the two teenage girls out the side entrance of my kitchenette, closing the door behind us then stepping past them, taking the lead. It was just then that I remembered that I had been through the stable wall door only a short time before, returning parts of the barricade, so how could it have possibly been locked?

'Look. A ladder stuffed in there,' Rose announced.

Did this girl miss anything? Perhaps she would end up working for the Old Bill?

158

We turned away from the millstream bank and rounded the corner of the tall Georgian building, crossing the smaller parking area where each winter Mrs H and I dreamed of assembling an illicit washing line. I literally led them both up the garden path to the top of the incline. The arched door into the stable yard was of course not locked, so I swung it in and one by one we entered the large cobbled stable yard.

Very quietly Nat said, 'It's like the door to the enchanted garden.'

'Oh blimey. Flip,' went Rose. 'This place is giant.'

'The stagecoach for London left from here in olden times but the guy who lived here before Marko was into his racehorses. The family had fifteen or more. Bred them up here. They probably used Foul Mile for running their horses, they'd just cross over to the gate into the fields along here. See the clock up there?'

They both obediently turned their heads upwards towards the ornate clock tower on the roof.

'It's stopped because when Marko was recording in this studio, its chimes could be heard in the background of the music he was making.'

'No way?' said Rose.

'Yeah. He could even hear it ticking too. So he had the clock disconnected.'

'Ha, ha,' Rose laughed with a sort of cruel glee. Petite Nat just held those biscuit-coloured eyes on me and smiled.

They fell silent, concentrating on my hands as I used the mortice lock key then the Yale to open up the exterior studio door into what was once the saddlery. They followed me into the smell of old incense and then down the new corridor where there was a small kitchen with grey plasterboard partitions which still required painting; we passed the small toilet then the first of two large storerooms. I thought of the fat accountant's words.

159

That building a studio was merely a means of concealing cash earnings with false and exaggerated receipts. Bloody philistine. What did he know? Mantovani, indeed. Then we entered the larger studio space with its higher ceiling and roof beams.

Nat said in a hushed tone, 'Oh look at all this. Man alive, you could just . . . Like you could have a band right now with all this stuff.'

We gazed over the amplifiers, a full trap drum kit with shining cymbals, cartwheels of cable, standing baffles and crowded corners of gathered microphone stands.

I said, 'Yeah. This is the best bit though,' and we walked onwards into the corridor which led to the second and larger equipment storeroom; but I paused and used another Yale to open the booth door. Inside, facing the long low strip of double-glazed window, sat the 24-track mixing desk that Marko had bought from Morgan Studios in Willesden. Hell's bells, the *Blind Faith* album had been recorded on that; this desk was history. It had been lashed in dust-proof plastic and sealed in a wooden box while the soundproofed booth walls were erected around it. It was a bit like looking into the cockpit of a 747 – an intimidating mass of dials and faders and indicators. Backed up against the rear wall were sound recorders with their silver tape reels like precious ingots.

'Wow.'

'Bet you can't buy one of these in Keelers,' I said to Rose, smiling, and she laughed. I explained, 'This is the mixing console – so you have the band out there, the music comes through the microphones to this desk and then you can control how it sounds as you record it down onto all these tapes. These are big tapes, much bigger than cassettes, eh? One-and-a-half inch. I mean, look at the size of that tape reel? That's because the tape is so sensitive in depth and sound and . . .' Actually my knowledge of recording processes ran out about there. 'It's a

24-track desk. That means without doubling up, you can have twenty-four different instruments coming into it. You could have forty-eight if you wanted to double up on each track. A bit like Mike Oldfield does, who is brilliant at that sort of thing. Do you know his stuff?'

'What? Is it music? No.'

'You've never heard *Tubular Bells*? Or *Hergest Ridge*?'

'No. What's that?'

'Oh,' I frowned, amazed. 'Doesn't your brother have *Tubular Bells*?'

'But the guy here had bells anyway, up on the roof here, eh?' Natandra quipped.

I laughed at her. 'You're dead right, he did. I never thought of *Tubular Bells*. Marko could have had another huge hit on his hands if he'd just kept the bells on. I'll need to tell him that.'

'Will you? Will you? Will you tell him what Nat said?' Rose asked.

'Sure.' I backed us all out of the booth though and I tested the Yale had relocked then we stepped a little further down the corridor. I unlocked the second storeroom then turned on the ceiling lights. There were no guitars there. There was just a new Fender Jazz Bass, one which Marko used for rough recording – expensive, but not worth much in comparison to his 1959 Les Paul and the two 1968 Strats. Marko doesn't trust his axes being way over in the studio, even his cheaper copies – when not on tour, of course – so he keeps every guitar across in the coloured light of the clerestory below the roof atrium in the manor house.

Over in the corner there were two Putney synthesisers but also, positioned up against the back wall on its support frame, was the graceful woodwork of a 1975 Minimoog.

'Oh. Wow,' Natandra whispered, and she stepped across to it. 'Can I touch?'

'Sure.'

161

'Has Gary one of those?' Rose also spoke in reverential tones.

Nat reached out her white fingers and gently pressed down the silent keys of the synth.

'Hey, will it not make all its sounds sound? Can you not put it on?' Rose spoke scornfully.

'I'm afraid not. Frankly, I haven't a clue how to work them. Umm . . . I could stick it into an amp but even then I'm not sure about all the settings. When I was touring with bands, I was just a bass- and guitar-amps backline guy. I'm still coming to terms with monitors. Keyboards are complicated. In fact, they're trouble.'

'Oh, that's no fun, I wanted to hear it all going.'

I smiled at her. 'Another day maybe.'

Nat turned to me, her voice returned to its usual doubt and caution, 'This doesn't look like Gary's ones.'

'I think he's using Polymoogs. Different version of this synth. This is a Minimoog. This one isn't that big either; Numan sounds like he has *big* synths. I'd need to ask old Gasser. That's a good machine though. You can get all sorts of sounds out of that contraption. Who knows? In a few years, maybe you won't need guitars. They could all be piled up on a huge scrapheap and burned at Guy Fawkes'. It might just be synthesisers.'

I suddenly fell glum at the thought; perhaps I even swallowed and the first phases of tearfulness were upon me.

Natandra turned and looked straight at me. 'This is brilliant. Thanks.'

I nodded. 'Okay. Come along then, we better be getting on.'

Natandra paused, still looking at me with those brown October eyes and said, 'Thanks for this, Mister. Honest. You've been dead nice to us.'

'Not at all, not at all.'

We departed the studio, the girls glancing back at various things, as if to retain the privileged sight within their memories.

Outside, I locked the main door then tested it. Once across the stable yard and through the wall, it was I who locked the arched door behind us with the big old key – hopefully to catch Dan Mullan out, but also to foil the furtive night movements of the lurker.

The girls had carried on ahead of me, down the gently descending path towards the main buildings, and I heard them quietly and carefully conferring but I couldn't make out anything they said other than Rose uttering a formal, 'Yes.' I stepped quickly after them.

They were waiting for me back at the kitchenette doorway where I quickly dropped off the stable courtyard key – because it is so big and awkward a key to carry in the back pocket of my Levi's. I placed it just inside the door but kept the studio keys with me, the bulge of them in the front pocket of my jeans.

'Thanks, mister,' Rose said. 'And thanks for saying you'll get them albums written on for my big brother. He was too scared to come up here. For years,' she laughed. 'But we weren't, were we? We came here. My brother is actually going to like me for once. Just as long as he doesn't try to give me a cuddle. Well. We'll need to be getting home now or we'll have Nat's mum on us – she'll be giving us a telling off if Nat's late.'

I smiled at them. 'How about I give you a lift back to the village?'

'What?'

'C'mon. We'll jump in my car and I'll drive you back to the village, it's only a few minutes really.'

'Cor. Would you do that? That's really dead nice of you.'

'Don't be silly. That road's dangerous for you both to be walking on. Come along.'

Natandra said, 'Thank you, that's really kind.'

'Yes, that's smashing,' said Rose.

'What's your name?' Natandra suddenly asked.

'Crofton Clark.'

'What?' Rose smiled.

'Mr Clark. Crofton. That's my first name.'

I could tell Rose wanted to tease me about my name, her mind trying to formulate some cutting barb about it; either she was too ineffectual or she had mellowed towards me at the offer of a lift in a car. Diplomatically, she said, 'I've never heard that name before.'

'It's an old English name. Usually it's a surname. My mam liked the sound of it.'

'I like it,' Natandra stated blankly with neither enthusiasm nor derision.

Fuck me if my heart didn't soar, pathetic dummy.

'Why, thank you.' I pretended to bow a little as we all walked back over the footbridge. 'Natandra's a lovely name. Quite unusual.'

Without expression again, she said, 'My mum is a bit of an old hippy.'

'Me too.' I held up my hand in the V peace sign.

'You're funny, actually,' Rose maintained. 'People say *I* have a good name as well. I'm Rose Weaver but as dad says I'm no good at flower arranging and that's what I should do when I leave school with a name like mine.'

I chuckled. 'That is a lovely name. There's all our roses over there.'

'Yes. I saw them.'

I said, 'They pong a bit at the start of summer, 'cause our gardener is forever chucking all sorts of dung in among them. He put horse dung on them last night but it's a bit dried up so you can't sniff it.'

Rose thoughtfully repeated, 'The gardener.' Then, 'Crikey. There would be a hell of a lot of weeding needed done round here.'

164

'There is, but we leave all that to old Worzel Gummidge.'

They both laughed in recognition at this.

Rose was soon looking around her again as we came closer to the manor house. She glanced scornfully at the wheelbarrow, the planks and crowbar which I had abandoned close to the bottom of the stairway. 'What's that?'

I looked up to where her jutting hand pointed and, to my amazement, I realised all that torn black plastic sheeting was still hanging down from the master bedroom windows. Somehow I hadn't noticed it before. I had just assumed Mrs H would have torn it all away, grabbed the strips and hauled them in by that point in the day.

'Ah. Nothing. Just a bit of painting was being done to the windows up there.'

Rose's interest had evaporated though as she suddenly called, 'Look, it's a bloody thing. A water thing. Like on castles, Leeds Castle on the school trip. I never saw it before 'cause it's all low down. Could you go swimming in that, mister? Crofton? No. Yeuch, it's all floating weed and stuff. Nah. No thanks.'

'It's a moat. From the sixteenth century when Shakespeare was alive.'

'No wonder it's all dirty and stuff.'

In a schoolteacher voice I said, 'Look up there, see how the stone changes on the wall here? See that? That's because the original bit, like this half of the house here, fell down before the last war, and they were going to just abandon the place and let it go to ruin, but this great English architect put in new concrete foundations and he rebuilt this half, so it's actually two halves. Half very ancient. Then this half built before the war. There's an old framed photo of it all fallen down inside.'

I was actually scanning all the windows to see if Mrs H was watching the three of us. Or the intruder? I glanced quickly around the grounds behind us.

165

Their doubtful faces nodded. 'Oh yeah. I see the join bit thing,' Rose said. 'Flipping hell. Half a house. Did he get the place half-price?'

I laughed as we walked past Mrs H's intrusively parked Triumph.

'Two cars, eh?' Rose observed.

I smiled. 'Marko has more than that.'

'I bet.'

'They're all locked up, back at the stables where you just were. Wait there a minute now, let me get the car keys.'

They stood at the bottom of the main exterior stairway where the stone ball was missing, watching after me as I trotted on up, opened the front door, reached in and took the Volvo keys off their hook. They annoyingly have to remain here, as one day years before, Auralie stated that she might need the 'silly old car' to 'jump in and pop to that town for some things'. She never has. Once. The total mileage on her 1976 Mercedes up in the garage remained at 877. Yet still the Volvo keys are officially hung here in case she needs the old estate car.

Sure enough, Rose had climbed up a few steps and was rubbing at the nub where the stone ball had broken off. I was surprised that somehow she hadn't already detected the stone, submerged in the murky water of the moat below her.

'How many cars does he have then?' she spoke upwards at me. 'My brother told me he has a right smart motor he's seen out on the roads round here a couple of times.'

'He does have a nice car. A Ferrari. And his wife has a Mercedes.'

'Oh, wow. Can we go in one?'

'No. This one.'

'Bags me front,' Rose yelled and she ran at the Volvo to yank out the passenger door, her feet crunching on the gravel. Nat just quietly opened the rear door and climbed in.

166

I walked round the front of the car and lowered myself in next to Rose who immediately picked up some of my cassettes from the space behind the automatic gearstick. She began frowning at them, reading the names to herself as she rotated the cases round in her hands. I started the engine up.

'Marko has another good car up at his London house.'

'What?'

'He has an old Rolls-Royce up in the garage of his London house.'

'He has *another* flipping house. Hear that, Nat?' she shouted out. 'He's got another house too.'

I reversed across the gravel.

'Flipping heck, man,' Rose said. 'I mean . . .' She turned her neck savagely and looked across at the full extent of the dwelling before her. 'Is this castle not enough?'

'Well, you see. He's advised by his accountants to make valuable property investments and he does a lot of work up in London. His record company's there.'

'He has a record company too?'

'The band do, yeah. We put out Fear Taker records now on our own record label. Senseless Ambition Records. All the good bands do it now: Stones, ELP, Moodies, Zep, Kinks, the Dead, all have their own record labels. You get a better deal by handling all that stuff yourself and cutting out middlemen who are taking percentages. Big record companies, all they really do efficiently is distribute records. Other than that, they just interfere with the artist.'

'What, touch them up and all that, like perverts?'

'No, Rose. I don't mean that.' I could feel myself colouring but I looked straight ahead.

Natandra giggled in the back. 'You're such a crackpot, Rose.'

'What then?'

'I mean they interfere in the important stuff for a band. Your music. Always angling for hit singles and stuff.' We were now off the low mush-sound on the gravel, curving up the tarred driveway around the cedars of Lebanon. I wound down my window to rest my elbow out.

'What's wrong with hit singles? Wow, electric windows. Check this, Nat.' Rose began to repeatedly lower and elevate her own window using the switch, which was a bit annoying, to be honest. Eventually she left her passenger window fully down and said, 'Weird gearstick too.'

At the end of the driveway as we came to a halt, I said, 'It's an automatic car. Rose, jump out please and go over to that machine there. You'll see a little silver pedal thing. Push it down once with your foot and that'll open the gates for us.'

'Oh, wow, right,' she opened her door then hesitated. 'This isn't a trick, is it? You're not gonna drive off without me, are you?'

'Like I would ever dare do that to you,' I said and tut-tutted. Nat chuckled in the back.

'It won't give me an electric shock, will it?'

'Course it won't.'

She climbed out and ran awkwardly across. I looked at her bum. She had on new-looking white running shoes splattered with mud and a green stain from grass. I turned round a bit so I could see Nat in the mirror. 'And Marko has a house up in Scotland as well.'

'Does he?' she said immediately.

'A big old house up there. In the countryside.'

'Oh.' There was a moment of silence then she asked, 'Whereabouts?'

'Ah. I've never got up that way but it's in the Highlands. The West Highlands. The county of Argyllshire. In the countryside. It's called Abbot's Isle, but it's not actually on an island, though the land includes a few little ones in the loch.'

'Oh. Nice.'

168

Quietly I said, 'Ever heard of the Sensational Alex Harvey Band?'

'Eh. No.'

'Right. They're Scotch.'

'Are they?'

The gates were opening and Rose screamed, rushing back to the car with her arms held out.

Nat laughed, ever amused by her.

As Rose climbed back in and slammed her door she said, 'That's brilliant. I wish we had one of them things on our gates; now we're on the main road we have to keep them closed all the time to keep Tanzania in. Tanzania's our dog. She's great.'

I said, 'Oh yes?' I drove ahead, checking the side lane was clear as I took the left and accelerated on down. An undetected troop of horses had shit all down the road again. Strewth. Then I remembered that I had forgotten to stop and close the gates behind me using the manual 'close' button on the keyboard. These nippers were distracting me and everything would be so much simpler if we just had more remote-control handsets.

'What a lot of horse poops are all on this road for your roses. Wasn't all here when we come up it. Sure that wasn't you, Nat? Ha, ha.'

'Shut up, you,' came Nat's voice from behind.

The main road was traffic free when we reached the telegraph pole so I turned right and accelerated alongside the hedge, the wide-open spaces of Foul Mile beginning away to our right. 'Yeah, all of this here is owned by the estate, but it's rented out to a farm at the top of the lane we just came out of and they use it for grazing and grass. I don't think they're allowed to grow on it which is good for you because you don't want, eh, oilseed or maize growing right up to your back gardens.'

'How not? You sound like my brother.'

'Well then you get cultivators and combines coming right up to your boundary every summer at five of a morning, and you can get all that dust. And pollen off the oilseed. It breeds up lots of field mice too. They like to hide in the growth. An open field and you have much less—'

'There's Mr Forster,' Rose stated, twisting her head round again.

A car had passed us going in the opposite direction.

'They live in the councils. If they saw me they'll be really wondering what I'm doing in this weird car.'

'I meant to say, girls. Don't go about telling everyone that you were up in the studio. It's just our secret. Let's keep it all to ourselves.'

'Why?'

'Well I suppose I'm not really meant to be showing people round Marko's studio, but I know you were interested, Nat. I mean it's up to me who is permitted in the place but don't go telling every Tom, Dick and Harry round the village and school you were up there.'

'But why not?'

'Well, I don't want all the local kids thinking they can just call round and get a tour of the studio. That was a special thing, just for you two. 'Cause. Well. You're cool, you two.'

They both chuckled.

'So don't go telling all your pals about it. Just let's keep it to ourselves. And who knows, when Marko's here, maybe you can come back up to meet him and he'll sign the albums for you in person. Wouldn't that be great?' I quickly added, 'But depends on how busy he is.'

'Okey-doke. We won't tell. Will we, Nat? If that guy does write his name on them and all that and we can't meet him, how are you going to get them records back to me? Will you post them? Rose Weaver. Number 4.'

'Oh, I hadn't thought of that. I mean if you can't meet with Marko and he signs them, obviously it would be easiest if I just dropped them off one day at your house on my way into town; but again don't go telling all the kids round here that you can just call round and get your albums signed or I'll have a fleet of them—'

Brusquely, Rose told me, 'I don't think anyone else round here is into that old band of yours.'

Ouch. That was that. We were approaching the village. I could see the name sign and, of course, before it, the row of new bungalows over on the right.

'Okay then, girls. I'll pull up on the pavement and you can get out but be careful opening your doors. There's no one coming now but they speed along this road.'

'Nah, you can go right into Nat's front bit. Can't he? At number 2. Their gates are always wide open.'

I looked in my mirror. 'Would that be okay, Nat?'

'I suppose. Mum's in, but our car's round at the side.'

'Okay.' I indicated right and there was the sound of that repetitive ticking.

'This one, this one here,' Rose was pointing, jerking her finger aggressively towards the rough, short driveway of a bungalow.

I carefully turned right, in through the entranceway. It was quite a tight fit.

'Ta. That was a good laugh,' said Rose. She had been holding my cassettes in her lap but she put them all back. In the wrong order. She got out but stood with the passenger door open.

I turned my head as I detected a movement on my left. A young woman had come round the corner of the bungalow and she strode quickly towards us.

Nat said quietly, 'Thanks a lot, Crofton,' and she got out of the car then shut the back door, standing beside Rose.

Because Rose had left the door open I clearly heard the woman hiss, 'Where have you been?'

The young woman was standing almost at the front of the car.

171

Nat's voice stated, 'Just up at that big old house place.'

I was staring straight at Nat's older sister. What a bloody stunner of a girl she was too. Taller, with the same face and dark hair. Blue jeans and boots that clung to her legs. Now we're talking, I thought.

She exploded. 'Get in that house, Natandra, and stay in it. And you better get home right now, Rose. I was worried about you both – as usual.' Nat's sister stepped right to the open passenger door, leaned down and looked in at me. Same brown eyes.

I said, 'Hi there.'

'What the hell do you think you're up to?'

I said, 'Sorry?'

'What the hell do you think you're doing?'

'I was just dropping them off. They turned up—'

She leaned far into the car, 'I bet you were just fucking dropping them off. And I'll have the police on you if I hear anything from them.'

'What are you talking about?' I said, 'They'd walked themselves all the way up the main road and it's dangerous so I was—'

'You know fine what I'm talking about. She's fucking fifteen years old, so you and your other weirdos up at your fucking big house or whatever it is, and whatever goes on up there, are nothing to do with her. Right? I hear anything from her I don't like and the police are up there to you in the next ten minutes. Right?'

'What on earth are you getting at?'

'Oh you know fine what I'm getting at. And, you can get your fucking car out our driveway now.' She slammed the passenger door so aggressively that I blinked and I felt like exiting the car immediately to walk around and check for damage. She leaned back down and stared in the still-open window.

I smiled, which was a mistake. It was the use of the word 'driveway' which was amusing for something which was hardly

172

the length of the Volvo. 'Look. If you're concerned about me driving them home, I think it would be easier if I explained to Nat's mother in person my reasoning. I'm sorry if you think there is any need for concern.'

Her brown eyes were on me. 'I am her mother, you silly-looking cunt. Get off my property.' She turned away and walked towards Nat who had paused at the corner of the house, looking backwards with a pained expression, observing this unfortunate encounter. The young woman I had thought was her sister took Nat by the arm and forced her away round the corner.

I could feel my face numb with affront and embarrassment, but also shock at the age of the mother. I mean, for Christ's sake, she was surely in her twenties. I suddenly realised Rose was still standing beside the car door across from me; she leaned down to the window and said inwards, 'Ooops. Bit of a cock-up there. Did you not realise she was Nat's mum too? Ha, ha! Does she look dead young to you too? My dad was the same, he even thought they were sisters. Ha.' She took a quick, almost manic chew at her gum. 'Nat's mum had her really, really young.'

'Blimey,' I said. 'You better get off.'

Without saying anything – almost as if we were old friends with no need of farewell – Rose simply walked away. I put the gear shift into R and looked both ways. I had to pause as a van was coming down from the Maxtelham direction, so I only reversed a few feet then halted. I felt as if Nat's rabid but beautiful mother could counter-attack at any moment, rush me from the house brandishing some harmful kitchen implement. I glanced nervously back at the front of the bungalow.

I noticed Rose was getting herself home not by leaving the property and walking up the public pavement of the main road, but insolently stepping sideways over the low divisions between the private gardens of her neighbours, striding across small hoops of green mesh wire and some recently planted hedge saplings.

173

When the van had passed, I reversed out onto the wrong side of the main road and accelerated a bit aggressively away, over to the correct side. I didn't look – as was usual – across Foul Mile towards the boundary walls of Kitchenly Mill Race. I was so shocked and upset from my encounter that I kept my eyes firmly trained on the road before me. I indignantly maintained I had done nothing wrong, but that didn't stop my paranoid thoughts repeating everything I had said to the young girls. All that 'this is just our secret' might well be construed in a deeply unbecoming way. I could almost hear the words spoken out loud, repeated to me in a law court. For some reason, I imagined Martin Dimelon as the prosecuting lawyer, his determined forehead thrust towards me with business-like intent. I shook my head. And it was that 'silly-looking c-u-n-t' which smarted worst of all, coming from the startling lips of that most attractive woman.

6

*Back on our side lane I had to manoeuvre the Volvo once
again . . . tea from a pot and a little talk from Mrs H
− restoration of a window − a shower cubicle − a Ferrari
motor car − uses of tarpaulin − a memento.*

Back on our side lane I had to manoeuvre the Volvo once again to avoid passing its tyres directly through the fresh horse droppings. I halted the car at the front gates. My hands were trembling, held high on the steering wheel. There was no mail in the box apart from a ridiculous typed circular which had been placed in our box, advertising a garden fete/sale of work at Maxtelham church. Could the intruder have put it in there? As if Marko would have attended such an occasion. I tapped in the code on the gate column.

Once through the front gates I again paused the car to get out and close them behind me. I parked the Volvo back where it had been before I had departed with the two girls, using the switches to wind up both the driver and passenger window which Rose had left fully down. As the windows closed I felt they were a symbol closing my friendship with the two girls and I was hurt and saddened by this. I had liked them. I sighed out loud and tried to concentrate on the chores before me.

They say in a time of crisis to concentrate on your work. You hear people say that kind of stuff, don't you? Things like: I don't know what I would have done without my work to lose myself in? So I immersed myself in my work.

But as I crossed back to the wheelbarrow I noted my eye being continually drawn towards the lane behind the screen of trees, listening for the approach of vehicles behind the brick wall – like in an episode of *Z Cars*, or *The Sweeney*, the spinning blue lights of the police would suddenly assemble. Rather than my conviction that the outside world was drawn to the secret inner world of Kitchenly Mill Race – now my attentions were wholly drawn outside this sanctuary to the more crude world beyond.

179

Conviction being the bloody word. But, strewth. I hadn't done a thing. In legal terms what had I done? Nothing. The feeling was exactly like when I was a nipper and Mam forced me up to confession at Saint Luke's: you wouldn't have minded all the fire and brimstone stuff coming at you if you had actually been committing some corking and outlandish sins. But I hadn't got round to committing any – as usual – as far as I could see. Other than glancing at Rose and Nat's very nice bottoms, Jesus knows I did that.

I found myself again kicking the toe of my shoe at the sawdust which I had spilled on the grass verge; but each time that I skiffed my footwear across, this served merely to knock the sawdust from the chevron blades of grass, driving it deeper in among the furtive roots. If bloody Mullan had the grass kept properly under control then this phenomenon would not occur, I reasoned.

I walked to my kitchenette and back again, cursing that over-sensitive, beautiful mother of Natandra Losey. Another gorgeous but barmy lady – like Auralie. I had fetched a tea spoon from the drawer. The spoon made me think of Creamola Foam.

At the bottom of the stairway, next to the wheelbarrow, I got down upon all fours with an air of repentance. Using my finger I could coax amounts of sawdust into the tea spoon and then toss these quantities outwards onto the moat surface. Soon I had cleared a mentionable amount of the sawdust. It was slightly irritating that the stuff floated on the surface of the moat but I was sure subtle currents would dissipate it. If the moat had currents. Yet it was at that moment that an ominous thought occurred to me with the approach of night-time.

There was a submerged moat light located very close to where I had accidently rolled the round stone into the water. What if at nightfall, this underwater light revealed the ball down there – clearly – for all to see? Like the crown of some ancient Egyptian reserve head submerged off the coast of Alexandria

180

and illuminated for the benefit of tourists; or the tip of an Easter Island moai, sunk in some long-obscure geological upheaval.

I stood up abruptly from my gathering of the sawdust and I peered downwards, squinting intently onto the moat-water surface. Over time, silt, growing roots and other debris tended to obscure the faces of the underwater lamps, so that once or twice a year on certain late summer evenings I would need to go round the moat and the edges of the millstream with an extended brush which I kept up in the stables especially for the sombre task. I would scrape clear the faces of each submerged waterproof spotlight – which were in truth designed for chlorinated swimming pools. I would wear Marko's Foster Grant sunglasses to counteract the dazzle over the hour this chore consumed, adopting an odd appearance of eccentric moodiness, seen wandering the grounds with the shades on but during darkest night.

Daylight reflecting on the brackish soup made it impossible to distinguish the light clamped onto its underwater brick support. I would have needed to go inside and switch them on in order to precisely locate it. Maybe the stone ball had pulverised the damned light during its descent? I hoped so – though that would give rise to further complications. If the lamp had not been destroyed and it did clearly illuminate the incriminating round ball – until I could devise a means to remove the thing from its resting place – I would have little choice other than to get down into the moat water wearing Dan Mullan's unpleasant waders and attempt to disconnect the telltale electric light.

I felt untold pressures were gathering in upon me. I got back on my knees and continued scooping out small quantities of the sawdust.

It was then I heard the front door open above me at the top of the steps. I looked up from my kneeling – well, crawling – position. Mrs H was there with her elbows on the stone balustrade, staring down at me.

'Crofton. What on earth are you up to now?'

'Hi-yah. Ah, I was doing a bit of wood-sawing here, so I was just clearing up this unsightly sawdust. I suppose I could ask Dan Mullan to run the mower over this section if that wasn't too much to ask but I was also thinking, Mrs H, if we used the extension cable could we perhaps bring your vacuum cleaner down the steps here and run it across this section of the grass?'

'Crofton, that's a ridiculous notion. I'm not risking dirty garden muck all up in our good hoover. The carpets have been dirtied enough.' She seemed quite angry.

'But what about that round-shaped hoover you have then, the one with the tube on it? Wouldn't that work?'

'No. Really, Crofton. The sun's going down; how can you see proper at all?'

'The sun's going down, is it?' I looked around at the imminent death of that day. 'Oh. Night will come.' I felt a horrible and irrational fear go through my body at the thought of this.

'Yes. I saw you at this game yesterday too, rooting about over there with tweezers like you'd dropped your pocket change. Was it to get every little bit of broken bulb out? Bless me. You're going to ruin your eyesight good and properly at these entertainments. I mean, when did you even last have your eyes tested? You worry too much about these little details sometimes. You do fuss about the oddest articles. I— Oh . . . What have you done with Jim's big ball? Managed to cart it away already, have you? My, my. Good show.'

I felt delighted at her misguided approval. 'Yeah, ah . . . I have got it out the way. So to speak. I'll need to start thinking about how we can get it put back up on there.'

'Well, Dan Mullan may have an idea.'

'I think we shall have to bring in a professional mason, Mrs H. I feel that might be the wiser idea. I mean, for starters, it wasn't built to the correct standard. With a finial, there should

182

be an iron bar protruding a few inches upwards to fit the ball down onto. Colonel Halmer was granted a shoddy job here. This was done on a lick and a promise. Very shoddy work indeed. The ball shouldn't have just been concreted on top with a slap of the trowel.'

'Would you like a nice cup of tea, Crofton? None of that fancy stuff, just a good Tetleys. Why don't you knock off for a moment, come indoors and we shall have a nice cuppa together in the morning room. Maybe steady your nerves?'

'Oh, okay then. Nerves? I'm not nervous. Not at all.' I glanced over towards the boundary wall to check if the police had arrived yet. 'Hey. We had some visitors. I don't know if you heard. Did you hear?'

'Did I hear what?'

'Did you not hear our young visitors? Two youngsters.'

'Youngsters?'

'Yes, youngsters. Youngsters with Fear Taker albums called round. The usual. Wanted them signed by Marko. So, well I hope you don't think it's . . . I don't know? A breach of protocol or something, but I allowed them onto the property? Nice young folk. They showed such a great interest in things. In Marko's music, I mean. Well. In his instruments.'

'Oh Crofton. You didn't take them up the staircase to the guitar things, did you? Trekking muddy feet from outside on that carpet for goodness' sake?'

'No, no, I didn't allow them into the house. I took them up to the stables' studio. They wiped their feet before going in. We all did. They wanted to see a synth.' I could not recall if any of us had wiped our feet on the studio doormat or not.

'A what? A cynth? They wanted to see some sort of flower?'

'A synth. A synthesiser. It's a keyboard instrument, Mrs H.'

'Oh. Well the kettle's boiled, the cups are warmed and the tea's in the pot; don't let it stew. Come along now.'

183

'You don't think there was anything wrong with that, do you?'

'With what?'

'Showing those kids Marko's studio?'

'Oh Crofton. If I've told you once, I've told you one thousand times. It's not Mr Morrell you need worry about round here.' She dropped her voice and looked all about as if she too was aware of that night-intruder's presence – she mouthed the words without speaking but I knew what words she mimed: 'It's Auralie.' She spoke at normal volume. 'Now look, instead of crawling around there in the garden on your hands and knees would you not help me a little instead? After a nice cup of tea. Would you please help me by gathering those silly, horrible plastic sheets in from the master bedroom windows? Be glad to see the back of the dashed things at last. I did lean out the window to have a bash myself but honestly, I wobbled on the chair and was quite giddy at the height. Anyway aren't those chairs costly antiques? I'm petrified of breaking things round here. It would be a year's wages. And, you see, I don't want to bring on one of my funny turns.'

'Oh yeah. Yeah. I was just going to get the plastic in, Mrs H, after I'd finished up here.'

'Well, shoes off, Crofton. Shoes off please on the big stairs in here.'

I stood, brushing quickly at my jeans then used my hands to sweep my long hair back over my shoulders as it had all fallen forwards. I also rubbed at my collarbone again where the crowbar hit and I winced. That was going to bruise.

I announced, 'I think we'll save on electric when night does fall and, for this evening anyway, I won't bother putting the garden and river lighting on? What do you think, Mrs H? Mind you, that means the prowler . . .' I muttered to myself. 'Oh, never mind.'

'Pardon me? You what? Just come on up here out of that gloom please.'

I made sure I wiped my feet on the mat entering the main air bridge door. All along that air bridge I was seeing two dusks gathering, one on either flank, as if I were being compressed between the subtle difference of each.

I slowly walked through to the morning room, under the 1602 lintel then by way of the wood-panelled walls as usual. Mrs H was pouring tea from a pot into two cups. She hadn't used the 'guest' tea cups kept right there in the sideboard – she had brought two of the kitchen tea cups all the way through.

Though I knew it was wrong of me to feel it, in some way that business with the tea cups really infuriated me. For Officers Use Only. The milk she poured reminded me of the milk I had poured into the patterned glasses for the nice young girls. She was concentrating, so I added, 'Yeah, friendly kids, Mrs H. Nice to come across kids like that. I dunno. Sort of makes you feel more optimistic about the future when you talk to nippers like that.'

She handed me my tea cup in a saucer and I perched – positioned quite far forwards – on the chesterfield, one hand balancing the cup and saucer on the slightly worn and dirtied knees of my jeans, being careful not to tip any tea into the saucer.

'That's nice,' she stated, and she sat down opposite me. 'I'm not so sure Headmistress Rowbotham from town who I meet in the club would entirely agree. Oh, good to get weight off my old feet.'

'Yeah. You take it easy. I'll do the curtains tonight and go upstairs and clear all those plastic sheets away.'

She leaned forwards and said, in a slightly conspiratorial voice, 'Gosh though. Isn't it peaceful?' and she laughed.

I laughed with her. 'Yeah. God yeah. It is peaceful, isn't it?'

'A bit of peace and tranquillity, that's what I like.'

'Well, me too. You're entitled to it. Have you had to do all the bed linen?'

185

'Yes. That too. And the ironing of the last load, though I must confess if there is one luxury about working here it's that the ironing board is always set up for you in the laundry room. Oh how I'd love a laundry room at home with an ironing board always set up. Mr Hilary is such a dear, he always gets out the ironing board for me, sets it up and puts it away. And here I have that nice wireless you got for me to listen to.'

'We should get you a portable television for when you are ironing in there. Just a little one.'

'I suppose that would be quite nice. So I have this load to do but I'll hang it out tomorrow, thank you very much. The weather's so good you can almost relax about drying.'

'Shall I hang the laundry this evening?'

'No, no. It's almost dark.'

'You keep saying that.'

'Well it is, son. You'll be falling over yourself up there on your own in the dark. That electric lamp that you and Dan Mullan jimmied up by the stables' arch doesn't really reach to the clothes-lines I'm afraid. It's a right muddle of shadows. Besides you never can tell with our weather. If there were showers during the night I wouldn't rest; it takes the fabric conditioner out. I can feel the stiffness of a sheet that's been caught outside in the rain, you know.'

'You see, Mrs H. That's a precious skill.'

She chuckled. 'Hardly. Do you need anything for your room, dear?'

'Everything's spick and span.'

'Well I left fresh sheets for you last week.'

'I got them, yes. I'll change them shortly. Thanks. Mrs H, what do you know about the new bungalows they've built just outside the village here?'

'What do I know about them? Nothing. Why?'

'I mean, did you know they were built on our land on the edge of Foul Mile? Where the war allotments used to be? I mean

186

Marko's land? He gave a chunk of the big field over so they could build those houses on them.'

'Did he ever? I never knew that. Comes to mind that was rather nice of him.'

'I suppose so. The two kids that came round; they've just moved into those new bungalows. Nice places by all accounts. A family from the village who were in a council house, and another family who have come down from up in the far north.'

'Oh. Were they nice lads then – not horrors? The language you hear out the mouths of some of these boys in this day and age. I said it to them straight – "Don't you get saucy with me" I told them, when their language was diabolical. I was standing at the bus stop in town just the other day and I assure you . . . it quieted them right down.'

'Oh. Quite right. No. These were two young girls.'

'Girls?'

'Yes. Just young girls. Teenagers, you know. Silly as brushes but nice kids at heart. Into music. Pop music.'

'I see.'

'Just girls. Still at school. One of them lives with her mother. Who is a bit unstable, let me say. Just the two of them alone, I think.'

'Oh that's a shame. Kids need a father in a home. I firmly believe in that, say what you will. Always said it to Mr Hilary though we were never blessed. Especially girls, or they end up as tearaways running with the lunatic fringe.'

'Yeah.'

'You need to be careful about letting children from the village wander around here though.'

'They weren't wandering round. I didn't take them in the house at all. Just escorted them up the stables to see the studio.'

'I see.'

'Frankly, they were quite good fun. It can get a bit dull round here.'

'Well, quite; you see, Crofton. You're not getting out enough these days. Are you, dear?'

'What?'

'Well. What happened to your walks? Gosh. I remember in the early days you used to walk for hours all around these parts. You'd walk to the village across Foul Mile and such like. You even walked all day once into town and back over the ridge bostal. And up Ablemyre Hill to see that eclipse thing. You're missing all of that in this splendid weather.'

'Oh, yes. Well I can't say I was ever one for outdoor pursuits. To be honest there seems so much to be getting on with round here. And partly, back in those days, Mrs H, I was checking the boundaries of the property for security. Examining the boundaries for weak spots with a practised eye.'

She chuckled. 'But Crofton, we don't even have a wall to the Maxtelham end of the gardens. People don't realise it. Even all those country rambler types. People don't believe it from this side of the road but from that side you can just walk straight into the garden.'

'I know that. I'm aware of that. You shouldn't make that common knowledge. But it's the impression. It is the impression of security you create which matters, Mrs H.'

She said, 'Fancy a Gypsy Cream? Mr Morrell has opened the packet, so they shall just go soft otherwise. I'll need to put them in a tin. That *cloisonné* box over there.' She chuckled again then let out an elongated sigh.

'No, thank you. Not for now.'

'I don't think you're eating properly, dear. See, Crofton, life is marching on and perhaps . . . Perhaps, perhaps you need a hobby? You should be getting out and about a bit more.'

'What? A hobby? What do you mean "out"?'

'I mean out, Crofton. Out of your little room at weekends and taking yourself away a touch more from this dreary old place.'

'Dreary? But I love it here. I love it more year by year.'

'I can manage fine with Olive. On some days, hopefully. I mean, I mean, what happened to all your friends, dear?'

'My friends?'

'Yes. Your friends.'

'Who?'

'Well that one. What was he called? Who used to come and stay over some nights. You'd play your records and even your guitars together? The nice quiet guitars. Not Mr Morrell's atrociously noisy ones. Norbert somebody.'

'Oh, old Nobby. Nobby Charles. Our acoustic guitars, yes. He was Marko's guitar tech. But Marko sacked him.' I laughed, which suddenly sounded very cruel.

'Oh. Did he?'

'Yeah. After the European tour last year. The Moon Over Europe tour. Very successful tour – wish I coulda gone across to the old Continent. But you know, probably have got driven mad. These Continentals, Mrs H, I mean. Little jumpers folded neatly over their shoulders, strewth. They're so . . . Continental. Anyway, Marko wants a new guitar tech now. I know why Nobbers got his books.'

'Why?'

'He asked for more bread. More money. Marko took a bit of the old moody and that was that.'

'But surely, you could still go and drop in on the fellow; pay him a little flying visit?'

'Yeah. Perhaps. But . . . He's very good. He's one of the best and a helluva guitarist himself. Not in Marko's league, of course, but knows his way round a maple-wood fretboard. I suppose he'll start working for another rival band now, probably quite a famous one and I would feel I was letting Marko down if I associated with him. In some way.'

'Oh, Crofton Clark.'

'What?'

'Now, you can't base your whole life, the rest of your life, around Mr Morrell. I mean . . . I mean, isn't it about time you had a new girlfriend?'

I was astonished. 'Mrs H, You know I confide in you. I hope you haven't been talking to people about all that.'

'No. I wouldn't. I know that young lady up in Stafford did the dirty . . . let you down badly, and I know it upset you.'

'She broke my heart.'

'I know, Crofton, but that was quite some time ago. Correct me – should I be wrong – but was that not almost five years ago? A young man of your age needs to get over upheavals of the heart like that. Bothersome as they may be. Well, when were you even last up to see your mother?'

'I was there at Christmas. Just after we got the tree up here.'

'That's over eight months ago.'

'So what? I'm busy here. I give her the odd tinkle. I dunno, things have been odd lately.'

'Whatever do you mean?'

'Well, round here. I sense . . . I sense an atmosphere. "Hysteric Atmospheric".'

'What on earth are they?'

'It's a song, by Fear Taker. Fourth album.'

'Oh. An atmosphere? Goodness me. What sort of an atmosphere?'

'I dunno. I suppose it's to do with Marko. I feel he has something on his mind.'

'Gracious me, Crofton. You can't be neglecting your poor mum because you think your employer has something on his mind.'

'He's not my employer.'

She turned sharply aside and looked towards the mantelpiece, sipped from her tea cup. She frowned. I wondered if she was trying to recall if she had dusted the mantelpiece or not. 'He *is*

190

your employer.' She spoke that to the painting bolted in above the large fireplace, an equestrian study in oils by David Morier. The horse looks all wrong and bendy. Apparently it was worth a bomb.

'He's my friend.'

'You've known each other a stretch of time, I will grant you that, but—'

'Marko hasn't been saying anything about me, has he?'

'No.'

I added, anxiously, almost a croak, 'And Auralie?'

'No, they haven't said a whisper, dear. I would tell you if they had.'

I frowned. 'Maude, then? Am I in some sort of trouble with Maude?'

'Far from it, Crofton. Maude thinks the world of you, that you're a wonderful chappie. And that's no bad thing, for her sharp opinions soon catch Mr Morrell's ears. But Maude was asking after you. She just seems to worry about you a little bit like I do.'

'Maude worries, about me? Mrs H, are you giving me the talk? I mean, what are you getting at here?'

'Nothing at all. Maude and I were just chatting over a lovely cup of tea and she believes you could be a little more outgoing. With regards to the world.'

'The world now, is it? Look I can't start going back to the local pubs. Not a man in my position; and if I go into town it's all nudge, nudge, and questions. Men in pubs can be funny to a fellow in my position. It all starts out civil enough but they know who I am – this house and all – and then the snarky remarks sneak in. Half an hour later, I feel the landlord's going to put me out the door. They think it's all drugs and sex up here, Mrs H.'

'Bless me.'

'Girls tied to the ceilings.'

'Oh, more dusting.'

I laughed out loud at her. She was an amusing old bird in her way. Though she was a bit of a rattle chops, telling Marko this and that behind my back. I went on, 'And it's no use trying to persuade people otherwise. Their imaginations run riot. They don't believe for one moment you and I are on the Tetley's and Gypsy Creams. Or else they are trying to bother me for a loan of a half-crown or getting me to buy them an ale. They assume I have money. That used to happen on a quiet Tuesday afternoon in town when I tried to nip in for a swift ale at the Team's Head Brass. People are funny around famous folk, Mrs H.'

'But you're not famous, dear.'

'I mean Marko. People are funny around the mere vicinity of fame.'

'Now what about that young lady from Mr Morrell's offices in London, who telephoned for you here?'

'Who? Nancy! Nancy's a . . . She just does the telephones and filing there. I mean, I mean she worked in accounts at Simpsons department store before she worked for Schillings. Another accountant. Too many of them about in this game. We never had a sniff of them back in the sixties.'

'What's wrong with a sensible head on steady shoulders?'

'She's not into music, Mrs H. She's not proper into her sounds. Honest. She's not even into the Fear Taker, though she works for them. It wouldn't last. Here, wait a minute?'

'What is it?'

'I've just noticed. Why hasn't Olive been in? She hasn't, has she? I haven't seen her about.'

'Oh, well, I felt we were getting along adequately without her. In fact Maude had a word with me about her the last time she paid us a visit.'

'Did she? About things getting pinched out of the fridge?'

192

'No. No. Not that. Be careful what you say about that. Actually I believe Maude was suggesting we maybe . . . Maybe . . .'

'What?'

'That I have Olive in a day or two a week too much.'

'What? Oh, come on. Olive's the daily. You can't have a daily who doesn't come in daily. Economising, are they now? Maybe they have noticed stuff disappearing from the fridge.'

'No. No, I don't believe it's that.'

'See? There's a funny atmosphere brewing round here. Even all this America business. I mean, the Taker have always, always, *always* recorded their albums in some old big house. You know? Every album apart from the first and the *In Concert* one obviously. They got it together in the countryside. Got settled in a splendid old rambling heap in the good old English countryside where nobody could bother them and they could just concentrate on their music, lock stock and barrel. Like when they went to Luxford. Statton-Smith's place, where Van der Graaf Generator record. That was a fantastic house over there. I went one day. Tape it down onto the mobile, then Marko and Gasser overdub solos in London; maybe a few new vocals on top of the guide, and Bob's your uncle. All their albums have been done that way, Mrs H, and now, when there's no pressure on them, like there was in the early days, they elect to go over the pond and record in some expensive studio with damned Yanks! They haven't even been in rehearsal yet to go through the new material that Marko's been working on. It's a bit distressing. I'm not sure I approve. I'm going to have a word with Marko about it. When I get to see him next. I mean, by Jove, at this rate they might make their first poor album.'

She looked at me.

'I mean I'm starting to wonder. I know you might baulk at the extra work involved, but wouldn't it be great for them all to record the next album here? Actually right here in Kitchenly

Mill? Why not? Chris Squire did a Yes album up at New Pipers, that great place he has – biggest thatched roof in England, they say. I know we would have to tolerate Alvin throwing people in the moat. But it would be such fun. There's room for everyone. We can park the mobile anywhere, set up the band – even in the house here. Even in this room! It's all about the drum sound, Mrs H, and we can find a good drum sound somewhere around here.' I turned my head sharply from side to side and noted I was unconsciously mimicking Nat and Rose earlier. 'The stairwell is a done thing for capturing a corking drum sound, Mrs H.'

She nodded very patiently.

'We can run the cables out over the moat bridge; or the whole album can probably be done in the stables. Certainly all the over-dubs can, the vocals and guitar solos. They'd have it down in a fortnight, three weeks at most, if they'd have a proper bloody rehearsal. That's how good they are when they come together and things just start gelling. It's pure magic, Mrs H.'

'I'm sure. Well perhaps those sort of decisions would be better left to Mr Schillings and Mr Morrell? I get the impression, and correct me if I'm wrong, but I get the impression Mr Morrell sees his home here as something of a refuge from his busy working life. When he spends any time in it. As they say, he might not wish to bring his work home with him.'

'It's art. Not work.' I noted that she had finished her cup of tea and when I looked down I had hardly touched my own. I'd spilled a transparent slop into the saucer too. I blurted out. 'So, you feel I should be getting out a bit more? Take walks?'

'Yes. A good old stroll every few days to blow away those dusty cobwebs.'

I involuntarily touched my free hand to my hair as if there really were cobwebs. There had been some picked up off the road barrier from the stables the night before. Then I realised she was utilising a common figure of speech so I shyly dropped my hand.

194

She added, 'Now what is it the schoolmaster made us learn? "I wandered lonely as a cloud? That floats on high o'er vales and hills."'

The moment she said it I thought of me watching those nocturnal clouds that night when I had first witnessed the bloody intruder.

'Tennyson, is that?'

'Wordsworth, Mrs H. That's William Wordsworth. Lord Tennyson is, eh, "linnet born within a cage, that never knew the summer woods", eh, "better to have loved and lost than never to have loved at all."' I felt a bit depressed already. '"One that loved not wisely but too well." Oh no. That's William Shakespeare.'

'You have to preserve your eyesight. You're a great reader of our classics, but you think too much, Crofton.'

'Think too much?'

'You see there you are dwelling upon all this record recording business. Now I don't know the first thing about Mr Morrell and all his making of his famous records but I do know this – that you shouldn't be worrying about it. For, mark my words, no matter how much you do concern yourself your thoughts will have no bearing upon what eventually happens.'

'That's a bit harsh, Mrs Hilary. Marko takes my general advice on many things. Many . . . matters. Why, I used to choose his houses for him.'

'Mmmmm. I feel Auralie might have filled that job vacancy by now.'

'Well, it's best if neither of us discuss what Auralie is and isn't. She's a scratch cat of a lady if ever there was one.'

'That's a bit bold now, Crofton. You mark my words. Don't get a mouth on you like Dan Mullan. Know your place and don't let me down. And you make sure you never get in between Mr Morrell and Auralie, for she will surely always win. And try getting out a bit more, taking an interest in things beyond these walls. I mean, Crofton, in May, you never even left the house to go to the polling station in Kitchenly village hall and vote in the general election.'

'The election?'

'Why, yes. The general election.'

'But . . . But politics isn't my scene, Mrs H.'

'Oh, Crofton. Even Mr Morrell went down there to cast his vote like everyone else.'

'Did he? Oh. I never knew that. Who'd you vote for then? Oh sorry. That's not my business either.'

'Never talk to people about politics or religion, Crofton. But I can tell you as a matter of fact, Mr Morrell and I both voted for Mrs Thatcher and I'm jolly glad we did. I think she'll make a fine Prime Minister. The state this country was getting in. Honestly.'

'Oh. Marko voted for the Conservative Party?'

She emitted that ominous chuckle once again. 'Of course he did. What do you expect? The tax he pays, now he's back living in the country once again and people without their dustbins properly collected. Mr Hilary did not play his part in the Dieppe Raid to see England brought to ruin.'

I had forgotten her old man was at that fiasco. And he was quick enough to remind you he was when you met him too. A bit like fat Jim and his accountancy tirades.

'Now, Crofton. There's something I really have to discuss with you.'

I looked up, my head held tensely. I had the bizarre notion she was about to invite me to the Conservative Club in town, to man a stall on the coming Sunday's fundraiser. Or perhaps a sponsored walk along the ridge bostal. 'What now?'

'All that nonsense with blocking up the air bridge last night. I mean, what on this earth were you thinking? Lucky for you, Mr Morrell and Auralie don't go down to that end of the house.'

196

'But I tidied it all up.'

'It's the fact you did it in the first place. Ridiculous performance. I'm afraid to say it.'

'No it wasn't. I was acting on information and have been for years — because Marko happens to confide in me — I was operating last night under the impression that his two personal accountants were never under any circumstances to meet.'

'And why didn't you know things had changed?'

'I don't get you.'

'Why didn't you know that Mr Morrell's position had changed on his two accountants?'

'I don't quite see what you're driving at.'

'Answer me straight, Crofton. Why didn't you know Mr Morrell's position had changed?'

I looked down at my tea cup. 'Because he hadn't told me.'

She said nothing to let the fact sink in.

'He doesn't tell you everything and you cannot go rushing ahead with your own outlandish escapades without asking Mr Morrell first. Now that's neither here nor there. I know you cleared all that ridiculous rubbish away, but, Crofton, you left two filthy stains, streaked all along the cream carpet in the corridor when you were shifting it all. Or lumbering it into the house. Goodness alone knows which.'

'Oh. Did I?'

'Yes, you did. The reason I didn't hear you with your — young friends — this afternoon was because I was a clear hour and a half getting the electric shampooer out and I was up and down that carpet, over and back on it with two good doses of the stain remover. Really. What a confounded nuisance. Lucky I got it all out and I'll give it a good brush and a vacuum tomorrow as well, to soften it.'

'Oh, I'm really very sorry, Mrs H. I never noticed. I'm ever so sorry.'

'Honestly, all told, Crofton, you make more mess around this house than Molly and Auralie ever do when they arrive. You really do.'

'Oh. Do I? I'm sorry. I weighed down the barrier with a little water in its base so it couldn't fall over, and I found I had to pull them to the bath to drain them out. I mean, I did that in the first place solely because I was afraid of spilling dirty water onto the carpet if I had drained them in situ – so to speak. Of course I did consider—'

'It's neither here nor there, Crofton. Let's not dwell upon all of your little details today. We don't have the time for it, I'm afraid. I know in your own way you thought you were doing the right thing, but those gentlemen were quite shaken up by the odd sequence of events last night and I am quite convinced they will say something to Mr Morrell.'

'Didn't little Molly get the blame for locking fat Jim in his room?'

'She did. But her mother and father aren't dim. When did Molly leave her room to do so? You know perfectly well she was in there with her mother all the time. How did the key get into the bedroom door in the first place, you might ask? But you did not. I had to hint with a little white lie that I had left the key in the bedroom lock and that I had been double-checking that key was the correct one for . . . whatever that silly room is called? We don't want lies going on. Lies are wrong, Crofton, and you should neither put yourself nor me in a position where we have to lie to Mr Morrell. Our employer.'

'I got a bit carried away, Mrs H. I panicked.'

'You panicked about something that's not your business, dear. You and I are here to welcome to this house whoever Mr and Mrs Morrell wishes to be here. And not anyone else. It's not your place nor mine to start deciding that for ourselves. This is not our house. Despite all the time we spend in it.'

'You're right. You're absolutely right. I keep doing silly things. Or silly things keep happening to me.'

'Well, you finish your tea then pop upstairs, try get those bits of plastic off the windows and that will be a big help to me.'

'At once, Mrs H.'

'No. I said sit yourself there and finish up your nice cup of tea. Or has it gone cold on you?'

'No, no.' I lifted the cup, which was shaking, and puttered my tongue into it like Corbisher licking at his saucer of milk. It was stone cold.

'I shall be off shortly.' She looked at her small Timex wristwatch which she wore that odd way, inverted underneath her wrist which women who work with their hands a great deal often do, to protect the watch face. I once saw Mrs H with a painful-looking cut finger and offered her one of the sticking plasters I keep for Molly. She scolded me that she used sinks and cloths and water buckets so much and all day long, that it was simply impossible for her to keep a sticking plaster on her finger during her working hours.

'Mr Hilary is at the Legion this evening, so Carrick Fergus will be expectant of his poached fish.'

She referred to her own voluminous Persian cat. A giant, badtempered bastard who resembled a skunk.

'Since we are at peace again, just leave your tea cup here and I'll clear the things away in the morning.' She was standing up now.

'I'll see you to your car, Mrs H.'

'That's very gallant of you. But we are not at a dinner dance. I do know the way. Off you get upstairs. And Crofton?'

'Yes. Shoes off. I'll see you tomorrow, Mrs H.'

'Yes. Night, night. You're all alone here again tonight so try to get a good sleep and I shall see you fresh as a daisy in the morning. A new start, so to speak.'

'Yes, Mrs H. Thank you for the tea; it was great.'

'Have a few of the Gypsy Creams; it's a sin for them to go to waste.' She sighed. 'Or Olive will be off with them by and by.'

'That's a very good point. I'll gobble them all up. Good night.' I had placed my tea cup and saucer on the side table and I made a show of immediately bending to unlace my Kickers. She left the morning room and I listened as she made her way through the corridor then her soft work shoes fell silent on the thick carpets. Distant as it was, I still heard the front door open and then close. I leaned back on the chesterfield and sighed. Suddenly I felt quite lonely.

To hell with them all, I thought. And to pot with closing all these barmy curtains as well. Perhaps, since I was all alone at Kitchenly Mill throughout the night, I would illuminate the garden lights and dash from window to window until I got a good spy of this blighter of an intruder? I thought upon this for a moment and didn't wonder if I felt just that tiny bit alarmed by the lurker's cowardly lurking. Did the intruder retain the potential for violence? Until all the house doors were locked, then even after, might it be prudent to arm myself with some implement for the duration of the night?

I looked over to the grand fireplace with its ugly Perspex spoiler which Marko was forced by the insurance company to fit, in order to prevent any escaping smoke and heat rising and damaging the large oil painting hung above. I noted the long poker with its brass handle. That would do splendidly as a weapon of self-defence, but I was no fool. I knew the other end would still be black with carbon from the last fire of early springtime, carbon which I would doubtless immediately smear a beige carpet with if I rested the poker for a moment in my line of duty. So I would take the poker outside on a patrol and wash the end quite thoroughly in the moat edge with a rag. I'd check the location of that moat light as well. I would also—

I heard the distant froth of Mrs H's car tyres moving across the gravel.

At the bottom of the main staircase I sat on the third step breathing rather heavily. Perhaps I should go walking again more often? I took off both my Kickers and threw the shoes down dramatically, feeling my stockinged feet cool on the huge and original Tudor flagstones, which are only covered by a large rug in their centre. I got my breath back then slowly went up the carpeted stairs in my socks, humming that evergreen Fear Taker classic, 'The Mental Trade Winds of Gemini'.

On the third floor, I opened the door to Marko and Auralie's master bedroom. The floor had been cleared of Auralie's many vestments and undergarments; the very thick carpet showed Mrs H's fine handiwork: the wheel-trace curvatures of a recent hoovering. The Chinese screens had been folded together and placed in one corner.

It was a very nice view from the master bedroom windows through the lattice diamond panes, so I stood for quite some time watching the blue light change in the garniture and groves beneath; a selection of the oldest glass panes distorted your view and twisted a wonky hallucination onto the specific vista which they framed.

Then I opened all the windows and fixed them on the widest nub of their securing arms. Like a gas, the last dribbles of bird-song came up and into the room; a natural harmony seemed to exist between the interior and the exterior – as if the entire building through its permanence in that place had generated its own calm equilibrium in this world.

I leaned out of the left north-facer and with a smart tug tore the black plastic sheeting inwards. It was easy to haul the stuff back and throw it to the carpeted bedroom floor behind me, but when I peered downwards outside I noticed a foot-long black strip of electrical duct tape had remained still attached lower down on the Tudor brick.

If you studied that old brickwork right up close you could note how hundreds of years of weathering had filed down the once-sharp sides and the arris corners into smoothly rounded edges. Their ochre surfaces showed minute sinkholes, powdery declensions and all the fustering of one hundred and fifty thousand days. In a strange way – if you reflected on the material matter of these bricks – (and I often did) you soon concluded that the house you looked upon today was not the house a human eye fell upon several hundred years ago. Not precisely. It was a bit like the ship of Theseus. Of course the basic structure was an archetype, but any ancient building is really an idealised essence undergoing invisible change. Through decades and centuries some 1/64ths or 1/32nd of an inch of the bricks' surfaces have been shed by the gentle rub of years, by their weather, their rotating days and nights. As skin cells lift hourly off the face of a most beautiful woman – Auralie or Natandra's mother – and are ever replenished, so her face of today is not that of several years before, or hence. So the facade of Kitchenly Mill Race was similarly undergoing a transformation of attrition too subtle for the presumptuous human eye to see. Though we would talk of the house having been here for centuries, my eye did not fall on the very same surfaces that someone admiring the house on the day of Waterloo would have seen. I was seeing a new brick surface fractionally unveiled to this demanding world – like a coast in its faithful work of eroding, the edifice was being worked down into some more base matter until one day – presumably – the bricks would be worn completely away to the fill-material beneath, placed there by hands four hundred years earlier.

Much the same as we look at the South Downs behind us and assume the landscape we see is unchanged for centuries – this is a human fallacy – the grass and verdure is all anew, a process of constant death and rebirth – trees grow and die, copses are cleared or flourish, even the shape of some gullies and stream edges have changed due to excavation, the particularity of wet winters, occasional frosts or summer floods. The world around us is in the process of undressing itself or, instead, of donning new cloaks, while we churn in the middle looking for permanence.

I had to use one of the two Elvetson chairs – which were designed specifically for the bedroom in 1934. They had been scattered through time but Marko sought them out at auction until he collected them together again. Standing on one allowed me to lean outwards then reach a full arm's length downwards without putting any pressure onto the glass frame of the fixed window section below me. I placed a hand on the outer stone sill, gripped the end of the tape and smartly tugged it free. I leaned back in and attempted to flick the sticky strip onto the floor but of course the tape adhered to my finger, refused to budge and I had to peel the blighter off. I repeated the process of removal on each exterior window with great success then began on the sheets of disposable bags fixed on the insides of the windows which acted as a second layer to the partial outer coverings. Again I had to peel the tape with the greatest of care. Some of it was affixed onto the upper wooden window frames where I had to stand on the chair.

Dan Mullan had been smart and respectful enough never to attach any of the sticky tape to the fragile gypsum plaster of the inside walls – much of which was original and could have been horribly torn away by this wholly frivolous exercise for pie-in-the-sky Auralie. Mullan had taped the plastic only onto the beautifully worn wood of the windowsills. I found the process of slowly pulling the black tape backwards very similar to that of removing annoyingly adhesive price stickers from the attractive front cover art on a long-playing album. My tongue came helplessly out of my mouth in concentration as one does not want the glue to separate from the underside of the tape and remain. I peeled the strips with agonising slowness, pausing at one moment as it grew darker outside to turn on the bedroom lights, using that light switch with its bobbled end which moves down with such gentle grace. I made an almost perfect job but in two places traces of the sticky adhesive remained on the varnish of the lower windowsills.

I went through to the bathroom and long walk-in wardrobe section which leads to the strange steam-room contraption. In what was once a cavernous and old-fashioned bathroom, Marko had – for Auralie's use – installed a long corridor of sliding wardrobes in G-plan style. I slid one open giving access to a succession of drawers with small handholds to place your fingers in and ease them open. They moved backwards with pleasing smoothness. I was faced with a shallow, flat drawer, like that which you might see in a jewellers, but festooned with layers of Auralie's pricey, attractive underwear, very neatly arranged. I felt I had no choice, so, using criteria which are complex to explain, I ranged my tender fingertips gently across her super-substantial knicker collection.

I required a slightly large piece of cloth so I can only report that the garment finally selected for the purpose was possibly what is described as French knickers – French-style underwear – in delicate blue and purple silk. It seemed somewhat blasphemous to be using this possession, but at the same time I required a sufficiently delicate cloth since it was to be applied to ancient woodwork. And, frankly, I couldn't be bothered walking back downstairs and through the house to Mrs H's glory hole of mops, buckets, cloths, detergents and cleaning fluids at the rear of the kitchen, by the pantries. Or larders.

I got down on my knees before the windowsill. It was perhaps at this point I felt there might be a little sweat on my brow from my concentrated exertions, so I took the silken knickers of Paris and I gently wiped them across my perspiring brow. What a feeling of pleasure. But on with the job in hand.

I had no choice other than to gently spit onto the lustrous fabric and then I began with a firm polish on the affected areas of the wood where the gum was tacky to the touch and visible on the worn, golden colour of the sill wood. By rubbing vigorously with just one finger pushed in behind the fabric – and using a little more of my spittle – I polished the troubled areas quite smooth. I ran a fingertip across it. Perfect. There was no trace of the sticky adhesive remaining there.

It was only then that it occurred to me that it might have been more considerate to have checked the griffen-footed bathtub side, or within the new large shower cubicle, establishing that no cloth flannels had been available for use instead of this intimate and costly garment, but it was too late to turn back.

A shower. A shower was a new item in Britain in those days. We all still used baths in the 1970s; showers in private homes were a recent American cultural import of the aspirant with a taste for luxury. I had only ever encountered showers in hotels, and only in American hotels did one encounter stand-alone, individual shower cubicles. In fact, that shower in the master bedroom at Kitchenly Mill Race was the first one I had ever seen inside a British dwelling house.

This got me thinking. For sure, I had a little sweat on my brow. Perhaps it would do my dwindling reputation – and of course that foul rumour of my personal cleanliness – a whole lot of good to make use of the now-available shower?

I wandered through and switched on the lights. Very inviting. The modern lamps were recessed into the varnished pine of the bathroom ceiling – including one light actually inserted into the roof within the large shower cubicle itself. I could only presume it presented no electrocution risk? I noted the shelf filled with

205

inviting-looking unctions, embrocations and lotions of differing colours.

I stripped off all my clothing with excited haste. But my Levi jeans fell to the ground with a heavy weight which actually struck my left toes quite painfully. Strewth, as well as the Volvo's, it was that big set of keys to the studio which had been in there all this while. I hopped for a moment then turned on the large – admittedly complicated – tap control and mixed a very agreeable temperature. The water fell down with a remarkable, almost aggressive gravitational force and I knew from back in the days of the builders being at work that this was because the cold and hot water tanks which fed this shower were positioned directly above it, so the force was both gravity-fed and mains-pressure assisted. There was no flannel and it would have been somewhat impolite and an intrusion of privacy to use a cloth flannel belonging to Marko – or Auralie – anyway, so I reached down and took up Auralie's underwear once again which I had dropped on top of my own clothing. I stepped in beneath that crushing descent of water. It was an invigorating torrent. I slid the smooth door behind me. What a feeling of exhilaration. Below the vertical downlight one could witness the individual droplets of steam condensation massing and circling so as to form shoal-like shiftings and undulations. I was puzzled by the many bottles and their potential functions – there was a right old apothecary; what could they all possibly be for? There was nothing as straightforward as a bottle of Head & Shoulders anti-dandruff shampoo.

The fall of the water was so overpowering it was somewhat difficult to see and even to breathe at certain moments; I rinsed the fabric clean of any adhesive then used a bar of delicious-smelling lemon soap (not, I took careful note, the standard Cussons Imperial Leather or Knights Castile hand soaps distributed on the sink edges throughout the rest of the dwelling:

Officers Use Only). Angrily, I lathered up a palm full of suds in Auralie's soft French knickers and I used this same garment to soap all my humble body: around my face, in my ears, under my arms, down my chest and reaching round my back. I lifted my feet to soap between the toes, then I gave the necessary attentions to my private parts. Round behind and in front too. Then round behind again to rinse the soap and again to my frontal anatomy giving special attention to all hidden crevices and covered glands. And again. With Auralie's glistening silk underwear sparkling in that vertical downlight; Auralie, who was so often naked just where I stood, completely naked with her upstart breasts hardly moving in her free-limbed haste and—

An accident occurred. An inevitable accident of gender-based biology. But I ensured I thoroughly rinsed her underwear in the convenient and hefty waterfall still descending upon me. And I would be sure to have the item properly laundered. Actually, that might be a little awkward – how to explain to Mrs H the presence of one rogue set of female underwear in an unrelated wash? I would personally take the garment to my own room and there give it a thorough treatment and hand wash using my tall tub of sink-side Vim. Then I would dry the silk ration on my little private clothesline.

I turned the shower taps off, squeezed the water from the light knickers and stepped out the shower. Now I was met with the challenge of selecting an appropriate towel. I found the cupboard where they were all neatly stacked and I searched through them. Sure enough: here was a large, stiff, starched white towel bearing the name and embroidered symbol of the Drake Hotel on Park Avenue, New York! I embraced it like an old friend from happier times, drying my body down thoroughly and roughly scruffing my hair.

It seemed a sacrilege to have to dress again in my own clothes after working hard in them. They had accompanied me through the tribulations of the day and frankly had accrued something of the exertions of these hours. I had been pissing sweat in them, hotter than a docker's armpit at times. It even crossed my mind to go through the wardrobes and – briefly – borrow some of Marko's own clean clothing. Perhaps some garments which were familiar to my eye from world-famous photographs of him? We were of similar build. Bollocks. We were not. We were of similar height but my Prince Hal lacked the slight, ever-so-slight distention of a healthy and characterful English beer belly which it has to be recorded here was considerably subsiding on me as my absence from pubs continued. So I dressed again in my own modest fucking garments.

I suppose it's a bit like that time I met Lowell George in – of all places – the Wheatsheaf pub on Rathbone Place. He'd lately agreed to produce the next Dead album, and Little Feat had been staying at the Montcalm Hotel up by Marble Arch – at that time a hotel much beloved of the music and movie industries, a hotel so exclusive it was not listed in the phone book nor in any London hotel guides. Sometimes I wonder if the place ever existed at all and might in fact have been a figment of my imagination, though many times I met Schillings and Marko in its lobby as they often conducted business from a suite there. Or did I meet them at the Montcalm? Was it perhaps in Blakes Hotel, Kensington, and I am confusing them? Anyway, Lowell was leaning against the bar of the Wheatsheaf. I'm pretty sure it was the Wheatsheaf. He was wearing blue denim dungarees and I said to him . . . actually, no. No, it was nothing like that at all.

I shoved my fingers through my partially dried hair to heave it all away from my face and it thumped the back of my Alan Parson's Project T-shirt with a dead weight. I had not really dried my hair that thoroughly. I placed Auralie's almost weightless, damp rag of underwear in the other pocket of my jeans – the one not containing the bunch of keys. The slight humidity of the fragile fabric resting so close to my crotch gave her underwear the feel of a deeply erotic totem with real potential, lodged in such close proximity to my loins.

I closed and secured the windows as it was now full darkness outside; with all the bedroom lights on I did not want any invasion of night moths, long-legged flies or other nocturnal insects and crawling things which emerge from the verdure of our . . . ornamental cultivations each summer.

I gathered considerable quantities of the black plastic together but then I devised a cunning innovation. The large towel from the Drake Hotel was now so damp from my drying, it formed an ideal and weighty cloak in which to entrap the multitude of black plastic and compress it all together into place. I was able to construct a large bundle within the towel. I clicked off the master bedroom light then outside I switched on the lighting of the Turkish staircase. I crossed to the balustrade and looked down.

Above me were the astrological symbols of the extravagantly painted ceiling. In the middle of the stairwell a long chain descended which emerged from the exact centre of the gilded, solar plaster ceiling rose, symbolic of the sun; it suspended a Murano chandelier which hung only halfway down the full height of the stairwell. With the burden of the damp towel and the rustling plastic filling in my arms – as if I was carrying my new bride over the threshold – I descended the stairway. The only bride I had was the humid silk in my pocket.

It had crossed my wildly adventurous mind to simply toss the bundle down the height of the stairwell to the ancient flagstones far below, but I did not. I saw the potential disaster in this act; if the package unravelled during its vertical decent and caught the chandelier on the way down, we would have yet more broken bulbs along with shattered decorative Venetian glass baubles. A forlorn piece of black plastic might remain hung from one chandelier arm, resembling some ugly, torn shard of deceased passenger's clothing draped on a shattered tree branch after a horrible air disaster, like that Turkish DC-10 outside Paris.

At the bottom of the staircase I sensibly placed the towel and plastic bundle down on the flagstones and here I laced my shoes back on. I illuminated the house lights through to the air bridge, picked up the package then moved onwards through the wood-panelled corridor. I paused again at the main doorway, for now came the moment of truth which I had been postponing.

I put down the towels and plastic then crossed to the painted wooden box on the wall which contained the switches for the external lighting. I opened the swift-moving little door and looked at those familiar switches, once again identified by small adhesive stickers in the handwriting of yours truly. *Driveway Lights. Garden Lights circuit 1 (moat and back slope). Garden Lights circuit 2 (mill race). Garden Lights circuit 3 (lower river).*

As indicated, these corresponded roughly to the moat and manor house area exterior lighting, the first and secondary mill house areas, e.g. the mill race extending from the first 'weir' as far as to the second footbridge, and the third switch controlled the river lights all the way down to the water's bend, and those small floodlights coloured by a green plastic film placed in by the weeping willows trunks – which make a luminous emerald tent of each of them at night.

I switched on only *Garden Lights circuit 1 (moat and back slope)*, then I stepped out the front door into the soft summer night. I peered carefully over the brick balustrade into the moat water.

Blasted damnation. As I had feared, that particular moat light was positioned precisely behind the recently submerged stone ball. The active cauldron of light was about one foot away from it. There the round stone ball was, almost as if the submerged moat light on its concrete support had been specially positioned only to illuminate the stone, and that the round ball was in fact a distinctive work, carved by a collectible sub-aquatic sculptor. It looked like the skull of Cyclops, his one eye about to lift clear from the moat surface, who had strolled across the bottom of some placid lake and was going to pop up and scatter a settlement of shoreside fishermen.

I sighed and whispered oaths at the hemisphere of darkness. I glanced around out into the garden, across the Volvo and car park, down at the kitchen doorway, frowning in fear of a crouching witness, then I turned back inside and slammed the main door closed behind me.

Then came my Archimedes moment. I found myself standing in the corridor staring down at the white towel which was roughly wrapping up the black plastic on the floor. It was this sight which inspired me.

I immediately stepped to the little wooden cupboard where the car keys are hung and I returned the Volvo keys, but at the bottom of this little cupboard are two thin drawers, only large enough to hold matchboxes, but with my fingers I plucked from one drawer an unmarked set of car keys and put them in my jeans pocket alongside the cool underwear.

I scooped the big towel swathing the plastic and I went on ahead, pausing to grunt awkwardly, having to push the large, bulky package in against the walls to allow my fingers to fumble for the light switches. Because I had not drawn any of the curtains that particular evening, it felt as if the illumination of the interior was throwing it open to examination from the outside. I began to regret not closing the curtains. The solution would be to switch off all the interior lights. I decided I might just kill all the electric at the fuse boxes and have done with it — illuminated moat and the bloody lot.

Down in the kitchen I began binning the plastic sheets in the tall reflective alloy container used for bulk items such as this. Much like a boxer, I took the towel and I draped it over my neck so the white cotton hung down the front of my torso on either side. I made my way back through to my kitchenette. I finally rehung the studio keys but selected the garage and stables sets instead.

I grabbed my rubbery night torch and my bravery was evident, since despite carrying no weapon of self-defence against a potentially violent snooper, I made my way up to the stables' main entrance arch – big enough for an old horse-drawn coach to have once moved beneath. I admit I had slashed the torch from side to side as I ascended the track in darkness. Mrs H was correct as usual. When I switched it on at the waterproofed light switch fixed to the arch pillar, the lamp hung on the archway did not extend its illuminations as far as the washing lines in their dip of garden. I would need to deal with that.

I used the keys to unlock the left-hand garage door which swung upwards with quite a considerable degree of rattling, metallic noise. But paradoxically this noise is a useful security measure so one might overhear any potential . . . etc., etc.

Before me was the number plate MM 717 and the curved, bulbous rear of the delicious Ferrari Dino.

I walked away though to the stables' storage area, unlocked the wooden double door unit, reached round for the light and went in. There behind the old threshing machine was the bulk of Colonel Halmer's vintage Wolseley. But what interested me was the tarpaulin material which had been draped over this vehicle. Yes. The material was strong: thick canvas but with a coating of modern polyurethane, and studded around its edges were a measured sequence of large eyeholes reinforced by metal washers. I tugged and heaved that dusty tarpaulin backwards, slapping free the matter which over the years had fallen from the roof beams above. It had been weighed down with a breeze block on one side only and came away free as I scraped it off the vintage car.

On the far wall – the southerly wall, if you would prefer to term it – were a selection of strings and tow ropes which Dan Mullan kept for various practical purposes around the grounds, such as for instance, tying sapling supports, lashing the Christmas tree or securing the silly little fibreglass rowing boat to the bankside when we cast off in it to do some maintenance work around the struts and underside of the track bridge or footbridges in the middle of the mill race.

I selected a series of thinner ropes, sensitive not to choose too thick a diameter which would be impossible for me to knot – but I still required one with considerable strength. I went back through to the garage and, using one of the stronger tow ropes, I got down on my knees and stretched out flat on the concrete floor at the rear of the Italian sports car. Then I knotted the thicker rope on the underside rear tie-down point. Not ideal, as it was not completely centred, but it would have to do. I tied a double knot then I secured the other end to one of the eye holes on the large tarpaulin which I had dragged out from the stables.

At this point in the operation I craftily walked backwards, taking the tarpaulin in both hands, sliding it across the cobbled stable yard, a movement which also laid out the tow rope. This would give me ample room to reverse.

I placed a selection of ropes into the foot area of the passenger seat and it was with considerable satisfaction – if not with a sense of confident entitlement – that I opened the driver's door of the Ferrari, spread the large towel from around my neck on the finely crafted leather to give it a measure of protection, then settled into the driver's seat of the coupé. I put in the ignition key and started her up. She fired first go with no need for even a mere shot of choke. Just the sound of a Ferrari engine igniting up in that enclosed garage space, like a mature elephant disgorging a rich bolus of giant hairball, made me feel a puff of pride towards my mate Marko and his achievements upon this earth.

It was impossible while in neutral not to touch again the polished chrome accelerator and to snarl out another herald of vast potential power. And again. Take that, silent Sussex night! Tremble and obey. I pulled the driver's door shut, which closed with that heavy, solid sense of craftsmanship applied across the whole vehicle.

Let me assure you that Ferrari gears are full of character and they take some getting used to – especially shifting the thing into second – you need a practised and gentle touch for it, or you don't get there easily, but I'd had plenty of experience around the driveways. I dropped the handbrake, angled the chrome-topped stick, watching the reverse lights illuminate the courtyard behind, then I drew just an inch of clutch – the wide wheels on those fat tyres oozed backwards from the garage interior. I had to be careful the unfurling rope being drawn in beneath the vehicle was not snagging in any fundamental way.

The Ferrari Dino sits low on the ground, you almost feel your bum could scrape the roadways. Leaning backwards you sense you could at any moment leap forwards uncontrollably – but I kept her in first and simply made off with a lift of clutch again. Even in first gear, kettle drums are all around you echoing in the stables' courtyard; the rope took up the slack and then, with a dramatic hiss, as if I were being pursued by some demonic herd of rattling crabs, twenty-five feet behind me the tarpaulin was towed, slithering over the cobbles of the stable yard.

The sound of the dragged tarpaulin was like a sinister, active avalanche or mudslide behind, as if urging me on down a gradient.

The headlights flashed on the glass of the attendant's booth and drenched the wide lawn beyond with a forensic spread of solarised illumination. I had to lean out the car with my cheek held curiously downwards, my hand loose on that fat, cowhide steering wheel. The following plastic made a shingle-like sound as if stirred by waves. I stopped the car just by compressing

214

the clutch, killing the engine but keeping the battery engaged for the lights.

I grabbed all the smaller ropes out the footspace of the passenger seat and hauled the tarpaulin over to the moat edge with both hands, my body leaning backwards as the huge sheet rustled and dragged gravel chips.

I began to remove all my clothes, squinting towards that submerged light. When I was totally naked, I tested the moat edges with my bare toes. Chilly. What bothered me most was anticipating the feeling of the reedy, mucky moat bottom on my soles and between my toes, so I jogged bollock-naked up the steps, leaned in the front door and grabbed a set of the wellies which are kept there. Strictly speaking, these were Marko's wellies, but they had often been put to communal use before. With the wellies on, in my birthday suit, about that dark garden, I must have made a fascinating rural study for any potential snooper, but to hell with him – or her, served them right – let this sight be my revenge on any rancid and prying eyes.

I moved my calves very cautiously and searchingly into the edges of the moat water and it was as I hoped – almost like a natural slope, the edge did not become sheer at any point, but gradually descended towards the moat bottom. A bit of a passion killer, as that moat water breached the top of the wellington boots, slopped and gurgled in around my bare feet. Summer or not, it was bloody freezing.

Oh, shall we dip at midnight?

Into the moat I gingerly and grudgingly went, the ropes draped over my shoulders as the towel had been, pulling the tarpaulin behind me like a mad king's train of robes. Tugging the resistant weight of the fabric slowly into the water actually gave me a sense of security, something to hold on to as the water came up above my crotch, but not quite to my

215

waist, though I knew it grew slightly deeper over towards the gabion shoring of the other embankment, beneath the manor house walls.

Essentially, I used the tarpaulin like a sling; there was enough of it so that I could submerge it, the dark water creeping in over its folds, having to duck in my chest or place my face very close to the surface. I pressed and tucked the fabric as far in under the stone as possible. More importantly, I could tug it snug round each side and then feed the smaller ropes through various eye holes to enclose the whole thing. As long as the tarpaulin was taut enough to capture the stone, and the stress from the tow rope on the eye hole was not too much, there was no reason why a car of such awesome power should not slide the stone up the sloped embankment and out.

I anticipated that the three-foot strip of lawn was going to be damaged – if not gouged out entirely by the stone traversing it, but I took the precaution of dumping wellington boot after boot full of water onto this segment of grass to give it adequate lubrication. At least it would put a final end to that damned sawdust and if I was questioned about any damage by Mrs H or Dan Mullan, I could claim I scarred the lawn trying to wash and rake every fleck of that sawdust out. I mean, that was a reasonable enough explanation, was it not?

I had to stand by the door of the Ferrari and try to dry myself off with the towel as best as I could, so I did not blemish the car interior. I was bloody shivering I can tell you, but England expects that every man will do his duty. I couldn't drive in wellingtons so I put my Kickers back on then laid the towel upon the driver seat and put my bare arse down on it, starting the engine up. I turned the steering wheel hard over, moved the vehicle slowly round into starting position, slightly taking up the slack on the tow rope which led into the moat and vanished beneath the surface.

216

I knew if the stone resisted and the car had to struggle, there was a real chance the rear wheels could spit out gravel chips in the direction of the moat, which might hit one of the ground-floor windows, but I was sure their trajectory could not be so. They would drop into the moat before reaching the other bank.

I kept the gears in first and slowly drew the car forwards to take up the strain. I tensed, waiting for the damned rope to snap. I felt the great vehicle slightly hesitate; its guttural exhaust rose a fraction and the moody RPM needle on the deep-set dashboard flicked up like a dismissive finger; my eye was rigid to the moat edge. The tow rope tautened, vibrated intensely from side to side then held true and dead straight. Before I even anticipated it, the bulky folds of the tarpaulin emerged from the moat surface, sloughing water aside, and, as smoothly as a blob of lard skidding across a hot frying pan, the stone, shrouded in its fabric cocoon, slid up the side of the short embankment and straight across the grass strip. I saw it embed a few inches as it entered onto gravel and there was a whooshing sound of it crossing the chipped stone.

I punched the Ferrari symbol, stabbing the car horn once, which sounded out towards the cedars of Lebanon. I jumped from the car, clenching my fist and pumping it in triumph – my crown jewels shaking. I called out into the night, 'You must imagine Sisyphus happy.'

The grass verge had been almost totally unaffected by the tarpaulin crossing over it! Other than the blades of grass being swept in the turning place direction and the muddy water which had discoloured it, there was no significant blemish.

I had feared the weight of the stone would not be distributed effectively and the tarpaulin might just sit down and fix itself in the gravel, but the tarpaulin had distributed the weight wide enough. Perhaps the round shape of the stone also cancelled out any distinct pressure points?

217

I got back in the car and slowly drew forwards again, heading towards the metalled drive; a long, obvious groove was being gouged in the gravel by the weight of the finial, but this could easily be raked back into flatness. I had also feared the friction on the tarred driveway being too much – the stone ball could rip through, or leave a telltale streak of stone up the dark macadam, but the towed burden slid across the tarmac easily and then I was soon off the tar and onto the grass and packed-earth track. The stone ball followed obediently behind in its shroud.

On the slight slope up to the stables' arch and the washing lines I gave it full clutch and a touch of gas; my odd convoy continued – as if I were pulling a stone ball to be loaded onto a medieval siege catapult!

I dragged the stone on past the stable archway then a short distance down the track which had been surprisingly well strimmed by Mullan.

Out of the car and totally starkers, I can assure you I scanned the side of the old stables' wall, looking for high-grown stinging nettles. I had angled the tarpaulin as far over to the right as I could, but I would still need it clear off the track before I could reverse the car back out. I was blessed again on this night. I found that by bending over and heaving up with real force I could actually roll the stone finial with relative ease off the fabric and into the verge. There it lay just as envisaged, off the track and resting by the wall – as if it had always lain on this spot.

I untied the tarpaulin and returned it by foot, dragging it backwards across the cobbles to the garage. It was a bit slimy and wet, it showed scorings on its underside, but I returned it inverted over the top of the old Wolseley and there it would dry out in a day – who was ever going to notice?

I ensured its interior was spotless and returned the Ferrari to the garage, parking it beside the Mercedes, draped the towel round my shoulders, selected a garden rake which doubled up

218

as a defensive weapon (should I be attacked in my undressed vulnerability), and I locked up, carrying all the keys back with me.

Naked under the starlight, I walked back down to the front of the manor house with the torch illuminating my path. I was whistling as I went. 'Jerusalem'. ELP's version of course, from *Brain Salad Surgery*.

It was a simple matter to smooth the gravel chips level using the rake then I placed the tool in the wheelbarrow. The wellington boots I would need to dry out in sunshine, but meanwhile I left them in the barrow, gathered my dropped clothing up from the ground and went back inside the front door of the air bridge, returning the Ferrari keys to their rightful place.

What a constructive night's work! I would tell Mrs H I had just wheeled the stone ball away in the wheelbarrow and deposited it behind the stables. If people would just leave me alone, I would have that house running correctly in perfect order. Surely I was deserving of some special reward for all this? I removed my shoes but had to struggle to put on my socks again, since my clammy feet had moat dirt between my toes and streaks of decayed plant matter clung on them and onto the rest of my naked, shivering body which was quite beaked up with muck. May I point out, I could not sit down on the stairs to put my shoes on. Of course I couldn't risk marking the stupid carpeted stairway – by leaving an inexplicable muddy bum print.

At the bottom of the stairs I had dropped my pile of clothing. I retrieved Auralie's underwear from my Levi's jeans then I slowly climbed back up the stairs to the master bedroom where I once again utilised the available shower to have a long, rather hot wash, using some of Auralie's strange shampoo on my hair.

This time I used a plain white towel to dry myself with – identical to the type I am regularly issued with over in my own quarters, so I knew I could hand it in as laundry which had been for my own use. The Drake Hotel towel, by then stained brown, I would conceal and launder privately.

I simply – and I feel justifiably – could not be expected to dress yet again in my dirty T-shirt. I knew Marko's trousers would not fit me so I had unwillingly pulled my own jeans back on, but I went through Marko's closely packed wardrobe for shirts. I recognised several garments, such as his zany jacket with sewed-on patches of reflective silver, which he had worn to the *Melody Maker* Awards in '74 or possibly '75? I also acknowledged the shirt which he was photographed in on the 1976 North American tour. I tried it for size but there were some challenges around my waist area. If you asked me, Marko should have thought about putting on a touch of weight. What he needed was a damned good surf 'n' turf dinner now and again with a knickerbocker glory or a banana fritter to finish off.

I found a corking shirt which I knew he wore on the '73 tour – it was made of some shiny material, but after a few minutes of initial enthusiasm this also was uncomfortably tight on me. A bit of a bloody pest this wardrobe was, to be frank. Very disappointing indeed. I had pulled out quite a few items and just by looking at them I knew they were unsuitable.

Eventually I came upon a neat black shirt from Nudie's with a slim flame of orange and red embroidery on its sleeves and up the front – and a fantastic long collar. I was pretty sure he had worn that shirt for an interview with the *New Musical Express* in 1976. The one when he was photographed at Trident studios round that alley where he had been mixing the *In Concert* album – but in that photo of Marko, the shirt was slightly obscured by a velvet jacket and a scarf. I would need to check my collection of old *NME*s later to confirm with certainty it was the same shirt. This shirt seemed a bit more capacious on me. If this shirt fitted me then why couldn't other ones?

220

I returned the other shirts on their hangers to his wardrobe, hoping they were roughly in any 'correct' order.

I tidied up carefully in the bathroom – had to flush some leaf matter from the plughole – and went downstairs carrying the towels, my dirty Alan Parson's Project T-Shirt and underwear. I caught my reflection in several of the uncurtained black windows and I thought I looked pretty damned cool in Marko's shirt with my damp hair combed back.

I went about locking the doors of Kitchenly Mill Race – ensuring the porch chandelier was left illuminated. I made my way back to my kitchenette where I put the plain towel in my laundry bin and concealed the Drake Hotel towel under the sink. I made myself a nice (hot) cup of cocoa. Ovaltine to be accurate. Or was it Horlicks? It was a bit like that time . . . no, it wasn't.

I sat at the kitchenette table on the chair where Rose had rested and I thought about those two girls. When the beverage was consumed, I locked the doors on that side of the house and went upstairs to my bed.

I had fancied giving my teeth a clean but had refrained from using Marko's electric toothbrush – much as it appealed. I do believe in regular brushing, so I went to my small toilet to the right-hand side at the top of the stairs. I stepped in the bathroom and switched on the light.

As I moved towards the sink something caught my eye: floating in the water of the toilet, a small chocolate-coloured and well-formed four-inch human stool – much larger, but thematically similar to some of Corbisher's own creations, consisting of individual pearls but firmly linked in a harmonic sequence; it was Natandra's poo, which I had heard so much about earlier that day. To me it was almost legendary.

I turned away for a moment in slight shame for the young girl that I had to witness this intimacy, then I stepped back and reached out for the flush handle. But I halted. I couldn't just

221

flush it like I had that guck from the moat in the master bedroom toilet. I looked down again at the oh-so-human remnant.

Then my degeneracy was saved by a purely poetic thought. This memento of that fair lass – the only memento I would ever have, it seemed – deserved a more noble fate than being flushed into the septic tank sunk at the rear of Kitchenly Mill; a large subterranean tank with a curved venting pipe, situated behind the tennis courts, towards the lower part of the boundary before the brick wall turns sharply east in an elegant right angle of fantastic craftsmanship. The septic tank never seemed to require emptying as Dan Mullan was a dab hand at tending its self-decaying properties. For instance, shortly after we had all settled in to Kitchenly Mill in 1973, I had been alarmed one day to witness Mullan carrying a lifeless badger by its back leg across the footbridge while I was at that moment standing outside my kitchenette door – snipping my fingernails if memory serves. I was shocked at the beauty of the long-snouted, dead creature.

'Christ, Dan,' I had called out. 'What did you do that for? It's beautiful.'

'Don't be such a city boy,' he replied. 'This brocker was done on the side of Maxtelham road, so I stopped for him.'

'What the hell do you want with it here?'

'Toss him into septic tank, boy,' he had said. 'A bit of wildlife breeds up those fat maggots nice and rich in there and keeps it all down. You find any dead creatures round here, birds, rabbits that the cats have taken, you be sensible and toss them all in through the tank hatch, even some chicken out your fridge that's gone off will do once in a while. But nothing breeds up the maggots good like a fresh bit of wildlife, that's how you keep the bacteria and the maggots up and the slurry down, eating away at all that expensive shit your crew make. Toss those cats in themselves for such as I care; feckless brutes – not even ratters them two.'

222

What a noble grave for the poor badger. I have made a point of never venturing near that damned tank since.

I went down to the kitchenette and rattled about in the cutlery drawer. There was an odd large spoon there with holes in it. I am no cook and I only used the thing on occasion to fetch a boiled egg out of the pot. I took the large spoon upstairs and I leaned over the cistern and gently captured the poo with it – like back in Stafford when the gypsy chaps at the fairground used to dip into their bucket to scoop out a poor little goldfish; they would place it in a little see-through bag for you to take home – if you had got lucky enough to stick three darts into the pinned-up playing cards.

I scooped Natandra's handsome little memento up and let the water which came with it drain off the spoon into the cistern. Then holding the spoon far out ahead of me very, very carefully, I began to go gently down my dark stairs and I took the interior door back through to the main house.

My intention was to carry her prim little deliverance out of the front door and over to the large triangle of roses in the garden; there I would toss it far into the centre of the blooms and what Nat had left behind would slowly contribute to those perfumed petals lifted to the sky.

I walked through the smaller air bridge, over the beige carpet. The bulb light from the Regency arch area behind me lit the way ahead on this section. I tipped the spoon a fraction too far forwards, lunged ahead to adjust and saw the turd fall straight down as a swift black blur; I hopped on one foot to avoid where it had fallen but I trod hard onto it with my right shoe.

'No. No. No.' I repeated. Probably more times than that. Many more. I sat down on the carpet and peeled off my shoe, holding it helplessly.

223

Once I had switched on the air bridge lights I looked down blankly. The human faeces had been trodden on heavily and plastered into the carpet fibres. It was specifically on the slightly bristly patch which Mrs H had shampooed clean earlier that day. I scraped as much of it as I could back onto the spoon and, in defeat, flushed the ruins of it down the toilet in the first bedroom.

I did consider getting a Stanley knife and cutting the affected area of carpeting out then replacing it with a piece of carpet I could also slice out from underneath a piece of furniture; but this seemed a doomed concept so I went to work with several basins of hot water and Sqezy liquid. It took me an hour or more to get the carpet blemish-free. In some ways it was a blessing that the unfortunate incident occurred exactly on the site of the previous stain, as any possible traces could be passed off as originating during the notorious earlier event.

I felt like another shower by the time I had finished but was too tired. On my way upstairs I noted that while my jeans were unmarked, I had got some shit on Marko's shirt, so it was off with that. The illicit laundry was mounting up.

I slept poorly and dreamlessly, but awoke towards dawn with a thick head. Sure enough, I had gone and caught a cold from my naked salvage operation. I dragged myself out into the grounds to ensure all seemed normal in daylight and, of course, despite how poorly I felt, I had to push and heave that damned wheel-barrow up to the stables with the crowbar and the rake, the wet wellies and all the rest.

Once I returned to my room I collapsed. I rose later in the day and shuffled through to the manor house in my pyjamas and Dougal slippers (checking the significant carpet-cleaning effort as I went) to tell Mrs H that I had caught a rather severe sniffle, and she was ever so sympathetic. She even made me some soup later and brought it over to me in my sickbed.

I learned Baraclough had telephoned and got Mrs H on the line (I had disconnected my phone due to my illness). Marko had taken up residency in his Chelsea house for a while and there was talk of him and Auralie returning to the United States once again before Molly had to go back to her school. Auralie had asked for certain items of clothing to be placed in a suitcase and sent up to her in London and Olive was handling this matter. A car was to be sent down at some point. I was far too infirm to deal with such trifling matters.

I often had the radio on at low volume during the period of my convalescence and strike me down if I didn't hear 'Cars' by Gary Numan. It was absolutely blooming brilliant.

7

The sun occupied the southern sky and some lengthy clouds rested above . . . a tree of aluminium – Ablemyre Hill view – Doris Boardman – a village surgery – a village hairdresser – in Foul Mile field – night walk into Kitchenly Mill Race.

The sun occupied the southern sky and some lengthy clouds rested above the ascending banks to the north, like a halted army. I was following the path to the village; crystals appeared to cling to my eyelashes, the sun seemed to leak silver on every surface, mercury droplets trapped in the folds of bitter dock leaves, molten liquid resting between the grass blades. It was so bright I squinted and frowned across the open heathland, then my face fell into relaxation when I came to the coolness beneath the trees. I had hoped to find some sunglasses around Kitchenly Mill Race – but people wore sunglasses sparingly in those times.

That path towards the village follows the northern and un-fenced boundary of Foul Mile, then it eases into the long declivity so the roofs of the village to the left fall down out of sight – even Kitchenly church spire sunk below that frowsy ridge. The new bungalows of Brockleberry Rents had also descended into the raised meadow, so I was at least hidden from them.

Some sheep grazed with their black faces fallen to the grass in the lee of Ablemyre Hill's initial slopes – even they were dazzling in their ivory wrappings. Why had they not been sheared to prevent dazzle? Didn't shearing occur back in the merry month of May? Was it sedge warblers who teetered out in brief sporadic alarms? And a car horn sounded a quick peep of greeting somewhere over towards the village. They all knew one another there.

I had met no other ramblers or even dog walkers. I detoured to the right, off the path to try and identify the beer tree again.

Some years before, a wayward drinker – a wandering tramp of complex lineage – had taken up an infirm residence in this grove. When he had drunk his fill of tinned beer he would attach those empties by forcing the can openings down onto the very tips of many of the thorn tree's more vertical sprouts and branches. After a period of a fortnight or more, the thorn tree was a bizarre sight, with its accoutrements and conglomerations of coloured cans – seemingly flowering from the many boughs. The tree slightly clanged in a breeze. People walked out from the village to witness the spectacle – I heard about the phenomenon from Dan Mullan. A whole variety of beer and cider cans in a range of colours covered the tree: strange fruit. Some of the cans had been attached impressively high up, as if stepladders had been utilised in the decorating process, which seemed unlikely.

When I reached that blackthorn tree I still recognised it but every can of its perverse crop was gone – doubtless blown down in the winters, or knocked away by bored, inquisitive children of the village shortly after the vagabond had continued on his inebriated ramble through this county. I admired him. Could he be the night intruder returned? I stamped around the tree in the long grass and sure enough I did come across at least one rusted can – its round, dull base less oxidised than its utterly withered and thin sides.

I turned my back on the tree, climbed back up to the route, and a short distance ahead the pathway divided. One way crosses the furthest extent of Foul Mile along the western boundary, which is fenced and where years of former cultivation in the next field have pushed up a chalky ridge of larger stones; that way leads towards the main road and the boundary of the village. I selected the other route which curves out around the boundaries of another landowner's field but then doubles back as it meets a long fence buried in a hedgerow.

I crossed the fence using the stile on the public footpath then took the sheep trail which curves gently but always ascending up the flank of the hill. It was a pleasant day to be walking, if

230

a bit bright. Within fifteen minutes I had moved so far around that the view showed the wave-like flow of slopes to the higher ridges of the north with the Iron Age earth fort at that far summit, from which you could look across the farms as far as British Rail Maxtelham; from there also you could make out the uneven line of bushes which indicated the double tracks of the railway line. But I left the sheep path and made ascent directly towards the summit of Ablemyre Hill with its small, conical concrete trigonometry point. In less than ten minutes I reached the top, which was scattered with those odd, stunted blackthorns.

A slight breeze suggested the idea of a higher summit but then the cool air vanished. I could command a satisfying view of the sunlit countryside around me – or certainly to the south. With satisfaction I could clearly distinguish the dark tops of our cedars of Lebanon, and the rolling, globular forms of the many deciduous trees of Kitchenly Mill Race, massed together like some bristling spot which God had missed shaving.

From that elevated vantage point, untutored eyes could make little sense out of the dwelling places – only the Tudor chimney stacks were hinted at, but from this new angle they were conveniently shrouded by a wall of young birch trees, which had heightened even in my time at Kitchenly Mill Race. The young trees ran from beyond that horrible septic tank eastwards until they petered out and showed the flat fields and the wooded spots which lay outside the property to the north of the main road. They shielded us from the unfortunate fact – as Mrs H had pointed out – that boundary walls did not actually exist on the eastern limits of the property. Something I emphasised repeatedly to Marko as a security issue when we first viewed the property that day with Colonel Halmer, but which Marko shrugged off with a surprised expression.

In the early days of our residency, over in the far copse which faces the open fields with no effective barrier, I had nailed up three **PRIVATE STRICTLY NO TRESPASSING** wooden signs on the thick trunks of three trees, spaced about thirty yards apart. Facing east of course – it would have been a bit Monty Python if I had fitted them facing west, towards the manor house.

It always bothered me that a random rambler, perhaps even a supremely alarming character like the itinerant tree decorator, could pass through those woods and even innocently and unknowingly miss one of the signed trees, and thus pass onto our property. It had seemed hysterical then to put up a sign on every single tree facing the eastern pasture – though my instincts had veered towards that opportunity. I accept that a trespasser into the gardens was still little security threat to Marko. The manor house is of course secured within its moat and entry to the network of dwellings is complicated. Any intruder would probably be encountered and challenged before they actually managed to come close to Marko or his immediate family. All the same – frankly – I would have preferred the construction of an extension to the perimeter wall; yet Marko just laughed it off.

Of course, for most of that advance from the east, any potential intruder would come upon the natural barrier of the lower river, which even widened and deepened at that point. But the river could be crossed at two points. It could be paddled across in warm summers down by the road bridge, using the pebble islands as way points. It could also be crossed higher up where an annoying and now disused pipe had been set across the river on ugly, tall brick supports. I had learned from Dan Mullan that this was originally constructed as part of some agricultural land-draining project in the 1960s when a pump was been fitted which had subsequently fallen into disuse. A valiant trespasser or pesky youth could have shimmied across this pipe, but really there was no point as by just moving a short distance to the north and through the aforementioned trees they could simply stroll through the copse onto our private property and be upon the northerly bank of our gentle mill race. Coming round the curve of the river as they cleared the bulrushes which flourished in that far corner, they would find themselves beside the sequence of weeping willows. Ahead of them they would suddenly see the secondary mill house and the charm of the well-maintained and painted lower wooden footbridge. Could a lurker be lured there at night by the enchanting and unintentional *son et lumière* of our stunning night gardens? What a delightful, breathtaking sight the night wanderer would haplessly come upon, rounding the river corner by the willows! The grass at their trespassing feet would suddenly be shorn and ordered and if they ventured just a little further inwards they would find themselves with a full view of the manor house and laburnum slope on the elevation over to their left. It had never happened. I had never witnessed a single trespasser even in daylight hours appear at that far end of the river's curve – standing like one lost, a mysterious traveller at the end of some long pilgrimage – a slight and haunted figure, the bright rambler's clothing highlighted against the greenery behind them.

I had still taken the trouble to have hammered into the ground a low-standing sign which had its face directed away from the dwellings and towards the outer world. As it was visible from the house, or could be passed by residents who might choose to stroll down this far-bank riverside, it was a more aesthetically pleasing and less stridently worded sign than the others – with the lettering burned artfully by a poker into a thick board of elm wood suspended on a short rustic post with bark still on it. **PRIVATE PROPERTY**. Mullan complained the sign made mowing difficult around that spot but I insisted the post was maintained. After all, someone could just stand there loutishly and snap photographs of Marko's private dwelling; we couldn't have that.

233

It seemed unlikely – especially during the hours of darkness – yet by what other invisible means could this intruder be entering into our grounds? It was possible to physically scale the boundary walls if one stood on the shoulders of an accomplice. But that would make leaving the grounds even more challenging. I had to admit the intruder had not been seen by me or by any other witnesses over the previous nights of my illness and recovery, but of course that did not mean the intruder wasn't there.

It had crossed my mind to set a trap in the area on the far estate side, by the bulrushes – dig a hole and cover it with thin bamboo scattered over with leaves and grass cuttings. Or string cans – beer cans perhaps – between some of the trees? But such extreme actions might backfire against residents of Kitchenly Mill Race themselves. Ourselves. I couldn't have Molly or even Marko falling into a deep pit with a scattering of fresh horse dung placed in it at the bottom.

Trying to avoid these defensive and belligerent hilltop reflections, I turned my sightseeing away from the distant gardens of Kitchenly Mill Race and faced the namesake village – and of course the strip of new bungalows along the roadside on the edge of Foul Mile's wide space.

Nothing seemed to be going on down in the cauldron of boredom that was the village, but I had a few tasks there. The grey church steeple stood like the trigonometry point next to me, mapping the spiritual framework of the county. On Sundays, bright Easter and Christmas days too, the bells of this village spire could be heard by the next village and vice versa, as all the church towers breaching on their broad horizons rang one to another and back again in some form of hope and thanksgiving, to my mind at least. They rang out the good news and at least some vague acknowledgement about strange happenings nearly two thousand years ago in Palestine – and this gave me good cheer.

234

Coloured vans and motor vehicles, a bread-delivery lorry and a short oil tanker were all seen to pass out along the road at the far end of the village heading towards town, small and perfect as Dinky toys; sometimes a chrome fitment would catch the sun and flash back at my location on the happy hill.

I sat down for a period. I even stretched out on the hard grassy ground, rubbed at the bruise on my collarbone then contemplated the skies above with my arms folded up beneath my head. I had some matters to reflect upon after my talk with Mrs H on that day before I caught the bad cold. This longing for something we have never even had. What was it old Eliot told us? I think it was: the boredom, the horror, the glory of life. I only retained and remembered pity, pity in the eye of a dog I came upon inexplicably dying alone in a wood outside Stafford town. I could not carry it home and I could not leave it so I remained until the end.

I have a broken heart, terminal case, no cure. Doris Boardman aged twenty from back up in Stafford. Worked in stocktaking at the biscuit factory, still living at home, smoked twenty-five Rothmans a day.

Always reading and rereading *Jonathan Livingston Seagull*. Mad about astrology – blown away by the zodiac. Every single day she did her 'charts', her 'Doris-scope', as she called it. Me: Leo with Gemini rising, her: early Libra; she said we were utterly compatible and it was meant to be. She did Tarot too, laying out those cards upon my bare chest.

All was going to be well according to those stars in her grey-green eyes. Doris Boardman aged twenty and her grey-green eyes. Eyes so big that when we strolled arm in arm in the country, together by the canals and waterways at Izaak Walton's cottage, or through the pastures down at Acton Trussel on a Sunday, with the obtuse applause responding to the click of the cricket balls beyond the hedgerows, I would see the whole sky moving

235

in her wide eyes. All these dashing clouds were long ago prefig-
ured in Doris Boardman aged twenty's eyes. Like she had already
mapped out for me England's low and moving clouds many years
before – they had crossed her dazzling pupils for my gaze and
now the regal clouds were merely playing back for me in the
form of a weak dilution in the southern skies. When I looked
up into the heavens it was her eyes I was seeing.

The white cheesecloth blouses she wore on her days off –
blouses with their small blue and pink flowers embroidered
round the collars and cuffs – these clothes actually seemed wrong
shielding her hard, twenty-year-old breasts, not just from my
greedy eyes and touch but from Nature itself. I was no naturist
but that was how it felt. Freeing both those breasts among the
buzzing insects, the trees and back lanes that first summer.
She held her still-lit cigarette vertically and I had to cautiously
manoeuvre the blouse collar over the burning ember. It seemed
an artistic move not a randy one to see those nesh tits come free.
This is the voice of an old man, but women seemed more beautiful then, they had tan lines from the Spanish package-holiday
fortnight and rich pubic hair which today seems viewed as some
sort of serious health hazard. On men too, it seems. Of course,
Doris Boardman aged twenty was already famous for being
caught sunbathing in just bra and knickers on the factory roof.

Doris Boardman aged twenty-one: and she got bored with this
man. She didn't get the music world at all – not for a minute was
she having it beyond listening to records. She thought the music
world was a daft southern affectation – she liked her sounds, T.
Rex, Bowie and especially The Move were her thing. But she
never took to Fear Taker though I brought her up every single
album – complimentary! – and one of them was signed on the
cover by the whole group. Offered her concert tickets but she
would only go if the band played Bingley Hall. Or Birmingham
at a stretch. And during that period they did not.

She shocked and hurt me by saying Side 2 of *Pascal's Moon* sounded like, to quote her – music for a French blue movie. I crumbled a little inwardly, wondering where she might ever have gained knowledge of or even viewed such a film, but that was Doris Boardman for you. Mysterious in her way for a Stafford biscuit factory worker in a white lab coat with a clipboard.

She was bloody open-minded too which was delicious. She told me straight out when we met that she would try anything once and she did. Trouble was it was exactly the once she would try it and then no more. She wouldn't smoke a reefer though because she said she didn't have time in between all her Rothmans. But I would have married her in a minute if she had hinted. My life would have been very different, wouldn't it?

Did Doris Boardman aged twenty-two leave me, or did I leave her? It now seems an astounding question – for at the time I felt I was royally dumped but I sometimes wonder. I had asked Marko if she could move in with me in the secondary mill house at Kitchenly and perhaps she could find work locally – buy herself a Vespa motor scooter, get around and into town for a little job in the shops maybe? But Marko wasn't cool about it. He looked a bit disappointed by the whole concept, frowned sadly and alarmed me by saying, 'Look, mate' – he definitely used the term mate – 'Look, mate, bring her down to visit for a couple of weekends – use one of the big bedrooms, Mrs H'll clean up, if you get what I mean' – he winked – 'but if you are serious on this bird I'll understand if you want out the scene, man. It's a shame, but I get it.'

I had to backtrack, fast. Explain and insist, not at all. We were in a relationship. It was great, but she didn't need to move in, it was just a thought.

Besides, Doris Boardman herself had no interest in moving 'all down south, duck', as she termed it. She had looked carefully at the Polaroid photographs I brought back to Stafford of my little dwelling and kitchenette, of the buildings, famous manor house and fine gardens at Kitchenly, and even one photo of me sitting on the bonnet of the Ferrari beside Marko who had his shirt unbuttoned quite far down.

As far as Doris Boardman was concerned it might as well have been Robert Louis Stevenson's house on Samoa where I lodged, rather than three hours away on the London train. All she did was turn to me and say Marko was quite dishy and that she didn't know I owned a Polaroid camera. Then using that camera she made me take some very rude photos of her naked, white and tan body, up in my old bedroom at me mam's. Very rude indeed. She didn't like those photos either, though she studied them intently for long hours, criticising aspects of her good looks and bodily features. In fact, using scissors she soon destroyed all the polaroids (including the Ferrari photograph) and she never gave me that harmlessly anonymous image of her firm breasts. Though when I studied the photos that she had furiously cut up into tiny triangles and thrown into a public litter bin on Stone Road – I had later surreptitiously returned to the bin and gruesomely tried to retrieve the multiple fragments – I was positive that one particular photo was definitely missing from the destruction and that she had retained it herself for obscure private purposes.

Doris Boardman aged twenty-two: face it, she saw my job as a threat. She stopped meeting me on the platform at Stafford railway station when I got off the train from Euston.

I started to obsess about her. I got down. I started to feel like I was one of that fellow's sculptures – was he Italian? That Giacometti – those big long, lanky, fragile fellows; limbs pulled out like tightropes. Or hangman's ropes. When I saw that bloke's sculptures I got them – poor radish man trembling and almost evaporating into nothing.

In the bitter last months, I said to Doris Boardman just-turned twenty-three, 'Doris, if you leave me I want you to always

238

remember this: when I die in a hospital bed thirty or forty years from now, it's your name I will be screaming out in the ward with my last breath and you won't be there.' She had frowned, momentarily affected by this, then reached for her next Rothmans and said, 'Crofton, you're so dramatic, duck.' She had a very strong Staffordshire accent, which you need to try to imagine. She blew out smoke and told me, 'Even if I was with you at the hospital, love, chances are I'd be outside the front door having a smoke.'

Pretty soon I heard through the Staffy grapevine she was seeing that smooth shit Rueben – the factory manager's son who had a bloody black Ford Capri.

It was in that hellish spate after Doris that I started my beef with Jesus. People get me wrong, though. It's a private matter but I am not a Jesus freak. It's true I did pray to Our Saviour: please please don't let Doris Boardman leave me for that shit Rueben in his black Capri. But the power of prayer didn't work out for me; same as the power of astrology, it would appear. I started reading the New Testament – even *The Singer* by Calvin Miller. I drifted into Mass now and again like a former addicted gambler popping into the betting shop three times a year.

People thought I was a Bible-basher, but I know exactly what I was doing; I was actually assembling a tight legal case against Jesus. Everyone, including myself, attacks the Christian Church for not living up to the high standards of Jesus and his Father. Yet what if the churches of this world are actually beautifully superior to Jesus? What if we are an audience at the Altamont Speedway which got too big for the band to cope with? Stage fright of two thousand years. Jesus as absent landlord. I never did understand why the Vatican didn't place a sign above the door of St Peter's: **BUSINESS ESTABLISHED SINCE YEAR 0000**.

There is something weepy about all these chapels, churches and cathedrals, the steeples of Sussex below me, waiting for the Prince of Peace who will never return. Maybe we are all better than show business? The messiah will not come back again despite what Roy Buchanan says on his first album. Every steeple is a monument to this bitter betrayal. Your Father forsook you and now you do the same to us. But it doesn't mean we cannot love him. I had a love as great as for Jesus but it was for Doris Boardman aged twenty to twenty-two and when I lost her I lost everything. In the end is humanity not more given to showing reliable and regular mercy than God is?

Why are we always screaming at God to manifest Himself? This is His one strength – His one genius is that He never shows himself – an ultimate mystic – He knows fine what would happen if He showed himself, or if his Son, the Prince of Peace, returned – we would rip Him to pieces – you know we would destroy Him. The saints knew this and they tried to take His place – the first rock stars – was it St Columba who had his acolytes walk supporting a square frame of twigs around his saintly self, so the peasants wouldn't mob him as they tried to reach and touch? What's the difference between that and Marko getting out of a limo drawn up by the Plaza Hotel while Death Threat Dave and a few heavies usher him inside past the porters and yelling fans?

In October 1975 I went back up to Stafford to see The Who at Bingley Hall with a couple of school acquaintances who I was losing touch with: Primrose Mike and Eisin. I was really looking forward to that gig. Five minutes in and I spotted Doris Boardman aged twenty-four, right up the bloody front with Rueben Bennett and he had his arm around her shoulder, across her white cheese-cloth blouse. There they both were in the changing colours of the stage show and the smoke which made the light look all powdery – as if a desert sandstorm was in progress somewhere outside the walls of Bingley Hall. The smoke got in my eyes.

I didn't make it as far as 'Tattoo', which I believe was the fifth song on that tour's set list. I had to leave Pete, windmilling and leaping (whom of course I had met at Emerson's lovely house) and dear Keith Moon too, RIP, shouting out in his Dickensian way between songs, cackling and slashing cymbals. I walked home alone through autumn streets of the north.

Eisin and Primrose Mike had been trying to support me, telling me to swallow it down. She wasn't worth it, hadn't I heard? Doris was getting a right bloody name for herself round the old town. Rueben and her did six legs in a bed with that tall Jessie Bunton from accounts. That update made me feel a whole lot better, did it not? What scenes had those green eyes reflected in the half-light? It was her who was swallowing it down. Another fucking accountant.

I wrote Doris many pleading letters after nicking the fancy, gilt-headed notepaper of Kitchenly Mill Race out of the antique Gillow desk Marko kept in the morning room, stuffed full of old *Melody Maker*s and *Disc*s which he claimed he hadn't yet read. In each letter I begged Doris to come back to me – though I was not even sure she had ever been *with* me. I received no replies to these letters. I kind of worded them with Rueben in mind to be honest. I knew she was reading them out loud to him in bed. Probably Jessie Bunton (who was gorgeous too) was also there, stretched across the crumpled candlewick bedspread listening to Doris pause in her recitations of my words to inhale on her latest cigarette.

Here is something else that . . . Strewth, too tired to form a full thought. Here is something else that you should know regarding the weather of my heart . . . Here is . . .

Kitchenly Mill Race was in a strange light, as grey and as green as Doris Boardman's eyes. I was inside the manor house, moving round the windows of the ground floor but I wasn't pulling any curtains across them, I was placing my palms against their sweating glass to test the temperature. Kitchenly Mill Race

241

was all at sea – an ocean, a biblical inundation had swelled up, swamping its acres; the new sea level came above the bottom of the ground-floor windows. Somehow all trees had vanished, so nothing showed of our once verdant grounds above the surface of the water; only an endless choppy sea surrounded the manor walls on every side, as if our household was a lonely lighthouse. I ran from room to room on the ground floor in my bare feet, but each window was now like a submerged porthole – the water was rising, lapping against the glass and, as in some giant aquarium, views were provided of activity beneath the oily surface – fish were there, an armband was semi-submerged, a giant octopus with its puckering mouth fangs, mussels and cockles adhered to the exterior window frames and there I was, trapped within, on the ground floor. I would need to climb to the higher levels for refuge; somewhere, I could hear a gush of water – a window had been left ajar or a pane had given in. I could hear Marko and Auralie up on the roof by the flagpole where she – wearing only bra and panties over a deep tan – had been transporting her finest clothes and handfuls of underwear too, salvaging them above the inevitable submersion of our house. Marko had lumbered his best guitars up there in their cases. A helicopter was coming in to fly them out but only Marko and Auralie were permitted aboard – with the guitars and clothes – because there was a weight restriction on me accompanying them. Officers Use Only.

I woke. Strewth. I'd conked right out in the warmth. I sat up. I don't wear a wristwatch, so I didn't know the time, but the sun had cranked around the castles of the sky and was over in the west with a diminishing power. I rose up, heavy with the weight of delicious sleep, but also stiff and very uncomfortable from the hard ground. I had to hobble to the trig point and lean my hands down upon its top to try and get some blood back into my wobbly legs.

242

Finally, I set off. My face felt poached by the sun and the heat. The path down off the hill which leads to the village emerges in an alleyway between two buildings, right on the main thoroughfare. Such as it is. I admit I paused there looking up and then down the pavements. Nobody who resembled Rose, Nat or her mum was about. In fact, the long street was devoid of any humankind. No cats or dogs either. There wasn't even any traffic; people had taken to their back gardens, or headed to the coast if they had a car. A thrush or a blackbird gave piccolo trills inside a vibrating bush in a small front garden.

A short walk to the west, past the empty village green, took me outside the pumps of the petrol station where there was a small shop purveying varieties of sweeties, ice creams, some basic groceries and household goods. You couldn't call it a 'corner' shop as the village was so small it didn't really have corners. I looked around for some sort of functioning timepiece which might reveal to me what hour of day it was – but there was nothing. Further on, before the bus stop, I crossed the road and here I went up the brief garden path which led to the modern extension.

The sign outside read: KITCHENLY SURGERY. The hours were posted on a board. They closed at six. With little hope, I put my hand onto the door knob to try, and it opened. I sort of stumbled inwards, finding my eyes struggling to adjust in that relative gloom compared to the fizz and dazzle outside. It was a wonder I didn't take a migraine. That surgery smelled odd too – not medicinal, more like damp, or even wood smoke.

I found myself in a small waiting room with some seats against a wall but nobody was in them. In front of me was a varnished, pine-fronted counter. At first I thought nobody was behind it then I noted there was a lady sitting there, small and old, with a lifted hairstyle of some description.

'Do you have an appointment? Dr Christopher is just about to leave.'

'Ah, good afternoon,' I said. 'No. No, I don't need to see the doctor. Sorry, but I wanted to ask you about, ah, this.' I tried each of my pockets on my jeans but I couldn't find it. Then I did locate the letter at the bottom of the pocket, under my house keys; the envelope had been folded over four times, while I was convinced I had only folded it once. 'Ah, I have received this letter and I want to ask you about it.' I stepped up to the counter and I placed the letter onto the Formica top in front of her. I started to notice how I had rural detritus adhering to my person. My *Tales of Topographic Oceans* T-shirt was rather crumpled. I brushed downwards with my hand at dry grass strands and aerial seeds which were clinging to the fabric.

The lady said, 'Yes, this letter is just informing you that from now on you won't be attending this surgery due to the new boundary changes, you will attend the Solham Street surgery in town.'

'Yeah, yeah, I see that but . . . well, I think there might be a mistake of some sort because, well, I have received this letter but other, residents at, eh, my address, haven't received this letter.'

She looked up at me with quite a jerk of her head. 'Oh.'

'Yeah, ah, my address is there? You can read this clearly: The Staff Flat, Kitchenly Mill Race, Kitchenly, etcetera.'

'Well what seems to be the problem?'

'It's just that other people residing at this address haven't received this letter and I can't understand why I'm being asked to go all the way into town if I need to see a doctor. Not that I need to see a doctor, but *if* I ever did need to see a doctor. Rather than just continue coming here. Not that I do. Ever come here. I've been registered here since 1973 and I've never been once. Till today and this is not a medical matter. But the others didn't get this letter.'

'Are you on any fixed prescription?'

'What? Eh, no, no I'm not.'

244

'You don't receive regular medication of any kind?'

'No I don't.'

'Let me look at our patient lists here,' she said. With surprising ease she lifted a large bound file up from somewhere beneath her knees. She spoke quietly, seemingly to herself, referring through her thick spectacles to my letter. 'Mr Clark, Mr Clark, yes. Kitchenly Mill Race. Staff Flat. Lovely day, is it not?'

'What? Yes. Oh yes, it's delightful.'

'And you say other residents at the same address have not received this letter?'

'Correct. I handle the mail so I know nothing has come for the others, and this came for me.'

'Could I ask you for the surnames of the other residents, please?'

I was surprised she didn't already know this from village hearsay. 'Oh. Well there's a Mr Markus Morrell, and a Miss, or Mrs, Kristensen. With a K. K for, eh, kettle. First name Auralie with an A. Though sometimes she goes by the surname of Morrell. When it suits her. And then there's Molly Morrell. Their young daughter.'

'Ah yes. A Mr Morrell,' she nodded, 'That name is registered as a patient but with no active file details.' She was going through the files, 'Ah, Krist. En. Sen. A,' she nodded. 'Yes. Same address. Well, they are all in order but . . . Do you perhaps share the same door as Mr Morrell and Miss or Mrs Krist-en. Sen?'

'The same door?'

'Do you perhaps have a different front door?'

'A different door?'

'Yes. Perhaps you live in a separate house from other inhabitants of the address; you know, a coaching house, perhaps, or a gate lodge?'

She seemed to be making up these theoretical locations, yet at the same time it appeared as if she was familiar with other large country houses which might indeed be arranged in just such a manor . . . no . . . manner.

Then she quoted, with a slow deliberation and, I felt, a sort of attendant sympathy, 'I see here: The Staff Flat?'

'So? Well. Yes and no, I mean it's all one house.'

'One house?'

'Yes, it is all one house, this is what's so puzzling to me. How can you decide that one patient in the same house goes to the town doctor but others go to the village, when surely the surgery catchment area is . . . well, we fall within it because we all actually live in the same house.'

'Well these are not our decisions, you see, Mr Clark. We are just the surgery. But you are aware that there have been boundary changes to the catchment areas of each surgery?'

'Yes. Of course, well it's in the letter. I'm aware of that, but—'

'Well Mr Clark, the new boundary line has to start somewhere; it appears that you fall just over the new boundary line of the catchment area.'

'But that, but that's . . . if you don't mind me saying so, that's a bit barmy. It's all wonky. Yes. I do technically have a side door other than the main door to the dwelling, but I literally, I mean, I don't use it that much. There are lots of doors. Lots of doors, I can readily assure you of that. We have a fine count of doors. I, I mean, my door leads into the same house as the other doors, I live in a—'

'No, no, Mr Clark. Look here.'

'What?'

'Well, your postcode: Mr Crufts? Cruffon? Sorry, my eyes. Crofton Clark. The Staff Flat. Your postcode has one different letter than the address of Mr Morrell and eh—'

'No it doesn't.'

'Yes, I'm afraid it does, see here: Mr Morrell and Miss Kristen-sen have a G and you have an F. Every house has a slightly different code.'

'But . . . But the mail all goes in the same post pox. Sorry, postbox; at the gate.'

'That's as well may be. But they are differing postal addresses; they bear different postcodes. So, in setting up the boundary they have been aware of that and made a distinction between the G dwelling and the F dwelling.'

'But, again, that's bonkers. I mean, I mean the GPO delivers to a single postbox up at the gate. Though I admit that is by request, for security and privacy. I admit the GPO would deliver to our doors. Our door, if we requested it.'

'That's as well may be. But at some point clearly the post office have registered your address as two distinct dwellings, thus, when the new boundary was made, I am afraid you find yourself on the far side of it.'

I told her, 'But it's only a one-hundred-foot difference. My door is one hundred feet from the main door and we all share that main door with great regularity. I mean . . . Hell. Nobody is asking at the post office what door I *leave* from, are they? It's all about what door I allegedly go in, is it? I leave from a whole variety of doors, let me tell you. And go in. Yes. Leave and go in. Different. Doors. The postman would be goggle-eyed at the doors we can have him knocking at. Regiments of them. He's lucky there is a post pox, box, at the top of our drive, or he'd be taking early retirement. We live in the same house, all together. I mean not all together as in some sort of, sort of strange commune affair or whatever. We're not hippies! I'm not inferring that sort of thing, but we are . . . We are a family with one pox. Box. I live only one hundred feet away – what does one hundred feet matter?'

She leaned back a little and considered me. 'No,' she spoke in a reprimanding voice. 'Mr Clark, one hundred feet is a significant distance in relation to individual postal addresses. Perhaps things seem a little different at a large, older address. Perhaps a larger house broken up into smaller apartments?'

247

'It isn't broken up into small apartments. Far from it.'

'In a high street just like here in the village, one hundred feet could contain . . . well let's say each doorway is four to five feet wide. In a street there could be a door every ten feet. That's ten doorways in a hundred feet, Mr Clark.

I felt a need to stand up straighter.

She went on, 'That's ten different addresses over just that length. Plenty of room for difference. I am afraid the health catchment areas are just the same as the school catchment areas. There has to be a dividing line somewhere; sometimes they can seem inappropriate, especially in relation to the nearest school, but that's as needs be – here we are and they have had to make a decision.'

I said, 'As needs be, yes, yes. Sorry to interrupt, but, no. Nobody has made a decision, that's the problem here. This is civil service bureaucracy at its very worst. Much like the colonisation of Africa, a line has been drawn on a map in an office somewhere. Some abstract idea is making the decision and it's potty to make a boundary line through the middle of a shared house. I live in the same house as the people that can come to this surgery and it's just a waste of everyone's time: myself, the health service, yours too, in dealing with this. It obviously would be more efficient if one household went to one surgery; surely that's just good old British common sense?'

'I can see your point of view, Mr Clark, I can perfectly see your point of view; however here are the new boundaries. We just have to adhere to them, I'm afraid.'

I said, 'I mean I can accept the boundary can fall between, say, two farms that are close together – one farmhouse has to go to the doctor in town and the next farm to the doctor in the village. I can accept that, although they are adjacent farmhouses; but I mean to say, within one building, to make a division, it's cuckoo. It's like saying there are two kids in a house and we'll say the dividing line runs right between their bedrooms, up the corridor, so the brother

248

has to go to this surgery but the sister to that surgery. I mean that's just things gone a bit potty now, is it not? How about these new bungalows at Brockleberry Rents. I bet half of them don't go to the surgery here and half to the . . .' My tirade sort of petered out; the lady had turned to look over to her right. I looked too.

A very large, elderly man – not stout – but simply tall and broadly built, wearing a dark-green, tweed-like suit, was standing there. He was a striking figure as he had a magnificently wrinkled face and a fringe of high white hair, but right up the middle of this long fringe, his silvery hair was stridently stained with a yellow streak. This was because the similarly yellowed fingers of his right hand held a lit cigarette, and as he stepped from his consulting room further towards us, I noted the fug of Capstan Navy Cut cigarette smoke which pursued his bulk.

The lady behind the counter said, 'Sorry, Doctor. I was just explaining these new boundaries to Mr Clark.'

'Mr Clark,' the physician said as if he had been expecting me for over a week. 'Step in. Please step in.'

'Uh, ah, no, no, Doctor. No, I don't even have an appointment to see you. Sorry, Doctor, I didn't come to bother you. I'm fine, as you see. I'm in fine health.' I held up my arms in a sort of Charles Atlas pose and I flexed my arm muscles then, suddenly feeling somewhat ridiculous, I dropped the pose. I also noted I had considerable dark sweat flourishes beneath the arms of my T-shirt. Deodorant sprays were not a great feature of the late seventies for me. 'I'm just confused.'

'Confused? We prescribe for that.'

I didn't know if he was joking. 'No. Confused by these new boundaries. There's nothing I need to see you about.'

The woman behind the counter spoke up, 'Are you quite sure you shouldn't see the doctor for just a jiffy? That's rather a dose you have there.'

I turned to look at her. 'I beg your pardon?'

'That's quite a dose you have there. Sunburn. That's a back-from-the-Canary Islands case there, is it not, Dr Christopher?'

'Sunburn? What?' I lifted my fingers to my face and, in areas, my flesh did feel hot.

'You do look like you've caught a touch of the sun recently,' the doctor informed me, dropping his face a little and looking at me over half-rim reading spectacles.

'I did just fall asleep, in the sun on Ablemyre Hill. For hours. Oh no. Do you have a mirror here, Doctor?'

'Step inside, Mr Clark.' Once again he indicated his open consulting room door. 'Step inside, perhaps I can interest you in something. What is life itself but the time between doctors' appointments?'

'Well it's not really necessary but a mirror would . . .' I walked straight into the doctor's consulting room.

Over to the right was a set of scales placed on the linoleum floor, and a long thin mirror was hung on the wall above them. I shivered. I have a horror of doctors and doctors' rooms, all initiated in childhood. No. Incorrect. I have a horror of ill health. I stepped up to the mirror but took care not to fully advance my feet actually up onto the weighing scales. I felt that would be in some manner committing myself to the jurisdiction of the medical environment which I suddenly found myself in. I slightly leaned down towards the mirror. 'Blimey,' I whispered. One side of my face was scarlet, yet the other side of my face had caught no sun at all and my complexion here was normal. If I have a normal complexion. Yet my arms, which must have remained folded behind my head while I had slept, didn't seem to have any tan at all – even on their fish-pale undersides. I looked like Roy Neary after he had been blasted by that alien spaceship's downward blaze of light, while sitting in his pick-up truck in *Close Encounters of the Third Kind* – one of my all-time favourite flicks which, the year before, I had journeyed up to London to see in Leicester Square – twice. I appreciated it so very much. Interesting to note in the film that Flight 19, the Bermuda Triangle aircraft—

The door shut firmly behind me and the doctor was there at my side.

In a low and thoughtful voice I admitted, 'I do seem to have caught a smattering of sunbeams on the left hand side of my face.' I lifted my finger to touch the red half of my forehead.

'Indeed, indeed, Mr Clark. But it shouldn't blister. I would recommend you take some good long drinks of water this evening in avoidance of dehydration. Now take a step forwards and let's get your weight on the scales, please.'

I turned around to look at him. 'But, why? There's no need, is there? What has my weight to do with a sudden case of sunburn? I'm really not here for a consultation, Doctor; I didn't even come here to see you about sunburn. In fact I got the sunburn by coming here. I didn't have sunburn when I set out this morning and I wouldn't have got it if I hadn't planned to come here in the first place.'

'Whatever you say but, to be truthful, Mr Clark, I like to guess a fellow's weight. I've finessed an eye for it, so I was just hoping you'd humour me.'

'Oh. Really? You can guess someone's weight, like at a fairground? All right. I don't have to remove my clothing, do I?'

'No need for that, just hop up. Ah. Just over eleven stone. I dropped my anchor right on the spot.'

I said quietly, 'Is that what weight you guessed I'd be?'

'Marginally. Yes. To hazard a guess and be exact is overpleasing.' He had crossed to his desk and although he had claimed my weight was of no significance, I noticed that he quickly jotted it – or some other detail about me – down on a notepad. 'Take a seat, do take a seat.'

'It's not necessary, Doctor. I really . . . oh, all right then.' I sat down on the seat positioned at a right angle to his desk; chairs for patients were always at this angle, so that they were not faced with the intimidation of being addressed by, or addressing, an authority figure across the barrier of a desk. Rather compassionate when you think about it.

The seat I sat on was a metal-framed thing but cushioned with fitted padding. It was actually quite comfortable after all my walking and my slumbering on hard ground under the open skies.

'So what is it I can help you with this afternoon?'

I laughed again, 'Really, nothing, Doctor, nothing at all. I'm not kidding you on. Just as I was saying, I only came along to enquire about these boundary-line changes. I seem to be getting sent to the town surgery, while others in the same house as me aren't.'

'Cigarette?' The doctor had lifted an old-fashioned silver cigarette case from within his jacket and opened it up, holding the frame of white cigarettes towards me – they reminded me of the ordered series of Corbisher's rack of whiskers. For a moment I wondered if this doctor would be at all interested in and willing to discuss Corbisher's bowel crisis of two years previous and his subsequent recovery, but that didn't seem appropriate. Not a vet.

'No, thank you, I don't smoke.' Which was true, since I had given up fat reefers, but I wasn't getting into a discussion about that.

'This confusion you have been experiencing. Has it been going on for long?'

I looked into his fine-wrinkled face. 'Only since the health service sent me that letter.'

The doctor laughed. 'Your sunburn, your confusion. It seems we are doing you great harm here.'

'That's not true, Doctor. Confusion set in a few days after my birth, I believe. Or even a few days before.'

'Oh it can be that way, Mr Clark. It can surely be that way. What is it you do for a living, Mr Clark?'

I sort of assumed he would already have known this, so it seemed unusual to have to explain myself. 'I am a retainer, a manager of a large property outside the village.'

'I see.'

I waited for him to ask which property but surprisingly he did not, so he must surely have known; instead he said:

'Mr Clark, can I ask you a frank question? A personal question, really – I hope you won't mind.'

I looked around me from left to right. This was an appraisal I deeply feared and had half expected, but not quite so soon and so straight to the point. Was it my general lifestyle he was going to question, or perhaps elements of a certain obsessiveness you might argue that my diatribe – which he had witnessed – concerning the boundary changes had revealed to a trained medical mind? I felt quite intimidated. What could he have possibly deduced about my ill health already? 'I suppose so,' I murmured.

'Mr Clark, do you sail?'

'Pardon me?'

'Do you sail?'

I asked, 'Aren't you confusing me with somebody else? Are you asking if I am in the merchant navy?' I looked down at my arms as if tattoos, or something being mistaken for tattoos, might be resting there.

'No, no, no. Do you sail? Do you sail?'

'Sail?'

'My wife and I, we like to sail. I am vice president of a yacht club down by Worthing – more small sailing boats, really – and we're always looking for new members and I wondered if you sailed? Or have had experience on boats? Even on our inland waterways?'

I frowned at him. 'Oh! Sail. No. Not at all, I'm afraid. Well . . .' I realised I was flattered to be asked to join his fraternity;

the man seemed utterly beyond prejudice in asking and that touched me. 'No. I mean, I have only a little experience of, eh, water-going vessels.'

'You have a little?' he leaned forwards, hopefully.

'Well . . . Well, on inland waterways, you might say. Around the property I work on. I mean, which I am responsible for. I reside there too, we do have a small, fibreglass, flat-bottomed, eh . . . Is it a skiff?'

'A skiff, yes.'

'We have a small skiff and on occasion we take it out on the moat or on the mill race to enable us to work.'

'I see.'

'On a bridge. The underside of the footbridges. Or to maintain the riverside lights, and to clear reeds or drifted branches away from the bridge supports.'

'I see.' The doctor lit another cigarette. 'I understand. Well there you have it, young man. You see, you do have boating experience.'

'I hardly think that applies to a Worthing yacht club and the whole open English Channel.'

'Not at all, not at all. I can see you're enthusiastic. We are really looking for new and younger members.'

I suddenly thought I got his game. 'Perhaps you mean my employer?'

'Your employer? Ah, your employer whose property you manage?'

'You want my employer to join the yacht club?'

'No, no. Yourself. Well, the more the merrier; if your employer would be interested as well, by all means. But you, Mr Clark. Let's get you out there on a seagoing vessel. Sailing is the most powerful tonic for good health I know.' He coughed once, richly. 'Come along and visit us. There aren't enough members round here.' He indicated the wall across from me.

254

I hadn't taken note, but several framed photographs were hung there, showing various craft with coloured sails, and the ecstatic faces of their crew members doing all sorts of nautical chores, tugging ropes and laughing with bright teeth. 'Well, there aren't enough sailors here, Doctor, because we don't live on the coast.'

'Oh that's not a barrier at all. We have members coming down from London. Now is there anything else I can help you with today?'

'Anything else? Well, to be frank . . .'

'Yes?'

'As well as this boundary issue, I actually came up into the village today for a spot of healthy exercise, but also to try and get a hair trim. I used to go to a place in town for a trim. Though few and far between were those trips as you can probably judge. I think I need a bit of a trim to be frank. Not an issue for the National Health, I admit.'

'I see.'

'Maybe even a bit more than a trim.'

'Yes.'

'I don't know if it's come to your attention. I mean, it's not a medical issue, I presume. Or perhaps it is. Well, blokes are wearing their hair a bit shorter these days, aren't they? Some guys even colour or bleach their hair these days, Doctor.'

It occurred to me this might have been an insensitive faux pas, what with his own unique brand of nicotine hair colouring, but I found myself ploughing on.

'I don't know if you're familiar with Gary Numan, for instance? The popstar? No? But now with this—' I turned back towards the mirror and I leaned forwards slightly, to try and once again catch my reflection from a seated position. 'Now, with this sunburn, I'm a little embarrassed to even be seen out and about. They may laugh at me in the barbers, but. I don't know the time, it might be getting a bit late in the day for hairdressers?

I hope this sunburn dies down. I look a bit ridiculous. Maybe you have something you could give me. Calamine lotion, is it?'

'Oh you don't need a prescription for that, Mr Clark. You could come by calamine lotion in any good chemists.'

I looked at him.

'Of course the chemist in the village here went out of business as I am sure you know, so I'm afraid you'll have to take any prescription . . .'

'Are you prescribing something? For the sunburn? Or the confusion?'

'It appears not. Not on this occasion; but if I *were* to prescribe, you would be required to go into town and go to the big chemist on the main street. So if you think about it, it isn't really that great an inconvenience for you now to be reregistered at a town surgery – was it Solham Street I heard? It isn't such a great inconvenience in the larger picture of things for you to be attending that surgery because any prescriptions you do require have to be dispensed in the town anyway. Do you mind if I have another; sure you won't indulge?'

'No. No, thank you.'

He lit another cigarette, lifting from his desk again, with both hands, a big heavy lighter, set in a stone. A green stone. Jade, was it? The colour of Doris Boardman aged twenty's eyes – another furious smoker.

'Did you ever take a pint up at the Babbacombe Lee, Mr Clark?'

I didn't know whether he might be insinuating I had a drinking problem, or if he might be asking me to go for a drink with him. Which I would have been happy to do. 'Well, not for some time now, Doctor. I am responsible for a large property and I feel it's not quite appropriate for me to frequent the local pub, if you understand.'

He seemed puzzled. 'Oh, really? I just ask because . . . Well, do you know where the name of this pub comes from?'

'Sure,' I said. 'John Babbacombe Lee, the man they couldn't hang.'

'That's right, Mr Clark. He survived the faulty gallows thrice, I believe, and the law in those days was three tries only.'

I nodded. 'Yeah. He was very famous. In fact for a time in England, in these parts – correct me if I'm wrong – you had Babbacombe Lee imposters touring the inns and alehouses pretending to be him, telling his story around the taverns. They say after the First World War interest in Lee fell off as so many men felt they had narrowly avoided death themselves.'

'That's right, Mr Clark. You know your history. So there's a man who survived the gallows three times. I tell my patients that we should think of him more often; and there is much evidence that he was innocent of his crime. Come here, come here for just a moment and take a look out of my window.'

We crossed the floor – my legs felt quite stiff – to the consulting-room windows which gave a view straight out across the fields to the south. Fields I was not overly familiar with, but fields all the same, stretching to the slow rise of the South Downs, spotted with what seemed to be lightning-struck elms, their naked, leafless boughs jutting out horizontally in a way that reminded me of the Lord Shiva dancing his Tandavam.

'Look down on the pathway there,' the doctor said. Against the dry coursing, a path of concrete slabs ran along the edge of the building. Marked on the slabs were three or four long scores of scratched lines – seemingly inscribed there by a stone. The doctor dropped his voice. 'Now don't let Mrs Greenhill overhear. I have a patient from a farm close by. Patient confidentiality and all that. In recent years he has suffered badly. Very badly, from stones and attendant ailments, swollen prostate, the works. I always see him last appointment of the day, just as you yourself are the last appointment on this day.'

257

'But I never made a—'

'I ask him to visit the Babbacombe Lee without using the gents lavatory before he arrives. Doctor's orders, as he calls them, so he always arrives jolly. Out the back he and I go, so Mrs Greenhill doesn't see, and I tell him to stand there on that division of the paving stones and to let blast like he was twenty-one years of age again. The marks you see there indicate the extent of his micturition; he reached as far as that one last spring, that one last summer and this one here is this summer. You see the prognosis? That's old age for you, Mr Clark. You remember those lines on the ground and enjoy your vigorous bladder while you can. Embrace your youth.'

'I'm pushing thirty, Doc.'

'That's young. Now, the barber.' Suddenly he shouted, 'Mrs Greenhill, please.'

With quite astonishing speed – I now suspect she was positioned on the other side, listening – the door flew inwards and Mrs Greenhill entered. Out from behind her counter she looked even smaller. I noted her bare arms; she had those spongy elbows which older women can develop if their arms are a touch short and heavy, so that when the forearm is extended straight, where the skin gathers on the elbow is like the sucking mouth of a squid. I thought of my recent dream.

'Yes, Doctor?'

'Mr Boniface still in the main street?'

'Oh, Daniel Boniface? I believe he and his sister still are.'

'Still barbering out of his front room?'

'Oh yes, I do believe he is. I haven't heard for a while now but I'm sure of it. Oh yes, I've heard the ladies of the village saying many of the farmers and their lads still come in to be shaved and barbered by Mr Boniface.'

The doctor turned towards to me. 'There you are, Mr Clark. What number would that be, Mrs Greenwood?'

'The Bonifaces have always been at 47, Doctor. Would that be all, Doctor? I've locked the front door. It is *Dallas* tonight.'

'Oh yes. Yes. It is *Dallas* tonight. Well look, Mr Clark. Have a think about the sailing club and you know where to find me. Don't bother your socks over all this boundary business. You are always welcome to pop in here if you have any thoughts about the sailing. Or indeed if you are feeling a smidgen under the weather at all, and want a little consultation to see how your weight is doing; anything else for that matter. Kept busy at Radding Hall, are you?'

'I'm sorry?' I said.

'At Radding Hall. Did you not say that was where you were working?'

'I'm not at Radding Hall,' I said. I was flabbergasted. 'You might be confusing me with someone else. Radding Hall is on the far, far side of the village, towards town; we're the other way, towards Maxtelham. I'm at Kitchenly Mill Race.'

'Oh, I thought it was Radding Hall, myself,' said Mrs Greenhill.

'But you just saw my address, Mrs Greenhill,' I sharply reminded her. 'Radding Hall *has* been divided up into different apartments. We're at the other end of the village. Our house is still in its original condition: a sole dwelling.'

'Kitchenly Mill Race? A sole dwelling,' Doctor Christopher repeated. 'Where about is that again?'

I was astonished. 'Just as you leave the village towards Maxtelham. The large house up in the woods, beyond those new bungalows, over on the left, after the very large meadow . . .'

'Oh, I think I know where you are now,' said Mrs Greenhill, nodding quickly. 'Up towards the farms. It's just trees, really.' She sounded disappointed – even disapproving. 'You don't see it from the road,' she declared, turning to the Doctor.

'Oh,' said the Doctor. 'I'm not from the village, Mr Clark. I live in Maxtelham.'

I pointed out, 'Then you pass us every day in your car as you come in here; we're up on that lane there on your right-hand side, a bit after the road bridge crosses the river. Our long high walls.'

'I see,' he nodded. He didn't seem entirely magnetised by the topic of the house and its location. 'It's quite odd, actually. The doctor at Maxltelham surgery, Doctor De Groot, lives here in Kitchenly and I myself, the doctor of Kitchenly, well I live in Maxtelham. Funny old world. Perhaps we should redraw our own boundary lines?' He laughed.

Walking casually but all the same, with a certain purpose, the doctor and Mrs Greenhill now ushered me towards the front door of the village surgery.

'Well, thank you so much for all your help, Doctor. And to you Mrs Greenhill,' I offered, though when I thought about it later, apart from directions to this barber fellow, I wasn't quite sure what they had helped me with.

'Not at all,' said the Doctor.

'Number 47,' Mrs Greenhill added, and I found myself standing just outside the exterior door. '*Dallas* tonight,' she reminded me, shut the door and locked it once again. Then she pulled a curtain across the glass in the door.

As I stepped up the path I turned around and looked upwards at the roof of the surgery. Sure enough, there was a television aerial there. But I still had a strange and overwhelming sense that rather than settling down to watch the latest episode of *Dallas*, Doctor Christopher and Mrs Greenhill were stripping off their clothes and falling on the couch together, wrestling in his cigarette smoke. An absurd thought. I actually shook my head a little to clear the images and the left side of my forehead stung. I also suddenly felt the bruise on my collarbone and it was obvious I should have brought this injury to the doctor's attention – what a missed opportunity! I almost took a step back towards the door to knock, seeking for a further consultation, but I had lost my moment, so turned on my heels.

I walked up the still-deserted main street and soon I came to number 47. It was a house much like that outlined by Mrs Greenhill in her theory about the compactness of front doors on a generic main street. She had a point. There were many doors in this vicinity. Number 47's door abutted directly onto the road with only one small front window, curtained.

I knocked. There was no answer. I waited and knocked again. There was still no answer. A lorry passed, clearly breaking the 30mph speed limit, its rear tightly lashed down with tarpaulin and ropes over some sort of concealed load; its slipstream rather buffeted me and my long hair lifted up and fell back as the dusty air bashed against the close-set brick wall of the terrace. I knocked again, waited, then, with relief, was just about to make my departure homewards when I heard slow movements towards the door from within. I knocked again briefly, to enforce the idea of my presence, then one after another, various locks and bolts were undone on the other side of the door. Slowly it opened inwards to show another small lady, but this time far in advance of Mrs Greenhill's years. This old woman didn't allow herself to look at my face which was probably just as well because of the distinctive case of sunburn – instead she seemed to strangely concentrate upon the logo on my T-shirt, frowning rather savagely at it.

'I'm very, very sorry to bother you so late in the day but I was wondering if Mr Boniface is available for a rather quick trim?'

She continued to scrutinise my T-shirt then told me, '*Dallas* is on in a moment.'

'Yes, I know. Shall I come back another day?'

'He doesn't watch it. Come along, come along then, or the cars blow the dust up the corridor.'

261

I stepped into their house behind her, and it was up to me to close and secure the front door. When I had turned around again the woman was almost exiting the front parlour, moving away through a curtain hung round a doorway. 'Take a seat,' she snapped then called out, 'Daniel. Daniel, that's one of your men still come back again. Will they never learn?' I could hear the sound of a television through in that side of the house.

I pursed my lip and glanced around the gloomy front parlour, which was ill lit from a pink glass lampshade on the ceiling. What I saw was less an operating barber's than what should have been a bloody museum. It was a linoleum-floored room with a single barber's seat in front of a small mirror and sink unit. Leather sharpening straps hung down both sides of the mirror, like the drying strips of pelt from some recently slaughtered beast. It was with growing alarm, however, that I noted the sink basin was not empty but in fact filled to its rim with a whole series of non-pertinent items: tarry light bulbs, an electrician's yellow-handled screwdriver, what looked like a flat tweed cap, bicycle clips and an empty brown beer bottle with a burned-down candle stub still stuck in the top.

Also, the Lord sayeth that this place shall know nothing of the brush nor of the mop – they shall remain mysteries here. More and more as I looked down at my shoes, I was suspicious that the white and curly hairs strewn absolutely everywhere across the floor, mingled with naturally occurring dust balls, were not those of a vigorous, curly, grey-headed human being, but were instead the snippings of a sheep's coat. So some shearing *was* done round here after all.

I turned, considering an immediate escape. But the woman had reappeared and with livelier gait came straight through the curtain. 'He'll be just coming. I've roused him.' She crossed directly to the front door before I could get there, re-slid the bolts then re-engaged the locks.

262

After she disappeared again and I heard the television volume being substantially increased, I had little choice but to sit on the barber's chair which was coated in dust – especially along its worn armrests where the custard-coloured sponge showed through the torn velour lining. This piece of furniture would not swivel from side to side with my urging but appeared as rigid and clamped in place as a Texan electric chair. I waited. And waited in vain. After a long period, with the sounds of the television reaching through the house, I searched for some reading matter. An old copy of *Horse & Hound* was the best I could do and it had many pages torn out.

After what must have been at least half an hour or more, the woman – was it mentioned she was the sister? – came back through and enquired, 'Is he not here yet?'

'No. He isn't.'

She returned into the interior. 'Daniel. This boy's hair is much longer than when he came in. Where are you?'

Waiting to have my hair trimmed back a bit made me think of that Crosby song, 'Almost Cut My Hair'. I felt a bit guilty. There was a time in the late sixties and early seventies when Marko and I would get spat at in the street by straights and squares (funny that both geometry terms apply) just for wearing our hair as long as we did. Especially up north, more than London. Blokes thought we were effeminate but, blimey, Marko was nailing more crumpet than they ever dreamed of. A bloke in a suit once shouted at us from the back of a taxi in Praed Street, that we should have been put in the gas chambers too. Imagine shouting something as abhorrent as that just because of someone's hair. But it happened.

Marko's hair was particularly long back then. Folk would get him between a street doorway and a taxi or limo. Nasty comments, sneers. Teds or mods would come up behind him and tug it, calling him a poofter, unless Death Threat Dave was with us, then they didn't try anything.

263

Nobody thinks about it now, same way as nobody believes that every man on the street once wore a hat, but longhairs like me and Marko really broke down a few barriers early on and we took the heat for it. Nowadays a fellow can walk up a street with hair down to his waist but it wasn't always like that. The punks got beat up too. Of course, Marko's hair was so long because he started growing it ahead of every other guy and he got out of Straight Street real quick; he didn't have to go to a workplace and endure daily teasing, and then suddenly he was up onstage, never using public transport – so he could let it grow out. Musicians always had the longest hair. Even in photos of Marko in '66, his hair is already long. Around 1975, blokes started getting their hair trimmed as it had become a touch unmanageable, but now I was going for a bit of a change.

Then like a stage act, I heard the deathly slow approach of Mr Boniface up the concealed corridor; he paused behind the curtain before entering. I could hear the disastrous breathing. He waited there as if expecting applause. Then the figure pushed on through the curtain. It seemed impolite to immediately swivel my body around on the static chair and look at him, especially as I could hear his progress was so impressively slow; so I tried a forlorn demeanour of casualness by continuing to read the magazine in my lap, which had been revealing a whole world of bizarre equestrian concerns. When eventually I did turn to look at Mr Boniface, I saw Sweeney Todd the snaggle-toothed murderer. He was still actually coming towards me, so slowly did he move. His own hair was no advertisement for his craft – it looked like it had exploded when he had his face in a cow's arse; his teeth were yellow dominoes and went every way. A look of pain – as if he were in permanent slavery to swift, seismic shifts in his intestines and bowels, swept back across his troubled face; cotton eyes above thick reading specs bore down on me in perplexed suspicion. 'You Cossley's kid? Christ you've shot up.'

'No, no.'

'What? You're not Cossley's nipper? What one are you then?'

'I don't believe we've ever met,' I told him.

'What?'

'We haven't met before.'

He frowned at me. 'Who're you then?'

'My name is Crofton. I live out at the old mills. At Kitchenly Mill.'

'Who lives out there?'

'I do.'

'Why?'

'That's just where I live.'

'Where?'

'Kitchenly Mill Race.'

'That's where you live.'

'Yes.'

'I know you do.'

'You do?'

'Yes. You just told me. What are you, some kind of under-taker? Coffin? What sort of name's that?'

'Crofton.'

'Never heard of you or your people. You say you farm there?'

'We just live there.'

'Live. What's that? Just live. Umph. Is Burtenshaw still out there?'

'Do you mean at the farms?'

'No, at the mill. Billy Burtonshaw, manager there once.'

I said, 'Colonel Halmer had it, did he not?'

'Ah yeah. I remember that blighter. That was the owner. I knew the father. But Billy Burtenshaw was managing the mill, that's a sure thing. A trim, she says. A trim, and you've as much hair on you as Crystal Gayle. That's a big job. Big problem. Like that tube of piping I dug out of Cossley's field that time.'

I nodded, perturbed. 'Just a trim. If that's at all possible. In fact just hardly touch it. Maybe tidy up the ends. Actually, look, I can easily come back another day if you're possibly too busy, right at this moment. With *Dallas* on, and suchlike.' I made to rise from the barber's chair.

'I don't watch women's nonsense; what do you take me for? Let me find my scissors here.' He began, slowly, to circle the chair, like a stoned Winston Churchill doing a Sioux war dance, reaching out occasionally to touch something beneath the mirror. He clearly couldn't see much as he craned in closer, looming over objects to confirm their identity and purpose. At one point he even picked up that screwdriver and squinted then dropped it, which made me more uneasy than I already was.

'Why don't you try looking in some of those drawers?' I suggested.

'What?'

'Why don't you try in some of those drawers?'

'Yes. Or I'll need to use something else on you.'

I coughed. I stood up and assisted him in looking. Without scissors he might suggest a razor.

He tugged other drawers with difficulty and each was crammed full of more random junk. Finally, he located the scissors. They were on the deep sill of the street-facing window. It seemed almost dark outside when he shifted that rigid curtain. I sat down on the chair again in my expected position and Mr Boniface came back at me, reached out the scissors with a firm jab and a snip. I felt my head tip over to the left with the weight loss from my hair. 'Whoah!' I yelled. 'You've cut away a lot there, Mr Boniface. And you haven't given me a gown thing to cover myself.'

'I never cut you. Did I?'

'No, not me, but that's quite a heft of my hair you took away.'

He made a breathing sound, a suck of saliva through teeth. 'Well we can even it back on this view here.' Snip – another

266

slab of hair slapped down onto my lap. 'That's a lot of hair. Don't you have a . . . a, what's it called? The thing you tuck into my shirt to keep hair snippings off?'

'Don't be sissy. Even John Botting's tup never asked for a cape. They had him in here for a bet and a trim. Meant to be in the newspaper but I never did see it. Most folks know to come here wearing their long raincoat and the hair slides off that nicely. Hold still now.'

So I was right about the sheep hair. I placed the *Horse & Hound* in my lap to try and catch some of the snipped hair. Being barbered by Boniface: abit like being eaten alive by a predator; it must be like that for the wide-eyed mouse being slowly swallowed by the snake. I grimaced, blinked, Boniface made that sucking noise and snapped out at me a couple more times with the blades, so I felt another part of myself fall away.

'Right, that's you. A weight off your mind.' He made a choking sound which must have been his laugh.

I could see myself in the mirror. Like I was recovering from skull surgery after injuries sustained in a downhill ski accident, and my hair was unevenly growing back in over my misshapen head. I had resigned myself already to asking for hair repair from Mrs H. She had once trimmed my barnet before, when I was going up to Stafford to take Doris Boardman out on a romantic date of a steak dinner.

'Thank you, Mr Boniface,' I said. 'And how much do I owe you?'

'Make it two quid flat. No, make it three plus tip is four.'

I took out my old leather wallet and gave him four pound notes.

'You've blushed pink as a girl. You must think you look lovely? But you've only rosed-up down one side, man. You must be headed for a bloody stroke or something. You want to see a doctor.'

*

With some difficulty operating the locks, he released me. I had been there so long it was dark outside in Kitchenly main street. I walked away rapidly, down the pavement with my nutter's haircut, hoping no loitering youths – Nat or otherwise – were hounding the village green, but luckily the place was still devoid of human activity.

The street lamps dropped down those huge medallions of mandarin-coloured light at regular intervals. I ducked in between the two buildings to take the path back across the night fields. I hoped I didn't meet any determined dog walkers operating by torchlight, a phenomenon I had encountered in the past.

The polished night sky above me glowed and seemed to show how northern hemispheres lean out into the space of the galaxy, and the stars were like fissures showing. The moon was a ping-pong ball first here then there, to my left as I took to the open lands. I stumbled down the paths, darkness at my feet, only keeping on track once I had cleared the fence by feeling the longer grass swipe at my Kickers to left and to right, which indicated I was straying and realigned me.

As I made my way back in the direction of Kitchenly Mill Race, I was looking forward to gaining the security of its confines and getting myself in front of a familiar mirror in order to assess the physical damage the day had bestowed upon my head.

Soon I had passed the beer-can tree, invisible in the obscurity, and I was ascending the path out of the dip, the starlight gently touching the roofing tiles of Brockleberry Rents bungalows as they slowly appeared. I noted electric lights showing in various window shapes so I stopped and breathed in the cautious air of the early evening, not yet cooled by the slow rotation of darkness.

I frowned towards those bungalows, attempting to calibrate the specific street number of the houses which had lights on in their windows. Rose's house at number 4 appeared to be in darkness but I was sure lights showed from a sitting room or

– perhaps – even a bedroom, further along at what could be number 3 – or, 2? Would I dare go closer though? Imagine if I was discovered by Natandra's potty mum.

The back of Brockleberry Rents faced directly onto this huge and vacant meadow with its considerable sightlines which now lay in dark night. The moon was up there but lowish and weak. Was it possible – unlike the regime of Kitchenly Mill Race – that the household at number 2 was considerably lax in regard to the drawing of curtains? And there was no huge illumination in the new rear gardens – no security lamps or back-door lights seemed to show, so this would allow the field that came up so close to their rear fences to conceal a careful observer. By a certain irony, the streetlights of the village had been extended along the new pavement to accommodate the bungalows, but these new lamp posts stood as empty poles, the lamps themselves not yet fitted to their tops, so this added to the profound blackness around the area on the roadside. Surely even a lit-up living-room window could only cast a feeble beam rearwards into the field, and one which could be avoided by moving slightly to the left or right?

I tried moving across the open pasture towards those low houses but it felt like walking upright into gunfire. It seemed reckless and dangerous, so while I kept moving, I found myself instinctively bending my upper body over more and more as I got closer to the main road. Then I advanced in a running crouch, exactly like a soldier under fire. Finally, I resolved to do what must be done. I got down onto my stomach and I began to crawl across the meadow grass towards where I considered number 2 Brockleberry Rents to be.

Perhaps I had begun my stealthy mode of locomotion a little too early as it really took a very long time to reach that distant point at crawl, rather than walking; but I continued on over the grass, wishing I had gloves, hoping no fresh animal droppings were encountered. When sparse traffic passed, going east or west, I lowered my head and lay still until the headlights had moved into the distance.

Finally, I came much closer to the row of houses; I was tense, by this point my body was absolutely flat against the grass. I moved forwards at a very slow and cautious pace; after all, I knew Rose's family kept a dog. Might the mutt not be tethered in the back garden and draw attention to my furtive scuffling, by its barking and whining?

As I came very close to the rear garden fences and tried to identify exactly what house I was positioned behind, I found myself looking into a harshly illuminated room. It was lit by a still-naked bulb hung from a ceiling wire with no lampshade. Beyond the intensity of the light I could see an interior area of wallpaper – an off-purple colour – but concealing most of that wall was a large poster, reflecting the bulb's glare; it was then I recognised the troubled figure of Gary Numan, his white brow frowning. I felt a pleasing burst of excitement, but combined with a deep feeling of perversion. What if Nat walked before the window in some state of undress and we were drawn together again into yet more obscure intimacy? Or was that what I wanted? Where was the youthful mother's bedroom? I would rather see underwear on her. I realigned myself and began quickly crawling east, along the fence edge to what I could see was another illuminated interior. As I cautiously came adjacent to it, I saw that the curtains were almost completely drawn over, but still there was a small gap where the two fabrics had not fully joined. Within, I could distinguish wallpaper or perhaps the edge of a piece of furniture. My heart was beating stridently. I remained there for some time.

I so wish I could report I saw something significant, even a glimpse of Natandra's mother in some compromising act; however, this is not a work of fiction but an accurate historical record, and I saw nothing but the telltale and familiar blue-grey

270

light of a television screen, shifting and recalibrating itself in odd, jerking, uneven rhythms. The feverish pattern of our era.

At one point I had intended to withdraw from the whole area but to my alarm, three hundred yards across Foul Mile, I saw the illumination of a small electric torch. A night walker – or walkers – making their way through that witching hour – and possibly accompanied by a pesky mutt which would root me out as these sniffers do. Though the distance between us was great, I couldn't risk much movement, and I had to remain low against the ground until that lonesome pilot light ambled on then passed away into the black.

I slowly crawled, retracing my previous scramble, to Natandra's bedroom window, hoping to catch a glimpse of her too. Instead I found myself studying Gary Numan's concerned visage. I strained, listening for his music but could hear nothing. I would be lying if I did not admit my imagination considered Natandra walking slowly up to the glass of the window, wearing only white functional underwear, reaching to take grip of the curtains quite high up, the almost-flat breasts vanishing above the fragile ribcage, the white briefs stretching as she stood on tiptoe and sharply pulled the curtains, zipping them together. Or better, Natandra in the state of undress previously described but bent firmly over Rose's two legs on a chair, as Rose grabbed Nat's black hair and gently but firmly delivered a series of sharp spanks to her taut bottom in tight white briefs. But the record states none of this occurred.

The path far behind me appeared cleared of the night strollers' torchlight so I crawled away, eventually pulling myself forwards on my elbows. I paused to look backwards over my shoulders then seeing that no movement or possible observer of any type seemed to be around the houses of Brockleberry Rents, I rose up onto my feet and ran ahead in a crouching position, my breathing heavy. I only fell over once. Some distance further

271

on, I straightened up fully but continued to run, squinting for the path ahead so I would not cross beyond it.

When I did find the path I stood gulping air but listening in both directions, for of course I did not want to meet a dog walker who may witness me behaving in this unorthodox manner, midfield in darkest night with hair of a stark raving lunatic. How to explain myself? Seeking buried truffles? Perhaps that I needed to relieve myself after a few ales in the Babbacombe Lee – much like Dr Christopher's sadly ailing patient with his kidney stones – so I had walked to the centre of the meadow to urinate, in order not to shock anyone traversing along the pathway? A bit elaborate but there we go. That would have been my alibi.

I followed the path beneath the haughty stars until it took me to the crossing style on the side road which leads up along the main boundary wall of Kitchenly Mill Race. However, it might surprise you to learn that I did not step directly to the main gates of Kitchenly and tap in the security code. Instead I walked on up the single-track road towards the upper farms, but at the corner of our boundary I stepped down off the roadside verge where a way exists beside the high walls which Mullan keeps trimmed back during summers, ensuring we have clear access to our brickwork, and also so brambles and overgrowth never build up against them. I followed the wall in the dark, sometimes putting my right hand out onto the bricks for support if I was a bit unsure of my footing.

The birch trees I usefully described viewed from Ablemyre Hill are over this wall, though planted a distance back from it to avoid root incursions beneath. Of course part of this wall running west to east forms the north side of the stables courtyard but I moved onwards below the stables on the slight downwards slope, where abruptly the wall ends without turning north or south. It just ends. A fence continues on but shortly after it too drops from waist height, sinking in a single, long, slowly descending wire into the ground. You are at the north-east corner of the gardens and it is here, by walking a little to the south, that you can simply turn and walk back into our private grounds.

I wanted to experience approaching our grounds at night with its mood lighting, just as the intruder did, so in I came, stepping between the trees and, sure enough, severed, sliced and chopped up sideways by transverse bushes, leaves and branches, Kitchenly Mill Race's floodlit night garden began to emerge from the moving black boughs on either side of me.

I had the curious feeling of being insubstantial. I was no more than a moving eye and the shadows and negative spaces of black were moving through me without physical contact. I emerged by the eerie green glow of the willow trees, lit from within their umbrellas like giant jellyfish; the reflective black slick of the mill race was silent and seemingly unmoving. The dwellings themselves, the mill houses, air bridges and the main manor all appeared dark within. Apart from the delicate framework of the two-storey porch, the chandelier within illuminating the small glass panes into a texture which seemed made of sugar. Mrs H had made a fine job of switching on the night lights, I proudly thought.

As I came up the limestone paving stones I saw Mrs H had drawn all the curtains but, either by overlooking them, or more likely, as a deliberate welcome upon my return, she had kept the lights in the main kitchen switched on and had not drawn the curtains on the windows which look out directly onto the moat.

Here I had another strange sensation. As I approached the yellow spaces of the windows, I expected nothing more than to see my own self through them; myself in the kitchen, moving meekly, helplessly from side to side, perhaps filling the aluminium electric kettle at the curved sink tap – and it was my former self I saw – or expected to see – unshaven, long-haired, not sunburned down one side of my face. Not this wreck of a thing I was – better off for me to stand outside, unworthy, looking in.

I myself had become the intruder.

8

What strange dreams. I was awoken that morning in my low-roofed room . . . waking from a dream – a further haircut – a letter – motoring to Halward Coombe – an enchanted breakdown.

What strange dreams. I was awoken that morning in my low-roofed room by the crush of Mrs H's Triumph on the gravel of the car parking area.

The night before I had assessed the vanity damage. Of course, the best mirrors were up in Marko and Auralie's master bedroom, so I had taken myself there and indulged in a hot shower, using another fine garment of Auralie's underwear for all of my purposes.

I found a sort of soothing cream among her battalions of bottled toiletries and I applied this white ointment to the sunburned portion of my face. Rather than returning a sense of equilibrium to my looks, the white cream instead made me look even more freakish: a sort of disfigured Marcel Marceau, Dylan on the Rolling Thunder tour. However, I discovered by applying the cream all over my face, my appearance became more uniform. In fact, with my pale face and my rough, short hair now violently slicked back – did I not, in a humble way, carry some resemblance to Gary Numan himself?

With this in mind, I found some of Auralie's white make-up powder which I transported a quantity of to my own rooms to experiment with, making my complexion more pale all round – and certainly to cool the strident scarlet on the burned side of my face. I had even slept in my 'make-up'.

I went to the telephone in my kitchenette and used the intercom button. This button simply calls all five phones simultaneously throughout the house. Auralie – when in residence – was a frequent user of this feature, to rouse me from quiet times in my rooms. Mrs H answered at her end. 'Kitchenly 4-3-4,' she said politely.

'Mrs H?'

'Crofton? Where are you?'

'Here. Just over in my place, one hundred feet distant.'

'Oh. How are you dear? You weren't home when I left; you were out on your walk still. I hope I switched on all the garden lights in the correct manner? I left the lights in the kitchen on for you, after I put the cats' food out. Did you get back all right?'

'Yes, thanks. I'm fine. Well, actually, I just wanted to say, I don't want you to be shocked when you see me, but—'

'Why? What is it? What's happened now?'

'Nothing. I just don't want you to get a fright when you see me, but I had a few adventures yesterday evening.'

'What is it now? Oh Crofton, you didn't go and get in a fist fight with local boys in the village pub, did you? You're above that kind of thing. You're far too clever for mixing with that rabble.'

'No, Mrs H. It's just . . . Well, it's easier if you see me. I'll come over.'

I walked through both air bridges, glancing at the concealed shit stain, under the 1602 lintel and through the Tudor panelling into the manor house, beyond the great staircase. I rounded the corner of the morning room and Mrs H screamed. 'God, the farm lads have sheared you and what have you got on your face?'

'Sunburn, but I put stuff on. I fell asleep up Ablemyre Hill then I got my hair cut by a lunatic in the village. I should have stayed in the house – this going out was your idea.'

Her face of pity now fell into one of bemusement and she walked up to me. 'Oh, poor Crofton. What a mess. I mean it's all in tufts and tuggles. Who on earth did this? And your face . . .' She peeled off her yellow Marigold kitchen gloves and lifted her bare fingers into my hair, examining the tufts and tugging at them, so my head moved slightly from side to side. It was rather pleasing to be touched so.

278

'His name was Mr Boniface, a right old Scrooge.'

'But that's Boniface the barber. Crofton, he's famous. Famous as a blasted eccentric. He hasn't had his barbers open since the death penalty was abolished and it shouldn't have been. For him. Miserable old so-and-so. Olive knows all about him.'

'I was recommended him by my doctor, who is also mad.'

'That queer Boniface was in the local papers back in May; he cut a sheep's hair for a Rotary Club charity do. There was a picture of him in the paper, I promise you. He even gave the poor sheep an awful haircut. Quite like this. Should have had the RSPCA straight on to him. Gosh, it makes you look much younger though, Crofton. Much younger. Let me get the hair scissors I keep in the kitchen for Molly and I'll tidy you right up some. Now that sunburn is quite nasty; you want a slap of oatmeal and some cucumber on that, my boy. Of course, there are no cucumbers in, or if there were, Olive has taken them, but I could drive to the village and get you some. They probably won't have a nice Dutch cucumber in that useless garage though. I'll need to go into town.'

'No, Mrs H, don't bother with all that. I cover it with this other stuff.'

She set a chair in the kitchen with old copies of the *Financial Times* and *Radio Times* spread out on the tiles. She went to work reconfiguring my hair, doing a rather swell job while I explained I wanted it a bit longer at the front then I would sweep it back with a comb and some Brylcreem. As she cut, I recounted a censored version of my experiences of the day before, carefully excluding my crawling episode in the meadow of Foul Mile and also skipping the fact that I did indeed find my jeans and T-shirt smeared with what I concluded was dog excrement as a result of those extensive crawling activities. Foul indeed.

She finished her operations on me by mixing oatmeal with a little milk and water, then commanding me to lie on my back on the sofa in the colour television room for half an hour with the strange unction plastered on me. Just as she was leaving the room to attend to more of her chores about the house, she said, 'Oh. There was mail up in the box which I brought down.' She left me lying there with some letters. One was a letter from the local authority rates board which I did not open, as my attention was immediately seized by a handwritten envelope with a second-class stamp on it, bizarrely addressed to me. I thought of Doris Boardman, but there was no Stafford postmark on it. As I lay there, I tore the letter open and saw curly, careful feminine handwriting in blue pen. I so prefer black ink.

2 Brockleberry Rents
Kitchenly
Telephone 386

Dear Mr Clark or Croftun (if you dont mind).

I am writing to apologise for all my behaviour and language last week outside our house.

After talking to my daughter Natandra I see how kind and patient and respectful you were to her and her new friend Rose Weaver after they called round without a invitation at the property you manage over there.

Natandra explained to me how you showed them round your place with a little tour there and even opened up a studio recording place for them to see things as the girls expressed an interest in music. Like many girls their ages they are music daft and it was extremely generous of you to treat them the way you did. I think you even provided them with refreshments.

More so than all this it was beyond the call of duty and very sweet and responsible for you to provide safe transport for them both back to here along what is – as you rightly pointed out – a busy and dangerous road for pedestrians. Especially young girls of their age alone. It was really really silly of the girls to walk along that road alone with all kinds of people driving the roads these days – if you know what I mean. I would happily have driven them to your property if I had been informed me what they were up to but as I am sure you know teenagers will be teenagers. I was like that myself. Very will full. If that is the right word or spelling.

Please do forgive my behaviour. I am afraid Natandra is at that difficult age when parents think the worst all of the time. I know I am extremely over protective about her as I am only her mum alone and there is just the both of us.

I have become one of them people who preach what they didn't practise themselves. But that is only my guilt and anger at myself that was coming out at you – if you get what I am on about. That was not a reflection on you it was a display of me and not for a moment should I have put you in that position which must have seemed really awful and cringey. Really sorry.

If you ever felt like going for a friendly drink sometime with me (Natandra safely at home with telly on and not allowed out ha ha ha ha), let me know. Just a friendly drink. Sort of to say thanks.

Again I am dead sorry for the way I freaked out and even if you cant be bothered to get back in touch I wanted to say all this and thank you.

A big hug. Sorry. Abigail Losey. X X X

p.s. maybe not say about this letter to Nat?

I looked up at the adjustable chrome lights on the ceiling of the television room for a long time. I couldn't understand it. God knows what an awful guy I am, crawling around outside this woman's house the night before, having smutty and wrongful thoughts about her daughter more than her. Why would an awful guy like me be rewarded and given a chance in this way? I really could not believe it.

I jumped up. A slobber of wet oatmeal slid off my cheek and onto the sofa. I cursed out loud but, when it is considered, the sofa itself is almost the same colour as oatmeal, so I didn't think the stain could be at all lasting. All the same, I went to the kitchen joyfully to get a damp cloth and tried my best to clean the mess up.

I intended to change my ways and become a better and cleaner person round that house.

I washed the rest of the oatmeal off my face in the kitchen sink. I rushed to my kitchenette, returning to the telephone. I dialled 386.

'Hello-oh 386.'

'Oh. Natandra?'

'Who's this, please?'

'Nat, it's Crofton, from Kitchenly Mill . . . the big house.'

'Oh. Wow. How did you get my phone number?'

'Eh, I got it from the phone directory, well not the directory, no – eh, directory enquiries gave it to me, 'cause I know your surname and address. Had to be you or your mum.'

'You're calling me or Mum? What's wrong?'

'Nothing's wrong, it's just, eh, it's been preying on my mind. I obviously upset your mum by driving you two home the other evening and she was entitled to be annoyed.'

'No, she wasn't.'

'She was. I really should have telephoned your mum first thing when you came over to the house here, just to inform her where you both were. That was my responsibility and I didn't do that, so I wanted to have a word with your mum, if you please, just to fully apologise.'

'We're not kids. Well I amn't, but I've been so embarrassed and angry at her. She just blew her top as usual at you, not at

282

me; it was crazy, and I've felt awful since you were so dead nice to me. Us. I'm really sorry for the way she is. The way she talked to you. I know she feels bad about it now 'cause I talked with her and explained it all. Think it should be my mum says sorry to you. And I think she will. Sometime.'

'Is your mum there now, so I could have a word?'

'Nah, thank goodness.'

'Oh. She isn't?'

'Gone to Marlborough for the day, coming back tonight. How are you?'

'Me? Oh I'm brilliant, yeah. Eh, hey, look. I heard "Cars"' on the radio. Man, it's so brilliant.'

She screamed down the phone, 'Wow! You heard it and you like it? How good is it? It's so brilliant isn't it?'

'It really, really is, and I'm not just saying that to try and pretend I'm some cool old guy or something. It's a really brilliant song. It will be a classic rock song, for sure. Hey, what are you up to just now?'

'Me? Oh, just messing around the house listening to the radio and that. Rose is away too; they've all gone to a furniture warehouse up near Guildford, or some crap.'

'Do you want to go for a drive somewhere or something?'

'What?'

'Do you want to go out for a drive and then I'll try and see your mum some other time?'

'What do you mean, see her?'

'I mean . . . I mean, I'd like to see your mum and apologise for everything. At some point.'

'But Crofton, Mum feels really bad anyways. Honest. I told her that you were this nice guy and she realises what a twit she looks after her big freak-out stuff, so I really don't think you need to say sorry to her and . . . What do you mean a drive? You and me go for a drive?'

283

'Why not? It's another nice day.'

'Oh, but I mean, where would we go?'

'Well, we can go wherever tickles your fancy. I mean, whatever you think. "We can drive down to Eastbourne and have an ice cream cone by the sea,"' I quoted.

She laughed a bit harshly.

I said, 'This really brilliant rock star guy said that to me. Keith Emerson, from Emerson Lake & Palmer; amazing player. There's a bloke with a few synthesisers. We can just drive down to Eastbourne, have an ice cream cone by the sea. Cool, eh?'

'I'm not ten years old though. I don't really like ice cream.'

'Oh. Hey, what age are you, incidentally?'

'What?'

'What age are you? Fifteen, is it?'

'Why? I was sixteen in May, right? I'm sixteen, and Mum can't boss me around and tell me what to do every minute any more. That's what I'm so pissed off about with her. She can be kind of evil.'

'Well, it's just, Rose is a bit cuckoo, eh, but you're cool.'

'Uh. Thanks.'

'Will I? Come round?'

'Well, I dunno. What would Mum say?'

'You're sixteen. But yeah, I don't think she would mind, but. Well don't worry – another time. Maybe I can take you *and* your mum out one day then, for a motor around?'

'That sounds rubbish. With her.'

'Well how about if I come round for just you right now and take you for a quick ride? What if I come in a really cool car?'

There was a silence. 'What, like one of that guitar guy's swanky cars?'

'Yeah. Like a really, really cool car.'

There was a pause then she said, 'Give us half an hour though, I want to get changed and that.'

284

'Great. Be there in a half-hour. I promise.'

I went to put on my make-up. I had been giving a great deal of thought to the Gary Numan look. I did have a denim boiler suit and had tried it, but there was something not quite right about it. I looked like an unwelcome plumber. But I had found this black shirt of Marko's in his wardrobe and, with my old jeans, I reckon it was okay. I knew not to overdo it on the powdered face, but I had to calm down that sunburn somehow. Blue Stratos aftershave. Not too much.

Of course, the normal noise involved in raising the garage doors and starting up the Ferrari Dino has been usefully reported earlier. I was very concerned Mrs H might witness my departure, but I would assemble an alibi.

I sat in that enveloping, solid leather seat and adjusted the car's mirrors to suit my own disposition and not Marko's, knowing I should be careful to change the mirror positions back to his requirements not mine; I took note of the variations best I could.

One of the great things about being the driver of the Ferrari Dino was having the remote-control box to open and close the front gates without having to climb from the vehicle every bloody time – though I admit I made matters worse for myself because of my bloody obsession with closing them.

I reversed out into the stables courtyard then was off, in first gear all the way down and over the Victorian coach bridge and up the curve of drive, seeing how far away the remote would work the gates – and it functioned very early indeed. I tossed the remote onto the passenger seat beside me then drove right on out, but looking both ways for bloody tractors and their smelly trailers. I turned the fat steering wheel with a single finger and onto the side road. No horse shit for once!

I focused on taking the wide, low car slowly all the way down the single track alongside the wall, just to savour acceleration when it came. At the A-class main road I turned – not as you might be expecting, to the right, towards Kitchenly and the bungalows of Brockleberry Rents, but instead I indicated left at the old telegraph pole and headed in the direction of Maxtelham where there were a lot of long straight sections of road.

Up into second, using those strange gears, the shift stick firm in its chrome grooves, that odd hesitation on the change up, as the entire car seems to resist the whole concept of going to another powerful gear – cautioning you. And I clutched her into third. And at last up to fourth. The pause of breath. The whole thing pushed me quite obviously back in my seat – the noise of curtailed power between the constricted combustion and the refined exhaust was so energising and I was touching 100mph on the straight in no time. Strewth. And all this on just six cylinders – who needs a V-12?

Two cars came the other way and it was impossible not to take a deep flush of inner pride to be seen by other witnesses while behind the wheel of such a machine, so I gave them both a cheeky wave. They would mistake me for Marko Morrell. Maybe. Or even Gary Numan!

I crossed the river bridge and took the long, pulled-out curves but I'm not a looner, so I took the speed way back down and continued at the steady pace of 50. I had to watch for officers of the law – but this was a thought, as an uninsured driver, which I cast out my mind so as not to spoil the overall experience.

About a mile west of Maxtelham there is a long lay-by sometimes used by suburban picnickers or caravaners. It is on the southern roadside and here I indicated and slowed, letting a lorry pass in the opposite direction before swinging round and coming to a halt in the lay-by, facing in the Kitchenly direction. I knew how the car looked to other drivers with its strange, limpet-like crouch, splayed wide as if hovering over the roadway on its radial tyres and its weight, moving as if in another dimension ruled by jump-cut photography as it hugged the corners. I just sat in the Ferrari for a moment and returned the remote-control device to the glove compartment. As an afterthought I put on my seat belt. There was no sense being silly.

I waited, making sure there was no traffic in either direction then started off homewards again, taking her much quicker up the gears this time. You were between 60 and 70 before you knew it. I could have reached Kitchenly in third, but there was a satisfaction in hearing that throat-clearing engine sound between the shifts, so I went up and down the gears again, checking in my mirror. My driving skills were quite innate, I thought. I was sure I was a better driver of this car than Marko was.

Kitchenly village and Brockleberry Rents came at me as if through a magnified and speeded-up screen, so I gently braked her down and swung over into the small driveway of number 2.

I checked my hair and general appearance once again in the rear-view mirror and, while in neutral, I stood on the gas a couple of times to announce my arrival. Sure enough, about two doors down a bloke working, bent over in his newly planted flower bed, rose up sharply and stared down across the other gardens towards me in my outlandish vehicle. Through my wound-down window I could hear the Weavers' dog starting up a bonkers barking frenzy along in their house, but at that moment the front door of number 2 opened sharply and the diminutive dark figure appeared in the small porch.

She looked at the post-box-scarlet car and she raised her fingers to her pale face. Natandra Losey smiled but she also frowned, noticing something new about my appearance. She walked very slowly towards my wound-down window but I clicked my tongue, pointed and reached across to swing open the passenger door. She leaned and looked into the car exactly as her mother had done when I was in the old Volvo.

'Crofton?'

'It is I. What do you think of the new me?'

'Where has all your hair gone?' she said in a voice both astonished but somehow afraid.

'It was chopped off by the mad barber of the village. Get in and I'll tell you all about it.'

I felt I was talking through cotton wool though, because since she had emerged from the door, I was highly aware of what she was wearing: a sort of tight black tunic jacket which hugged her small body and was sealed up with these beautifully shaped velvet buttons – slightly Hendrix-like. She also, most noticeably, wore a very skimpy black skirt, the brevity of which was highlighted by bright-white tights in a weave pattern all down her slim legs, to boots which on this day had some kind of heels on them. When she had visited Kitchenly Mill Race she must have had her hair pinned down in some way, because I previously assumed it was bobbed or shorter than it was, and now she had formed it into a black ponytail of some sort, in which she had secured a white lace scarf. Her eyes had black make-up drawn at their sides.

'Your hair's got longer and mine's got shorter,' I stated. 'You look like a fantastic French film star,' I told her.

She still hadn't got in the car. 'Uh, thanks. Have you got make-up on?'

'I have to wear it for my sunburn, look. I got sunburned yesterday. Quite badly, so I have to glam up.'

She started laughing with a fascinated edge. 'You look sort of cool. Mad. But cool.'

'Why, thank you.'

'What a bloody car.' But she spoke keeping her eyes on me, not in any way scrutinising the car with its dashboard or leather, metal and wood as any male would surely do.

'Are you getting in?'

'Oh my.' She eased herself down into the passenger seat, putting the white legs out in front of her; she looked around the cramped interior. She pulled the car door carefully to her but its own weight closed it with that heavy, laden sound. The legs, the white lace on the pale flesh. 'You can't get much of a suitcase in here,' she told me.

'You need to put your seat belt on. It packs a bit of a punch this motor.'

'Oh. Okay.' She reached around and pulled the seat belt out of its taut hanging and I took the tongue from her fingers and pulled it across and down to the chrome securing buckle between us, clicking it in.

I asked, 'Is that okay?'

She smiled, nodded, looked at me, 'What car is this then?' But I could see she was coming to terms with my appearance.

'It's a Ferrari Dino. Italian.'

'Can it go dead fast?

'Well it can, but not if you don't want to.'

She shook her head. 'I can't get over your hair and everything. You look . . . Well, like someone different.'

'It's still me. I couldn't help it. I was told to go to this old hairdresser in the village who was blind as a bat and he had hacked half my hair off before I could stop him.'

She laughed. 'Wait till I tell Rose.'

'It was quite scary, actually. They say he cut a sheep's hair once that they sat up in his chair.'

She laughed again, an odd, throaty and masculine chuckle. She had on red lipstick too, for sure.

I said, 'Let's get the show on the road, kidda.' I craned round, looking both ways and reversed out slowly, facing the long, low bonnet towards Maxtelham, then I took off. I didn't overdo it but I did go gently up the full gears, noting her head which moved in an involuntary manner, a little way back and a little way forwards.

'Weee,' she said, as she turned to me and smiled, but as the speed built, I saw her being fully pushed back in her seat, as

289

if cruelly and by my own hand; she held herself more tensely. I slowed down and just took it easy instead of trying to be flash. I hummed the opening melody and recited the first lines of Gary Numan's 'Cars'. She laughed and she sang along for a moment, then we both laughed. I didn't know all the words, so I couldn't go on for long.

I declared, 'We'll go up to Halward Coombe.'

'What's that?' With the windows down she had to shout a bit. I saw how the slipstream from outside tossed at her ponytail and scarf.

'It's like a beauty spot. For a beauty.'

She looked straight ahead but smiled.

We cantered through the fine day, into Herstmonceaux with the Pevensey Levels way out to our right. Far off, I think we could see Firle Beacon at the end of the South Downs. I drove pretty slowly, following another car which was motoring at a leisurely pace, until the one long straight spot I was anticipating; I checked my mirror and kicked the Ferrari out and quickly up the gears, standing on the accelerator – the hidden nature of the car burst forth as we just soared by that slowcoach Ford Cortina.

As I carried on up the wrong lane, accelerating and then easing back over to our side of the road, I heard a small, frightened peep of exclamation from her, so I slowed back down again.

I looked over and laughed, 'Are you all right, love?'

'That's a bit scarily fast.'

'All right, no more fancy stuff.' And I slowed down to an almost comical pace, since no one was behind us. She looked over at me and laughed.

'What's your mum doing in Marlborough?' I asked, speeding up a bit again.

'Mum? She's from there. Visiting Nan. I couldn't be bothered going, which pissed her off.'

I nodded.

'My Granny Losey can be good for a laugh though. She is eighty-seven and I asked her the secret of her long good health and she said to me, "Silly girl. I have felt ill every day of my life."' Natandra looked at me with an oddly mature eye and added, 'Make of that what you will.'

I laughed away at this. I found this lass genuinely smart and funny. I said, 'We'll pull round here to Halward Coombe then we can double back to get home over the little farm roads, so I won't be going fast, okay?'

'All right. I suppose.'

We drove on for ten minutes or so then we came off the A road onto the B road which climbs up, trees lining the roadside all the way. There was a sign for the car park but, as I suspected when we turned in, there were only two other cars there and some folk over by the picnic tables. I circled, pushing in the clutch and revving the car once then twice, higher. In reaction to the noise Nat turned and smiled at me. I could see the family over by the picnic table looking towards us, but I aimed the bonnet towards the Coombe depth, halted then switched the engine off, ratcheting the handbrake up. Birdsong could be detected despite the Italian outburst; leaves moved in the trees above.

She looked ahead, profoundly unimpressed. 'What's this place?'

'Well a coombe is where there's a dip in the ground. It's not much of one. Not like the Devil's Punch Bowl.'

'What's that?'

'That's a big one up by Petersfield on the A3. That's a good one. A spooky place.'

'That sounds good. Like that big spooky house you live in.'

'Well maybe we'll drive up to the Devil's Punch Bowl one day?'

She turned round to look out the low strip of the distinctive rear window with the black rubber sealant round its shining chrome. 'There's no back seats; you couldn't have brought Mum if you wanted.'

291

'But you could sit on her knee.'

'Get lost, you. The very thought.'

'No room for Rose either,' I said.

'Just you and me,' she said. I had a frightening but dizzying thought she was going to reach out her tiny hand and put it on my leg. She did not. Her twisting, restless body had really pushed that skirt up over one thigh but I was a man of nearly thirty years and I firmly looked ahead towards the green coombe. 'Want to get out for a stroll?'

'No way. You know what Gary says. Safest to stay in your car with the doors locked.'

I grinned.

Then she said, 'I've got heels on, these.' She twisted her gangly legs around to reveal the footwear. But now the skirt was virtually, surely, hoisted to nearly the crotch of her tights. 'I'd fall over. A dip in the ground,' she announced. 'Scotland is nothing but huge dips in the ground and giant mountains. Down here people get all excited about the slightest little hill.' She straightened up and yes, both hands went to the hem of the skirt and gave it a quick, good little tug downwards while she minutely hoisted herself.

'I wanted to ask you about Scotland. Must be nice up there? I've never been.'

'It's all right. Rains. Thing is, I'm interested in the views of the future.'

'Oh. That's an interesting thing to say.'

'Is it? Cities and stuff. Where the future is. I do my drawings of them. Spaceships in the sky that are taxis. All this green, it gives me a headache. I'm interested in machines and robots and stuff. I'm a right tomboy.'

'Do you read about that?'

'What, the future and stuff? Yes. I quite like these sci-fi books. I've a few. It's interesting. Nothing about now, just what will be.'

'What books do you like?'

'I have a few. Read bits of them. I tried to read them all the way through, but they had too many pages and all that. Bit boring. I really like the covers on them all though; I copy them a bit in my own drawings and make up bits to add on. That's what I would like to do. Covers to books.'

'What are the names of the books?'

'I can't remember. No. Something with Rama?'

I said, *Rendezvous with Rama*. Arthur C. Clarke.'

'That's it. Wow. How did you know that?'

'I read a bit of sci-fi too. About eight years ago it's all I read. The usual stuff: Albert Bester, *Dune*, *Stranger in a Strange Land*.'

'What's that?'

'A book.'

'That's me, isn't it, stranger in a strange land?'

'No. You've made a friend already.'

She turned and looked at me. Smiled and chuckled, 'You're so sweet. Dunno why, to me. Your hair is so weird now. Like I had an image of you in my head and now it's gone.'

Was she trying to be intimate? What was I doing there with this child? I coughed. 'Well. My hair was too long. Out of date. Like me.'

She laughed. 'It was quite long. Let's see your sunburn.'

I cautiously turned my head around a bit so she could see, but I was looking in her eyes. I said quietly, 'I've been so tired lately I fell asleep on a hill when I was taking a walk and got roasted.' I coughed, 'Have you seen *Close Encounters of the Third Kind*?'

'No. I wanted to see that.'

'It's great.'

'Yeah. There was no cinemas in bloody Scotland. They were all a hundred miles away and stuff. Honest.'

'What kind of place did you live in there?'

She looked at me, 'What do you mean?'

293

'What kind of house?'

'A place in the countryside. Like here. No bloody cities either.'

'A big place, was it?'

'The village? No teensy-weensy. Mum worked in a hotel so we had accommodation from them at first then she got a rented house. We had some help though. My father and that.'

'Oh.'

'Yeah, Mum was a receptionist and bookkeeper.'

'Really?'

'Yeah. What's wrong with that?'

'Nothing. That's impressive.'

'Nah. Nothing special. I was away at school a lot. That school was a big old place.'

'So your mum was working up there and just took a brain-wave to move here, did she?'

'Well, yeah. She likes the south coast and there's more hotels for work and she goes on about getting me into a university.'

'She's from Marlborough up near Swindon?'

'Yeah.'

'Is your dad around, Nat?'

She looked down at her snowy December legs. 'Nah. Well I mean I met him and that, a couple of times, you know? Mum hates him, she was so young and he was older than her when he got her in trouble, so she had me; he's never been in my life. It's all a pain, actually.'

'And what does your dad do?'

'Well I hardly think of him as "Dad". He's just this smarmy bloke. A right plank actually.'

'Oh. What does he do?'

'Do? He's quite rich.'

'Oh, is he now? What does he do?'

'You really want to know?'

'Yeah, of course.'

'It's poxy and embarrassing. He owns a whole lot of dry-cleaner places round Northampton and that. He always had a fresh shirt on.'

I laughed. 'I'm not going to go on about it. I know it bugs you. Sorry to be asking. What it is, is. You're a great kid and I find it hard to imagine how a geezer can just sort of, not want to be round you. Be with his own daughter, you know? I'm a bit old-fashioned that way.'

'Mmmm. It was hard for them both. Mum said that, and the families ganged up on them and that was that. I was lucky I wasn't, you know . . . Fostered out and stuff. Might have never known my own mum. They did stuff like that back then, didn't they? Mum had me and Mum struggled on. I mean, she's my mum. I love her and that, and she's always been there for me. Even if she's a pain.'

'He hasn't been there for you?'

'Well, he has provided money. How come you don't have kids and sort of a wife and all that? You don't have a girlfriend, do you?'

'No. Nobody. I had my heart broken years ago by an idiot.'

'Oh, shame. I'm sorry about that.' She sighed. 'I had a boyfriend last year. He didn't break my heart or anything, but he certainly pissed me off. I wish I'd brought something to drink, like – there's this bottle of Blue Nun I have hidden for me and Rose. Know what Blue Nun is?'

'Yeah. It's a strong wine.'

'I should have brought it along and got blotto eh? But nowhere to pee as usual but trees and bushes.'

'Yeah.'

There was a long silence. There was a little bump on the roof and she looked up. I knew what it was, a leaf or twig from one of the trees above perhaps dislodged by a bird. Face it, I was jealous about the boyfriend. Suddenly she asked, 'Do you have to look after your boss, 'cause he's dead famous and rich and all that? Are you like a body guard?'

'No, no I'm not but I'm very conscious of his personal security. You have to be. Back in the early days of our band this nutter got onstage and pushed Frank Zappa right off the stage at the Rainbow up in London 'cause he thought Frank was making eyes at his girlfriend – nearly killed Frank.'

She laughed a bit harshly, 'Who's Frank Zipper?'

'Never mind. In America you have nutcases with guns who want to assassinate rock stars. And my boss is a big famous rock star. He's rich.'

'Yes, I know. I'm sitting in his dead swanky car.'

'When you have my job, security and the preservation of boundaries . . . Borders. They are vitally important.'

'I understand. Gary must have to have people like you too, to keep freaks away from him. Well, people like me.' She let out a joyous, high-pitched giggle. 'I would never do anything to harm Gary, but I know there is probably mad girls who would, so I understand what you're saying.'

'But there has been an intruder in our grounds at night. Maybe in daylight hours too.'

'An intruder? God.'

'Yeah. I've witnessed an intruder, I think; seen figures, shapes and someone else has too. I think I've seen it. Or him. Or her. The intruder. I've seen someone a few times. I think. Actually I can't remember now.'

She frowned, 'But look that's a bit crackers. How would anyone have ever got into your big gardens place? It's got all massive walls round it and that clever electric gate thing.'

'No, no, look Nat.' I turned more round to face her on this topic. 'People don't realise but there are no walls on the far side.'

'There are no walls?'

'Only on the roadside. Look . . . Say at night, you left your

296

house at Brockleberry Rents and you just climbed quietly over your back fence there, so no one in the house heard; you cross the field there; you find a path on the far side of the great meadow. You go along that path to the right and follow it for a while to the end. You come out over an easy stile, right at our main gates. Now if you had examined the place thoroughly in daylight and circled the property, you would find out you can easily wander in round the back. You can just walk in. Anybody can.'

'Really?'

'Yeah. You go up to the left and you find the end of the wall. Go round it and there's a path there. At night you can't see a thing. There are no streetlights up there but you could use a pocket torch all along that wall and I would never see it, because you would be hidden behind the tall wall. If you walk on along there – it's a pathway. Then you'll come to the end, okay?'

She whispered, 'Okay?'

'You turn right at the end of the fence, you find yourself in trees. Go carefully through these trees and in a few moments you are at the bend of the river. What we call the mill race. That's where the water was funnelled into a channel to drive the old mill wheels back in olden times, long ago when it was a full working mill, grinding the golden corn from the fields of good old England. Now as you come out of those trees, you are in our private gardens.'

'Really?'

'Yeah. And because we have the garden all lit up at night it's really lovely and a sight to see, it's all illuminated by coloured lights and carefully arranged spots and beams, and floodlights. Like a posh, ferny Blackpool.'

She whispered, 'Oh I'd like that.'

'You would. We even have lights in the water, in the river, and we have them all round the moat. It's really beautiful, magical at night. So you don't need your pocket torch any more. You just

297

stroll around at ease. Up the path there and you will come to the kitchen, by crossing over a footbridge and going on round the corner. There is grass verging, so you can move silently.' My mouth had gone dry. 'Carry on to your left there and you see the turnaround area, the front door of the house and the parked Volvo in the darkness. Now if you were to go hard right and cross that footbridge, quietly, where you were the other day, you would be right outside my place again. Where I live. There's two doors. The one into the kitchen where you were with me and Rose. My rooms are there where you . . . Well, you went upstairs there.'

'Yeah. Thanks for letting me use your loo.'

'That's how easy it is just to walk in. It's really easy for you to come in there at night.'

'Uh-huh.'

'I've always been angry at Marko that he didn't seal off the rest of the grounds. I would if I were him. Seal yourself in, like Gary in his car. But Marko's very laid back about security. Doesn't seem to worry him. It falls to me to worry about it. I dunno. Jesus, maybe I'm just jealous of other people having access to him. Maybe it's not to do with security, it's to do with me being possessive over this guy I admire too much. Maybe I'm a fu— flipping mug. Same way as your mum freaked out at me the other day. What was she doing? She was being protective of you and she regretted it. It's the same for me. My mind thinks all the wrong thoughts, not the right ones. Who even knows what right and wrong thoughts are any more?'

'There's protecting and smothering. You don't know her. And when you did meet her she just chopped your head off. Who do you think it is then? Who is the intruder?'

'I don't know. Maybe . . . Maybe there isn't one. Maybe it's all in my head. Paranoia. I mean I never got a good look at any intruder.'

'Mmmmm.'

'I know it sounds potty. I don't want to scare you, 'cause it's only meant to be in the house.'

'What?'

'Well. Like every old place in bloody England, the house is meant to have a ghost.'

'Oh, shit. No way? That's brilliant.'

'Yeah Sir Lawson Starley. He was stabbed to death at the top of the house in one of the oldest rooms. You're meant to be able to see his blood on the floorboards under the carpet. I saw it before the carpets went down in 1973 and if you ask me, someone just spilled a pot of Dulux there. Mrs H, the housekeeper, says he was behind her one day when she was making a bed and she took a week off. She doesn't like to go up to the top floor.'

'Have you ever seen anything?'

'No. Well. Once though, I heard a light switch go on in a room. Not the haunted room, one of the new ones, and when I went in the light was on. I switched it off. But then the next night when I was outside, I looked up at the window and the light was on again. I promise you that is true. I didn't go up till next morning, I admit. And when I did, though I was alone in the house, the light had been turned off.'

She said, 'Flip. That's creepy. But I suppose he'd be fascinated with electric lights.' She mused. 'So he's taken to wandering the gardens. Maybe all your lights out there have got him confused?' She laughed.

I smiled. 'Let's go,' I said, and I reached for the ignition keys.

'Oh. Okay then, I suppose,' she shrugged. She looked glum.

I started up the car and we circled the car park again.

Up and down the small hills we went, the shadows of trees brushing over both our faces like garden bonfire smoke. I took the far farm roads then we churned forth, north, up the last spine of the hills before they descend into flatness. We'd just

299

reached the summit before the route dips and curves downhill, under hedgerows and below banks all just yards away; it's a two-way road there, but narrow with rough, tussocky verges. You have to watch for tractors coming out of the fields. I geared down, gave the Ferrari some gas as we reached the top then the accelerator went slack. I pushed on it but I seemed to have come out of gear. I forced the stick down into first and the clutch slowed her abruptly, but when I gave her the accelerator there was just no response.

'What's wrong?' She turned her face to look directly at me.

'Uh, dunno.' I gave the car gas again and the engine noise escalated crazily, then suddenly there was no power going to the wheels. 'Oh shit.' I braked to a halt. I pushed the accelerator down and the engine didn't respond. I came out of neutral into first then opened the clutch and she moved forwards fine, but the revs just remained static as the first gear carried us along. The accelerator had ceased to function. I couldn't get any revs to put her into second.

'The power's gone on the bloody thing from the accelerator. It's just the clutch carrying us. I don't get it. Honestly, Italian junk.' I stopped again and put on the handbrake. 'Shit. Shit and shit.'

We sat on the flat section with a clear fifty yards of hill still to climb. Then a half-mile more on these lanes before the turn onto the main road to Kitchenly.

'Maybe someone will come along?' she quietly said, looking around.

Then I thought out loud, 'I think the accelerator cable has gone again. It went once before and Marko had to have it towed in, but we're in the middle of nowhere out here, bloody five trees from nothing.'

'Someone will come along, won't they? And help us?'

'I dunno.' I looked towards the west and already there was an aureate tannin to the sky. 'I can cover a bit of ground using the clutch and first gear but I won't be able to gear any higher and we'll, eh, certainly draw attention to ourselves on the main road at twenty miles an hour for sure. I'm not really meant to be driving this car, especially if the rozzers are about.'

'You aren't?'

'Not at all. It's not insured for me. If we get towed in, Marko will get to hear about it and I'll be in the boiling pot.'

I took off my seat belt.

'Someone will help us, won't they?'

'Maybe but . . .' I turned my neck and shifted my body around to look back down the hill. I was no longer cocky about being associated with the ostentatious vehicle. 'We need to get you home safe before your mum is onto us.'

I pulled the bonnet toggle and got out, glancing both ways up and down the road. I opened the heavy bonnet off its clasp and took a long look at the impressive machinery. The accelerator cable was hanging loose. You could see where the line reached the carb lever above the hub and the section between them was missing. I frowned, staring along the road behind us. I could walk back down, but even if I found the missing segment, how could I ever reattach it?

'Is it bad?' she called out.

'Yeah. Accelerator cable that gives it gas has gone for a burton. I can't just go along in first gear all that distance without a touch of gas on the main road to speed us up a bit. If I could give it gas I could, but. I need string or rope to tie onto the carb lever.'

I checked in the small rear luggage compartment but there was nothing apart from copies of *Vogue* and inexplicably, a clean coir doormat – perhaps kept by Marko in anticipation of inevitably having to clamber beneath the vehicle on a repair job?

Her sweet voice called out, 'What do you need string for?'

I got back in beside her. 'It's a bit desperate, but I could tie the string to the gas lever, then I could accelerate the car by

301

leaving the bonnet open an inch, my hand out the window. I
give the end of the string a tug, and vroom-vroom. That way I
could make it home easy in first gear with a car this powerful,
be a bit slow but not too bad because it's a Ferrari. But we need
string to knot it on and it needs to be quite strong.'

'What about my tights?'

I looked at her. 'You're joking.'

'No. I'm quite lanky. From the end of one foot to the other is
quite a length and they're nylon so they don't rip.'

'That's a bit embarrassing for you, Nat. And it'll ruin them.'

She shrugged, 'I'm not embarrassed. What a laugh. Would
it work?'

'Huh. It might.'

She glanced forwards and backwards up and down the road
and then got out of the car; standing there between the fields
and the high weeds of the verge banks she pulled off first one
boot then the other.

'I promise not to look,' I said and put my hands over my eyes.

'I don't mind.'

I watched. She looked both ways once again, pushing both her
hands up the front of her skirt. I saw panties then she started
tugging and wriggling a little bit, the middle crotch section of
the white nylons came lower onto her thighs, then she tugged
them on over her bared skin, first advancing one leg then the
other; she stepped free from them on her right foot, balanced
a moment and pulled them off the other foot as she raised her
heel. She reached in and held the snowy garment across the car
interior at me. I laughed.

'Well?' She started pulling her boots onto her bare feet again.

The woven heel and foot section with its darker reinforced
toe tied perfectly onto the carb lever and the length of both legs
stretched all the way back to my wing mirror by the driver's
door, which was enough. She giggled when I gave the length

of white lace a tug and the growling engine responded, once then twice.

'Sturdy tights,' I observed.

I had to jam the opened bonnet up an inch using an RAC road map from the glove compartment, but otherwise, with one hand out the window and the other on the steering wheel, I could control the car in first gear up the ascents and then declutch and let her roll down.

As we travelled onwards once more, we often looked at each other and laughed. My hand held her taut nylon tights like a fishing line which had a huge and turbulent fish hooked on the other end, responding moodily but compliantly to each tug I gave.

When we reached the main road I was lucky as it was traffic-free. I could swing left and cruise along quite smartly and though one car passed in the other direction and the driver gave my hand a fascinated glance, we met no resistance. Soon we were over the river bridge; the trees of Kitchenly Mill Race showed up to the right and the roofs of Brocklebery Rents rose ahead.

'I so hope your mum isn't in, or this will take some explaining. I mean, your tights came off for purely mechanical reasons. Right?'

She laughed. 'If she's in, I'll see the car, so drop me ahead. No, it's okay, she's not back yet. Just drop me outside, if you please.'

I stopped by their gateway.

'That was brilliant, see you then,' she said.

I nodded.

'I'll, eh, endeavour to return your tights,' I said, and I gave two tugs of throaty acceleration.

She looked in at me and chuckled. 'Your new hair is kind of fanciable,' she said then she straightened and slammed the passenger door, walking up the small drive in her high footwear, her bare legs with long, slim muscles. I pulled on her pantyhose and went on down the road, promptly indicating left.

303

Reversing would have been a risky proposition so I drove on to the wider road section as you reach the village – just beyond the *Welcome Kitchenly* sign. Here, with care, I executed a U-turn. When I passed Nat's house on the way back she had already gone inside, which made my heart dip a little.

I nursed the Dino home in first gear with no mishaps and parked up in the garages. I would need to try and get the accelerator cable repaired before Marko's return. I tried to rearrange all the mirrors to Marko's settings. With tender care I unwrapped Nat's white tights from the accelerator lever and dropped the bonnet. The right leg of the tights had been horribly stained with oil and murk, but the left leg remained gloriously pristine. Amazing, after their cruel over-extension to the limit of their length, what a small fabric they compressed down into.

I made my way directly to my rooms where I anticipated washing the tights with the greatest of care in my sink.

9

Ceilinged by noctilucent cloud, off to the west a sinking sun unbalanced our broad world . . . motoring to The Mumbleton Arms – a dinner date at a supper club – an encounter in a public saloon bar – an incident and a misunderstanding.

Ceilinged by noctilucent cloud, off to the west a sinking sun unbalanced our broad world.

In the old Volvo, I had collected Natandra's mum that evening from number 2 Brockleberry Rents. She had emerged looking overwhelming. The Stevie Nicks style: knee-high floral dress finished in white doily on the skirt hem and on the cuffs, so a laciness lay like individual snow crystals on her tawny upper arms. Her perm fuzzed out momentarily against the surrounding sunset, like the complex tributaries in some water-system diagram; leather boots compressed the unmown lawn among the peppering of daisies, themselves like unique, fallen frills.

She said, 'What have you done? To your hair?' She pulled the passenger door closed behind her with a gentleness, perhaps in self-conscious apology for the way she had previously slammed the same car door.

I felt relief; obviously Natandra had not spoken about our illicit afternoon of motoring together. 'That time you first met me,' I said, 'I was wearing a wig. This is my real hair.'

She stared at me hard then looked ahead, laughed in a way which made it a genuine, private laugh – as if she were alone, watching Dave Allen on the colour television set of her front room. I glanced uneasily at the house windows all the same. I could sense Nat was spying on us from somewhere, disgruntled and resentful.

Then there we were, motoring along. It was so reminiscent of driving with her young daughter that it was a déjà vu; windows wound fully down by the life-filled verges, disappointing to look into the gladdening light ahead – instead the need to steal leftward peeks at her haughty profile held there against

309

the passing green field of Foul Mile. Like young Natandra, her mother's face was so flat, the nose a neat button. Her eyes didn't wrinkle when she smiled; they had a strange way of seeming to fractionally elongate backwards around her skull, as if sweetly agreeing with all which came before her.

In my high nervousness I changed cassettes too often – in fact I replaced them constantly, one after another. As soon as a tune commenced playing, that music felt horribly inappropriate: not romantic, or perhaps not reflective enough. I ejected cassette tape after cassette tape in the course of what was inevitably going to be only a very brief journey – it wasn't as if we were eloping together along the coast to the ferry at Dover then driving south for Saint-Tropez.

Initially, I even awkwardly attempted to replace the cassettes in their appropriate cases, holding the steering wheel with one hand, but ultimately I didn't persist with the fiddlesome task – I just launched every rejected cassette smartly backwards between Abigail and my shoulders; not even onto the rear seat, but further, and with such force that the cassettes crashed all the way to the end of the hatchback vehicle, so when we rounded that series of corners by the water meadows at the rear of Ablemyre Hill, those tapes and their cases slithered and clattered together, first this way then that, across the bare metal of the boot base.

As well as Pythonesque showing off, I was making nervous utterances – at one point I said aloud, 'No Mac. I don't have any Mac.' I glanced across at Abigail who was watching – looking amused, but nervous. 'I don't have any Fleetwood Mac,' I told her. Though I had no evidence she favoured the music of that group, just because she looked like Stevie Nicks. We travelled on ahead.

'How have you been?' I suddenly yelped.

'Oh, all right I suppose.' She sighed. 'Nothing happening. Visited my parents.'

'Where are they then?'

310

'Marlborough.'

'Oh, yeah. I mean, are they? And how's Nat?'

'Being Nat. Locked up in her room or wandering.'

'They do. At that age, don't they? Wander. Or locked in a room. Mind you, up in the house there, I seem to find myself spending more and more time in my own room. The housekeeper told me off just the other day.'

'Did she? Housekeeper? *Upstairs Downstairs.*'

'Is a bit like that, I suppose.'

'Are you positive you aren't just avoiding housework like most men?'

'That is . . . so true.' I looked over at her and we both laughed together.

'Why so short? Your hair?'

'My pelt was scalped by the village pillock.'

Giving up on the cassettes, instead I briefly told her of the manic barber, an account which largely covered the extent of our early evening outing by car. As I spoke, she laughed that same private laugh, like little onwards encouragements to propel my story. I concluded, 'The dangers of not getting your barnet properly snipped since, I dunno, 1972? Whenever I moved down here to the sticks where all the pretty women live.'

She looked at me, then straight ahead. 'Shucks.' Then, 'Ooooh. This is ever so nice.'

'Hope you haven't eaten anything. I'm taking you to dinner.'

'Dinner? You're taking me to dinner? I thought this was just a drink? It's pricey to eat out.'

'All I make is beans on toast. I burn the toast and stick the beans to the pan.'

'But it looks so posh and swanky. I haven't had a sit-down dinner in years. I work in hotels. Reception, a bit of bookkeeping. Perhaps we could make a good impression and I shall be offered a job here?' she said, smiling at me.

311

'It's only the Mumbleton Arms.'

I steered the old Volvo into the hotel's elongated car park which extends from that long sequence of dormer windows along the Victorian façade with the flat-roofed modern extension of the Victory Rooms.

Already the floodlights in the flower beds were switched on, glazing gold tungsten stains onto the lower red brick of the hotel walls, yet there was still enough general light so that these beams didn't constitute a real illumination. The moment was all about the consistency of fluctuation between what was day and what was night.

It was the blue hour with all of its strange luminescences – brilliant glints of flying insects creating strange networks. Across the lawn and patio came drooling sun spills through the trees, beyond that new conservatory which I knew to contain a colour television for hotel residents who dozed before it.

We both found ourselves rising up from the car, closing its doors, small bird droppings and prints of peeled-off damp leaves on its long roof. I tugged down sharply the sides of my dark-green velvet jacket, gripping just beneath its pockets. I had not worn the jacket for some considerable time. Possibly years. I was concerned it retained a smell of the wardrobe.

I had my same old Levi's jeans on, which I'd neglected to throw in the washing machine, but I was wearing a crisply fresh though unironed Uriah Heep T-shirt. Or was it Jethro Tull? The Heep or the Tull. Understandably one gets them mixed up.

We walked forwards together towards the main hotel entrance which faces the road. I could sense her skirt swirling around quite above her knees. I suddenly stopped after just a few strides across the car park. 'Sorry, but did I lock the car?' I had to step away, tug the secure rear door then walk back over towards her as she waited for me. That wasn't very romantic. Who would steal the old, jiggered Volvo? Who would nick

312

my battered cassettes? I walked ahead of Abigail as there was simply no room on the grey paving stones for us to walk side by side, whereas I should have gestured 'Ladies first', but too late, and the grey paving stones were absolutely identical to those Dr Christopher had marked up at the rear of his surgery in Kitchenly village – where he got his patient to project his urine ahead as far as he could.

Just beyond the main entrance, a short distance ahead of us, a single figure had emerged from the public saloon bar and he moved across the space to the side of the road by the cast-iron bus shelter there. When the saloon bar door had opened, Abigail and I had both clearly heard the general hubbub and human chatter, the babble of a considerable clientele within – until the door swung back shut again.

We entered the hotel lobby where you could no longer hear the public bar and came side by side up to the polished surface of the reception desk. Despite the season, a wood fire burned under a mantelpiece; you would have expected a pleasing, smoky aroma to permeate, and there was some of that, but there was also something else: that strange and – to my mind – slightly bovine scent which was always present in the Mumbleton Arms.

I raised my hand to ring the bell on the reception desk. Abigail was turning her curls from side to side to observe things, but before I could lower my palm on the bell, a short man in shirt and tie with rolled-up sleeves stepped out from the back and immediately said, 'A room for the night?'

It was Harry Marley, the manager – mentioned by Rose, I recalled, sometime previously. I felt myself physically flinch at his question and in a way it was knowing that Abigail had sensed the physical flinch which made me flush even more with mortification. I tried my best to give him a steely look. 'Actually, it's dinner. The table is Morrell.'

313

Without a hint of apology he stated, 'Dinner, is it?' And shot out a hand to grab a ledger. 'Morrell, yes. If you just want to go through to the dining room along the corridor.'

'Yeah, to the right. I have been here before,' I sniffed and walked away.

I was sure she was sniggering to herself, but I led Abigail down the carpeted corridor towards the dining room. Reproductions of landscape paintings hung on the long walls: muddy, swarming deviations on *The Hay Wain*.

The dining room was not dimly lit – it was stridently ablaze with low, thickly bulbed chandeliers, as if all residents floundered in the slightest poor visibility.

The dining room was empty. I looked left then right: nobody. Seat backs faced each other across the tablecloths, set cutlery, glasses and place mats.

'This is nice.'

'Could do with a bit of livening up.'

'Bit bright, isn't it?'

'More and more, I need a pair of sunglasses,' I said.

A schoolgirl waitress came striding down the corridor behind us, adjusting an apron on her front. I got the impression she had just been upstairs turning down beds. She was wearing flat shoes and a shapeless skirt long enough to destroy the sense that she possessed any lower legs whatsoever. The skirt made her seem excessively short – possibly disfigured – in the area between her knees and the tops of the flat shoes.

'Hiya.'

'Evening,' I replied.

'I hear you've come in for dinner,' she told us, as if this was staggering news. I thought she might be about to add that chef had met with some rural mishap, but she snatched two menus bound within thick green covers from the top of a lectern by the door. 'This way, please.'

We began following her tapping ponytail on the back of her white blouse towards the far bow windows, but just before we reached there she swerved left to a small table for two, pressed against a pillar, with a single-bulb wall lamp in a red velvet shade fixed directly above it.

'Can't we sit at that table?' I pointed.

In a hushed tone she replied, 'But that's a table for four. You reserved for two.'

I replied, 'Well, after I made the reservation I asked two friends to join us as well.'

Abigail looked at me, puzzled, but I gave her a sly wink. 'They should be along later. If they do turn up that will make four of us, won't it?'

The schoolgirl waitress looked at me. 'Four,' she repeated.

'I accept you have to walk a little further to reach this table but there again, if my friends and I drink an extra bottle of wine or two, it's going to be worth it for the old hotel, isn't it?'

She looked at me. I thought she might burst into tears. Just for a split second she slid her lower lip inwards over her bottom teeth and gave that lip the briefest of little bites with her top teeth, then she slid the lip back into its normal position. 'So you want to sit at a table for four though there are just two of you?'

'Yes. But, our two expected friends might come along at any moment. Two plus two equals? Four. And look, we'll be able to spot them through the window here, won't we? And give them a little wave as they arrive. That'll be nice.'

'Mmmm. Need to ask Mr Marley.' She turned smartly, walking away, taking the menus with her.

I stepped to the table and I pulled out the high-backed chair for Abigail. She seemed a tad taken aback by my behaviour, and as the young girl disappeared out the double doors and round into the corridor, Abigail said in a low voice, 'Watch out, I think I recognise her from when Nat joined the high school. She might

315

be a pal of Nat and Rose. Thank you,' she added as she sat in the seat I held for her. In my defence she said in the same quiet, wondering voice, 'I don't really see why we shouldn't have this table though when it's so quiet.' She looked around herself and the empty dining room but with some unease.

I circled the table – which was large – and sat down in the chair to Abigail's left, next to her, but the round table meant there was a polite distance between us. It wasn't as if I was crowding her. 'An old trick of Marko's worth remembering,' I told her. 'When he was dining out in the good old days he always told the restaurant that there would be a much bigger party than there actually was. Means you get a nice big table. You say your friends are running late, then after twenty minutes you say you don't think those friends can make it after all; the restaurant aren't going to shift you off the table by then because you have already ordered drinks and the bread might have been delivered. That's what we always did when we had an Indian at Nirvana on Central Park South, so we always got a huge booth.'

'That's telling a lie though. Where is that?'

'Central Park South.'

'Where's that? Is that in Brighton?

'New York.'

'Goodness. You've been to New York? I've never met anyone who's been to New York.'

'Haven't you? Sure I have. Many, many times. With the band on concert tours. Staying at the Sherry Netherland or the Drake or the Plaza. Well, I was at the Drake and the band were at the Plaza. Nirvana is a great Indian restaurant just next to the Plaza. I remember once—'

Harry Marley was crossing the dining room towards us followed by the schoolgirl waitress.

'I'm sorry, Lorraine tells me I am to understand you are actually a party of four?'

316

'That's what you are to understand,' I told him.

There was a silence.

'You're awaiting your other dining companions, are you?'

I looked straight at him. 'That is correct. Mr Morrell and his lady friend, Auralie. We're expecting them down from Heathrow this evening. They are coming in on Concorde but I have to be frank with you and say, they might not get here for a spell. Might be headwinds. Yet at the same time they might arrive at any moment. Tailwinds. We'll all have to just wait and see, won't we? I know that's a terrific ask – but there you have it. Of course they won't be requiring a room either. We have a residence nearby.'

'I see. Concorde.'

I ducked my head a bit and pretended to look out of the window towards the car park. 'No sign of the old Ferrari yet. I expect Mr Morrell will be paying with Diners Club. You do accept Diners Club in this little hotel don't you?'

He nodded curtly, 'Yes.'

I said, 'How about a nice bottle of Liebfraumilch to get the ball rolling then?'

He glanced insolently at Abigail, but it was then I realised I had ordered the wine without consulting my date for the evening. A touch imperious. I quickly turned to her and asked if that wine would be all right with her.

'I'm sure,' Marley answered for her, and he managed to say it with a real snap of venom.

Marley retreated, knowingly beaten by a better class of customer. The teenage waitress paused a moment, still holding on to the menus, a bit like an officious border guard, clutching our passports for too long before finally relenting and handing them back to us.

'Thank you,' Abigail said to her.

After the child had left us alone, Abigail looked at me and said, 'That was a bit of a fib you told, was it not? A white lie, wasn't it – there's no one else coming, is there? But you seemed to put him in his place.'

I leaned back in my seat. 'That's just Harry Marley, the minority owner. Pretends he doesn't know who I am but he certainly does.'

'You booked it under another name from the start though, not yours?'

'Yes, yes, that is an old habit. I mean obviously there was a time when I made constant restaurant bookings for Marko, so I have just got in the habit of booking tables in his name. Not that he eats out much any more.'

'What is he like to work for then? Like a big pop rock star. Like David Bowie or something? Is he a bit weird like they all are?'

'No, he's brilliant, he's down to earth – I mean I'm so lucky. I go way back with him to when we were both pretty broke, sharing a flat behind Paddington station, him practising all day – it's odd. Obviously, I am both his closest friend and also I work for him, but Marko is one of the greatest English guitarists – if not the world's – he's up there with Garcia and El Becko and Carlos and—'

'Are they all Spanish then or something? Castanets and all that?'

'What? No.'

'Is New York like *Kojak* and *Starsky & Hutch*?'

'Ah, well. Well, sort of, I mean, it looks a bit like it but that's all a bit, well, yeah I suppose.'

'Here comes the wine,' Abigail told me.

True enough, the waitress was approaching with the wine in her hands. I noted that, though full, the bottle had already been opened. Obviously if I had been in New York – say at Lutèce – I would have immediately sent it back. You don't open a bottle of wine before you bring it to a table. Lutèce with

318

chef André Soltner. When we went to the States for the great '73 tour, Marko and Auralie loved to go to that restaurant to pick at the food and took me along. Once. She would just sit there with a faraway look, staring at the other diners; when the dishes came out Auralie had a way of never quite starting them as well as never quite finishing them. She did the same at the Russian Tea Rooms. I knew fine that Marko and me just wanted a good plate of fish fingers, peas and chips with lots of ketchup, but let's admit it, we were curious. Fucking oysters and trout with nuts sprinkled on it, so you think it's bones in your mouth. Bloody Continentals with their jumpers folded on their shoulders, they're just so . . . Continental. No wonder we had to win the war for them with the Yanks. And that's why we and the Yanks have the best music.

I admitted the schoolgirl waitress would most likely have cocked it up if she took a corkscrew to a bottle – so it made sense. We watched the girl pour the clear wine, first into Abigail's glass and then mine. There was no pretence of us tasting it. I don't like a silence at a table when waiting staff are serving, so I repeated, 'Yeah, New York is great—' but the girl interrupted me.

'Would you like to order?'

'Oh, I'm so sorry,' Abigail said. 'I haven't read the menu at all.'

'I'll come back.' She pulled a tight smile and left us again.

'Cheers,' I said to Abigail. 'Thanks for coming along.' We gently clinked the wine glasses together and she actually looked me in the eye. I always felt people were about to reprimand me or laugh in my face if they looked me in the eye, but this woman did neither.

'Cheers. It was me that invited you in my letter.'

'Well, I can't say I would have had the guts to invite you after the last time I saw you.'

She laughed and drank from her glass and I drank from mine.

I said, 'But I'm totally flattered you did.'

319

'Well, I did say just a friendly drink. I wasn't expecting dinner, and by the way we can split this bill.'

My heart sank a bit at this. 'Oh no. I won't hear of it. I've been saving. For years. I have nothing to spend my money on down here.' We were both looking at the menu. 'What will you have?'

I was a bit surprised when she immediately and rapidly replied, 'Prawn cocktail and the chicken in a basket.'

I couldn't help feeling a bit stumped, for that was exactly what I would have ordered off the menu if she hadn't beaten me to it. I took another few swallows of the wine. 'That's just what I would have ordered. I guess if you are having the prawn cocktail then I could try the soup. But I've never known what mulligatawny is. It always sounded like a town in Ireland to me.'

She laughed. 'I think it's Indian.'

I added, 'And I don't know what cock-a-leekie is either and I don't want to think about what it is.'

She tightened the corners of her mouth a fraction. Swiftly moving on, I said, 'Strange thing is I have had both soups in the past more than once but afterwards, I just forget.'

She smiled and loosened up. 'These soups must do something to the memory.'

I laughed at this. 'Yeah they must, and another thing, what is vichyssoise and what is bouillabaisse?'

'What page is that one on?'

'No, it's not on this menu. Just in general, what are they? I think one is a soup and you have it bleedin' cold. What's that all about? Friggin' foreigners.' I said this quite loud and I found myself frowning at my wine glass. I had drunk most of it already I was so nervous.

Suddenly she said, 'But look here, look at this in sweets. Rum baba. I've never had a rum baba.'

'You've never had rum baba?'

'No, never. I've always wanted to try rum baba but I don't go out to restaurants much. Obviously. Never had rum baba. I never had a rum baba in my whole life and it just . . . sounds so good. Rum baba.'

'Never had a rum baba and never met someone who's been to New York. Well then you must have one this very night. It's fantastic. You can get blotto there's so much booze in it. Let's order them up.' I looked across the table at her but I suddenly felt even more tremendously nervous. I saw how good-looking she was. She wasn't just good-looking, she was beautiful. This woman was all-out lovable and her daughter was a great kid. I could care for this woman; I could have a life with this woman. Mrs H was correct: what on earth had I been doing with my life?

'Ready to order?' The child waitress had arrived without me noticing. She gave me such a fright materialising beside me, I blurted out, 'Soup! No the prawn cocktail, no the soup. No. Sorry, no. Abigail, excuse me, you order first.'

Both women were now looking at me. Abigail said, quietly, 'The prawn cocktail, the chicken in a basket and the rum baba please.'

The schoolgirl was writing it all down.

'The same,' I said. 'I will have all the same stuff. And another bottle of . . . this stuff.'

There was a pause then I said. 'Look, just to be different I'll have the soup as well.'

'The soup instead of the prawn cocktail then?'

'No. No. The soup *as well* as the prawn cocktail. I'll have two starter courses.'

'Two starters.'

'Yeah.'

'Well what shall I bring you first? The prawn cocktail or the soup?'

'Well, obviously . . .' They both looked at me. 'The cold dish first then the hot. The hot prawn cocktail, sorry the hot soup after the prawns.'

Out came the lip again and the little uneven teeth came down upon it. This instruction was written down. 'Okay then.'

'Oh, and don't forget those good old rum babas; two of your finest rum babas for myself and my very good friend here.' I smiled and stuck out a pointed finger at Abigail.

'Eh, yeah.' The waitress went away. Hard not to feel subconsciously that she was pissing herself at me. Not even subconsciously.

'Soup and prawn cocktail?' Abigail smiled.

'Look: a bee.'

Crossing the centre of the dining room some distance from our lone table a honeybee flew across the space at about six feet of height, flying in that strangely slow lumber, where their rear seems to drag lower in the air – perhaps weighted by delicious nectar?

I stood and moved from our table, towards where I had last sighted the bee.

'I love bees,' I called backwards.

Suddenly the schoolgirl waitress appeared carrying a tray inexpertly with two fists and held in against her belly. I had an instinct to assist but I didn't want to embarrass her. On the tray was the new bottle of wine and the two tall ornamental glasses filled with the telltale green and light pink of prawn cocktails.

Moving my legs swiftly, I attempted to beat the waitress back to our table which was not difficult as she walked so slowly. She looked up at me oddly, clearly flummoxed by my idle meandering around the dining room.

'There's a honeybee in here,' I told her, pointing my finger around in the air while I shuffled behind the round table until I was next to Abigail. The waitress placed the wine bottle in the

322

middle of the table and then distributed the two prawn cocktails – serving Abigail first. As the waitress committed these actions she commented: 'Your wine. The . . . Prawn . . . Cocktail . . . There,' she concluded, seemingly with some delight.

I didn't know if I wasn't starting to find the young waitress attractive! Once she was gone, I drank some more wine and I topped up both of our glasses from the older bottle.

Abigail had been talking. What she was saying was very interesting indeed, and while she talked she did not pick up her fork to approach her prawn cocktail. She spoke about her youth – a tale of misunderstandings on the streets of Marlborough. I was listening – of course I was – the carefree days of youth are so important – but something else was dominating my concentration. Napkins! I have problems with the management and monitoring of cloth napkins. I always lose them halfway through any meal; I usually find my napkin to have slid off my knees and fallen to the dirty floor beneath the table, or resting on top of my shoes. I was intent on making a good impression on Abigail, so it was very important I concentrated on my napkin and was aware of its location at all times. I cast a nervous eye at Abigail's napkin, still tucked tightly in its brass ring by her hand. She was chuckling and I followed her into a chuckle – suddenly with her lovely fingers, she slid her napkin from its polished brass ring and lowered the cloth down out of sight onto her thighs. Naturally I copied her action – making sure my napkin was positioned quite high up on my own thighs, so movement of my legs would not shuffle the napkin lower towards my knees and hence permit it to fall forwards onto the ground.

I took up my fork and with my other hand copied Abigail in squeezing the lemon slice onto the top of my prawn cocktail, watching the viscous nature of the juice insinuate itself down the insides of the glass and how it pooled clearly on top of the Thousand Island dressing.

'Do you know— Oh, sorry.'

'No. Go ahead.'

She had actually been talking and I had interrupted her. 'Sorry. I was just going to say that there is this strange rumour that Thousand Island dressing – this – was actually invented by Phil Spector.'

'Who?'

'Phil Spector, the record producer.'

'Oh.'

I took another few gulps of wine. Checked my napkin. On my fork I lifted some prawn cocktail – the watery shards of crisp lettuce, the slug-like prawns, flavourless but for the lemon and the cloying, powdery cream sauce clinging to them.

I took another long swallow of wine ensuring I did not leave telltale lip marks of the sauce on the rim of my glass.

'I don't know who Phil Spector is.'

'Really? He . . . He's a great guy. A very innovative record producer. He produced George Harrison.'

'Mmm.'

'From The Beatles.'

'Yes. I know who George Harrison is.'

I said, 'Sorry. I need to go to the toilet. The bathroom.'

'Oh. All right then.'

'Excuse me.' I stood up.

I felt a bit flushed. Steady on, old chap, I told myself, as I walked a little waywardly across the dining room to the doorway and turned left. It occurred to me, rather than crossing the lobby past that oaf Harry Marley, I could instead simply nip to the gents in the saloon bar. I turned sharp right into that corridor and pushed aside the opaque glass door.

The noise and the airlessness of the smoky public house was quite surprising to me. Heads turned towards me, to note my presence, especially from those local regulars standing or seated

324

on stools along the bar. Wild-haired rustic types – I suppose until my recent haircut I looked like one too: bleedin' Wurzels.

I stepped forwards, crossing the carpet next to the old wooden plough which they had lashed up on the far wall. Seated in a booth to my right, about seven feet away from me, was Dan Mullan and Marko's mother, Maude. Leaning together. Just the two of them. My surprise was so great and complete I found myself rooted to the spot in a completely involuntary manner. Grotesquely, Dan Mullan was wearing a tightly knotted mustard tie and a white linen shirt, in some crazed attempt at transforming his identity. Maude as usual was in one of her many, trim, three-piece ensembles, like a sexy member of the royal family with a south London accent – she leaned slightly into her version of Mellors, but what was most appalling was that they were leaning together to enable them to link arms, and from thigh to shoulder they were pressed together in an astonishing – especially for people of their age – display of public affection.

A glass of beer poured from a bottle, and a dainty sherry glass sat in front of them on the dark, round table. For a few seconds they were submerged in one another's company then they became aware of my still form – I had somehow shifted a block of the stale air or displaced the previous arrangement of shadow. Both of them looked over at me simultaneously. I realised that neither of them had immediately recognised me with my new hairstyle. I should have stepped ahead and left them wondering: who the hell was that; looked familiar?

Then Dan Mullan said aloud, as if I were not within hearing, 'It's daft Crofton. Crofton, you loop, what happened to all your lass hair?'

Maude smiled. Something was wrong with her mouth. Lipstick! Very light in colour and application, but nonetheless she was wearing it.

Maude was talking at me. I stepped towards her.

325

'What have you done to your hair?'

'I cut it,' I said abruptly in the tone which indicated a stupid question had been asked, and then I added in a voice that seemed to come from my last year at high school, 'What are you two doing here?'

A truly senseless question since all was so apparent.

Maude smiled that patient smile. I expected her to look distractedly to one side and reach to a bunch of flowers in a small pot on the next table to deadhead a shrivelled petal. But no such flowerpot existed.

'Why, I am having a little catch-up with Mr Mullan, Crofton.'

'What you doing up this way then?' Mullan bluntly asked.

'I was meeting a friend.'

'Didn't think you had any,' Mullan said and turned to Maude with a smile.

Maude both tutted and shushed him. 'You look very smart indeed, Crofton. A very tidy haircut. Mr Mullan and I were discussing some important changes to the flower beds for next spring. Out with the violas and in with the pansies on the far side of the river, we are thinking. Markus will like that.' She smiled imperiously, making the power structure at work more than clear, with her arm still firmly placed in that of the grizzled gardener.

I so just needed to ask, to know how long this had been going on for under my stupid nose. My mind was electrified with the implications of this most dreadful sight displayed before me, which so explained Dan Mullan's cockiness over recent months. Eh, years. Yet I found myself turning on my heels and leaving the saloon bar.

Halfway across the dining room floor I called on ahead to Abigail. 'Any sign of that bee yet? You will not believe what just happened to me. Oh, I see the soup has arrived.'

'Eh, hi. Yeah, she came while you've been at the bathroom.'

The bowl of soup was beside my largely untouched prawn cocktail. With a jump I realised I suddenly didn't know what I had done with my napkin. Abigail watched as I touched aside the tablecloth which hung down over the edges of the table; I bent slightly to peer in underneath the table into the gloom, perhaps as if I were trying to look at her bare calves on her crossed legs. Which of course I was not. I promise. I stood upright, tapped the side pockets of my green velvet jacket and sure enough, I had placed the napkin there in the right-hand pocket.

I sat back down but then I immediately stood up.

'What has happened?' she asked in a hushed, timid voice.

'Oh.' I placed the cloth napkin neatly back down on the table after folding it carefully. 'I have forgotten to go to the bathroom,' I told her. 'But, let me get this off the table, I don't trust that young girl to deal with this.' I took a long drink from my wine glass which had recently been topped up from the new bottle, but the first bottle was now empty. I lifted this bottle and I placed it down on the carpeted floor by the edge of the table. Perhaps I was slightly confused by the way Mrs H lined up the empty wine bottles down on the polished linoleum floor by the swing bins beside the pantry or larders of Kitchenly Mill Race? I added, 'I'll just let my soup cool off for another few moments; back in a tick.'

I walked quickly down the dining room corridor and then across the lobby by the open fire. Harry Marley was there of course; from behind the reception desk his suspicious, blunt face followed my sure trajectory toilet-wards. For the hell of it, I yelled out, 'Hey-up. Our friends have decided to take a drink in the bar for the moment.' I jerked a thumb in that direction. 'I must say Marko and his wife are looking a bit the worse for wear. Must be the in-flight meal on Concorde.'

I raised my eyebrows, signalling a mutual and weary familiarity, but kept walking to the toilet door.

327

I peed in the cubicle. I hate peeing at urinals for reasons I could usefully summarise for the historical record – but at another juncture. I washed my hands medium-thoroughly and tried to stick up what fringe I had with my wet fingers which I then wiped on the bum of my old jeans. It was at that point I thought about rewashing my hands, for after all, these jeans had been with me for some time, but what the hell, it's not as if I would be eating with my fingers.

I came back into the dining room with my head fairly swivelling from side to side in search of that bee which no one else appeared to have seen. 'Hi there, you won't believe who is in the saloon bar.'

In a voice, spoiled I felt by a touch of the deadpan, Abigail said, 'Not our Nat, I hope?'

'No. Of course not.' Still standing by the table I picked up the soup bowl and brought it carefully to my lips. I blew on it to tease the surface and test the temperature, but I blew a little too gallantly and in fact sputtered some drops over the lip of the bowl which landed rather close to Abigail's place mats. 'Oh. Confound it,' I said, 'I am sorry.' I took a step forwards but I had forgotten about that empty bottle I had placed down on the floor and I gave it a good kick, so the bottle shot forwards, hit the central strut beneath the table and made a swift crunching sound, as if perhaps the neck of the bottle had slightly shattered. This kick led to a stumble; a large globule of soup was thrown forwards and over the edge of the bowl which landed with a slap on the centre of the table, covering the salt and pepper stand rather badly. 'Oh blast and tarnation,' I said. I lifted the soup bowl gently to my lips and slurped a goodly ration more from it in an attempt to further lower the hazardously high surface level. I glanced round the soup bowl at some point to look down at Abigail. I know I had soup around my lips but using both hands to hold the soup bowl, obviously I couldn't reach for my napkin. In fact, where was my napkin?

'It's not too hot,' I mentioned. Then I placed the bowl carefully back on the table and sat down next to her. I snatched my napkin up from where I had so neatly and sensibly folded it, but I wasn't willing to use this napkin to clean the spilled soup off the salt and pepper pots – for this, I selected one of the unused napkins intended for the missing guests around us. I dabbed at the soup spillage and cleaned off the condiment pots.

'So who *is* in the bar then?' she asked.

The schoolgirl waitress was approaching us again across the dining room with a large tray, spreading out her small arms.

'Lorraine!' I called. That was her name. 'It's the chicken in the basket and there is the basket for sure.'

The schoolgirl waitress had to lay the tray on the edge of our table to offload the breaded, fried chicken which lay on chequered paper cradled in woven baskets with the browned chips in these wire frying trays. I nabbed up a single chip from my wire container with my fingers and nibbled at it. I took another drink of wine then I picked up one of my pieces of breaded chicken in my hand and tore at it because it looked so good to eat. It was a bit hot but good.

'It's my damned boss's mother who is in the bar.'

'His mother?'

'Yeah the randy old so-and-so. She's been carrying on with the gardener.'

'The gardener?' She raised her fingers to her smile.

'It isn't funny.' I realised I had snarled these words at her. She blinked.

I said, 'He's just a bloody old dirty villager. She's been having an affair with the bloody gardener and they are both sitting there proud as punch in full view. It's a disgrace.'

'Will I take these away?

I looked up. The waitress was still standing by the table despite my verbal outburst. I looked dumbly ahead. She was indicating the unfinished prawn cocktail and the soup. I waved my hand at them, 'Yeah, yeah.' She placed them on her tray. I seethed until she had departed. Sitting there with my arms folded.

After the waitress had gone, Abigail asked, 'Goodness. You seem to have had a shock. What age is she?'

'Marko's mam? Oh I guess in her, eh, late forties, early fifties maybe? Quite well preserved; an all right-looking woman all things considered.'

'Says you.'

'But him . . . Bred on the midden, born in the dungheap, that guy. Straw in his boots to dry out the cow shit. Daughters of his own he has shared out to local farmers' sons round Maxtelham to get his interest in. A right sly Johnny Fox, this bastard. Been gardener at the Mill Race since time began of course, so there is no telling him anything. Now he's doing the how's-your-father on Marko's mam, there'll be no end to it all.' I paused. Picked up another bit of chicken with my fingers and bit into it. 'I dunno, even if Marko is aware of it or not, nor how I should break the news to him. Absolutely shocking. I have a good mind to go back into that bar and give them both a piece of my mind.'

'Why's it shocking? Is she married? The pop singer's mum?'

I looked across the table at her and she was staring at me.

'She is widowed. Well, it's her poor choice in men.'

Abigail let out a laugh and kept looking at me.

'The guy's a real berk. A . . . just a total berk. A subtle bully too. You should try having to work with him. Just the other day he deliberately cut through a lawn mower cable so they could lounge about.'

Abigail said, 'But that's quite the thing among the posh, is it not? For the lady of the house to have a fling with the gardener?'

'She *isn't* the lady of the house,' I snapped. 'That's Marko's wife. Not that she's much better.'

'Here I am being taken for dinner with the . . . The what? What are you? A steward is it?'

I let out a polite cough. 'Estate manager. And incidentally, Marko is not a pop singer, he is a virtuoso guitarist.'

'Estate manager,' she had to repeat.

'And she's not posh either, they grew up in Sutton and the old man was just a bus driver. And—'

Her eyes were following some new development behind me. Rudely I stopped talking and I turned around to observe what: the teenage waitress was approaching yet again, but this time she was accompanied by the chef, in his whites and chequered trousers, the white tube hat up on his head. As the chef approached he said, 'Evening. I am so sorry – I know you have both ordered the rum baba but my commis has fouled up this afternoon and there is only one rum baba left. I am so very sorry. Am I able to offer you something else? I have a lovely, fresh apple crumble with double cream perhaps?'

'Sure thing. Sure thing, Chef,' I said, 'Bring us a rum baba and some of your finest crumble.'

'Sorry about that,' the young waitress said.

'No, no, darling, don't you worry about it at all, it's not a problem.'

Chef said, 'I hope you don't mind me asking, but I've been led to understand you work down at the Mark Morrell place. I am a bit of a fan of his music.'

'Really? That's great.' I leaned back in my chair a touch, perhaps I gravitated towards Abigail an inch or so, as if she was my regular lady. 'Yeah, yeah I work for old Marko and have done for yonks. He's not here at the moment, he's been back and forth to the States looking at recording facilities for the new album.'

The chef looked excited at this and nodded. His hat didn't move. 'Oh, great.'

331

'What's your favourite album?'

Quick as shot he came back, 'I'm A *Pascal's Moon* man, but I like the live album. I've never seen them live but you know . . . Hopefully one day.'

'Sure, sure. I'll give you a nod when the next tour is announced but it's probably going to be after Christmas. Well, look . . . If I'm passing by here sometime I'll try to get you a copy of an autographed *Moon*. I always know where to find you, eh? What's the name?'

'Oh, wow, that would be something else. Yeah, Andy. I'm Andy Hewitt. Head chef.'

'Andy. Okay then, Andy.'

'And you know – if he, if Mr Morrell is at home he's always more than welcome up here for lunch or dinner, it would be a pleasure to cook for him.'

'That's kind, Andy. I'll be sure to pass that on to him but he is a busy bloke.'

'Yeah, sure. I understand. I'm so sorry again about the rum baba situation.'

'Take it in our stride, mate.'

The waitress and the chef walked off together. I turned round and looked at Abigail. 'Yeah, I get a lot of that of course; you know, got to be diplomatic and all that, goes with the territory.'

There was a silence at the table. I took up the new bottle of wine and topped up my glass but when I went to do the same with Abigail's I was surprised as she silently placed two fingers over the top of the glass to prevent me doing so.

Now the waitress reappeared and descended onto our silence. She was bearing our desserts across the dining room with regal passage. I looked at Abigail and I said, 'How dare they? How dare they not tell me about themselves carrying on like that?' I was shocked myself how much bile my voice was impaired with. I suppose in my way, I felt possessive about Maude. I knew she retained a soft spot for me – well, felt sorry for me. All the same,

332

I realised now I probably felt some attraction towards Maude. An attraction I hadn't owned up to, that I would have loved to have pulled up her tweed skirt in the kitchen one afternoon and lay my face down on her fine-formed features – the great cheekbones that Marko had – which you could still see in little Molly. It would have been amazing to have a physical relationship with a woman who has been round the block like that – who would be sure of her fine trim figure and her breasts pressed flat against herself in those neat-fitting tailored jackets of hers. If anyone had a right to be carrying on with Marko's mum it was me – not that dung-spreading peon we had inherited like a faulty boiler system.

The waitress and Abigail nodded politely as desserts were placed before us. I grabbed up my spoon. Then I slammed it down hard on the tabletop. Where the fuck was my napkin this time? It was neither in my jacket pocket nor on the floor. I slapped aside the fabric of the tablecloth quite violently so the cutlery jiggled and chinked on the surface while I took a look underneath. I had broken that bottle. I found the napkin stuffed in my jeans. I tugged it out and folded it in place in my lap, lifted the spoon and dug it into my rum baba. Wow, it was a strong one. What a Caribbean kick, dripping in the booze. I lifted another huge spoonful up to my mouth and swallowed that too – it was fiery and annihilating in my mouth.

Abigail was watching me again over her crumble. She had an unsettling habit of just staring at me, silently. It made me nervous and I took another spoonful of dessert. At least the dessert was something I was embracing with enthusiasm. I had kind of wasted that other food. I took the last spoonful and scooped up some of the gathered alcohol by tipping the bowl – as I had been taught was the right etiquette – away from me.

I said, 'I believe it's polite manners when eating soup or a dish in a bowl to always tip it away from you as you scoop it out, not towards you; it's something you might want to pass on to Nat.'

'It might have been polite manners to let me at least try a taste of your rum baba,' she said. 'I told you I was looking forward to having one since I've never ever tried it.'

I looked down at my plate. 'Fuck,' I said aloud. 'Strewth, I am sorry it just sort of . . . I sort of forgot and you only have the crumble. Oh, I'm so sorry.'

I had to carry on making a good impression, so I lifted up my napkin from my lap and gently dabbed round my mouth. I am a messy eater, I admit to that, and I didn't want food particles in the corners of my mouth. 'I am so sorry about the rum baba, my bloody mind was on those two idiots in the bar.' I folded the napkin neatly and put it down.

For once Abigail had stopped staring at me and she was frowning. Frowning at my napkin on the table by my empty plate. I looked down and saw I had just wiped my mouth with and folded up that pair of Auralie's purple and blue French knickers.

We both looked at the intimate undergarments lying on the table. 'Ah. They are not your daughter's,' I said.

'Pardon me?'

'They aren't your daughter's. Knickers. You can probably believe that by the exquisite quality of these. You see. I know it looks unusual but the reason I had them in my jeans here, I got them mixed up with my napkin. The reason I had them is . . . Well, first things first, they belong to Auralie. My boss's wife. That's the reason I had them on my person. Well, obviously not *on*, on my person, I don't wear them or anything – for God's sake don't think that. I had them in my possession. You see, I use them to polish furniture. More especially, eh, the wooden windowsills in the masturbate bedroom. The master bedroom. I mean I should point out that those windowsills are original Elizabethan wood. I mean it's quite incredible when you think

334

about it. I had to remove some adhesive material from electrical tape which that fool in the bar there had stuck on the wood. Bloody oaf. So I was rooting around looking for the softest, most delicate material. Anyway. That's what I was using her knickers for – on a regular basis – and I've gone and popped them back in my jeans and forgotten about them. Got them mixed up with my . . . I started tapping at my pockets on my jacket again. 'Napkin.' I lifted up the knickers and had to stretch forwards a bit to force them down, back into the pockets of my jeans. I felt my napkin fall off my knees onto the floor underneath the table.

There was a silence.

I nodded at her dessert. 'Are you going to eat any of that? It looks good. I'll have some if you don't fancy. Oh listen.' I turned around. 'There's that bee. Hear that?'

10

Two days later, around three thirty in the afternoon . . .
Kitchenly 4-3-4 — a future dreaming — in a night garden.

Two days later, around three thirty in the afternoon, I was walking out of the Elvetson morning room where I had been reading the new *Melody Maker*, which, as has been usefully narrated, came weekly on subscription. I was feeling a bit clemmed and on my way along to the kitchen, trying to find Mrs H to enquire about a sandwich to eat, the phone rang. I picked up, I would say, almost casually.

'Kitchenly 4-3-4.'

'Crofton?'

'Marko. How are you? Sorry I missed you when you were down.'

'Just wanted a bit of a word.'

'Sure. Look, I'm sorry about the Volvo.'

'Yeah. What happened then? All okay, are we?'

'I'm fine. Not a scratch. I don't think we'll ever know, Marko. I was coming round on the far side of Ablemyre Hill, just where the water meadows are and it just went on the corner there.'

'Where? Where's that about then?'

'On the road down behind Ablemyre slope, there are a few tight corners.'

'That's the road down from that hotel place, yeah?'

'Ah, yes.'

'Yeah. Yeah, I heard. You were up at that hotel. Having dinner or something. I heard.'

'Yeah, a bit of a bite to eat. Mrs H was telling me to get out and about a bit more.'

'Was she?'

'Yeah. I'm so sorry, Marko. Maybe it needed new tyres or something? It had been a while. So the car just crossed the road on me. I wasn't going fast, it was just a corner that kept coming

339

and I lost it. It bumped through a fence but I think what done for the old car is that it was quite steep off the road there, so the chassis got bent when she settled.'

'Yeah. I seen the garage report on a fax machine I got. Totalled.'

'I guess so, Marko, the car was getting on a bit though. I left all my cassettes in it so they're gone too. The garage just took it away.'

'Sorry about that. I heard you were up the hotel with someone but she wasn't in the car when you wiped out, was she?'

'Ah, no. No. Lucky she had left a bit earlier in a taxi. Just a friend.'

'All right. Well, Mrs H will just have to use her bleedin' car when one is needed for now, I suppose.'

'Yeah. Well, unless you want to insure the Mercedes for me and I could use that till you get us a new car for the estate?' There was an odd silence in response. I added, 'Everything here is up to date as usual, no need for concern. Letter from the rates I left in your desk, or I can send it on to Schillings? I have it all under control here as usual. What happened with the studios over in the States, Marko? I never found out from you.'

'Oh that. Started to turn into a bleedin' drag as well. Can't really go into it right now. Look, man.' He paused. And he coughed. 'We are going back to the States right now. Tomorrow. I mean me and the old lady . . . back over with Molly before school starts. To be honest, be good to get a break from the old Baraclough Effect here. Know what I mean?'

I laughed. 'Yeah. Yeah, I had a weird phone call from him a bit back.'

'Did you? Weird in what way?' he very suddenly asked.

'Well, middle of the night, he was telling me you were all coming down from London. But he was, you know, nippy. Disrespectful. All okay with the house up there?'

'Disrespectful, eh? Uh-huh. Oh yeah. Everything's cool. With the house.'

340

'Oh brilliant. First class.'

'Look, Crofts, want to talk to you about something.'

'Fire away.'

'Pardon?'

'On you go. Fire away.'

'Oh, right. Yeah. Well this first one is one I have to trust you on. It's a bit bleedin' heavy, man.'

'You know you can trust me. Remember that time—'

'Let me finish. This is one I need to trust you on. It's a bit of a biggie. And I need you to keep this one tight to your chest for, I dunno how long. A week. A fortnight. I'm counting on you now. No talking to your mate, what's his name, at the fan club?'

'What is it?'

'Fear Taker's splitting, man.'

'What?'

'Yeah. We ain't releasing a statement yet. Nothing. At the moment; but that's it. You have to play it careful so you can't let it beyond your lips, but look – and I want you to remember this. I come to you and I told you first. Almost first, Crofton. Because you were with us there in the beginning and you're here for the end and there's not many left apart from us – the boys I mean, even fuckin Alvin – that can say that.'

My hand was suddenly shaking. 'Marko, I'm going to have to sit down on the carpet here, my legs are going wobbly.' I did slump to the floor and I put one hand to my face, holding the receiver in the other. 'This is a mistake. Don't do it. I mean, why? Why now? You can't. Ten years, man, and you know the band can do another ten years. Why? The Who kept going after Moon. Don't do it.'

'It's sweet you care, mate, but nah. Nah, it's bleedin' everything, isn't it?'

'What do you mean? You've got new material ready to go; America is waiting for you guys. It'll be a sell-out tour again.'

341

'Oh man, don't guilt trip me. Nah, leave it out. It's everything. Not just all this bleedin' new wave shit, and this sales headache; it's Alvin too. I mean we always knew he was an asshole, great front men usually are, but we didn't think he would be crowned king of all assholes. I don't know if I can stand beside him onstage for another tour and feel honest. Besides, that wanker's gonna bleedin' scorch my carpet on the next tour, chuckin' his fag ends so near it; just does it as a wind-up on me. He had to boot one away on the last tour. I got down on my knees to examine if there was a burn mark, right in the middle of a song – looked a bit of a plonker, didn't I?'

I pointed out, 'Yeah, carpets are a liability. Who thought we'd ever end up fussing about carpets, like our mums?'

I realised I'd offended him but he ignored me.

'Wants to do his solo album with bleedin' cissy ballads. Our piano tinkler wants to do an album with bleedin' strings and orchestra. I don't. Styxie thinks the new album should be a rocker with only short tracks. Rick doesn't talk at all now with this new bird of his. I wouldn't mind trying a solo album myself, then get a new outfit together, some new guys to blow with, stretch out my solos a bit on a tour; yeah, I tell you, mate, I feel it in my bones that it's time to call it quits. We done all right.'

'I'm gobsmacked. I support you in everything but my heart's breaking here.'

He chuckled. 'Yeah, you always loved the band, I'll say that for you. Now Crofton, you can't be letting this out. We have to control it with the press and make sure no backbiting, and different quotes from different folks start up. Don't want it to get all messy. Everly Brothers. No guitars breaking over heads.'

'Sure. I understand, but I am close to tears here, man; I can't believe it. I mean is this coming from you alone or from Alvin too? What does Schillings say?'

342

'Oh Schillings is shitting himself, silly git, 'cause he just bought that fucking boat in France before the US tour was booked and all his bread is tour percentages. We had a meeting. So look, Crofton. Look, there's going to be some changes.'

'Yeah, sure. Of course. But I'm devastated. I know bands break up, it happens, but I want to say: you have your talent. It's still there. You have it, your fingers are slick as ever.'

'Nah, leave it out, mate. Don't embarrass me. So listen, Crofton. There's going to be some changes here and there. Auralie and I have been thinking. We don't know the way ahead so clearly now, so I'm going to be doing some, eh, some streamlining at the house here in London and down there I might just have to, yeah. Make a few changes.' Thoughtfully, he announced, 'Maybe no more bleedin' giant Christmas trees for a bit. We'll get one of those big plastic ones from Woolies this year.'

'Are you going to finish work on the studio here? Look, Marko. I wanted to say. I thought of something. Just a joke. You should have kept the clock bells above the studio. You might have had a new *Tubular Bells* on your hands. Huh? Eh?'

There was an atomic silence.

I reassured him, 'Just a joke.'

'Huh. Well, I'm afraid, mate, that I think times have changed, things have moved on a bit, have they not?'

'What has moved on? Music, you mean?'

'Yeah well, music yeah, like, fuckin' hell, these gobby new wavers and all these new bands. Man! What is this bleedin' Devo? What is this Devo? I don't understand. Devo. I mean I'm quite afraid of those guys. They freak me, man. What do they mean? Devo? Thing is, they scare me. These Devo guys really are fuckin' deviants, dressed up like production-line workers at bleedin' British Leyland. Those guys should be arrested. Devo, I mean, I don't know what charge, but they should be arrested. Taking the piss. Where'll half of them be in ten years? I'll still be out there in some shape or form, making music and protecting what I gone and built up. But thing is, we are going to have to let what's her name, her that comes in every now and again to help out Mrs H?'

'Olive.'

'Olive, is it? Yeah. We're going to have to ask her to leave and I think we'll need to let you go from the big house there too. Sorry, mate.'

'What?'

'Yeah. I mean, come on. It'll be the eighties soon, man, we've all got to battle on.'

'I don't understand. How could you not want me here any more? I mean, where the hell else am I going to go in the operation?'

'Well, there you go, mate. Exactly. This is bleedin' it. It's high time for you to be figuring that out for yourself and getting on with it.'

'But . . . I can't believe it Marko, really.'

'Why?'

'Why? Why? Well. What'll happen to Kitchenly Mill Race without me here, to keep an eye on everything?'

'Nothing will happen to it. Ah Crofton. Croffie, can I ask you? Straight up, man. What do you do down there all the time?'

'What?'

'What do you do there? At my house. What do you do?'

'How can you ask that? You know fine what I do. I run the place. I . . . I control security. I keep up your side of the equation.'

'You what?' he actually laughed.

'I'm your, eh, caretaker. I'm the retainer. I'm a faithful retainer of this house that I love, Marko. I love this place and I care for it and I watch out for it. I appreciate its character. I don't even look at my month's salary, let alone spend it, I'm so devoted to life here.'

'Yeah, exactly, but that's it. You're devoted to life there, but you don't actually do anything there, mate.'

'What do you mean?'

'What do you do? You sleep over in your digs, sleep all the time it seems. I heard you just had a common cold and took to your bed for three days. Mrs H and old Mullan keep the place up, and you . . . I don't know what you *do* any more, mate. When we moved in, it was a high, I admit it. And you were there with me and you helped us get it together in the country. I offered you a job in the office at Senseless Ambition a few years ago and you actually laughed at me. Offered tour positions, and you turned them all down. You just seem to think, as the years go by, you can sit on your ass in my house and do sweet fuck all, while I pay for it. I know you love the music, mate. But loving the music isn't enough.'

'Loving the music isn't enough?'

'No, it isn't. When I come back from the States there, you didn't even get out your scratcher. Even to come say hello to little Molly. You weren't to be seen, apart from bugging my accountants when they come round. I was told by one that you were crashing about the house at bleedin' midnight, being short with the geezer for turning up. He said there was other stuff, but he didn't tell me what. Just as well. I mean Mullan's an old grump, but he says you don't do nothing any more either. You helped with the painting of the bridges, I know. That was a year and a half ago, Crofton. A year and a half. Oh, and by the way, I see you still ain't give a lick of paint to the bleedin' flagpole. I'd be ashamed to fly the union jack from the thing. Think you're in the Sex Pistols, do you? Mrs H is great, you know it and I know it, but as far as I can see you sit in the little mill house playing records and I dunno, I've heard over the years you watch a lot of *Top of the Pops* and *Whistle Test* and tennis. On my colour telly. You don't help old Mrs H with carrying the washing down. You open and close the gates a helluva lot, I'll give you credit for that, but that's 'cause you went and lost the gate remote-control button thing, didnt ya? I got a friggin' machine does it, Crofton, ain't I? Opens and closes the gates. I don't need you. Now you've totalled the bleedin' car and it sounds like you were pissed up. Lecturing my old lady about different kinds of cow shit.'

'Horse shit,' I corrected.

'What sleeping draughts my old lady should take or something. I can't work you out any more, mate.'

'I do lots, Marko.'

'Well you must be a true bleedin' artist, Croffie. A poet contemplating the clouds or something, 'cause I don't see it. Maybe it's a northern thing? You clean the outside windows? Once a year if I'm lucky. You painted the pump hutch, but you got a bloke in to fix it. You didn't even take a look at it yourself. And you lectured me about fitting an on-and-off switch, so you don't even need to leave your bleedin' lair. Look. Everything that is needing doing in that place, the gardener and the housekeeper do. You're like a throwback to the late sixties when we all sat around smoking reefer and staring at Sirius. You're surplus to requirements. I'm a guitar player, Crofton, but I've got to be a businessman too, or I'll go down, mate. I'm a company director, mate. And I ain't going down again for the tax man or for you. That happened to me end of the sixties when I thought I was finished, just before we got the Taker together. And I ain't going down now that the band has gone to pot. You've said it to me yourself, Croffie. At the end of the day it's all about ego and money. But you don't make any. And you got an ego for no reason. The sixties and seventies happened suddenly, mate, we were both there. You took the risks and you hung in there, and we all came out tops, but now, mate . . . It's just run its course for you, man. And—'

346

'Marko, please. Give us another go and I'll get—'

'No, man. Let me finish. You've taken my money for years, now at least let me talk. You decided to hang around. That was your choice. You set up in that mill house and I was okay about it, for a while, but then you sort of . . . You sort of appointed yourself lord of the bleedin' manor. You pull the curtains some nights. And not all of them. I bloody know when I'm away that the curtains ain't getting pulled, 'cause Mullan told me. So I've asked you now, what do you do in my house that's of use? And you can't answer me a sensible answer. I can't employ you to circle things that are on telly in the bleedin' *Radio Times*, mate. To be frank with you, I just felt a bit sorry for you. I just asked you to do that to keep you busy, mate, and you don't need to do that *Radio Times* shit when I'm not there but even when I was, still you'd get the days wrong for *Bagpuss* and stuff.'

'That's not true. You like everything on telly and, eh, that car horn stuff to tell you when something was on telly was . . . Has Auralie put you up to this?'

'What? Don't pin this on my old lady, bud. She's cool. She's put up with you hanging around there for bloody years as well. You know the place is meant to have that ghost chap, well that's what she calls you mate, Sir Crofton the Creepy, bloody household ghost, wandering the corridors at night. She's seen you standing out there in the garden alone at night. Just standing there for no reason at two in the morning and stuff, staring straight ahead of yourself. Or looking down from your bleedin' bedroom window thing at all hours. She seen yah, through the telescope, man! That's creepy. She asks if you can be exorcised. Just like you were saying. Your joke. Like in that Mike Oldfield bleedin' scary movie. She tells you to take some empty suitcases up from a car and it takes you all bleedin' day. Anything Mrs H wants, it's always: I will ask Crofton, and guess what? It doesn't happen. And when things do go wrong,

347

you're calling in tradesmen from here, there and everywhere for jobs Mullan himself can do. He's a handy old geezer. Don't forget, he's been there longer than all of us. What about that time, without asking me, you called in a builder to get an estimate for a fucking sixteen-foot wall to be built down on the riverside? They charged me a couple of hundred nicker just for that stupid bleedin' estimate and that was for tens of bleedin' thousands. I never requested that. Never requested it. You did. What do I want a new wall for? And now I'm seeing that the other day you called in some stonemason from Haywards Heath to come and look at some bleedin' stone bleedin' ball that come off somewhere.'

'That was your accountant that knocked it off.'

His voice was rising. 'What? He nicked it? Leave it out, what are you even on about? They've bleedin' charged us for the visit already, we got off a fax here, but when my assistant here phoned, I hear they haven't even come round yet. Leave it out, mate, what's that all about?'

'They are coming on Tuesday because I was available then . . .'

'Put a sock in it, mate. Available? What you doing the rest of the bleedin' week? Got the queen's bleedin' crown to polish, have you? Pinning all this on my old lady is low. You've pinned it on yourself. I'll be honest with you, mate. I think you might be losing your glass marbles a bit, cooped up down there. What was it used to say when you come to London? Gone barmy on the crumpet, was it? I think you have. Or lack of it. Too much of the country can be bad for a town boy, that's why I have the place up here and it's why I never get up to Scotland any more. And I got probs with my fucking tenants up there too, taking bleedin' liberties. Just like bleedin' Nobby started. Too busy, mate. Too busy by half. Gotta earn a buck. It'll do you good to find something new. Get back up to London and find a job in the music game here. Something. Back up north. But you can't just sit it out in my house waiting for Elvis to come back. Or Jesus. I'm sorry, Croffers. Schillings will bring your salary through at the end of this month and the next one too, and we'll stamp your books as usual, but that's it, buddy. I'd appreciate if you arranged to get all your clobber out the small mill house by the end of next month. Use one of our bleedin' tour trucks, why don't ya? Won't pull your salary next month. Wouldn't do that to you. You want references for anything, I'll make sure Schillings gets one to you. And a good one. There won't be a bad word in it, mate. But for your own good, get going. Get your life together. I feel blue hitting you with this and the whole Taker spilt thing on the same day but in a way they're tied together. Ain't they? Time for a new chapter, Crofton. For me and for you. I'm gonna make that solo album. *Stratified*, was it? A year down the line and you'll see I was right. I've got to go now. Meetings. You take care of yourself.'

I whispered, 'Okay, Marko. I'm really sorry. I'm sorry.'

'Nah, leave it out, mate. Take care. Peace and love.' He hung up.

I stood unsteadily, unsure if I was devastated about the demise of the greatest band on earth, or for myself. I began to walk, trembling along the panelled corridor, over the worn flagstones, under the 1602 lintel and on down those familiar air bridges towards my rooms. But though it was too early, I did pause to switch on all the exterior garden lights of Kitchenly Mill Race.

I remained in my rooms. Sometimes I looked out my window in the afternoon sun, down to the front door, glaring at the missing stone ball and the point at which, on that night, I had first seen the apparition – that figment of my ill and wasteful imagination.

The falling sun made a six-foot shadow out of almost every object it could reach. Eventually Mrs H departed in her car without coming to bid me goodnight, which she always did, so I concluded she had knowledge of Marko's call to me.

349

Soon enough I took Natandra's tenderly hand-washed tights from the drawer. All I did was hold them in my hands, between my fingers. Pathetic, of course. The ghostly pale tights were the brightest thing in the room. They did seem to retain a faint phosphorescence in their being.

I fell asleep later and I dreamed of my future – truly a prophetic dream. The only one in my life I have ever experienced. I saw houses, white modern houses, spreading out on a plain of clay land and brindled heath.

On the very fringes of Stafford, in the early 1990s, a rash of new-build housing began to spread. Right out on the very edges of town, to its north. Far over to the east was the mainline railway and beyond that the M6, which could just be heard at rush hour some mornings. On the flat land by the railway, single wild beech saplings rose – but as if planned in their ordered spacings – ten feet apart with weeds between.

Those housing developments always ended in a circular loop of road with four detached houses. Exposed pipes emerged from the gouged soil, and a row of three white porcelain toilets still sealed in their manufacturers' plastic sat in the open air. The edges of foam insulation, which had not been snipped back, fluttered out of the walls round the window spaces. There were the breezes of that zone which had no mature bushes or trees.

It was here I started to recognise that emerging landscape foreseen in my old Sussex dream over ten years before, and I was to know that vista well, because after my eleven-year stint at the Royal Mail sorting warehouse in Stafford ended with redundancy, I worked as a nightshift security guard for two years around those house shells, with their water and electricity supplies still to be connected. At least I had Mam's old place. A faithful retainer still, as I wandered and prevented theft of fittings and vandalism, in and out of those door-less and window-less dwellings of two and three bedrooms which would soon contain families and all their hermetic complications. Families, those cowering defence mechanisms which form their own little units of aggression against the world around. But are usually, one day, torn apart effectively by attrition, divorce, entropy. I wanted one myself and was just bitter.

On summer dawns, in those clean-lined property developments, I would stare over to the north where virgin England still began anew for us each day, begging us to know its history. I would tug up the collar of my donkey jacket. That land would be powering up out of the dawn grey among those wild birch saplings which reseeded each spring by being blown from the west.

Birdsong. Old merrie England was still there. A merrie England people should know, though we cannot define it. A dear England I thought I had found inside the boundaries of Kitchenly Mill Race. I made the mistake of believing I encapsulated some values, but what were those values, bought so cheaply from a few books and vain thoughts – values which I had allowed to lead my life and to knock it astray?

In that dream I saw beyond the birches, where lay the dark spread of older trees and heathlands, and later I would take walks there. Sometimes, after it had been freshly raining, the ground was like God's waterproof, sloughing off the water to where puddles like burnished metal had gathered in the corners of the fertile fields.

That was when I was to be happiest. Back in the town, the fields and outskirts of my boyhood, with no illusions or vanities left.

The music press disappeared, but I would still hear, through the scattered telegraph, news of the lost rock world which had been. Now tours got sponsored by Pepsi-Cola; a long way from

Woodstock, while I tossed parcels in the sorting office. The odd postcard from Death Threat Dave, or Nobby. After Marko got off the brown, which he hit bad in the early eighties, they reformed Fear Taker to tidy up financially. He had been right. The good old bands had become historical artefacts in themselves. They had become articles with provenance, as valuable as all those antiques which filled his big houses. They started making more money touring in the 1990s and 2000s than they ever did in the 1970s. Lower income tax too. I never got an invite, nor did Nobby or Dave.

Marko divorced Auralie in the normal manner and took up with a twenty-two-year-old; flogged off Kitchenly Mill Race in 1988 and it got broken up into seven or eight apartments. You can still see up-to-date photos of it today on this internet, with about fifteen sports utility vehicles lined up in the old turna-round area which they have now tarred over. Up at the top of the driveway that could do with being resurfaced, there are about thirty recycling bins in different colours, representing each individual apartment, and the Elvetson gates have been removed.

As previously and usefully pointed out, we could never tar over the gravel car park because of the great elms and their thirsty roots. Well, these trees were gone. The famous hurricane of 1987 hit Kitchenly Mill Race hard. It funnelled in round the South Downs. The Tudor stacks were eternal, but the clock tower came off the saddlery and down in through the roof beams; and the wrath took all the glass off the roof atrium, throwing it high into fragments which fell like rubies and emeralds into the moat and the grounds; the hurricane took down almost every mature tree in that garden, cedars of Lebanon, elms, the lot, whether it stood before Waterloo or not. The younger birches with their thin trunks had their branches thrashed bare, but survived. It was like the garden was undeserving of history and so was stripped of it all. The moat overflowed, taking the laburnum

352

slope with it, the lower footbridge turned wrong way-up, got minced by the wind, and its white parts floated off downstream towards Maxtelham. I even heard that the lock broke loose and the millwheel started turning in the force of the wind alone, as if the bloody thing was making up for lost years, churning up the startled mill race water like a Mississippi paddle boat, before its central bolt snapped off and it sat down and disintegrated on the bottom.

On my single bed I woke up from that dream of future Stafford housing developments. I looked across at my Mickey Mouse alarm clock. Close to eleven. The young girl's tights lay forgotten at my side, as bleached as the peeled skin of a pale fish. That dream seemed so mysterious to me in 1979, but it was only over a decade later I saw that it was a dream of my future, which defies all logic. I promise you I saw those brash new modern houses, simmering on the edge of an older England where my humble fate awaited me.

I stood up slowly and I crossed over to the window and looked down on the now-cursed beauty of that selfish, hidden night world. I looked hard and then I saw the movement of the intruder.

She was sitting on the bottom step of the stairs up to the main entrance, beside the missing stone finial, and even at that distance I saw the familiar motion of her tipping back the long slim bottle of Blue Nun towards her face. The intruder was as insubstantial as ever in the powder of the gloom, but she was there. The bottle even glinted in that moat light. She was there – she was no phantom.

I put on shoes and went downstairs and out through my kitchenette door. I crossed the footbridge and then I openly stepped onto the car park gravel, my Kickers crunching. Neither of us spoke as I approached.

353

She was wearing that jacket and that skirt again but this time with those woollen kinds of tights which darken and lighten on the skin with movement, due to the weave. She was smiling and I could see her white teeth.

'Natandra Losey,' I said.

'Crofton Clark.'

I said, 'Sir Crofton the Creepy, the resident ghost of these parts.'

She laughed and rolled back on her arse a bit, and said, 'Drink?'

I took the bottle from her hand and swallowed some down then returned it to her.

'I knocked and knocked softly at your little gingerbread house, but you never answered. I was scared there were other people about here but there aren't, are there?'

'There's no one else here but you and me.'

'It's like you said, it's just flipping beautiful this place. Much nicer at night. I think it's like a dream world, like it's always Christmastime here. I saw that, all hanging light thing in the big glass box round there, it's kinda beautiful.'

'Is it switched on? Mmmm. That's the old porch and they put a huge Christmas tree up in there every year. Or they used to.'

She nodded and she took the bottle of Blue Nun in both her hands to swallow some more down.

'I'm sorry, I was sleeping. You must be cold by now. Sat out here.'

'Nah, I'm okay. I knew, I knew you would wake up. I'm drunk but I knew you would wake up and look out your little window and see me sitting here.'

I nodded. 'I knew you would come one night. I felt it.'

'Did you? I suppose I sort of felt, when you explained all about how someone could get in here and stuff, you were kind of telling me to come one night.'

I sat down on the stone steps beside her. 'You were always welcome. You're a great kid. I just had a strange dream and then I woke up and I knew you were here.'

354

Suddenly she tilted her head sideways, so it fell onto the side of my right arm in a caring way, then she lifted it quickly away again. 'Sir Crofton the Creepy, I'm drunk. I kind of thought . . . you would look out your window at night and you would be haunted by seeing something. Someone. You thought it was maybe something that came from the past, a ghost thing, but that's when I realised. I am it. I was always what you were seeing.'

'What? I don't get you.'

'What you were seeing when you saw them things in the garden. It was me you were always seeing. It was something from the future. You were seeing something from now that I've come to be. It was me you were seeing all along, and here I am, so you won't see them things ever more.'

'That's a beautiful idea. And you do like the future, don't you?'

'Yeah,' she said. 'Do you believe it?'

I said, 'I do. Yes.'

There was a long silence. We looked out together over the lawns and night garden before us; the crush of quivering starlight beyond the treetops; the inky hopelessness of the doomed elms and cedars.

'But what now? What now?' she said in the profound, ominous voice of an adult.

'Yeah. What now?' I said.

I sat on a while then I pointed, 'See that stupid glass booth thing?'

'Oh yeah.'

'He had that built for me to sit in like a monkey at a tea party, to direct traffic. He would have parties, big parties, forty, fifty people and their cars would come down from London. F. Scott Fitzrock'n'roll. Rich, famous bastards, but some were okay. Coming and going on the carousel of fame. People either show off all their lives or they get fed up showing off. What is all this house or any big house but a big show-off?'

'Yeah and for who? It's just for us tonight.'

'Yes, it is, Nat. Five hundred years, but it was just waiting for this one night. For you.'

'You say the sweetest things.'

'Are you not a bit cold?

'If I say yes, you might ask me in and that would be weird for you. Mum's away tonight. She stayed over in Marlborough again. Next thing we'll be moving back there. I hear your date together didn't go too well.'

I laughed. 'I'm glad at least you didn't bring nosey Rosey along.'

'We've had a falling out for a few days. But I would never have brought her.' She nodded once.

'I'm going away soon,' I said. 'I haven't got her records autographed either and I don't think I'll be able to. I'll post them back to her.'

She looked at me. 'What? You're going? With the band or something, or on a holiday?'

'I've been on holiday for years. Naw. I'm going away for a bit. What did you fall out with Rose about?'

'A boy in the village. She fancies him and he likes me.'

'Yeah. That happens.'

'I don't fancy him, but that doesn't count, you still get the grief.'

'Yeah. Reckon you can find your way back out of here?'

She looked at me. 'What if you'd answered the door?'

'I would have asked you to come back out here onto this step, so I could see you from up at my window. Like you said, so I could see what I had been seeing was an image of the future. I would have watched you from my window. That one up there. That's my bedroom window and I've been looking out of it far too long.'

'Okay.'

'But I'm way too old for you to hang around with me; and worse, I'm not that much of a man.' I said, 'I'm going to do the right thing now, Nat, for once in my life, and go in. Do you want me to bring you out a blanket or something to put over your shoulders for the walk home? I can't drive you back in any cars any more. I'm back on the bus.'

'No, no. I want to walk back, that's the way it should be if you are chucking me out. Past the rabbits, past the owls and the night creatures.'

'I'm not chucking you out.' I stood up and so did she. 'You finish this,' she told me.

She walked towards the white wooden footbridge and lifted a small pale hand against those gauzy stars of heaven. 'Maybe see you about?'

I held her half-empty bottle of wine, both fearing and hoping that she might do a teenage walk straight ahead, in through the open door of my kitchenette, shedding the skirt and the rest as she went, and up into the single bed; but the intruder took a right, and her lithe figure disappeared into the darkness forever, far down towards those river bends, through the colouring lights, until she could be seen no more.

I remained in front of Kitchenly Mill Race. I myself became that dark figure of my own devising, motionless and seated on the night-time steps. When the bottle was finished, I didn't even bother to chuck it over into the moat. I walked forwards and on the gravel I fell to my knees and gave thanks – I don't know to whom, I never have known – always felt confused whether we were talking to Jesus or his father. Bit of a crossed telephone line. But I just gave sincere thanks for all good things. Never been more sincere in my life – and it was about time.

THE END

357

Acknowledgements

Lee Brackstone, Ellie Freedman, Georgia Goodall, Seán Costello, Luke Brown, Mark Edward Geyer, Wayne Price and Ali Lumsden: thank you. Hazel Warner (for great hospitality), Simon Reid, Brian Hamill at The Common Breath website, Will and Jenny Lawson, Fred MacPherson, Allan McEwan, Ruth Thomas, Sandra Schmidt, Hildegard Schmidt, René Tinner, Paul A Taylor, Andy and Niki Pryde in the tech bunker, and Tula and Benji.